Hailiorea Revolt

Adam J. Austin

Aswain Books

www.Aswainbooks.com

To freedom lovers everywhere, past and present.
To my parents, my brothers and their families.
To my closest friends, thanks for your encouragement.
To my buddy, Jaxon.
And, as always, to Vivien, my pride and joy.

Chapter 1

I felt sick to my stomach the instant I stepped off the boat.
Chills raced down my spine as beads of sweat trickled along
the sides of my face. Oh Christ. I asked for this. This was my
own doing, my idea. I bought the ticket, willingly boarded the
passenger ship and endured the journey back into GU territory,
the Global Union. Now the boat was docked and I could only
go forward. May whatever god existed take it easy on me.

The place was even worse than I remembered. Everything
felt wrong, twisted, deformed and evil. Colors seemed off,
they were dull and the outside light was dim. Even the ground
felt weird under my feet. The air, which stunk by the way,
carried an eerie essence of fear I could actually feel. It wasn't
my imagination. Neither was the anxiety that pressed down on
me like a damp, smothering blanket. Common sense screamed
at me to turn around, run and hide. But, as was often the case
in my nightmares, I continued on despite the strong risk of
capture, suffering and death.

Stupid. It was stupid being here. I was stupid, lost,
confused and hardly able to think clearly enough to walk. My
resolve had been so strong just a few hours ago but now the
last bits of courage were quickly evaporating away into the
paranoid, depressing air. The place stirred up horrible
memories that flooded my spinning head. Memories of the god

awful asylum, my old military unit and the general pain everywhere. I'd left the relative heaven-like Aswain for the corrupt, hellish, one world nation of Tehlasrin. The word meant unity. Yea right, united in sadness, misery and fear.

Someone from behind me lightly nudged my back, pulling me from my thoughts. I turned to see a frightened looking woman brush by me and then head away from the boat. I stared at the back of her head, blankly, wondering what I was even doing here.

No. You know why you're here, so stop it. Enough of that crap. Wake the eff up!

The internal voice was like a cold slap to my face. I spared a few seconds to focus on my breathing and to concentrate on clearing my head. My fear's grip had started to weaken. I couldn't spend too long, though. Standing still in the open would get me noticed.

Regrouping, I leveled myself off and remembered who I was and what I could do. I remembered why I was here. I remembered who I was here for. I recalled the strength and the drive that helped destroy the monster on Ravenfall. I wasn't alone but, with my help, we managed to come out on top despite being unprepared and outmatched.

I *had* to rescue David. He was my best friend. He'd saved my life several times and I owed him my sanity. Helping him was simply the right thing to do. It was my duty. There was no alternative. Of course he was worth the risk.

The horror I knew my friend was going through had been at the forefront of my thoughts ever since he fell under the sway of the now dead Samantha Forrest. Eff it, I couldn't and wouldn't turn back. This was it, do or die.

I let out a deep exhale and followed the especially somber bunch of people who got off the boat with me. We quietly marched toward the security checkpoints as the Sun slowly set behind us. I spared a glance at them. They each had their own reasons for coming here and I bet none of them were happy ones. No one with a properly functioning brain would prefer to be anywhere in the Union over Aswain. The group kept their heads down and watched their feet as they plodded along.

The only sound, other than those of the sea and the wind, came from obnoxious speakers planted atop posts throughout the pier. They continuously rattled off their controlling, fear based, propaganda filled mantra.

"You've entered the Tehlasrin Sunset Port of northern California." Yea, California didn't even exist anymore. It was once a part of the old United States but was now just a name that covered a vague area on maps that were all one color, Tehlasrin's color. It amazed me to think that not so long ago there were so many independent nations and in some of those, like the US, there were states, each with their own unique freedoms. I didn't understand how people could ever willingly give that up.

"Follow the yellow lines to the next available checkpoint for identification and background inquiries." I looked down at the lines of yellow paint under my shoes. They were chipping and flaking away, appearing old, dead and worn out. The lines matched the rest of the place. The Union had only been around for about eight years and was already in a sad state of decay. I scoffed. That's what happens with such blatant corruption. The murdering, bloodsucking controllers have nearly drained all the life out of the world, leaving junk for the rest.

"For our continued safety and prosperity, immediately report any suspicious activity or items to your nearest security official or other authority personnel." I nearly spat with rage. 'Official,' 'authority,' security guards and police were once public servants and protectors in the days before I was born. That's how they were on Aswain, that's how they should be. Here? Hell, why not just call them gods?

Report, report, report. How many innocent people had been put to death or locked in a cell for the remainder of their days simply due to suspicion? Guilty until proven innocent and only deemed innocent if, and that's a huge 'if,' you were ever given the chance to defend yourself. God, this place sucked.

"You've entered the Tehlasrin Sunset Port of northern California." The loop started over again.

I risked another curious glace at my surroundings. This was the same port I passed through on my way to Aswain a month ago. Then, under Fier Wren's directions, I was so obedient, nervous, tired and out of whack, I hardly took in a single detail. Now, I registered just how gross the place was.

Trash littered the floor, everything was caked with a thick layer of grime and scattered packs of disheveled guards stood around eyeing the people that walked by. They were mostly young men and the majority looked depressed with hollow eyes and sad faces. Others had a dangerous, predatory edge to their stares. Those were the ones I kept a special note of. I could tell they were pathetic, ego maniacs who got off on the power their status gave them. I'd seen their bunch more times than I cared to count. Hell, I murdered a small group of them after they slaughtered my brother. The memory caused me to shiver.

It took a long time to get over my brutal act of revenge but recent history seemed to help heal the old wounds. My past didn't upset me like it used to. Who knows, maybe I was still bolstered from my part in killing that monstrous creature, the osilea, that wanted to destroy Aswain. Maybe the knowledge I'd gained about what I am, a hailiorum, helped rationalize my actions. Or maybe I just didn't care anymore. At any rate, I didn't hate myself for killing the bastards anymore. Was it wrong? Probably. They were killers too, though. Live by the sword, die by the sword.

I took another glance at the nearest pack of sloppy, grungy guards, almost making the mistake of locking eyes with an especially twisted looking one. Some of them were predators, fishing for a nice, ripe victim to rob, humiliate or torture. Only the finest for the honorable Global Union.

My palms started to sweat as the checkpoint dew closer. I was on such dangerous ground here. One little slip and I'd be back in the asylum or someplace similar… Well, that was if I let them take me alive. The drumming of my heart echoed in my brain and I wondered how others couldn't hear it pounding away. *Calm down, Jason.*

The situation felt oddly similar and at the same time completely different from my entrance into Aswain. Then, I had David with me to help calm my nerves. Now it was just me against a world that had me tagged as a traitor, a murderer and a mental patient. All I had was a bag of clothes and five thousand GU dollars in my wallet. The Union had been trying to phase out paper currency for years. It'd be easier for them to control and track people electronically. The agenda hadn't taken full effect yet and that was fine with me. The less I had to plug into the system the better.

There were also two etherpistols in my bag, within easy reach. It probably wasn't the brightest idea bringing those but what the hell. Better to be armed then not in the event something went wrong. Firearms were banned for the cattle population but I wasn't technically a citizen of Tehlasrin anymore and I had my fake identification. According to the PDRI, thanks to the Aswain security team, I was Aaron Waters, a mid level soldier from Prospous County.

At least I hoped that still remained true. It'd be quite an unfortunate and wickedly comical turn of events if my leaving upset August Cross enough to where he set my registry back to Jason Sworn. I'd find out soon enough.

In similar regard, I was fortunate Aswain's bank was set up to communicate and work with the Union bank. It made sense due to the extremely high volume of trade between the island nation and Tehlasrin. As such, I'd have access to my account which included the other forty-seven thousand plus Aswain Gems I was paid from old man Crow. The exchange rate was still roughly two GU dollars for every one Aswain Gem. So, if things got dicey, I had the chance of buying my way out.

August Cross. Breathing and taking in the hell hole around me bolstered my appreciation of the man. I'd gone from thinking he was an elitist prick, to a dictator and then to freedom lover just trying to escape the Union's evils. I still wasn't positive I had the guy figured out but for the moment he had my respect. Everything he'd risked and fought for seemed to have paid off. Deep down, though, most believed Tehlasrin would clamp down on him one way or another. He couldn't stay in the favor of such a corrupt group forever.

Thinking of the corrupt, I was nearing the front of the line. My ears strained to pick up any tidbits from conversations going on ahead of me. They were limited and brief so it was hard to make anything out. The interrogators showed about as much enthusiasm in their jobs as the trash littering the ground.

God. Another wave hit me of how drab everything was. People were like zombies, locked in a daze, all enjoyment gone. It was hard to believe I'd never noticed how sorry everything was until I finally tasted freedom. Strange, it was then and there that it dawned on me my brother, Mark, realized this all along.

"Next."

I snapped out of my daze and stepped up to face a short, stocky, tough looking woman with ratty, black hair and thick arms. Her dark eyes, though cloudy and dead looking, stared into my light blue eyes with sinister intensity, like a shark examining its prey. I waited.

"Place your thumb here for a blood scan." She spoke in a robotic, neutral tone and gestured to a thin plate with a small needle coming up from the center. I almost complained. The thing was dirty and I didn't feel like catching any diseases but I refrained, not wanting to rock the boat. Christ, I was already acquiescing, accepting the tyrannical union procedures.

After the brief pinch, my data flashed up on the small screen on the woman's podium. My heart and breathing felt like they came to a standstill.

She looked at me, expression unchanging. "Aaron Waters. What's the purpose of your visit?"

I nearly smiled but, thankfully, was just barely smart enough not too. I fought to find my voice. "I'm here to visit family in the old Michigan district."

"How long will you be staying?" The woman droned on, not at all caring about me or my family.

I raised my eyebrows. "Just a couple weeks."

"Place your bag on the scanner by your feet."

"Um." I started.

The guard's expression finally changed. "What?" I could sense a sudden nervous and excited tick in her body language.

I shook my head. "Nothing, it's just that I'm a security guard and I have two weapons in my bag."

She stared at me, unblinking, not saying a word.

"Pistols." I continued. "I hope that won't be a problem." I tried to keep my voice both friendly and bold at the same time. Didn't do a good job at either.

"All firearms for non Tehlasrin security and military are banned." She spoke with authority in a monotonous tone, like she was reading a script.

I swallowed. "I'm sorry, I wasn't sure if I'd be ok with them since I'm also in the armed forces."

"No firearms for any non Tehlasrin security or military official." The woman's tone was slightly agitated. "They'll need to stay with us."

I paused and kept my face still, not moving a muscle. My brain, on the contrary, was a whirlwind. *Idiot, you should never have brought those pistols! What am I going to do? I have to hand them over; I'll never get through with them. Tehlasrin shouldn't have etherpistol technology! Damn, I effed up. Maybe I could fight my way through. You moron, there's no way. Melt them, set the self destruct. Yea right, good luck explaining that one...*

The thoughts danced in my head for all of four seconds but that was far too long, my silence was creating suspicion. I nodded my head. "Of course. Is there any way I can get them back on my return trip?"

I might as well have asked for a billion dollars. Her face showed the slightest smile at the stupidity of my request. "All materials left behind become Tehlasrin property."

I nodded again.

"Stand still." She reached down, grabbed my bag, slid it over to herself, unzipped it and began rifling through everything. "Where are they?"

"Near the bottom, in the side compartments that are zipped up" I wanted to slap myself. The thought of these goons taking my weapons, new technology, secret weapons at that, was blood curdling. The only good thing was that they weren't loaded. The energy capsules, ammunition for the guns, were in another part of the bag. I hoped the guard didn't think to ask for them too.

She pulled the weapons out and looked at them. For a brief second, life flickered in her eyes. The woman looked curious and interested as she ran her fat fingers over the weapons. Then she looked back at me and nearly gritted her teeth. Oh damn, I knew that look. She was jealous, envious I'd been in possession of such pretty things.

Painful silence held on for a few moments. Then she spoke. "Gather your belongings, and proceed through the body scanner."

I obeyed a little too quickly, eager to get out of her focus and still angry at myself for loosing the etherpistols. Cursing myself, I headed for the body scanner.

"Enjoy your stay in Tehlasrin." The guard's voice was dull and foreboding, she was still studying the pistols.

I licked my lips. "Thanks."

After breezing through the scanner I headed out past the security station. There were still guards here and there and cameras everywhere but I'd made it. I was now roaming Tehlasrin, ready to rescue David.

Laid out beyond was an especially dingy looking rail system with several trains sleeping in wait to transport passengers, and prisoners, to their intended destination. I turned to the south and saw a small airport. Air travel was especially limited in North America. I wasn't sure how the rest of the world was set up but I knew planes were only for the rich and government personnel. For the commoners, traveling by road, boat or rail were the only options for getting from place to place. Not that many ever had the means or permission to travel at all. Most people were bottled up in filthy mega cities throughout the continent or pinned down on large farmlands to serve as serfs for the royal elite.

I saw a few roads that lead away from the port. They were no doubt peppered with checkpoints. This wasn't going to be easy. Hell, nothing ever was. I hoped I'd be as good as Fier at bribing checkpoint guards.

I chewed on my lip, planning my next move and pulled a sheet of paper out of my pocket with a list of Fier's contacts in the area. I glanced around for a payphone and hoped one of the contacts would help me on my way to Denver. David was back at Morbal's so that's where I had to go.

Someone called me from behind. "Aaron Waters."

I turned and saw a tall, lanky, dirty man in a Tehlasrin military uniform with insignia that showed he was a Captain. He was flanked by two armed guards, one on each side.

"Yes?" I asked.

The Captain smirked. "Come with us, we have some further questions."

Mothereffer…

-

Time dragged on but I guessed it had only been fifteen minutes since the officer and his pawns left me. I was in a small, blank, boring room, sitting in an uncomfortable, plain, plastic, beige chair at an equally plain table with two chairs on the opposite side. This was obviously a room for questioning and deeper interrogation. What wasn't so obvious was what the Captain was doing while I waited. Why did he stop me? What did he know?

They had my bag and were surely riffling through it. I hoped they wouldn't find the etherpistol capsules but, all things considered, that should've been the least of my worries. More likely than not, they knew who I really was. Things weren't looking good.

I used the time to try to plan my next move, to figure out what I should say. It was best to act stupid and to keep my defenses up without looking like I was hiding anything. Also, I'd need to be courteous, not my usual unpleasant self. Any defiance or 'attitude' would only flare the guard's anger and predatory instincts. There was no sense squirting blood around when being circled by sharks.

I drew in a deep breath and held it for a moment before letting it escape. There was the money in my wallet. If things went sour I could always try to bribe the guy. If that didn't work… I clenched my fists. The anticipation was surging in me when the sole door to the room opened.

The Captain from before and one of his guards entered then shut the door behind them. They took the seats across from me and the leader placed my etherpistols on the table in front of them. He noticed my interest immediately.

"Nice place, that Aswain." He began, speaking in a slightly southern accent. "Never been there but I hear it's quite heavenly."

I set my jaw then released it, mentally reminding myself to play nice. "Yes, it is. You should visit sometime."

The Captain motioned the weapons. "Interesting toys. How do they work?"

I smiled, trying to play along. "Sir, I just use them, I don't make them."

"Fair enough, but don't play dumb with me, son." His tone grew a bit more serious. "I don't think the leaders over there would give such fancy weapons to just anyone without them knowing how they worked."

I glanced between the two men before speaking. "They fire a high energy beam. The dials on the sides set how powerful the blasts are. The highest setting can kill, the lower settings can easily stun a full grown man."

"Ah." The Captain nodded. "Very nice." He picked one of the pistols up and pointed it at me while thumbing the setting down to the lowest level. He squeezed the trigger and nothing happened.

"WHAT THE HELL?!" I yelled.

At the same time the Captain raised his voice, "Nothing happened!" No doubt upset the gun didn't fire. He didn't realize it needed to be loaded.

Trying to shoot me set me over the edge. My 'Mr. Nice Guy' demeanor vanished. "WHY AM I HERE?" I barked.

The second soldier didn't like my tone and stirred in his seat while the Captain slammed the etherpistol back down on the table. "You lied to me? HOW do these work?"

I set my jaw and glared into the Captain's eyes. "Tell me why I'm here and then maybe I'll explain the gun more."

"Maybe?" The subordinate started, with raised eyebrows. "You pathetic, son of a -" His outburst was cut short by the raised hand of his commander.

The Captain relaxed his muscles and smiled. "Right, I'll play ball." He nodded. "You're blood set off a little red flag in the PDRI. The alarm is hidden to most. It seems you're of interest to an important person."

My left eye twitched. "Who?"

"But the information doesn't match, there's no record of Aaron Waters being wanted." The officer went on.

I fought to gather my wits enough to regain control, reminding myself to keep my cool. "Ah. Well it must be a mistake. It's not like anyone can manipulate the PDRI. The database is tightly controlled by the high government in London."

"So." The Captain motioned me, expectantly, like he wanted something.

I shook my head. "Who's supposedly interested in me?"

The other snorted. "Nah, ah, ah. I gave some information, now you give me some. How does this weapon work?" Each word grew less civil.

Damn it. I had to play along, couldn't think of any way around it. "It needs to be loaded, where's my bag?"

"Brian, get Mr. Waters's bag." He spoke to the guard without taking his eyes off me. The other man stood up and headed out of the small room.

I took the alone time as an opening. Cool, stay cool. "So, I'll show you how to use the weapons and then, ah, I'm hoping you could let me go."

The Captain only smiled.

"I'd be most grateful and would offer my thanks." I smirked.

The man studied the weapons again. He spoke in a nonchalant way. "What kind of thanks?"

He caught on. Good. "How about five thousand?" I nodded at him. "Not a bad exchange, huh? Besides, this is all a glitch in the system anyways. Silly actually."

He laughed and licked his lips. "You have all these 'thanks' with you?"

"I wouldn't have offered them otherwise."

The guard, Brian, entered back into the room with my bag. He went to sit down when the Captain stopped him. "Drop the bag and leave us. Wait outside."

The other paused.

"Understood?" The superior gave a no nonsense look.

Brian shook his head. "Yes, Sir."

Perfect, it looked as though my bribe was going to work. The Captain didn't want any witnesses. There was no loyalty or trust among the GU military. If the subordinate knew about the exchange, he'd want a piece, or he'd nark his commander out. No honor, no sense of duty. It was all so pathetic but it was my ticket out of a messy situation.

The door behind me closed again and the Captain spoke. "Ok, so. How do we load these?" He paused as I reached for my bag. "And no funny stuff. I know how to use this just fine." The man motioned his regular handgun.

"Right." I said casually, almost friendly. "This is a business exchange. No tricks. I'd hate for anything to go wrong."

"Speaking of which, why don't you grab those 'thanks' while you're at it."

I looked him in the eye. "First, tell me who's interested in me. Please."

"Big wig with the North American government." The Captain said with a smile. "There're rumors he's looking to run the whole continent."

I pulled out the etherpistol energy capsules and felt a chill run up my spine. "Does this person," I swallowed, suddenly feeling ill, "does he have a name?"

"Lord Dr. Morboro or something to that effect."

The words stung like an icicle through my heart. Maledro Morbal. I fought as hard as I could to keep a straight face. So there it was. The doctor had been keeping a watch out for me and wanted me back. Forrest had planned to send me to the son of a bitch with David. Why he was so interested in me? There were plenty of other hailiorea out there and lots were more powerful than I was.

The Captain's eyes narrowed. "You know him?"

I shook my head. "No." I made myself laugh. "That PDRI is seriously screwed up." I changed the subject. "Now, let me show you how to load those and then I'll give you my thanks and be on my way."

"Sounds like a deal, Mr. Waters. There's no guarantee I'd receive such thanks from this Morbo guy." The Captain sounded especially genuine and I was sure the bribe was working as intended. Then the door opened back up and the officer's expression changed. His face went pale.

I turned around to see a tower of a man in full Tehlasrin military dress standing in the doorway. His face looked like it was chiseled out of stone under perfectly combed blond hair. His brown eyes blazed. The officer's cap was tucked under his left arm and the insignia on his shoulders showed he was a Colonel.

I silently screamed in rage and heard a chair screech across the tile floor. Half turning back, I saw the Captain was on his feet, saluting his superior.

The Colonel spoke in a dignified and lethal voice. "At ease, Captain. Thank you for holding Mr. Waters. I'll be taking over from here."

"Of course, Sir!" The Captain said quickly with a quiver in his voice. "Though, I was hoping to deliver him myself."

"Indeed." The senior officer raised an eyebrow. "But that won't be necessary." His eyes drifted over the etherpistols and seemed to sparkle. "And I'll take those as well."

Reluctantly, the Captain handed the weapons over.

"Gather your belongings, Waters, and follow me." He looked at the Captain. "You're dismissed."

I stepped out of the room and was immediately surrounded by the Colonel's entourage, two men and a woman. It wasn't clear where they were taking me and I didn't have the stomach to ask. All I could think was, 'Why me?'

Chapter 2

My captors led me to one of the popular armored security vans Tehlasrin used for both troop and prisoner transportation. I'd been in similar vehicles a lot during my time in the military. They were tough, sturdy and surprisingly quick given their size and non aerodynamic shape. The Colonel had his guards direct me to one of the two prisoner seats near the back of the vehicle where they shackled my ankles and wrists. I expected brutality but was surprised at how loosely they left the restraints.

After everyone settled in we filled up on fuel (which I knew was etherspring by the sound of the batteries charging up), moved through 3 different security points and then headed north. I determined our direction by the last remnants of light from the setting Sun. The golden color seeped through the two rectangular windows on the large side by side doors that made up the back of the van.

The Colonel sat his commanding presence down in the spacious back section with me. Two of his guards were with us, an old man and a young woman with wild, intense eyes that looked red in color. It was hard to tell in the dim light but she also seemed on the verge of smiling. Another woman, older than the first and previously unseen, drove the vehicle with one of the men who'd escorted me serving as her copilot.

No one spoke for what seemed a good three hours. Uncomfortable with the situation in more ways than one, I broke the silence with some questions a few times but never received any answers. I tried to make eye contact with the soldiers and their commander, but all to no avail. On each try, they'd quickly look away or swivel their seats so they faced forward. Fine. I sat in silence, in the back of the van trapped in my thoughts.

This wasn't at all how I'd planned things but I had to admit I wasn't surprised. My actions and hopes of saving David were foolishly comical. Within ten minutes I was captured, pinpointed by Morbal and on my way back to his hellish asylum. That was if we'd changed directions from north to east. The Sun's diminished light no longer served as a compass.

At least I was heading toward David. That was the point of my being here after all and the main reason I kept from putting up a fight. Powerless, all I could do now was wait and wonder. I wondered how far a bribe attempt would get here. Judging by the Colonel's professional demeanor, I figured it would only get me a nice slap across my face. Mostly though, I wondered how my friend was holding up.

With things being the way they were, I was intrigued by how relatively calm I felt. The fear from my uncertainty and the unknown back on the dock had vanished. Now I knew where I stood. It wasn't a good place but at least I could see it.

A month and a half ago I'd have been losing my mind by now, lashing out, sweating and quivering with dread. Now, somehow, while trapped in the grips of the hated Union, I was only mildly anxious. It was a strange and unfamiliar but welcome state of mind. Panicking wouldn't help me any and I was ready to bet a week's wage against a used tissue my calmness had to do with my hailiorum blood.

I tugged my arms against the restraints. They held nice and fast. God damn. Part of me still had a hard time believing all the 'specials' stuff was real but I couldn't deny what I'd seen, fought and felt. It was all real.

And so was my current situation.

We passed through several other checkpoints and I guessed the stations were set up about every fifty miles or so along the main roads. Each time we stopped, the Colonel breezed past me out through the back of the van to chat with the guards. I imagined he was showing his credentials, passport and checking up on operations. Everything seemed especially fluid and still none of my captors spoke. Their communication was limited to glances and nods. It almost seemed like the five people were of one mind.

Bored and sick of speculation, I began to consider closing my eyes for a nap. After all, we could be on the road for several hours still. Needless to say, I was more than surprised when the copilot spoke.

"We're clear. Finally." He let out what sounded like a sigh of relief.

The Colonel nodded, grunted and swiveled his chair to look at me. The old man and young woman did the same. "Thank God."

A soft dome light turned on so we could see each others faces. I squinted a little then raised an eyebrow. "So, you want to talk now?"

It looked like the Colonel's left eye twitched a little. Annoyed perhaps? He made the slightest of gestures toward the old man, leaving his eyes on me. "Read him."

I quickly focused my eyes on the other, wondering what 'read him' meant. The old man chuckled and shook his head. He looked to be in his mid sixties and had a strong, stern face with a slightly large, pointed nose. Small rows of lines rested under his eyes, showing his age, but his stare was intense. His hair was grey and long, pulled back in a clean ponytail. He spoke in a soft, slightly nasally voice with an educated sounding English accent. "Are you sure? Once I open the gate to his full consciousness it can't be closed. The flow will only increase over the coming years. It can't be stopped."

"Do it." The Colonel barked quickly.

Now I felt even more uncomfortable. "Wait. Do what?" I looked between the two of them, then at the young woman after she giggled. She seemed cute in an odd way and had short black hair pulled back over her ears. Again, her eyes looked reddish-orange. Her teeth showed noticeably sharp canines and her eyebrows each formed small upside down V's that were just as sharp.

"He's not prepared." The old man said with warning. Then he lowered his voice. "And is it really fair? Is it right?"

The commanding officer slapped his hands on his lap. "Oh come on. We've all been through it." He gestured in my direction with a nod. "We'll be doing him a favor." He paused. "And I need to know who we're dealing with."

"Ok, what the eff are you talking about?" I'd had it with being in the dark. "What're you doing? Where're you taking me?"

The old man raised and waved his hand in the air then shook his head. "Shh, it's nothing. I'm going to read you, your story, your thoughts, aims, goals, dreams. Try to relax."

I instinctively tugged at my restraints. "RELAX? No! You have no right! Stay the hell out of my head!"

"Jason Sworn, twenty-eight years old," the man started with his eyes closed, "he'll be twenty-nine next month. May fourteenth."

"Oh eff," I said in a defeated tone, all but surrendering. They had me and this old guy was going to pick every little nuance from my brain. Great.

As I continued to be 'read,' I felt myself drift off into an odd relaxed state. I saw old memories play over in my head as my eyes stared blankly into space. I focused on every word the old man said. His speech was more like song now and I could almost feel a soothing breeze wash over my face. If I didn't know any better, I'd swear I was being hypnotized.

"He's a good man with great potential." The reader went on. "No wonder Cross holds him in such esteem."

The mention of August Cross almost snapped me awake but not quite. The old man went on. "Hm. His confidence and drive have been strengthened by the destruction of the osilea."

"Demon slayer." The Colonel said with approval. I only vaguely registered the leader's voice. More so, images of the creature's demise showed themselves to me. I felt powerful and fulfilled.

The hypnotist went on. "Still, there is a lingering pain of loss. The death of his brother and the capture of David Holt." A pause. "He and Holt have created a powerful bond, they're brothers in arms. Hm. Quite tragic."

David... It felt like I could almost see him. I had an idea, a vision he was somewhere dark and cold. Somehow I knew he was both happy and terrified at the same time. Odd. The happiness came from some strange new found sense of purpose. The fear was from something that was with him.

My heart sped up. The fear David felt was a blend of respect, envy and hatred. He held a sort of corrupted reverence for someone or... something that was with him. What was happening? They were connecting in some way. Why? The person or thing was more evil and powerful than the osilea that died on Ravenfall, ten times more sinister. It was very smart and even more devious. It was... *Oh god! It knows I'm here!*

"Easy, Jason. You're safe." The old man's voice pulled me back to the van. My nerves calmed and my heart stopped pounding.

"What is it? What just happened?" The Colonel's voice asked, anxiously.

He answered. "The mention of his non blood brother, David, opened his mind's eye." His next words hummed with warning. "I told you, he's not ready for this."

"Continue!" The hypnotist's superior spoke with even more fire and determination. "He's a man, a hailiorum warrior! He can take it."

"Yes," the old, accented voice went on soothingly. "A hailiorum warrior. His blood brother, Mark, was powerful and brave as well but never knew what he was, never learned his potential. He fell needlessly."

Now I saw Mark, lying face down in a pool of his own blood. My anger started to grow.

"Enough of that!" The man said, pulling the images from my brain. "Unfortunately, Jason hasn't had any real training either. He hasn't learned how to grasp his gifts. Up until now it's all been instinct and raw talent."

The Colonel scoffed. "What the hell has Cross been doing on that island? He should be working with his people."

"It's typical, I suppose." The old man said. "Jason wasn't on Aswain very long."

"Hmm, true." The commander agreed. "I suppose he would've learned more with time and had some training. At least I hope so. We are talking about August Cross." He chuckled. "Go on."

The reader drew in a deep breath, eyes remaining closed. "He hates Tehlasrin and learned to love Aswain." A smile. "A fan of freedom and justice."

"Good." The Colonel spoke the word so slowly and with such passion it almost made me laugh.

"He's a straightforward man, honest and trustworthy for the most part. That is, if he trusts you. He's impulsive and quick tempered, partially a byproduct of frustrations in his life. A bit bullheaded too." He stopped, smiling again. "Not unlike you, Michael."

"Oh, no need for insults. No one's as bullheaded as me." The big man laughed.

"There's a frustrating conflict of interest inside him. Jason's hailiorum blood yearns for justice and action. It wants to protect and help people. However, at the same time he's often distant, dismissive and detached." The old man furrowed his brow. "He's always searching for something to believe in or for a sense of belonging but hasn't found it yet. So he's quick to give up on ideas or groups. Part of him wants to be left alone, doesn't want anything to do with anyone. A hermit of sorts. Let me look a little deeper…"

The last word sent my thoughts soaring through memories and feelings I'd had as far back as I could remember. They moved all the way back to when I was a kid.

"His parents were both oblivious to what they were, no knowledge of the hailiorea. They weren't at all pleased to have children." The words left a bitter sting in my brain. "They lived and worked in constant fear, envious of those who had more than them. They saw family as a hindrance and might've only stayed together for financial reasons. Shame. As so often the case these last few decades, the state raised Jason and his brother. Mark saw things differently; he was a rebel from the start, unsatisfied. Jason learned to surrender, he learned it was best to not be noticed. He learned that people were trouble and often wanted to hide, retreat."

I remembered my teachers, classmates, so called friends and enemies as a kid. I wished I couldn't.

"Tell me more about his parents." The Colonel ordered.

The old man nodded. Richard was it? "I was headed there. One moment." He almost paused long enough for me to break my daze. Everything started to seem way too weird and invasive. "It's amazing they were able to actually have two healthy children. A testament to their hailiorea blood."

My brow furrowed as I spoke. "What do you mean? Two kids isn't a lot."

"Look around, Jason." The big man said in an almost soothing voice. "Humanity is thinning out. We're dying. This is part of the demonic plan. It's easier for the controllers to manage a smaller slave population. We're being sterilized through war, depression and poison."

I shook my head. "Last I heard there were too many people in the world."

The Colonel laughed. "Well, you were lied to, like the rest of us. Even at our peak of over eight billion people you could fit everyone in the old state of Texas. The GU doesn't release census numbers, but last I heard we're down to fewer than four billion living people."

"What?" The information startled me. Partly due to absolute hugeness of four billion deaths but also the fact that I'd never even thought about it before. "*Four billion dead*? You're lying."

"NO, Sworn." The Colonel boomed.

"Yes, let's get back to Jason's parents." Richard opened his eyes and looked into mine. "Focus, Mr. Sworn."

I looked at him and almost instantly fell back into the relaxing fog.

"They're descendents… Oh, lovely."

"What?" The commander, Michael I think it was, asked quickly.

Richard shook his head the looked at his leader. "They're *both* descendants of protection. Amazing. The blood has thinned through time and ignorance but they are. Jason here is of the prime protection line."

The men exchanged looks and both remained silent for a few moments. The Colonel broke it. "Now I see why Cross asked me to save him. Aside from his unwavering kindness he wants me to protect and no doubt train him."

"Huh?" I managed to get out. "August Cross asked you to save me?"

"Well, at least we know this isn't a total waste of time." The woman from behind the driver's wheel finally spoke. "Maybe this *is* worth putting our operation on hold."

"What a joke." The copilot commented, wickedly.

The younger woman, sitting across from me turned her seat around and punched the back of the man's seat. "Stop that!" She turned back toward me and smiled, showing her fang like teeth.

By now I was back to reality and found myself frowning at the older woman driving the vehicle. "What did you mean?" I glanced at everyone in turn. "Who are you people?"

Richard spoke while keeping an awestruck gaze on me. "With the right training and some delicate unlocking, Jason here just might be able to reach his potential. Interesting."

"We'll see." The Colonel said, skeptically. He stared me down. "Just relax and don't do anything stupid. We're driving down an exposed line here and I don't want any outsiders effing things up."

I chuckled and hung my head.

"Hey!" The Colonel said sharply. "What's so funny?"

I exhaled. "Nothing, you just sound familiar."

Richard laughed. "You remind him of Chief."

"How did you?" I snarled. "Stop reading my thoughts!"

"I'm trying, young man." He laughed again. "It's not like a light switch, you know, I can't just turn it off. I need to ease out of your mind."

"CHIEF?" Now the Colonel laughed. "That blowhard? He's a great warrior and I'd have him in my corner in a scrap any day but he and I live in different worlds."

"How do you know him?" I was growing so tired of these people not answering my questions. "How do you know Cross?"

The Colonel gestured and looked like he was about to answer but was interrupted.

"QUIET!" The copilot suddenly hollered. "We're coming up on another listening zone."

The old man, Richard and the wild eyed woman swiveled their chairs away from me again. Before the commander did the same he put his finger to his lips and whispered. "Now shush. Tehlasrin has ears."

The overhead light shut off and I sat back in my seat confused and annoyed.

-

I wasn't sure if it was due to the time of night, the stress, the hypnotic session or just plain boredom, but I managed to doze off for a short nap. It wasn't very restful, though. Images of David played through my head. He was below ground somewhere, around pipes. It looked like an old boiler room or sewer of some kind. He seemed to be alone this time, no sign of that other... thing.

He seemed excited. Ready to do something he believed was extremely important. Something big, fantastic and awful was about to happen. Then I woke up.

"Oh oh."

I determined it was the co-pilot who spoke. The Colonel sat up straight, eyes aimed forward. He reached over and nudged the old man with his right hand. "Richard! Wake up. I need a read on them."

Instantly all business, the old man, pulled out a small pair of glasses and put them on. He was also looking ahead at something beyond the van's windshield. I couldn't see anything from my angle.

"They're not on the normal checkpoint channels." The copilot said with a slight quiver. It didn't sound like fear in his voice, more like excited determination. His face was aimed downward, like he was reading something in his lap. "They've received some high security level transmissions. It looks like they're preparing to send one back."

The Colonel grunted. "Richard?"

"They're anxious." The old man hummed. "They're ready for us. It's a trap."

"Like hell they're *ready* for us." The large man stood up and quickly took his military dress jacket off. I could hear some of the fabric rip as he tore it away. "To hell with this crap. Sally! What's our ETA to target?"

"I'm slowing down a little," the driver answered. "At this rate, they'll be on us in two and a half minutes."

The commander swore and switched the dome light back on. I was baffled but even my, usually dense, brain was able to put some of the pieces together. These guys were either friends with or worked for Cross. They obviously weren't Union military at all and now it seems they've been caught. Which meant I was caught for real this time. Still, I wasn't sure I trusted them. They kept me strapped down like a prisoner. It's hard to like anyone who keeps you in shackles. They were also slowing me down, preventing me from helping David.

"Richard, take this effing mask off me, I'm sick of looking like a damned Nazi." The Colonel, or no, he probably wasn't a Colonel, turned away and opened some compartments on the driver's side wall of the van. He pulled out a back harness with holsters for two impressively lethal looking blades. He slid the swords in their sleeves behind his back and turned around.

My jaw dropped. The man looked completely different. His skin color changed to what looked olive in the light, a mix of yellow, brown and beige. His hair turned black, buzzed short all around. He had a small patch of black and grey hairs on his chin, dark eyebrows and jade green eyes. He didn't seem quite as tall as before but now looked more muscular, thicker and meaner.

"What the f -" I started.

"Load up!" The man, Michael, barked.

I became slightly aware that while the leader completely changed before my eyes, the rest of his team were busy loading weapons and preparing for a fight. The red-eyed woman spoke. "What's the plan, boss?"

Keenly interested, I focused on the leader.

"We'll do like we did in Pittsburgh." He smirked while nodding. "Liv, you send them a fire grenade after Sally makes her move. Burn the living hell out of their communications post." A pause. "They most likely have ear killers set up. Plug your ears good and Liv, melt that effer too."

"Got it." The young woman said while loading what I recognized as a hand held grenade launcher.

The older woman also agreed. "Right. I'm gonna break and move in sixty seconds."

"Drew, plug who you can. Once I'm loose, you and Liv cover me." Michael stretched his arms, preparing himself for battle. "Sally, you'll rush in and join me on the front as backup after my first attack."

"Yes sir," the chorus came from all three.

Richard grunted. "What about Jason?"

Michael looked at me. "Watch him. Plug his ears, hold on to his etherpistols and stun him if he tries anything." He raised an eyebrow. "Unless he's trustworthy?"

The old man looked at me, looked in me, then back at Michael. "Not yet."

I gritted my teeth. Why should I be trustworthy? They sure as hell weren't. I was the one restrained against my will.

"Let him loose if things go bad and fight your way out." Michael snorted. "Alright. Hands! Quickly!" He knelt down behind the driver's seat and put his right hand out, his left was on the driver's shoulder. The others, except the woman driving, each put their right hand on top of Michael's.

"Lord. I ask that you protect us as we enter battle." His head was dropped as he spoke, quickly and softly.

A prayer? It was the absolute last thing I expected. I never really cared what people believed but religion wasn't my thing. It all seemed so... dumb.

He went on. "I know I'm a weak man. I know I've sinned. I've killed and now I'll have to kill again. I ask forgiveness. You know why we have to do what we do. You made us your warriors of justice and righteousness. I'm your soldier and I'll defend goodness at all costs, even my own soul. We stop those who worship darkness and do evil." He stopped and turned his head upward. The others remained silent. "If I'm doomed to burn in hell for my actions then I accept my fate. We love you and serve you, God. Thank you. Amen."

The others said amen and then Michael raised a fist in the air. "For a better tomorrow!" The others repeated him with boisterous shouts.

A second later, the van's tires screeched across the road as it rapidly decelerated then made a sharp, short left turn. The red eyed young woman, Liv, literally screamed past me with her grenade launcher leading her out through the back double doors. I sat there, shocked, excited and dumbfounded while the old man shoved cold, heavy plugs into my ears.

Sounds were partially muted but I was still able to hear explosions from the woman's grenades and then Michael's roar. He exited the van with remarkable speed that matched the crazed, wicked Samantha Forrest and her puppy faced inventor back on Aswain. How some hailiorea could ever move so fast boggled my brain.

Liv came back to the double doors and shielded herself behind the passenger side one. Her eyes actually glowed with an odd red light, like two small stop lights. She let out a wicked, sharp toothed smile as she stared ahead, not even flinching when bullets whizzed past her face.

Speaking of bullets, I heard the copilot fire off a machine gun of some kind into the unseen fray. I looked at Richard and the old man nodded. Apparently, this type thing was nothing new to him. He spoke without looking away. His voice was small but between what I could make out and reading his lips, I picked up, "Sally, dear. I think it's time you joined Michael."

"Right!" The woman yelled. "Cover me!"

I wasn't comfortable with Richard's stare anymore. "Stop looking me."

He obeyed and my eyes drifted down to my lap. Since I couldn't see anything and my hearing was stunted, I decided to wait and let my imagination play out the battle. I'd been in enough to know how things went, I knew the sounds and feelings of war. The longer it went on without any enemies coming at the van, the better. I knew Michael's team was winning. I rationalized that the group were either some extremely powerful hailiorea, or they were extremely lucky. Maybe both.

Liv fired her pistol, drawing my attention back. She gritted her teeth as she shot. A few moments later she and Richard removed their earplugs before taking mine out.

"We're clear." The copilot said.

Richard let out a relieved sigh. "Liv, honey. Please release Mr. Sworn from his chair. We'll need to get moving."

"Sure thing." The woman bounded back into the van and worked on the restraints binding my wrists and ankles. She looked at me and smiled. Her eyes faded back to normal, well, as normal as they could be. "That was fun, huh?"

I grimaced and shook my head. Fun? Two years ago and I could have been one of the guards who, judging by the sounds and the copilot's announcement, were just mowed down for simply guarding a post. I sighed, trying to grasp a little perspective and reminded myself that Tehlasrin were the bad guys. Instead of answering I asked, "Why do your eyes glow like that?"

"Just the way I am." She winked. "I'm good and blowing things up and burning what's left." She tapped my wrists. "All free."

"Thanks." I stood up and hopped out of the van, glad to be outside. The night air smelled of smoke and gunpowder. Light shined from the still burning checkpoint.

"By the way, my name is Olivia. Call me Liv." The young woman said from inside the van. She was busy packing a bag of some kind.

I nodded. "I'm Jason."

"Yea, I know."

Richard exited the van. "Come, Jason. We'll need to get moving soon." He looked at the carnage. "Even though it's dark, that's a big smoke signal."

I agreed and found myself meandering through the wreckage. Several dead Tehlasrin guards littered the road. Some were missing limbs and others were shot up or hacked to pieces. Jesus. The poor bastards had no idea what hit them. And I only vaguely did.

"This is America." Michael said, startling me. I looked at him and squinted a little from the light. He stood in front of a blazing fire. His white t-shirt was blotched red. It matched the swords he held, one in each hand, dripping blood into small puddles by his feet. "Welcome home."

Chapter 3

"Here. Eat this." Michael pulled something out of his pocket and tossed it to me in mid stride. "You need to keep your strength up."

Luckily, my eyes had adjusted enough to the night so I was able to catch what turned out to be an energy bar. I tore off the wrapper and gulped it down. The thing was as bland as bland could get but it felt good at the bottom of my stomach. Now I was thirsty.

We'd been walking in silence for what seemed a good hour or more, heading away from the scene of carnage that was once a Tehlasrin checkpoint. The night air was damp, cold and biting but I blocked it out. Instead, I thought about which questions to ask, nervous to do so in case the GU had voice sensors in the woods.

The small group ransacked the Union van, snatching anything of value they could carry; weapons, food and other devices before heading out. They returned my etherpistols which I immediately loaded before putting one in each of my front pockets. Now I followed along like a lost puppy dog, lugging my bag, still foggy as to who these people were and what they wanted. It was risky going with them but it was better than waiting for Tehlasrin troops to pick me up.

Michael had changed into new clothes so he no longer looked like he'd just butchered something. He put on a fresh tee shirt and then a sweater with his blades and their harness strapped over everything for easy access.

"Where are we?" I asked finally.

Michael moved closer to me while stepping over what looked like a small bush. "Northern Oregon."

I snorted, pissed that I was still so far from David. "I need to get to Denver. Who are you people?" My voice raised a bit and I quickly told my self to quiet down.

"Shh." One of the men, Drew I think, scolded.

"Shut up and listen." Michael began with an edge even though he kept his voice low. "I'm Michael Vistaer, the man ahead of you is Drew Olsen, behind us is Richard Sands, to your right is Olivia Miller and up further ahead is Sally Borris."

I rolled my eyes. It took long enough to get everyone's names. "Hi."

"Hello!" The young woman, Olivia said happily.

I made a face at the woman before turning to Michael. "So, you're all hailiorea?

"Jesus Christ." Drew, mumbled, shaking his head.

"Yes, and in case you haven't guessed already," Michael went on, "we're part of the wide network of resistance."

"Don't be modest, V." Olivia said with a giggle. "That's not your style. You're the leader of the resistance!"

Michael ignored her. "I've known Cross a long time, before the GU formed, even before he unveiled the cell truth. I think he's a bit of a coward and weak, but -"

He paused after I unintentionally stopped walking. "Cross is not weak."

"Keep moving!" Michael rumbled. "I was going to say I owe the man my life many times over so I'm bound by honor to do favors for him from time to time." He paused and I think he smirked even though it was hard to tell in the dim light. "He asked me to help you so here we are."

"Ok." I replied. "I have to get to Denver."

"So I'm helping you." He went on, ignoring me. "But on my terms. I need to get to Seattle as soon as possible. You've already held us up long enough."

"Hey!" I snapped. "I didn't ask for your help, damn it."

Michael laughed. "You helped kill a demon on Ravenfall. Don't diminish that feat by acting like a fool. You'd be in shackles for real if it weren't for us so enough about you not needing help."

I bit my lip, suddenly annoyed and a little embarrassed. He was right, I was stuck.

"We all need help, Sworn." Michael's tone suddenly held a gentleness that didn't match the image I had of him standing near a mound of flame holding two blood covered swords. "Don't worry. You'll get to Denver soon enough. My team's headquarters is there, another reason Cross contacted me."

I guessed my wits were a bit slow from everything that'd been going on but the name 'Sands' finally hit me. "Richard Sands?" I turned to look behind me while continuing to move forward.

"That's correct." The old man said. "Does the name ring a bell? Do you know my son, Joshua? He works for Cross too."

Of course! Learning Josh's father was with this group made me feel a little better. "Yes, he was actually the one who admitted me into the island."

Richard laughed. "Small world. I don't believe in coincidences so I'll take that as a good omen."

We pressed on a bit more with only the sounds of forest debris cracking under our feet before the old man spoke again. "Can you tell me more about your parents? Your family?"

"My parents?" I almost spat. "They never gave a damn about Mark or me. They worked and slept, annoyed anytime I asked for something. So I learned to ignore them."

"Hmm," Richard hummed. "A pity. They could've taught you a lot, including how to love and be loved." I heard him sigh from behind me. "Are they still living?"

"I think so." My dull tone showed how little I cared. "I haven't seen them since I joined the military. Mark kept in touch with them but, well, he's gone now."

"I see. It'd be good for you to see them again someday." I turned to glare back at him while still walking, doubting he could even see my face. He went on. "Hailiorea strengths and gifts run strong in our families. Seeing them again now would help your spirit grow and increase your talents."

I shook my head, feeling my temper flare a bit. "Yea, whatever."

"Forgive me." Richard said before clearing his throat. "And what about the lovely Miss Fier Wren?"

The mention of her name made my heart skip a beat. I swallowed. "What about her?"

"She's a wonderful woman, Sworn." Michael's deep voice echoed through the woods.

"You care for her, yes?" Richard asked even though it was hardly a question. The guy was still reading my mind.

After a groan, I said, "Yes. She's great. She's my friend. And I betrayed her."

"Oh Jason." The old man chuckled. "She's more than a friend. You may very well love her. It's dangerous to love in these times, I know, but you mustn't deny it." A pause. "And you didn't betray her, you just used her resources. I believe she'll get over it."

Michael moved closer to me. "Does she love you?"

"I don't know!" I snorted. "Jesus, enough with the questions."

"If she does," Michael went on, "then that's good. Love is *not* dangerous. Love is what makes life worth living." I could almost hear the smile in his voice. "If she cares for you that means you're a good man. That makes me feel better about helping you."

I snorted then turned to Michael. "So what are we doing? Are we walking all the way to Seattle?"

The big man let out a small laugh. "Drew," he called forward, "how far?"

I saw a light come from Drew's hands and realized he was looking over a map. "Not far, about another hour."

"We're fortunate to be close to Free Arbor." Michael addressed me. "Otherwise you'd be right, we would have to walk the whole way."

"Free Arbor?" I asked.

The old man trekking behind me giggled.

"We're in what Tehlasrin calls the wild lands, Sworn." Michael drew in a slow, deep breath. "What they call wild, we call free."

Richard cleared his throat. "And some truly are wild, ferocious even." A pause. "We know how to find the more civilized groups."

My brain tried to absorb everything. It was hard to do especially when walking through a dark forest, trying to keep from tripping every other step while carrying a bag that grew heavier with each passing second.

"The Union is weak, spread thin and afraid. That's true more so in North America than anywhere else." Michael spoke with pride. "Their strength is concentrated in key hub points over big cities."

"Right." I knew that much.

Michael hummed. "But in the spaces between them, freedom is blooming. There are camps of resisting freedom fighters everywhere. Free Arbor is the closest one to us now."

"That's great," I started, "but I can't believe the Union isn't running sweeps everywhere. They could find these camps pretty easily and bomb the hell out of them." I paused, feeling sick and resentful of my past. "I had to help with things like that when I was in the military."

"Don't be ashamed." Michael soothed. "You're a new man now and more importantly the world has changed in the past couple years. People are finding their strength and they realize Tehlasrin is weak. We're tired of being ruled, sick of having our children and loved ones taken from us, fed up with being abused, manipulated and controlled. We're learning we're the ones keeping the walls of our own prison standing."

I shook my head both glad and surprised the Union could be so incompetent.

"Rebellion is everywhere." Michael stated. "The pathetic Union doesn't have the courage to run sweeps. They've suffered so many losses they're trying to tuck in and secure what they still have."

"But," Richard began, "don't let that fool you. They still have the upper hand. The war is still an uphill battle for us."

"All we need to do is organize." Michael replied. I turned to see him nodding his head. "Which is why I need to get to Seattle."

-

Finally, after traipsing through the forest for another chunk of time, we reached Free Arbor. Once there, we were greeted by smiling men and women holding flashlights and shotguns. They were both delighted and awestruck when they saw Michael. The new group regarded him as a sort of hero.

We were led to what I guessed was the center of the camp, a ragtag construct of broken down mobile homes, beat up vehicles, generators and dim floodlights. The people I saw wore dirty, ragged clothes but seemed to be in high spirits and were glad to have visitors. Despite the late hour, children and armed adolescents rushed to join in greeting Michael and his team.

The friendliness between the groups made me feel uncomfortable, like the outsider I was. I put on a fake smile and stayed close to Michael. These were hard people who'd seen rough times. I didn't want to step out of bounds or get on their bad side.

"Well, well, well. Michael Vistaer." A short, burly man with a thick beard said as he power walked toward us. His coarse voice croaked like a frog that had swallowed cement. "What the hell brings you here?"

Michael smiled and moved to embrace the man with a hearty hug. "Roman! Good to see the camp is still strong."

They released their bond. "Strong as ever, Mr. TV star."

My brow furrowed. TV star?

"We took a little trip to pick up Jason Sworn here." Michael said, still smiling.

The squat man regarded me. "Oh?"

"He's one of Cross's men. He helped kill a demon a few days back."

"Oh!" The man, Roman, repeated, excitedly this time. "Is that so?"

I nodded. He stretched an open dirty hand my way and I shook it, nodding again.

"We ran into a welcome party on the road a few miles back and we need to get to Seattle. The heads are having a meeting that *I* called for." Michael spoke with a wisp of urgency. "We need a vehicle."

Roman took his eyes off me and focused back on Michael. "Of course, but you can't leave until you've eaten something."

"That's not necessary." Michael said with a smile. "I don't want to bother you any more than I have to."

The shorter man laughed and slapped Michael across his face. "Nonsense! The crap out there is tainted, poisonous."

"I know." Michael said quickly.

"Well then sit down and have some real food. We've got meat, bread, vegetables and cold milk." Roman boomed and I thought I saw him wink. "Freshly freed from a Tehlasrin farm nearby."

"Poisonous?" I said out loud with the intention of keeping quiet. I wanted to get moving rather than sit around for a picnic with these people. David was out there and Michael was planning to drag me all the way to Seattle. I nearly growled.

Roman looked back at me. "Ah, still a greenhorn, huh?"

"Seems like it." Michael answered.

"The effing Union has been drugging us with poisonous, sterilizing food and water for decades." The tank of a man spit on the ground. "We get the stuff they grow for those elite controllers and their special bootlickers."

I exhaled sharply, grasping another devious side of the Union. "Why? Why poison people?"

"Oh, for control and population reduction; keep us sick, weak and dumb. Same old, same old." Roman spoke in a nonchalant way, like he was describing a plain pair of socks. "It's all old news but too many people are still clueless, some intentionally so, sad to say. Can't deal with the true horrors."

"They're monsters, Sworn. The Union elite." Michael stated. "You're surprised?"

I realized I wasn't. "Not really."

"Let's eat!" Our host led the way and we all sat on weak, broken down chairs around flimsy plastic tables. The food was odd but not bad. The fact that I was starving helped it go down quickly.

Michael's group talked cheerfully with our hosts while I remained quiet, trying to get my head around everything. These people at the camp, a camp like many, many others I learned, were barely getting by, poor and living off dirt. But, through it all, they lived partially free from Tehlasrin. I hoped for their sake things stayed that way.

I wasn't really included in any of the many conversations during the meal so I took the time to pull Fier's contact list out of my bag. Sure enough, Michael Vistaer was listed. That further helped put some of my lingering suspicions of the man and his group to rest.

The thought of Fier left a twisted feeling in my gut. I really liked the woman and had left on shady terms. I knew she was pissed at me but I did what I had to. When I saw her again, I hoped I'd see her again, there'd be hell to pay.

After an hour of eating and socializing, we were led to the vehicle we'd be taking out of the camp. The thing was an old school bus, refitted to transport grain and livestock. I almost laughed when I saw it but had the wits not to.

Roman gave Michael an overlay of Tehlasrin checkpoints and operations in the area between Free Arbor and Seattle. Pointers were given on which routes to take that had the fewest stops. I even overheard him note areas where there were Union guards who were sympathetic with the rebellion. Some were even part of it. Say what you will, these rebels had their act together. At least I hoped they did.

"Thanks for everything, brother." Michael said finally. "By God's grace I'll see you again."

The men hugged again. "You too, Michael." He regarded the rest of the team. "Keep Mr. Vistaer out of trouble, now." Then he looked at me. "Good luck, Jason the demon slayer. Take care."

"Thanks." I reached to shake his hand again before the big man surprised me with my own hug.

I felt awkward while climbing into the bus and sat myself down in one of the remaining benches. Moments later we were off again, headed towards Seattle. I accepted things as they were but remained disappointed I wasn't headed toward David. Above all, though, I was exhausted. After about ten minutes, with a busy, full stomach, I fell asleep.

-

David was about to do something horrible and at the same time wonderful. No, it was evil, it was murder but he was happy about it. Why? What was he doing? It was dark and damp but images of fire danced in his head. He felt absolutely thrilled and was full of excitement. Jubilant. The euphoria tickled his gut and he couldn't keep from giggling as he lit a cigarette lighter and moved it toward a fuse…

I opened my eyes and rapidly blinked myself awake. My heart was racing.

"You say what you will, Michael," Richard said, seemingly in the middle of a conversation, "but I'm old. No way around it." He laughed. "How are you going to get by after I'm gone?"

Michael groaned. "Stop it."

"Yea!" Olivia piped in. "You know I hate it when you talk like that!"

I grunted and sat up, rubbing the sleep from my eyes.

"Morning, Sworn." Michael said in his deep voice. "Nothing quite like a little battle, a hike and a good meal to knock you on your ass, huh?"

I raised an eyebrow. "Something like that. Where are we?"

"Almost there. Welcome to Seattle." The group's leader said the last bit with a snort as he slid his arms into a brown trench coat. Surprisingly, it concealed the blades on his back quite well.

Olivia bounced into the seat next to me. "You missed the whole trip! Nothing much happened though." She sounded disappointed. "We had a couple stops but you know what? The guards were on our side! They love Michael as much as we do."

I yawned. "Great." Outside my window were the slums of what had once been a decent city, or so I was told. The place was packed with sorry, depressed people, trudging through dirty sidewalks as a heavy spring rain pelted them from above. The bus we were in crept along behind a long line of vehicles. Cameras were posted every forty or so meters, watching the grim display of everyday life.

"Most of them are stuck in food and ration lines." Richard narrated. "The Union keeps everyone tied up in all the big cities. If they aren't working twelve hours a day for minimal wages, they're waiting in line to spend what little they have on scraps the government makes available." He grumbled under his breath. "Pathetic."

I only watched. I'd seen some of this before my time in Morbal's asylum but here and now, things seemed even worse. Patrols of Tehlasrin troops rushed through the crowds. In contrast to the dead looking masses, they seemed especially alert.

"Eff." The driver, Sally said. "I bet they're all keyed up over Brenner." I saw her shake her head and had no idea what she was talking about. So, rather than wondering, I turned back and continued to study the people outside my window.

No one smiled and no one acknowledged each other. Each of them were trapped in their own private hell; cramped, hungry, cold and miserable, all the while afraid of the eyes that were always on them. Those eyes, be they biological or digital, lustfully hunted for anyone that stepped out of line. There was no trust in each other and no care. It was one of many super-cities where people were packed in, monitored, watched and controlled. My jaw tightened. This wasn't much better than the asylum.

"Turn off here." Michael ordered. "Head down the first sub parking structure on your right."

"Ok." Sally said, nervously. "Where should I park this thing?"

"Somewhere dark with enough space to fit us." He glanced over his team then looked at me. "Once we park follow me and keep quiet. We've got a base set up in an old building at the end of a nearby street. Don't fall behind."

I nodded, not much caring for being spoken down to like a child.

Moments later, after finding an adequate spot, the bus came to a stop. I grabbed my bag and filed out behind the others. Automatically, I slipped into military mode and traced Michael's team perfectly. We shot up a set of stairs and breezed through a door that led to a sidewalk outside the parking structure. There, we were instantly surrounded by a mob of wet, dirty, depressed Tehlasrin citizens. No one seemed to notice us and some even blindly ran into me. Christ, they were like mindless drones.

"Keep your head down, Jason." Richard whispered in my ear. "Keep your bag low and don't smile for the cameras."

"Right." I obeyed working to keep my anger in check. Things were so pathetic here, it seriously pissed me off. I wanted to knock the effing cameras off their posts, I wanted to wake the people from their daze and beat life into their brains. Instead I just focused on the back of Vistaer's head. Before I knew it, we reached our destination.

Michael quickly swiped a card over a dirty plate, glided through the door, moved into the shadows and held it open. "In." He said quietly.

I stepped into the dark room followed by Richard then Michael shut the door. I heard a click and then the big man let out a deep breath. "Made it." He spoke in a normal tone now and I guessed we were free from any visual or audio monitors. "This way."

It was hard to be sure but the place looked like an old furniture store. There was lots of space and everything was covered in dust. A musky, mildew smell filled the air until the moment we walked into the backroom warehouse. Here, things were brightly lit, the air was fresh and there was a computer station set up with several monitors displaying information. Two men hovered over the screens, studying them until we showed up. They looked at Vistaer and nodded.

Beyond that, down a somewhat long hallway, was what looked like a conference room holding a number of people. A woman, middle aged, athletic and good looking with a long, swooshing, brown ponytail, bright eyes and a beaming smile hurried toward us.

"Michael!" She rushed to the man and they embraced then kissed, long and passionately.

I looked away, feeling odd.

Michael called my attention when he released the woman and spoke. "All our guests here?"

She shook her head, slightly. "Erica isn't. We couldn't get a hold of her. Too much going on I guess."

"Damn it." His eyes dazzled with a brief intensity. "What about Rigel? Rigel's here, right? How's our guest?"

The woman laughed. "Brenner's tied up nice and tight. Can't say the puke is enjoying his stay but oh well. Rigel was the first to show and he's quite pissed having to wait all night and this morning."

Michael looked at me with an annoyed expression. "Hannah, this is Jason Sworn. Jason this is Hannah Fisher."

"Hello." I said and nodded. She cocked her head to the side and gave me an awkward smile.

Michael went on. "She commands the resistance in the entire northwest area of North America."

I raised my eyebrows, surprised at the woman's authority and responsibility. Not because she was a woman but because she looked so... I don't know, calm, relaxed or friendly.

"Jason Sworn, huh?" Hannah said. "Cross speaks highly of you."

I laughed. "Glad somebody does."

She graced me with a laugh of her own. "You can set your bag over there." She pointed to a small couch against the wall. I gladly tossed the thing, sick of carrying it.

"Hi Hannah, good to see you." The woman, Sally spoke softly as she drew nearer. They exchanged a meaningful hug.

Hannah pulled back, smiling. "Been taking good care of Michael I see." She quickly glanced in turn at the rest of the group. "Richard, Liv, Drew. Great to see all of you."

"Good to be here, Ms. Fisher." Richard said, regally with a slight bow.

"C'mon, let's go." Michael said. He was pulling off his large coat and already heading toward the conference room. Hannah and the rest of us followed.

The bright atmosphere helped me get my first real look at the group I'd been with since leaving the port. Drew, with long black hair and reddish skin appeared Native American.

Richard seemed out of place due to his age and demeanor. His walk was a gliding stroll with perfect posture. Sally looked especially average, about five and a half feet tall with short reddish-brown hair. Olivia, Liv, had a bounce to her step and didn't look a day over eighteen years old. Before now, I only really noticed her red eyes and pointy teeth. Michael looked even bigger in the light and more exotic, a blend of African, Asian and Caucasian. I guessed his ancestors were from all over the globe.

The conference room was large, spacious, brightly lit and decorated with several plants. A big, oval table rested in the middle of the room with about thirty basic fold up chairs placed around it. Some of the seats were taken and others had men and woman standing near them. From the looks of it, everyone was armed.

"Well, look. Michael Vistaer." I turned to the man who spoke in a snide, sarcastic tone. He'd been standing, leaning over the table resting on his palms before standing straight. The man was shorter than most, balding and had a trimmed red beard covering half his face. "You make us wait here, unprotected after you went ahead and announced to the whole effing world who you are?"

"Relax, Sandstrom." Michael said with a deep rumbling voice. He curled his lip. "Thanks for coming."

The red bearded guy extended a hand toward a young man sitting at the head of the table. "Rigel. You've been quiet on Vistaer's little publicity stunt. Help me out here. We're not ready to come out in the open!" He shook his head and let out a sharp exhale. "The god damned Union is going to clamp down even harder!"

Before the other man could speak, Michael swooped over to him. "Rigel, thank you for being here. Sorry for the wait."

Rigel, stood up and nodded. He was well groomed, average height and had what looked like a mildly muscular build. His blonde hair was perfectly combed and his eyes were deep grey. He had what I'd consider a normal looking face, nothing stood out except his chin was a little too large. Most noticeably of all was his expression. He had the confident look of someone both burdened and prided with responsibility and power. "Right."

The two shook hands and then Michael spoke, somberly. "I'm sorry about your parents. They were the best of us. We wouldn't be where we are now without their work."

A shorter man in dark sunglasses stepped up from the wall behind Rigel and stopped and arm's length from Michael. The guy had a tough looking, thin build, tattoos on his arms and extremely short hair. His sharp, pointed face was aimed at Vistaer.

Michael turned to him. "Who're you?"

"This is Morrison." Rigel said, smiling and turning back for a flash. "My team found him on the road between battles." He looked back at Michael. "He's a strong, loyal and especially protective hailiorum. Sort of reminds me of a younger you."

I could see the wheels spinning in Michael's head. He obviously didn't like Morrison. It was so obvious even I could tell and I'd just met him. Or maybe something about the sunglass wearing man rubbed me the wrong way too. He made me think of a deadly snake, a cobra, ready to strike at a moment's notice.

There was an uncomfortable moment of silence and I took the time to do a quick once over of the other faces there. It was a diverse group that looked proud, bold, eager and alive. Michael had told the coarse man, Roman back in that back woods camp, he was going to meet the heads of the resistance. These must be them.

Richard sensed my curiosity and spoke softly in my ear. "Rigel Brass is the leader of the largest part of the resistance. His parents built an underground army over the years but were recently killed in a raid in old North Carolina."

"Thanks for the kind words, though." Rigel said with a sigh. He looked young but held himself like someone who'd grown up early. "My parents were always fond of you. They respected everything you've done for the resistance." He looked at the red bearded man, Sandstrom, then back at Michael. "But I agree with Gary. Your broadcast over the network was rash and dangerous for us all."

Michael shook his head. "No."

There were murmurs from the group and Rigel raised an eyebrow. "No?"

"We've hidden in the shadows for eight years." Michael addressed the entire group. "The time is ripe. The people are ready."

"Ever the rabble rouser, Vistaer?" Yet another man spoke up. This one had what sounded like an Italian accent. He sat in a chair as far as possible from the rest of the group. I nearly gasped, the guy was actually wearing a suit, tie and everything. His black hair was slicked back perfectly and he studied the fingernails on his right hand while he spoke. "Bless you for your work but you're like a wild animal sometimes, acting before thinking." He pursed his lips. "Not good for business."

Michael walked around Rigel and Morrison then stepped closer to the guy in the suit. "Business? Is that what you call it these days?" He gazed down on the man who, as far as I could tell, wasn't the least bit intimidated. "We all appreciate what your crime syndicate has done for the cause but I'm not going to pretend to trust you."

"Eh." The suave man shrugged his shoulders. "You're trust doesn't profit me either way." He slowly turned to look at me then pointed. "Who's the new guy?"

Michael held silent an extra moment, keeping his eyes locked where they were before finally turning to me. "This is-"

"I'm Jason Sworn." I interrupted, sick of others speaking for me. "I was on August Cross's security team. I'm here to track down a friend."

More murmuring. A woman spoke with a French accent. "Cross is a good man. He's helped us a lot too." She nodded, gesturing the group with open arms.

"So now you're bringing strangers to our meetings?" Sandstrom barked. I was quickly finding myself not liking the guy. "Are you trying to get us all killed?"

I thought I heard Michael grit his teeth. He wasn't loved by everyone here like he was at Free Arbor. No, I got the impression the others viewed Michael Vistaer as a bit of rebel, a free spirited loose cannon.

Rigel spoke and the others quieted down. "Michael wouldn't have let Jason Sworn in if he didn't trust him." The man sized me up, smirked and nodded. "At least I hope not. Welcome to the revolution."

I let out a small laugh. "Thanks." I wasn't here for any revolution, I was here for David but I kept that to myself. The thought set me on edge, reminding me how much time I was wasting. Things were urgent and my friend was in trouble. Each moment he remained captured could ruin him. I took deep breaths and tried to keep calm.

"And Michael," Rigel went on, circling things back, "Raphael's *crime* syndicate has helped keep my army fed and equipped for years. It's the same for all our forces. He's in this as deep as any of us."

It looked like Michael rolled his eyes. He was about to respond when two more men entered the room. One was a thin, young black man with thick glasses and the other was an older looking, short, well built guy with oriental features.

"Michael!" The younger said.

Vistaer smiled. "Mike, Chin. Hello."

"They're part of our team." Richard narrated in my ear. I focused on the word 'our.' Did that include me? Did he think I was part of their team?

"Ok, everyone." A low voice said. It came from a very dark skinned, black man with short graying hair. He looked to be in his fifties and stood a little away from the group, leaning against a wall on the opposite side of the table from me. "We all have things to do back home. Can we get this meeting started? Vistaer called us and now he's here. How about we get on with it?"

"Right." A seated Hispanic man said. He turned to me and the group of people standing around. "Take a seat everyone. You all standing behind me makes me nervous." He chuckled.

I followed Richard and took a seat next him near the far end from Rigel, close enough to smell Mr. Fancy Italian's cologne. Most of the group sat down but the snake guy, Morrison remained standing behind Rigel, staring straight ahead like an emotionless, robotic sentry.

Michael paced around the table as he spoke. "There are several points I'd like to cover." His green eyes blazed and he seemed to relish having everyone's attention. "First off, it's been too long since we've all gotten together. We need to keep our movements and strikes coordinated, especially now that the Union is so close to falling."

Sandstrom, a man I now tagged as a complaining cry baby, scoffed. "Our movements? You went on live god damned radio and telescreens and showed the world who you were without *coordinating* with any of us!"

Michael stopped walking and balled his hands into fists. "We've been over that already! The people need confirmation of light at the end of the tunnel and I -"

"Easy, Vistaer." Rigel hummed. "Many of us share Gary's concern but what's done is done so let's move on."

"Hmm." Another man rubbed his chin. He realized many eyes were suddenly on him. "Oh sorry."

"What's on your mind, Aiden?" Rigel asked. Michael was obviously annoyed he wasn't directing the meeting any more.

Aiden furrowed his brow, thinking before he spoke. "Vistaer says the Union is close to falling. I know they're weak here and there and I hope he's right but we don't really know. Europe, Asia, Africa the Middle East and South America are all in turmoil but Tehlasrin still has a firm grip."

There were sounds of agreement throughout the group. The man went on. "It's obvious they don't have as much control in North America."

"Thanks to all of us and everyone else who's resisting." Michael bellowed. "Most of all your parents, Rigel."

I saw the young leader nod. Part of him rubbed me the wrong way. He came off as arrogant. Michael appeared to like him but then again, I wondered why Michael's opinion should mean anything to me.

"So," Aiden continued, "Say we do somehow manage to overthrow the Union in North America." He shook his head. "What'll keep Tehlasrin from bombarding or invading us?"

"Excellent." Michael said, waving his right index finger in the air. He started pacing again. "I wanted to cover this since I hear Kasire's concern everywhere I go." I gathered Aiden's last name was Kasire since Vistaer motioned him with an open hand.

The Italian laughed. "Perhaps you, how do you say it, hailiorea will protect us?"

Two things dawned on me at that moment. First, I'd all but forgotten not everyone knew about the hailiorea and second that a good number of the leaders present were normal people.

"The true, uncorrupted hailiorea are here to defend liberty and spread justice." Michael stated. "We'll protect and help who we can when we can but don't mock us or think we're anything special. We're people too and I know full well most of us aren't hailiorea." He glanced at Rigel while pulling something out of his pocket. "Our future needs the guidance of all good men and women regardless of what's in their blood. If we follow this," He held up a small booklet, "the United States constitution, we'll be fine."

"Books and paper won't shield us from bombs and bullets." The older black man from before said.

Michael let out a small laugh. "We won't be obliterated by Tehlasrin after we gain our independence. No." He shook his head. "One, as Kasire said, the Union is preoccupied with the rest of the world and it doesn't have the manpower. The fires of revolution will spread once we're free. Two, our lands supply food and materials the world needs. We'll open trade. War would stop the flow of things. They don't want that."

Sandstrom laughed. "Our lands? You're such an idiot."

"THREE!" Michael roared. "We all know August Cross has had the Ether Targe up and running for months now. The effing Union," he spit, "can't hit us with any missiles without them blowing up in their faces." He chuckled. "I'd almost like to see them try."

"What?" I asked.

Richard put his hand on my shoulder. "Later."

"And four." Michael stopped and leaned in on the table, eyeing everyone present. "It's up to *us* in the end. Each citizen will need to show Tehlasrin that we're willing to endure any pain, any consequence to maintain our freedom. We'll show them that we're not afraid, that we'll suffer and die to stay free. We'll never surrender!"

A good number of people present clapped, Liv loudest of all. I saw Hannah smile with her big, glossy eyes locked on Michael. Rigel squinted with a small smirk on his lips. The room was silent for a slice of time afterward.

"So this is it? This is why we're all here?" The Italian asked. "We need to coordinate and now after a few words from Michael Vistaer we're supposed to no longer fear hordes of Tehlasrin troops coming at us from every direction?"

Michael looked at Rigel. The man motioned someone in the back of the room. "You'll each be given an outline of strike zones and times we believe will cripple the Union's communication and organization." Rigel said. "Since we're all here, except Erica, I know you all have the plans."

People glanced over the plans as Michael spoke. "Raphael Zappa." The suave, suited man looked up and met Vistaer's eyes. "You and I have something in common. Neither of us commands an army like others here. But we're still important parts of the resistance. We know how dirty the front lines are better than anyone else. Whether you or I like it or not, we're leaders too and leaders need to synchronize. So don't tell me this meeting is a waste of time."

"Did I say it was a waste of time, Vistaer?" The man said with raised eyebrows.

Michael turned away and swept his gaze over the group again. "There's another matter we need to discuss." He waited for everyone's attention. "Rigel's parents are dead so now he commands our largest force on the continent. I know there are rumblings of who our leader should be and some of us doubt Rigel Brass because he's young."

"It's true," the older black man said.

"He's a good man." Richard whispered in my ear while pointing at the man.

I watched the other guy nod. "I've heard from my people that some are afraid you won't be a good leader, Rigel. There are even plots to have you removed."

The group started murmuring until Michael stopped them. "Well I can't think of anyone better than Rigel to pick up his parents' mantle. We need to get behind him." He looked at Zappa. "It doesn't matter to me that he doesn't have any traces of hailiorea blood."

The majority of the group agreed. I studied Rigel. He looked as though a heavy weight had been lifted from his shoulders. Maybe he was an alright person, maybe he was just nervous about his place after his parents' deaths.

"Now, let's open the discussion up for everyone's thoughts and concerns," Michael said before finally sitting down, "and then Hannah and I have a surprise."

Whatever Michael had to say might've been intriguing but mostly I was growing seriously impatient. How much longer would this take? Denver wasn't a short ride away and I wasn't even moving.

Chapter 4

The discussion over the next hour covered a series of issues which included the deployment of food and supplies to different resistance armies spread across the continent, maintaining the power grids if and when the GU was overthrown and then jobs for people after everything settled. The list went on and on, covering a wide gambit.

I spent the time trying to figure out who was who. Not that I really care who everyone was, the knowledge didn't matter. The exercise simply helped keep me from dwelling on the impatient rage brewing in my gut.

The key players were Rigel Brass, whose forces primarily occupied the south-eastern part of America. Hannah Fisher's group based themselves in the north-west, Gary Sandstrom covered the north-central area, Kevin Jones, the elderly black gentleman from before, and Aiden Kasire focused on the center of what was once the United States of America. Lucy Plante, a delicate looking woman with a French accent, operated in eastern Canada. Last was Martin Gomez. He ran operations in the southern reaches of North America. Raphael and Michael moved about the country but from what he told me, Vistaer's team mostly stayed in the Denver area.

Raphael Zappa gave an inventory of recent scores and mentioned he'd been helping supply various groups spread out in the wild lands, camps like Free Arbor. Michael didn't like the gangster but the group agreed the man served a much needed purpose. I wondered, if everything went as well as Michael hoped, what the smuggler would do in a new North America. He sounded like a criminal. My skeptical brain figured he'd probably end up running the place.

Absent was a woman named Erica Wood. She was actually a Tehlasrin controller who secretly worked with the resistance. She controlled the Southwestern part of the US and some of old Mexico. I was interested to learn the resistance actually had influence that far up in the Union's hierarchy.

Finally, Michael called for everyone's attention. "Ok, now there's one other reason I asked you all here. Three days ago my team got a hold of Elias Brenner, the Tehlasrin controller of these parts."

The group drew in a collective gasp. I snapped back to the present and raised my eyebrows. They actually had a controller held captive?

"You may have heard about him going missing in the news." Michael chuckled.

Sandstrom stood up. "Are you effing insane?! The Union is searching like mad for him!"

"Where is Brenner now?" Rigel asked, calmly. "Dead?"

Michael looked at Hannah and nodded. The woman pressed a button on a panel in front of her and the wall behind Rigel slowly slid open. Behind the wall was a thick pane of glass and beyond that was a man in expensive clothes sitting in a chair hunched over a cheap plastic table.

"Oh my lord." Jones mumbled.

Sandstrom slammed his fist on the table. "He's here? This is too much!"

"Damn it." Rigel said, quietly, shaking his head. "You've gone it alone again, Michael. We need to get out of here, this is too risky."

"Wait!" Michael boomed raising his hands in the air. "Don't worry. We have a teleporter standing by. If things get too hot you can get out of here, right Mike?"

The young black man with glasses nodded his head. "Ah, yes, Sir. It's charging up now."

Michael smiled. "I wanted everyone here for when we questioned him. We're bound to get some information and having us all here keeps everyone up to date."

"Quickly, Vistaer," Rigel hissed. "This is making some of us nervous."

The man, Kasire, groaned. "Just kill the bastard and let's go. Brenner's a monster. We all know he's a sadist and a child molester." He curled his lip. "We won't get anything from him but trouble and lies."

"Hannah, we can hear what's said in there, right? Out here I mean." Michael spoke, completely ignoring the other leader.

She nodded then Vistaer was off toward a door in the corner of the room that led into the interrogation area. After he stepped through, everyone in the conference room stood up and moved closer to the wall. They were each visibly nervous about having the controller here but both intrigued and interested at the same time.

"Brenner," Michael began. "Been a good guest?"

The captive slowly turned to look at the big man. "Eff you, Vistaer." His labored voice was a tired groan.

"You remember my offer?" Michael asked, ignoring the verbal assault. "It still stands. You've had time to think about it. So?"

"How many people are behind that wall?" The man asked in a cool tone while gesturing the glass. Now more alert, his voice was nasally and filled to the brim with arrogance. "How many of your stupid rabble did you bring along for the show?"

Michael pulled a pistol out of his pocket and pointed at it with his left index finger. "This is the easy way out." His tone was cold as ice. "What are Tehlasrin's plans for the resistance? How are they going to strike back?"

Brenner smiled. "Your resistance is a pack of animals fighting over scraps." He stared into Michael's eyes. "You don't know what it's like to truly live. You're a pathetic little worm who doesn't understand or appreciate real power."

"I'm offering you a chance to clear a part of that disgusting, twisted soul of yours." Michael hissed. "I'm not going to get pulled into any of your little mind games. You're a sick, murdering, elitist who's so far from any shred of decency you don't even deserve my mercy."

"MY MASTER HAS GIVING ME THE RIGHT TO DO AS I CHOOSE!" Brenner screamed, instantly losing his controlled demeanor. His face was beet red and looked like it was about to explode.

Michael growled but kept his tone normal. "Your *master* is a treacherous, grotesque demon who doesn't give a damn about you! You just use that as an excuse to slaughter and torture innocent men, woman and children."

"You don't understand anything, Vistaer." Amazingly, Brenner was perfectly calm again. I figured the man was utterly insane. Not that I really cared. It was clear he was a psychotic monster like Forrest and Morbal. Eff him. "You want information?" He continued. "Fine but don't you think I believe I'm leaving here alive."

"Oh you're not." Michael said plainly. "I told you I was going to kill you and that's what I'm going to do. My deal was to offer you a confessional before I send you to hell."

Brenner laughed. "Hell? Hell is only living life as a deluded fool like you and your cockroach friends. The world of man is a sorry, diseased place that deserves to be raped, beaten and whipped into submission by those with power. That is, until the master finally consumes it."

Michael drew in a deep breath and aimed the gun at Brenner's head.

"Men, women, children?" Brenner mocked, speaking a little quicker. "They're insects! Poor, inferior, weak bags of meat and blood." He shook his head and mumbled to himself. "You and your compassion, what a masochistic joke."

The controller smiled again, more evilly this time. "Look at what we've done to you. In the few years leading up to Tehlasrin and through the past eight years we've destroyed everything humanity once held dear. Your pathetic families are dead, hollowed out shells. Your faith is gone and you've lost the will for freedom." A pause. "Humanity is beaten and the masses have accepted their role as our slaves. The conquered have no right to anything better."

Michael stood silent for a few moments. From what little I knew of him, I figured it took a lot of self-control to keep from ripping the controller to shreds right then and there. The big man huffed. "Who's going to lead North America? Who's taking control?"

Brenner gazed at the glass, even though he couldn't see through to our side, his stare directly hit Rigel. He shrugged his shoulders. "What do I care, none of you will do anything of consequence anyways. Control is being fought in a little political game between Steven Ark, Erica Wood and Maledro Morbal."

A cold chill seemed to suck the air out of my lungs. Morbal was in line to rule North America? Rage flooded every ounce of my body and I could only barely contain myself. I wanted to march out of the conference room, steal a vehicle, speed to Denver and put a bullet between the man's eyes.

"Erica?" A woman next to me said, pulling the heroic, dark fantasy out of my head. It was the French-Canadian woman, Lucy. Then it dawned on me. Not only was Erica a controller with the rebellion, but now she was in line to head North America? It sounded too good to be true.

"Once the Lord or Lady of North America is assigned he or she will easily rally Tehlasrin's forces and stomp you all to the ground. Like bugs." Brenner laughed.

"Who'll they be assigned by?" Michael asked. "Who decides?"

The man lazily looked up at him. "Are you that dense? Doesn't your hailiorum blood tell you the answer?"

"You're a hailiorum too." Michael's eyes glinted. "How have you fallen so far?"

Brenner shook his head. "No. I used to be a hailiorum but through illumination and understanding I've become much more, better. I'm free. Free of care, sympathy and empathy. I became free to do what I want."

"So, then. It's your sick little demons who'll pick the ruler of North America?" Michael tried to get back on track.

I didn't notice Rigel move but at that second the resistance leader entered the interrogation room. Brenner raised his eyebrows when he saw the newcomer. "Well, well, well. How're mom and dad?" He actually giggled.

"I don't believe any of that crap about demons." Rigel's voice was heavy with anger, ignoring the personal jab. "We live in the real world. Who'll really pick this so called Lord of the continent?"

"You're even more ignorant than Vistaer." Brenner taunted. "The master will dictate to the Tehlasrin heads in Europe. Once done, you'll see an army like no other burn everything you hold dear. That is, unless you skitter away and hide like the vermin you are."

Michael gave Rigel a cross look then gritted his teeth, pulled a paper out of his pocket then slammed it in front of Brenner. "Which of these points holds the chemical plants the Union uses to poison our food, water and air?"

The man looked at the map and laughed. "You've done your homework, I'll give you that. It's surprising you fools can think at all after how much we've dumbed down and engineered you." He paused then slumped his shoulders. "Fine, again, it doesn't matter, it's too late for all of you. They're all in use. All those plants. Working hard to shut your little delusional, troublesome brains off."

Michael looked at Rigel. "They all need to be burned."

The young man didn't take his eyes off Brenner. "They will."

"Why not just accept it?" Brenner asked. "You're not the master's chosen. Just turn off, go to sleep. Die. The inevitable is much less painful that way."

Rigel roared and punched Brenner square in his nose, busting it wide open. "You son of a bitch." His voice remained calm. Then he punched the man again, and again.

"Rigel!" Michael yelled. "Enough."

"You're coming with me. We'll get some real answers out of you." Rigel grinned.

"No." Michael said flatly.

The two men, Michael and Rigel, held an intense stare down for several heartbeats.

"Look at you!" Brenner exclaimed. "Fighting amongst yourselves like disorganized children. So amusing." He laughed.

Michael's attention was back on Brenner. "What does the Union know about the Ether Targe?"

Brenner laughed. "You think you really have something there don't you? It's nothing but a slight nuisance. We'll find its source and dismantle it soon enough."

"So you know nothing, then?" Michael almost looked like he was going to smile. "You bastards love to gloat, you'd tell me if you knew."

Brenner nodded. "Only a matter of time. Rigel Brass." He looked at the young man. "Your parents died for nothing. Now they rot as they lived; foolish wastes of space. Or did you burn their corpses? Remove the evidence so you could take power."

Rigel snarled and looked ready for another strike.

"You're out of time, Brenner." Michael said, devilishly.

"He's coming with me, Vistaer." Rigel barked, nodding his head.

Michael looked Rigel in his eye. "So you can torture him?" He shook his head. "No. I gave my word he would NOT be tortured. Torture is a tool of the mother effing demons we're fighting. I WON'T allow it. We're better than them."

"I think you forget who's in charge here, Michael." Rigel spoke with warning.

Michael shook his head. "Not at all. But Brenner is my prisoner and I won't allow it. I gave my word."

"Enough!" Rigel raised his voice. "We're taking him."

"NO!" Michael roared, aimed his weapon and put a hole through the controller's head. He died instantly. What was once contained under his skull now plastered the floor behind Brenner's slouched body.

I instantly gritted my teeth and nearly hollered with rage. The controller didn't deserve any mercy but seeing the brains of a defenseless man blasted to bits didn't sit well with me. I pulled my weapon out not sure what to do.

Richard grabbed my arm. "Calm, Jason. It was a mercy kill."

I was about to argue when Rigel spoke. His hands were balled into fists. "UGH! Damn you, Vistaer!" He shook his head, fighting to collect himself. "Think of what we could have learned."

"I gave my word." Michael droned. "You wouldn't have learned anything. He respected me in some twisted way. You're people? He would've lied and corrupted them. He was a powerful, horrid hailiorum."

Sandstrom entered the room. "That's it! Rigel, arrest this son of a bitch."

"Back off, Gary." Rigel ordered. "I think this concludes our meeting."

With that, sirens went off and snapped me back from the shock of what I'd witnessed to the here and now. Beside me, Olivia visibly jumped a good foot off the ground like a startled cat. I looked at Richard who was looking at Hannah.

"Oh no. We've been located. HOW?" She yelled the last word as she headed out of the conference room. The others and I followed behind her.

A man from the computer station called back. "Something sent a signal out just a few moments ago. It came from the interrogation room."

Michael and Rigel were right behind Hannah and me. The younger spoke. "The bastard had an alarm beacon of sorts rigged, probably to his heart. It went off the second he died."

We all looked at Vistaer and I could see the 'oh crap' look of guilt wash over him. It only lasted a few seconds before he collected himself. "TAFT!" He roared. "Ready the teleporter, set it for Rigel's base in Atlanta."

A faint voice from still inside the conference room said, "Got it!"

"Oh god!" The other man at the computer station cried. "We've got incoming projectiles heading right for us!" He aimed his worried eyes at Hannah. "We're effed."

"Calm down!" The woman hissed.

Michael nodded. "Cross's targe will protect us. Chin, Drew, Sally, Liv; we're heading outside to draw their attention away from the base while Mike gets the portal open." He spoke while checking his gun's clip before slamming it back in place. "Headsets on! Rigel, keep the group in the conference room. Once the portal is ready we'll head back and get the hell out of here."

Rigel nodded and silently slipped away.

"Jason, you stay with Hannah and Richard." Michael went on. "Hannah! Put your guards at all warehouse entrances."

I instinctively pulled my other etherpistol out of my pocket so I was doubly armed, ready to fight. I wasn't at all happy about staying behind. "Eff that. I'm going with you."

"NO!" Michael yelled. "Stay here and protect the leaders. You'll slow us down."

"Missile coming!" The man at the station squealed.

I looked at the monitor just in time to see a line of light suddenly meet the cursor that signified the missiles. The rockets disappeared.

"They're gone!" The man delighted.

I shook my head. "How the hell?"

Michael ignored everyone. "Move!" And then he and his team were gone.

I followed Richard back into the conference room while Hannah worked on getting her defenses in place. There were multiple discussions going on and none of them had anything nice to say about Michael Vistaer.

"What the hell is this Targe thing?" I asked Richard.

He ignored me. "Mr. Taft is being swarmed. Come." He led me to the young man frantically working on some device that looked like a small laptop computer with a couple antennae shooting out the top. "Clear off!" Richard hollered. "Give the young man some room to work."

"Screw you!" Sandstrom barked while shoving Richard.

Before I could act, Richard straightened himself and merely stared at Sandstrom. The short man immediately clasped his hands on his own head and let out a string of obscenities as he collapsed to the floor.

I followed Richard's lead and shoved several bodies away from Mike. I used too much force with a few and tossed them to join Sandstrom on the floor. Oh well.

Then there was the small, thin, wire like Morrison standing in front of me. I couldn't see his eyes behind the thick, dark sunglasses, but he smiled, daringly. "Back the hell off!" I warned.

Morrison didn't speak. He cocked his head to the side and raised an eyebrow.

Rigel's voice carried over the group. "Calm down! We're stuck here and Mike Taft is the only one who can get us out. Leave him be."

The snake like bodyguard took three steps back on Rigel's command.

"Fine mess Vistaer has gotten us into." Raphael said, coolly. He was seated again with his feet up on the table. "This'll get us all killed."

I don't know why I defended Michael but it felt right. "Hey! He didn't know this would happen." I looked Rigel in his eye. "Would you rather have found out about the beacon back at your base?" My gaze shifted back to Raphael. "He's out there, risking his life."

Sandstrom finally got back to his feet, visually shaken by whatever mental attack Richard blasted him with. He snapped at me "You're just like *Him*, aren't you? Just like Vistaer!"

I puffed my chest out, stood up straight and stared him down. He backed off.

"How much longer, Son?" Richard asked Mike with a soft voice.

The guy didn't look up from his work. "Almost there."

The room grew silent enough to where I could hear fighting and gunshots from outside the building. My senses were on full alert.

"Calm, Jason." Richard soothed. "We'll be out soon." He could tell I wasn't taking his advice. "The ether targe is a defensive shield August Cross's team created. It covers all of Aswain and most of North America. The device fires a high powered ether blast that incinerates anything it hits."

I looked at him, amazed at what I was hearing.

"The targeting system is mainly designed to hit any projectile explosives launched in or onto the protected area." Richard continued. "Young Mr. Taft here helped create it."

"Mmhmm." Rigel hummed. "Cross is always planning. Genius man."

"Sir," Mike called to Richard. "It's almost ready, the coordinates are all set for Brass's base. Right now I can only open a portal for a couple minutes. We'll have to wait a bit longer for Michael and the others to get back."

Richard moved closer to Mike, "Shhh."

"It's ready?" Sandstrom said. "Let's go, now! Start it up! I'm not dying here."

Mike looked at him. "No, not yet, it won't -"

Rigel was standing now. "We need to leave. Open the portal."

"But Michael and the others!" Mike pleaded.

I put my arms out, nonverbally trying to stop everyone. "We're not leaving them."

"You can stay if you wish, Jason Sworn." Rigel said. "But we're going, we can't wait any longer. The resistance will end if we get killed or captured." He nodded at several armed men around him. They immediately aimed their weapons at Mike. "We have to leave now. Open the portal."

Richard sighed. "Better do as they say, Son."

I stared past the loaded weapons and studied Rigel's face. "You're really doing this?"

"There are bigger, more important things then one man and his team." He squinted. "My parents taught me that."

"Very well." Richard said smoothly. "But, Mike, the teleporter and I are staying."

"Me too." I said.

"As you wish." Rigel said, nonchalantly. His eyes dropped to Mike. "Ready?"

"Opening now," The young man said with a defeated tone. "Stand clear."

Kasire spoke. "What about the body back in the interrogation room?"

"Not our problem." Rigel said coldly. I was really beginning to dislike the man.

In the seconds that followed, a beam of blue energy shot between the antennas on the device and then a line moved out from it about a meter and half away. The line stopped in mid air and created a flat, misty, glowing, cloudy, rectangular monolith about three meters high and two meters wide. The form hummed.

"It's ready." Mike said, somberly.

"Head through, one at a time." Rigel ordered. People stepped into the mist and disappeared. Before he stepped through himself, he looked at Richard and me. "So long. Good luck."

Not ten seconds after the last of them left the portal vanished. Mike slumped his shoulders and buried his face in his hands.

"None of that." Richard commanded. "Power it back up and set it for our base in Denver. Quickly!"

"I, I don't have enough energy, not enough etherspring." Mike shook his head. "It'll take time."

Richard raised his eyebrows. "Do it! Use what fuel you have left, the remaining etherspring, that electrical outlet there and your own brainwaves. You're a brilliant hailiorum alchemist! Get it done."

I furrowed my brow. "What the hell?"

"I can explain some other time." Richard said quickly. "We need to let Hannah know our status and then we need to inform Michael and the others."

"Wait." I said, turning to look at Mike Taft. "You need etherspring? Will this help?" I took the clip out of one of my etherpistols and tossed to the young man. "These are powered by the stuff."

He tried to catch the clip but failed, the thing bounced off his fingers and clattered on the floor. After picking it up his eyes boggled. "I know. I helped design the weapons." He paused a second. "Yes! This should help! Thank you!"

I turned back to Richard and saw him smile. "Let's go." He said and took off, moving fast for an old man. I shouldn't have been surprised.

-

A pair of bullets whizzed past my ear. I growled out a curse while ducking down behind the cover Vistaer's team whipped together. Sparing a glance, I saw three uniformed Tehlasrin soldiers working their way through the doors. Someone from Michael's team quickly knocked two of the guards down. The shots were loud as hell and well aimed, hitting our enemies square in their throats.

The third dropped to the ground with a startled scream before opening up on us with every bullet his weapon had. When that ran out, he grabbed one of his fallen companion's weapons and began emptying that too.

Someone nearby swore in between the sounds of bullets ricocheting off metal, wood, hard plastic and concrete. I blew out a quick breath and aimed my weapon. There wasn't much to shoot at. The guy was tucked away good but he didn't count on his adversary having an etherpistol. A beam of light blue energy rocketed from the barrel after I squeezed the trigger. The blast sizzled through the air and pegged my target on his helmet, directly over his forehead. The energy coursed through the soldier's body and he was unconscious in a heartbeat. My shot wasn't set to kill and I wasn't sure why I powered down the weapon. I guess I felt sorry for the soldiers, blindly following orders. They were trapped too.

"Sworn! Enough with the damn light show! Use that thing as a last resort." Michael scorned with a rumbling whisper. "You'll give our position away."

I curled my lip. "I got the prick, see?" It would've been nice to receive a little praise instead of criticism. I looked at the two dead soldiers and the stunned one. "They're going to find us soon no matter what."

"Shut up! That's one of the reasons I use these." He motioned the lethal blades resting on his back. Blood trickling down the holsters, showing they'd been used recently. The gun he'd inspected earlier was resting inside the holster on his hip. "They're quiet and won't light up a damn room."

I barely nodded. It was true. Etherpistols did give off a trail of light that was easier to track than the sound and sights of standard firearms. That was one downside of the new weapons. The upside was that Kevlar, helmets and other body armor did very little to protect the person against the ether blasts.

Something nudged me in my side, just below my ribs. "Here." I turned to see Sally. She handed me a conventional handgun.

I took it. "Thanks."

Michael spoke softly into the microphone attached to his headset. "Chin, what's your status?" I couldn't hear any response since Richard and I were the only ones in the bunch without headsets. Vistaer nodded then spoke again. "Hannah, ask Mike how much longer."

Richard and I had relayed with Hannah Fisher after Rigel and the others left. She contacted Michael and most of the group collapsed back to the seemingly abandoned furniture store gallery. Our make shift wall was quickly built out of old, musty furniture and then we laid low. Whatever distractions Vistaer's bunch had made earlier seemed to have thrown the Union off our scent. So far, the three soldiers from before were the only ones who'd found us.

"About ten minutes and we're out." Michael updated. An explosion went off not far from the building. "That's Chin. He's got those morons running in circles. The bastards will get their heads out of their asses soon though. Sworn's right. They'll find us just like those three." He motioned the soldiers lying on the ground by the door.

I spared a glance over our makeshift barricade, out through the shattered, dirty windows that lined the wall separating us from the outside. The rain had stopped and the Sun shone on the grim setting below it. People were crouched down behind cars, huddled in corners or lying flat on the ground. Their faces were a blend of terror and rage. I related to the angrier, frustrated ones. They were desperate people that wanted to fight back. Who they wanted to fight, I had no idea. The GU? The resistance? Maybe everyone. "Jesus."

"I said my prayers already, Sworn," Michael whispered, "but you go ahead."

I looked at him and almost rolled my eyes. "No, it's just those people out there."

"Cowards." That came from Drew. "Why don't they get up and fight?"

Olivia slapped him. "Shut up, Ass!"

I gave the man a cold look and he only glared back. "You're tucked in nice and safe." I noted with attitude. "Go show them how it's done."

"Stop effing talking!" Michael hissed. "Richard! Get you're old ass over here."

The man scooted up between Vistaer and me. "Colorful."

"Sworn's right." Michael nodded. "Those people need inspiration."

Richard pulled back a bit. "We'll be gone in less than ten minutes. Let them lay low and this will pass once we're gone."

"No." Michael shook his head. His face showed the same determined look he had when telling Rigel he wouldn't let the now dead controller be tortured. "This'll never pass over. They need to know Brenner is dead. Besides, we need to get Chin back here."

Just then Michael put his hand to his ear. "Go ahead, dear." He nodded, listening. "Ok, get the hell out of here. Tell Mike to keep working and to stay low. We'll pull back in five minutes." Another pause. "Ok, take care. Love you."

I heard others with headsets whisper goodbyes into their microphones. Void of the details, Richard and I looked to Michael. He sighed. "They're zeroing in on us. A large group is heading down the street. Hannah is getting her team out of here through a secret route."

"Shame to leave her base and equipment behind." Richard said with a downbeat. A second later I could hear small explosions, banging and smashing coming from the old store's backroom.

"She's trashing her hardware so those pricks can't have it." Michael snarled. "Chin!" He looked off into empty space. "Work your way back here. Your distraction's over. We're warping out in five minutes."

"Why don't we just head back there now?" I asked. "Or why don't we go with Hannah's group?"

Michael nodded. "No, not until the portal is ready. I want to give Mike plenty of space and we've put Hannah's team in enough danger. We need to keep the army off their backs." He looked at Richard. "Any ideas?"

"Oh yes." Richard smirked and I'll be damned if his eye didn't twinkle. "You want to inspire these people? Well, let's inspire them." He situated himself into a better sitting position then gently placed both hands on Michael's head while closing his eyes. "The old multiple illusion trick should work."

Michael nodded. "Right." His eyes darted around. "They know we're here, hiding is pointless now and will only further pin us down. We need to slow them. Sally, take the team, get Chin and keep them busy. Five minutes then we're gone." He paused before closing his own eyes. "Sworn, stay with Richard and me."

I snorted. This staying behind thing was getting real old. With a couple deep breaths I told myself to relax and remembered I was here for David. Sally, Drew and Olivia crept off toward the door and as I looked beyond, I saw a wave of Tehlasrin soldiers heading toward us. They moved quickly but cautiously.

"Almost ready." Richard droned. "Here we go."

I couldn't believe it. Suddenly there were several Michael Vistaers standing around me. I made sure the Michael I'd seen before, the original Michael, was still sitting in front of Richard. Yes, he was there. He was also behind me and to my left and right. He was everywhere!

"Begin." Richard ordered.

I watched the original Michael as he spoke. "Hello. I'm Michael Vistaer." Every Vistaer in the room spoke at the same time and volume.

Gasps, roars, cheers and gunshots suddenly filled the air outside the store. I looked out through the glass and was astonished to see dozens of Michael Vistaers scattered all over the place. The few shots came from Tehlasrin troops trying to kill the illusions. From what I could tell, the soldiers were as baffled as I was.

"I'm sure most of you have seen me on telescreens or heard me over the radio." Michael continued in a smooth, friendly and diplomatic tone. "I know most of you share my dream. Most of you want to fight. Most of you want to be free. I can't do anything alone. My team can't do anything alone. We need each other. Only by working together can we overthrow the evil that Tehlasrin has become. Now is the time to stand up and take action. I'm talking to all of you! Citizens, guards, soldiers! Fight the abomination that steals our children, controls us and uses us as slaves."

I watched Michael deliver his speech. His eyes were still closed and his hands were clenched in tight fists. He gritted his teeth and snarled. Turning again to look outside, everyone was at a standstill, completely dumbfounded. I didn't blame them. Suddenly a wanted man, one of the leaders of the resistance was everywhere delivering a speech the Union would consider treason.

"WE ARE HUMAN BEINGS!" Michael's roar sent out an echo that seemed to reverberate through the entire city. "I'm sick to death of the Union's tyranny and would rather die than live under it any longer! I've removed Elias Brenner. He's dead and gone. Now you're free to start over. Defend your freedom before another monster takes his place."

Michael's tone softened a bit. "Guards. I beg you, please. Stand with us, with freedom. Let the spirit of liberty wash over you. I don't want to be your enemy. I don't want to fight you. Many of you want a better world than the one the Union has to offer. You, like me, want a better life for your friends, families and yourselves. This… this hell we've trapped ourselves in isn't natural. We're NOT supposed to live like this. Join with us and cast off the repressive controllers. That's all I have to say. The time is now. The place is NOW. CHOOSE!"

And then, the world outside the old furniture store became a wash of chaos. It started with more cheers, then roars, then orders from Tehlasrin guards telling people to drop to the ground. From there rocks were cast, punches were thrown and shots were fired. All hell broke loose.

In the distance I could see Sally and the others fire on the troops. I saw most of the people who'd been hiding charge the Tehlasrin guards, attacking those who weren't already fighting with their fellows. Michael Vistaer's words had whipped people into frenzy and managed to shift the allegiance of nearly half the Union's guards I could see. The guards that had changed sides removed their helmets in what seemed a show of defiance. I wondered if this, as wonderful, horrible, shocking, liberating and dangerous as it was, was what Michael wanted.

"Don't be shocked, Jason." Michael's deep voice rumbled as he stood up. The instances of gunfire outside increased. "I told you people were ready for something new. Help Richard make it back to Mike. We'll be there shortly."

"Help Richard?" I looked at the man who appeared much older than he did two minutes ago. He was having a hard time standing up.

Michael suddenly put his hand up to his ear and pressed it against the headphone. "Repeat?!?" He said, urgently. "NO, Sally!" In a flash, he tore the lethal twin blades out of their holsters and headed for the madness outside.

Confused, I looked down at Richard. The man nodded. "Go, help him. Don't worry about me. GO!"

Without thinking I rushed to follow Michael who was already outside literally slashing through any Tehlasrin guards that remained aggressive toward him. I stopped for cover behind a parked car, surveying the scene.

The three times I lined my weapon up to fire on enemy soldiers, Vistaer darted in for a brutal kill. He was quick as lightning, ramming his blades through the chest of one man and hacking away at the neck of another. On the third, he came up from behind, stuck his swords through the soldier's back, lifted him up into the air and tossed the body away at a small group of his enemies, knocking them all to the ground. In an instant, he was on them too.

Finally, while Michael was busy with two soldiers, I was able to fire on and incapacitate a woman soldier who appeared to have had her weapon locked on Vistaer's head. She dropped and Michael quickly turned to me. "COME!" He yelled over the chaos, either oblivious or ignoring the fact I just saved his life.

I followed as best I could through the smoke, gas, bullets, explosions, fighting, yelling, screaming and crying. At one point Michael halted his dash and used his weapons to end the lives of several other unfortunate soldiers. Standing still, out in the open, would quickly get me killed so I ducked for cover behind a beat up car. From there I shot 2 soldiers who were firing on a packs of civilians.

Vistaer was moving on but before I could follow, a woman's scream from behind me demanded my attention. I turned and saw a helmeted Tehlasrin soldier, in a black uniform, towering over a crying young woman who was down on her bloody hands and knees. Judging by the size, I guess the soldier was a man. He had a handful of the woman's long, scraggly, brown hair and was beating her across her back with a nightstick he grasped in his free hand.

The devil itself surged inside me. It's the only way I can think to describe the rage, disgust and hatred I immediately felt for the soldier. The angle I was at didn't give me a clear shot so I tucked the gun away and charged, quickly and brazenly, inconsiderate of all the dangers around me. The man saw me coming once I was a couple arm spans away. He released the woman and took a swing at me with his nightstick.

Had I not been so furious, I might've appreciated the fact or been amazed that I actually caught the club in mid air with my left hand, ripped it out of the guard's grip, tossed the weapon to my right hand and then slammed it, with as much force as I could, against his head. The helmet shattered into several pieces and the man stumbled to the ground. My fury wasn't satisfied. I fell on top of him and pinned the man down while pummeling him with his own nightstick until he stopped moving. I don't think he was dead but he was most definitely unconscious.

"THIS WAY!" Vistaer roared at me. I turned to him, surprised he came back to check on me. Without giving it anymore thought, I stood up, dropped the stick and pulled my pistol out, following the man again. I was satisfied to see the young, mud covered, woman I'd helped scamper off to a group of others that looked just like her. They greeted her with open arms then ran off together. A moment later I saw Olivia's ruby red eyes blazing just a few meters ahead. She was launching a volley of bullets at our enemies.

Michael hollered over the sounds. "HOW IS SHE?!?"

My eyes scanned the group and I saw Chin shaking his head looking down on Sally. The woman's eyes were closed and blood covered her face.

Drew roared and when I looked I saw tears in his eyes. "SHE'S DEAD! LET'S GET THE EFF OUT OF HERE!"

Michael holstered his swords and I could faintly hear him say, "We're not leaving her here." He crouched down and scooped Sally up in his arms. Then, without another word, he quickly turned and headed back for the furniture store. I followed with the rest of group and seemed to be the only one of the group still aware of the madness everywhere. Luckily, we made it back without incident.

We rushed toward the backroom and passed Richard along the way. The man was hobbling along and I helped him through the last half of the hallway, tucking my right arm under his left armpit. I grabbed my bag with my left hand when I passed it, only really thinking about the additional etherpistol ammunition.

Someone must've told the guy, Mike, we were close because the portal was open by the time we reached the conference room. Michael went first, still carrying Sally. Olivia, Drew and Chin went next. I helped Richard step into the misty, swirling rectangle leaving just Mike and me.

"Go!" The young man urged. "Don't worry, it's instant," he paused, thinking while I nervously studied the portal, "actually quicker than instant. Christ, MOVE!"

I stepped through and everything, my surroundings, the whole world, instantly changed. It was like waking from a vivid dream. Somehow, I was back in Denver.

Chapter 5

A slew of questions circled through my head like race cars on a track. Where was I? How did the portal I just used work? What exactly was that targe thing? What came of the chaos Michael Vistaer just helped create in Seattle? What would happen to the people fighting there? What happened to the other leaders? Everything, it was all too much to grasp at once. I struggled to narrow my thoughts down to one specific thing at a time. Regardless of all that, though, given the current situation, I had enough sense to keep my mouth shut. Sally, one of the members of the seemingly tight group, was dead.

"MARIE!" Michael yelled from a short distance away. The room, or building, we were in was similar to the small base we'd just left. There was lots of open space and several computer terminals scattered about. This place wasn't as clean or as brightly lit, though. The air carried a damp, almost musty smell of soap. It reminded me of a laundry room. Looking around I saw the far wall had several makeshift clotheslines set up with various garments hanging on them.

"Marie!" Michael called again not as loudly this time. "It's Sally! Hurry!"

Mike Taft magically appeared through the still swirling portal before rushing off in Vistaer's direction. The big man was gently laying Sally's body down on a large, old, beat up, brown couch. Others came into the room from different doorways and rushed to join their friends around their fallen companion.

The portal vanished, making the room's light even dimmer. A woman screamed as she fell to her knees next to Sally. She placed her hands on the slain woman's body and I guessed she was trying to perform a healing. I grimaced, it wasn't going to work. My bag numbly slipped from my fingers and fell to the floor.

"NO, no, no! Nothing! I can't feel her, I can't heal her! Michael," her slightly accented voice quivered as she looked up to meet Vistaer's eyes. "How? How did this happen? Why didn't she block the shot? Why?"

She started sobbing and Michael held her in his arms. "Shh." The woman buried her face in his chest and he gently stroked her hair.

"She tried, Marie." The tall Native American looking man, Drew, said somberly. His head hung low, shaking. "There were so many... too many."

Michael stood and pulled Marie up with him. "Come on, Honey." The words were heavy with sadness. "Come on." He looked back at one of the men who'd joined them. "Chris, keep watch on the base. I'll fill you in later."

The new man nodded then turned, noticing me and no doubt wondered who I was and what I was doing here. I stared back; something about him reminded me of David. His hair was a different color but they had similar builds and facial features. Rather than saying anything or asking any questions, he quietly moved on.

Michael took the sobbing woman back through one of several doors in the far corner opposite from where the portal had been. Chin and an older looking Hispanic man, who was crying rather heavily, scooped up Sally and took her through another door.

I didn't know what to do with myself so I stood where I was, thinking about Vistaer. In the short time I'd known him he'd been friendly, rude, compassionate and impulsive. He was so tender with Sally and now Marie it was hard to believe that just moments ago he was hacking and slashing through people like a barbaric machine. A half hour before that he put a bullet through the head of an unarmed prisoner.

"He's a complicated man for sure, Mr. Sworn."

I eased out of my daze and turned to see Richard Sands sitting in a chair, slumped over a nearby table. He looked both tired and sad. In a flash, though, my eyes immediately and involuntarily locked onto an absolutely, stunningly beautiful young woman who sat next to the old man. My heart raced and I think I blushed. The woman had strikingly shiny hair that was so blonde it looked white. Her face was soft and friendly, despite the sadness she no doubt felt for her lost friend. Most lovely and noticeable were her large eyes that were deep blue like mine only a hundred times more enjoyable to look at. I wasn't usually so focused on details but the woman, who I guessed was about the same age as Olivia, demanded it.

She gave me the slightest of smiles and her eyes glittered with fresh tears. My heart felt like it weighed a thousand pounds. She was beautiful and vulnerable. I wanted to help her. This girl, a complete stranger… I paused and it dawned on me. I immediately rubbed the back of my neck.

The young woman and the Richard both smirked but otherwise ignored my action. He nodded and pointed off behind me to my left. "She's watching you."

"What?" Confused, I slowly turned. A dog was standing not three feet away, intently studying me. I nearly jumped. I'd never had much interaction with dogs and had no idea what breed it was. She was bigger than most dogs I'd seen but not huge. Her fur was short but curly, a deep caramel color with patches of black on her back. She had a good size snout and her mouth was covered with a scruffy beard. Her large black nose and deep, dark eyes formed a perfect triangle. Those eyes stared right into mine. I swallowed.

"Don't worry," Richard said with mild amusement. "She won't hurt you unless you're a threat to one of us. She's just observing."

"Her name's Chickadis." The young woman said in a soft, dreamy voice that literally tickled the back of my neck. "She's Michael's dog. She's an Airedale. Come sit down."

I turned back to look at the cute young woman and smiled. "Are you talking to me or the dog?"

She laughed. "You."

I walked over to the table, a little weak in the knees, and sat across from her and Richard so I could see both their faces. The girl laughed as she looked at something just off to my right. The dog was right there, sitting again, still staring at me.

"Why don't you pet her?" She asked.

I bit my lip. "I don't have any experience with dogs."

"There's a way to remedy that, Jason." Richard said, nodding toward the animal.

With a slight nervousness, I reached out and pet the dog's head. She brought her snout up and rubbed her cold, wet nose against the palm of my hand then licked me with her large, pink tongue. It tickled and I nearly laughed.

"I think it's noble what you're doing for your friend."

I turned away from Chickadis and looked at the young woman. "You know why I'm here? How?" My gaze shifted to Richard.

The old man smiled even though his sharp eyes were still heavy with pain and fatigue. "Questions, questions, questions." He smiled. "They just never end, do they?"

Never, I thought and then nodded. "Things have been insane for weeks now. It's hard to keep up." I snorted. "I can't even decide which questions to ask."

"The targe, the teleporter, who we are, what we're doing here, is David ok, where is he, how will you save him, how do I know so much, how did I perform that enchant..." Richard listed the questions like he was plucking them right out of my head, he probably was. "... Is Michael Vistaer a good man, is he insane, what's his relationship to August Cross and why does he think the man's a coward, how is Maledro Morbal in a position to rule the continent, who is this young woman sitting by me, is the dog going to bite you?" He raised his eyebrows.

"For starters, yea." I said, mildly amused. Normally, I'd be annoyed by having someone read my thoughts but, right now, I didn't care.

"Michael's like a son to me." Richard said. "Perhaps even more so than Joshua but that's my own fault I suppose." There was a hint of regret in his voice. "As I mentioned, he's complicated, Michael that is. He contradicts himself in some ways and he's a slave to his passion. Love and rage burn equally bright. I admire his drive and I believe in him. He holds honor and compassion in high regard. The man yearns for liberty, for us all, and he'll continue to fight for it until he's won, or dead." He smiled. "I'm honored to help him, to fight with him."

Locked in thought, my eyes wandered back over to the woman's face.

"And this is Claire White." Richard said, putting his right arm around her shoulders.

She pulled away and I saw her left eye twitch. "Lilly." She looked at me. "My name is Lilly."

Richard swallowed. "Ah yes. Sorry, my dear. Like they say, it's hard to teach an old dog new tricks."

"See, that right there." I said quickly, pointing at the two. "What was that? Why was, Lilly," I nodded at the woman, damn she was hot, "obviously so upset about being called Claire? And why do you," my gaze was back on Richard, "suddenly seem so disturbed?"

"You're quite observant." Richard dodged the questions.

I huffed. "I'm usually not. I just want answers." Silence hung in the air for a few seconds. "Look, I'm sorry. You both just lost a friend. I don't want to impose but I have a friend of my own that needs to be saved."

"Very noble." Lilly said, softly. "I'm sorry I was so rude a moment ago. You're our guest. I should behave better."

"Rude?" I squinted. "No, no, you're fine. Don't worry about it." My eyes studied her lips… they were like a sexy combination of soft rose petals and fresh, plump cherries. When my thoughts dwelled on licking, kissing and nibbling them, I knew it was time to administer another deep massage to the back of my neck.

Lilly smiled and winked. "You'll need help, Jason." She sang her words like a soft lullaby. "Your friend is in Morbal's asylum." She turned to the old man. "Richard, you can help, right?"

Damn, the old guy looked dead tired, barely able to keep his eyes open. I expected him to tell me how foolish I was, how hopeless my aims were, that he couldn't and/or wouldn't help. His eyes still studied me and he groaned when he spoke. "Yes. Of course I'll help him."

I raised my eyebrows. "Great. How?"

"Someone going to Morbal's?" A young woman's voice said from behind me. I turned to see Olivia. She bounded up and plopped herself in the seat next to me, pulled out a cigarette, lit it then looked at Lilly. "Hey there, Butterfly."

"Hello Liv." Lilly said. "I'm glad you made it back safe."

Olivia nodded. "Sucks. I can't believe Sally's dead. Just effing sucks." She turned in my direction and looked past me. "Heya Chickadis, you rascal. Howwu dowwin?"

Baby talk from a red eyed, sharp toothed woman with black fingernails and cigarette smoke steaming out of her nose. I chuckled. She looked at me. "If Richard wants to help you get into Morbal's, I want in." She looked at the old man whose eyes were nearly closed. "He's just the tops. I love him."

Lilly sighed. "Love." My heart nearly broke as several fresh tears ran down her sweet, soft, rosy cheeks. "I'm sorry. I'll leave you all be." She stood and glided away. I was sad to see her go.

"See ya." Olivia said with more cheer than the situation called for.

Richard pulled me back to the present. "You've seen me do some things lately, Mr. Sworn, that I'm sure you consider quite remarkable. I can help you get in and out of Morbal's but not now. I'm utterly exhausted."

I sighed with frustration. A sudden, agitating wave of urgency tingled through my body. I didn't want to wait any longer. "Well, thanks anyways. I need to go. If you can't help me I'll head out on my own. Don't worry about it."

The old man's eyes were wide open now. "Nonsense, Jason Sworn. I won't allow you to get yourself killed or captured. Not when I know I can help you and not after all the trouble we've already been through."

I curled my lip and straightened myself in my seat. "Hey, I appreciate everything you've done and the offer to help me but it's time to move." I smirked, smugly. "You can't stop me."

Olivia giggled as she blew out another plume of smoke.

Richard sat back in his chair. "You need to recharge your energy too. The group is in mourning and I'm sorry but the answers you seek will need to wait. I'll see you in the morning."

My anger started to build. "Listen -" Everything went dark.

-

The next thing I knew, I woke up lying on a small, uncomfortable mattress in the middle of a tiny room made up of the bed I was on, a door, which was open, a small dresser with my bag sitting on top of it and a dirty oval mirror hanging on the wall. People were moving about and talking outside the room I was in. A faint smell of coffee reached my nose.

I sat up and tried to gather my wits. There weren't any windows I could see but it felt like morning. That might've been due to the coffee smell. I still had on the clothes I'd been wearing since getting off the boat and felt especially grimy. It was safe to say I didn't smell too good either.

After getting up, I studied my reflection in the mirror which caused a wave of memories to race through my brain. Images from dreams I'd just had played over in vague sequences. They were of David again, leaving somewhere on a boat, a very fast boat. Waves rocked by and wind blew in his face. He seemed proud, feeling successful. Behind him was what looked like an island engulfed in a raging inferno. The whole thing was burning. Flashes from explosions went off in random places like dances of light in a lightning storm.

What was going on? David's face was blurry but I knew it was him. Why was he so happy? What happened? What did he do? Where the eff was he?

Giving up, I shook the images out of my head. They were dreams, no point in dwelling on them. I'd once dreamt I built a flying machine out of a lawn mower. No truth in that, just random absurdity.

Pulling back to my image in the mirror, I was pleased to see that, despite the stubble on my face and my short but disheveled hair, my eyes were bright and alert. I guessed I'd just gotten a lot of sleep and had the energy to find David.

Richard had done something to me, knocked me out. That was obvious. Now I wasn't sure if I should be mad at him for doing so. I supposed that would depend on how much and how quickly he could help me.

Hungry, I followed my nose and eventually found my way to what passed for a kitchen. The dog, Chickadis, found me and trailed behind. I stopped and turned to look at her. She stared directly into my eyes, studying me. Not sure what to do or think, I turned and continued toward the kitchen.

The room was a fair size with four round tables in it which could each seat 4 people comfortably. It was lit by several fluorescent lights in the ceiling and had a tile floor. The walls, aside from one that was made of a sink, refrigerator and stove, were covered with clips of paper. I took a closer look at the nearest wall and saw newspaper headlines about rebellion. Next to them were pages, I learned with a little investigation, from the old US Constitution. The Bill of Rights were scattered about. Glancing around, I saw the list was a theme throughout the three walls. I blinked, wishing I knew more about history.

Chin stood up and walked past me, "Morning, Jason." He exited the kitchen and pet Chickadis on his way out, leaving just me, the guy who looked like David and, much to my approval, Lilly.

I studied the pretty young woman, now able to look at her with fresh, alert eyes. She wore a pair of well worn blue jeans and a nice, form fitting sweatshirt. Cute. For a fraction of a second I thought I saw odd, bright, little flames dancing around her head. Something about them, about her, right then and there, made me almost believe David was in the room with us. Strange. I shook my head and rubbed my eyes.

"Sit down." She hummed. "I'll make you some eggs."

I took the nearest seat. Chickadis parked herself right by me and licked her nose. "Thanks." I said finally.

The man in the room with us set his fork down on his empty plate. "I hear you're heading into Morbal's asylum." He had a southern accent and wore a tight fitting flannel, short sleeve shirt that appeared to be missing a few buttons. I looked him in his eyes. He nodded and raised his eyebrows. "My name's Chris."

"Jason." I said.

He chuckled and smirked in a friendly way. "I know."

"Here you go, Hun." Lilly set a cup of steaming coffee in front of me. "Sorry, out of cream and sugar right now."

I looked up to meet her eyes. They were as big, blue and beautiful as ever but still glossy and a little red from crying. "Thank you." I watched her glide back over to the stove, marveling at her lovely shape. The urges I felt weren't as strong as they were the last time I saw her. I was still attracted to her but maintained my wits, no need to rub my neck.

"It won't be easy," Chris pulled me away from my thoughts, "but you should be ok with Richard's help."

I blew into my cup then took a sip. Not bad. The coffee wasn't like what like the stuff on Aswain but I'd had much worse. "It's why I'm here. For a friend."

Chris nodded slowly and pursed his lips. Somehow, I knew he was thinking about Sally. The word friend set off some subtle emotions in him. I changed the subject, feeling a bit uncomfortable and odd at being able to read the man so well. Something was different about me, I felt it.

"So," I began, glancing again at Lilly's adorable frame, "what is this place?"

Chris set his cup down. "Our base for the time being. We're in the back room of an old toy store. We move around a lot but always try to stay in or right around the city." He paused, thinking. "Denver is sort of the capital of North America now. We get a lot done while infiltrating here."

My brow furrowed and I looked around again at the walls. "You move around a lot? Seems to be a lot of decoration for something temporary."

"It's a pain each time we move. We need to soundproof the walls to keep the Union's ears away and we have to screen out our heat signatures in case there are any investigations by air, though those are less common thanks to the targe." He gestured the wallpaper. "The decorating was Michael's idea. It's good to see the fruits of some of our labors. They remind us why we're fighting."

"Yea." I agreed and then looked back at Chris's face. "The water, the electricity. How do you keep them on? I doubt you guys are paying bills."

Chris smiled. "It wasn't always like this. Hasn't always been so comfortable."

I thought about the stiffness in my neck and back from the little bed. Comfortable?

"But this place is a sign," Chris went on, "that we're making progress. We've got sources deep in the infrastructure helping us out with things like utilities and information."

I took another drink of my coffee, burning my tongue a little, made a face. "It's amazing how hollow and pathetic the GU seems these days."

The man stood up and I saw a large knife holster strapped to his left hip. The handle of what I figured was an impressive blade stood out prominently. "Wasn't always that way either." He looked around, thinking again. "But the tide's turning. It can't be stopped now, all we need to do is press on. See ya around, Cl-Lilly." He headed out of the kitchen then stopped, looking at me. "Oh, Drew doesn't like you."

I squinted, immediately on edge and ready for a fight. Damn short fuse. The dog seemed to sense my aggression and grumbled a little under her breath.

"Don't take it personally," Chris added. "He doesn't much like anyone, especially at first. Just try to stay out of his way."

I wanted to tell Chris to tell Drew to stay out of *my* way but kept that thought in my head. Instead, I shrugged and the other man moved on. I turned back to Lilly and wondered how, given the setting, she managed to look so heavenly.

"We don't have showers here." She said with her back to me, still working over one of the stove's burners. "We make due with the sinks in the restrooms." She turned to spare a quick look my way. "You can shave and get cleaned up after breakfast."

I was puzzled by the woman giving me permission but brushed it off. "Ok."

She brought over two plates, each carrying a good stack of steaming, scrambled eggs, set one in front of me and then sat down across from me with her own serving. "I'm sorry, out of salt and pepper too."

I took a bite and was pleased with the taste. I was so hungry I wanted to pile them all down quickly but forced myself to match Lilly's pace. "These are great, thank you."

"Not as good as the eggs you get on Aswain, though." Lilly said with a little smile.

I stopped midscoop. "Have you been there?"

She raised her eyebrows. "Aswain? Of course. August is almost like family." She shrugged, "An uncle of sorts. I spent a lot of time there when I was a kid."

I froze, deep in thought for several moments and watched her eat.

She leaned her head to her right. "I really hope you find David. I admire your bravery, Jason." I swallowed, feeling a little odd. "You're a beautiful man."

Now I outright blushed and laughed defensively. "I've never been called that before. Maybe you should wait until you know me better before you decide how *beautiful* I am."

"I know you, Jason." The look on her face was both dreamy and serious.

I was momentarily lost in her eyes but still managed the word, "How?"

She whispered back. "Don't worry about that for now. Just believe me. The world is an interesting place and the way things work is even more fascinating." She paused long enough to have a couple bites of her eggs. "Do you miss Fier?"

My face flushed again. "Fier? I guess." Thoughts raced through my head. It hadn't been that long since I saw her, just over a day, but yes, damn it, I did miss her. However... having a sexy young woman like Lilly showing interest in me stirred up several questions. Fier was attractive, honest, strong and lively. But. She was back on Aswain and I knew I might never see her again. And I knew she'd be more than angry with me.

Lilly, on the other hand, was right here. I mentally shrugged the thoughts away. I was here for David, not to score any young women. Besides, I told myself, the young beauty was probably just being nice, not at all interested in me. I focused back on my breakfast.

Lilly laughed, capturing my complete attention again.

"What?" I asked.

"You're funny." She said. "Always thinking, trying to figure things out. Sometimes it's easier to just feel and give the thinking a rest." Lilly blinked then bit her bottom lip. "I'm sorry, Jason. I don't want to burden you. You have enough on your mind."

Now I laughed. "You need to stop apologizing for doing nothing wrong. And I wouldn't say I'm always thinking. I'm not much of a thinker."

"You are though." She nodded. "Ok, enough about you, it's unfair I know so much about you and you know so little about me."

I swallowed another mouthful. How the hell did she know anything about me?

"Go ahead," Lilly started, "ask away. What do you want to know about me?"

I really wanted to know why this sexy young woman was being so nice to me but I tried to be a bit more tactful. "Ok, um," I thought. "How old are you?"

"Twenty." She blurted immediately.

I pulled back a little, still trying to grasp how open the girl was. "And you're a hailiorum." It wasn't really a question.

"Of course, we all are."

Fair enough. "Alright, how did you get mixed up in the revolution? How did you join Michael's team?"

"Finally." She said. "Some real questions." She set her fork down. "My father was very close with Michael from the time I was born. He died when I was thirteen."

I dropped my gaze down to the tabletop. I never knew how to react or sympathize with those who lost others. "I'm sorry."

Lilly reached over and grabbed my hand. Her skin was like a warm slice of velvet. There was also strength in her hand. I met her eyes again and she went on. "It's ok. They worked together with August and others, trying to sabotage the Union as much as they could before it even got started."

I nodded, always impressed to hear that Cross had helped keep Tehlasrin from being even worse than it already was. There was no evidence other than the words of others but I chose to believe them. It felt right somehow. "I see."

Lilly slowly pulled her hand away. "So you could say I was born into the resistance." She said. "I've known Michael as long as I can remember and I like to think my talents have helped him and the others."

I drew in a breath, feeling nosey. "What can you do?"

"My gifts?" She smirked. "This and that. I can heal a little but not as well as Marie. My illusion skills aren't as marvelous as Richard's. I sometimes have telekinetic abilities but they're not reliable." She paused, her blue eyes opened a little wider. "My real gift to the team is the inspiration I help create in others. I help build positive thoughts and fight despair."

"Interesting." I spoke in dull tone I didn't mean to let out.

Lilly laughed. "You're mocking me?"

I shook my head quickly. "No, not at all!"

She laughed again. "Inspiration for hailiorea makes them better at everything they do. Michael and Richard, and August for that matter, have said it's one of the greatest gifts a hailiorum can have."

I considered that. "I see now." It wasn't a lie, it really did make sense. Hailiorea could be even faster, stronger, heal better, everything. I looked at Lilly and smiled. The smile faded when I suddenly saw a dark cloud, a strange mist around her head. It vanished as quickly as it arrived. I wondered if I'd imagined it or not.

Lilly spoke with a downbeat. "But, something happened that's nearly taken that gift away. I can't inspire like I used to." She looked at me and a tear dropped from her left eye.

Now, without thinking, it was my hand reaching out for hers. I rubbed her soft fingers with my thumb. "What happened?"

"So sweet." She said softly. "I'll tell you some time. One of the reasons I stay here, now, is so Richard can help me."

The next question was out through my lips as quickly as it popped in my head. It seemed important, like it made a huge difference in Lilly's life. "What about your mother?"

She looked at me without speaking for an uncomfortable amount of time. "She died recently."

"Jesus, I'm sorry." The poor girl was filled with tragedy and my dumb ass kept bringing up painful subjects.

"Don't feel bad, Jason." Lilly said, sounding better than she did a few moments before. "I told you to ask me anything. I was never very close to my mom. She died and now…" She snorted.

I didn't want to pry so I just moved my hand away from hers and ate the rest of my eggs.

Lilly worked on her own plate. "I had no idea the bitch was bound to me."

Hearing her swear felt oddly out of place, like hearing an opera singer sing about pornography. I was more shocked than confused but still managed to ask, "Bound?"

"You don't know about that." Lilly stated. "Some hailiorea can bind part of their essence, their being, their soul to their children. Sometimes even siblings or very close friends or companions."

I took a drink of coffee, again amazed at what I was hearing. "How is that even possible?" Hell, I didn't believe in souls but I couldn't accept that Lily would lie to me, nor did I think she was a fool or crazy.

"The world is a mystifying place." She said calmly. "Now part of my mother is in me. We're bound." Tears welled up in her eyes and her lip quivered. "It's why I'm so emotional. I don't like it at all and I'm not sure how to deal with it. I'm trying though."

I had absolutely no idea what to say. I just sat there like a big, dumb idiot. Lilly stood up and took her plate to the sink. "Thanks for having breakfast with me. If I don't see you before you go, be careful at Morbal's. Don't get hurt."

I only nodded and scratched my head. Chickadis rested her snout on my lap and I patted her head without thinking.

Chapter 6

"This is stupid." Michael Vistaer fumed with contempt, leaning against a wall across from me with his arms crossed. He'd been carrying on for a while and was really starting to piss me off.

I tried to ignore him and focused on Richard who was seated across from me. "You've gotten some rest. Good." He nodded with approval. "That'll help. You seem as ready as can be. Still," he glanced at Michael then back at me, "your consciousness is expanding as I predicted. Don't let that distract you."

"What?" I had no idea what he was talking about. He was right about me being ready to help David though. I'd slept, ate, shaved and cleaned up as best I could. The restroom could only go so far. I was clean in a sense but the facilities couldn't rival an actual shower.

Now it was nearly seven o'clock in the evening and we were in another room that was tucked away in the back of the toy store. It was small but had enough space for a fold out table and a few chairs. Michael, Richard, Olivia, Drew and a young Asian man, who didn't look a day over sixteen, shared the space.

Richard studied me. "The reading I gave you back in the van. Your mind is open now." He raised his silver eyebrows.

"Been seeing things? More observant? Been having any revealing dreams?"

I grimaced. My dreams about David were odd and seemed real but I didn't put much stock in them. "Maybe."

"Don't dwell on them." Richard said with warning. "You need to keep your mind clear if my illusion is going to work."

Michael snorted. "Waste of time and energy." He looked down on me. "You really think you can help your shattered friend? You'll probably get yourself killed."

I set my jaw and stared at the big man. "It's why I'm here. Why do you even care, anyways?"

"Because it's stupid." He hissed. "We have bigger things to take care of. You're a selfish fool."

I snapped, pounding my fist on the table and bolting out of my seat. "He's saved my life more than once, god damn it! I'M GOING TO SAVE HIM!"

Michael growled and stepped toward me. "I should order Mike to open a portal to Aswain and toss your ass through it."

"Eff you." I spat.

Chickadis, who was sitting next to Michael grumbled under her breath.

"And you shut up too, dog." I curled my lip at the animal.

Olivia laughed.

I heard Drew step up behind me. "Looks like Mr. Demon Slayer is getting cocky."

I turned to look at the man, hands instinctively balling into fists. "What are you going to do about it? Why the hell are you even in here?"

"Enough of all this nonsense!" Richard raised his voice and shut everyone up. "Jason, I said I'd help and that's what I'm going to do." He turned to Vistaer. "You can leave if you wish, Michael. You too, Mr. Olsen."

The big man huffed and took his spot back against the wall, eyes fixed on me. Drew backed off too and Chickadis licked her lips then hung her head low, cutting her eyes around the room.

"Now, let us go over the plan." Richard's tone was calm and relaxed. I sat back down. "You're wearing the keeper uniform supplied by Mr. Lee."

I looked at the baby faced Asian man. He was visibly uncomfortable with the tension in the room and stood close to Olivia. The clothes I wore, dark blue shirt and pants to match with a black belt and shoes, were tight but they fit. The things must have been baggy as hell on the thin Mr. Lee.

"Who are you anyways?" I asked.

He swallowed then attempted a smile. "I'm Sean Lee. I've been working at Morbal's for a little while as a keeper but I'm done with that place." He looked at Olivia and she smiled at him. "Thought I could make a name for myself but that place is evil. My father was right. I'm going to work with him. He runs a super center here in Denver."

"Yep." Olivia said. "My man's practically royalty."

Super center. So Lee's dad was one of the few that could still be considered middle class. Not rich like the corrupt controllers but far better off than most others. The young man was a keeper so naturally my instinct was to hate him. I'd dealt with my fair share of keepers. Most were sadistic assholes and vicious control freaks. The only one that ever helped me was Berg and he'd been bribed.

I put the thoughts out of my head, tugged on my shirt and looked at Richard. "Ok, so how does this help me?"

Lee fought to find his tongue, only managed a mumble.

Richard spoke first. "You're wearing a uniform he supplied and you have his identification, pass and shock gloves." He paused. "These things will help you get in but won't get you far beyond. That's where I come in."

Something about the man's tone spooked me a little. I looked at Sean. "Have you seen David Holt? Do you know where he is?"

"Who?" The young man shook his head. "No, sorry."

I swore under my breath.

"Jason, eyes on me!" Richard snapped. I gave him my attention. "I'm going to weave an illusion enchantment on you. It'll work as long as you allow it to work. Keep focused."

Michael shifted his weight. "It never works that way with me."

"That's because you never stay properly focused, Michael." Richard's tone was full of scorn. He focused back on me. "An aura will surround you that'll keep others from making any special notice of you. To them, you'll be as noticeable or troublesome as a soft breeze. So long as you even somewhat believe and keep a modicum of mindfulness, the vale should last a couple weeks. Now, if anyone does try to zero in on you, you'll look like Mr. Lee. That effect will only last twenty-four hours."

My rational mind didn't want to believe what Richard was telling me but I was learning to give reason and logic a rest. I'd seen too many bizarre things in the past few weeks to dismiss anything at this point.

I studied the standard issue shock gloves resting on the table. They could be lethal but didn't offer the security I really wanted. I looked up at Sean. "Hey. Can I sneak my etherpistol inside if I tucked it in one of those gloves?"

"You can't survive a firefight against them all." Michael droned, speaking down on me like I was an idiot.

I was tired of everyone doubting my abilities. "Oh, so I should go in unarmed? Yea, that makes sense."

Vistaer sighed and rolled his eyes. "Whatever."

I looked at Sean again, waiting for an answer.

"Uh, a what?" He asked.

Annoyed, I let out a slow, deep breath, "This," and pulled out my pistol, setting it on the table.

The young man thought for a moment then picked it up. "So light." He looked at me. "What is this?"

"Can I get it inside if I hid it inside one of the gloves?" I asked again.

He chewed on his lip. "They have metal detectors set up but this might not register." He shrugged and set the weapon back down. "Maybe. I dunno."

I looked back at Richard, deciding then and there to give my smuggling attempt a try. "So how does this illusion work?"

Richard smiled ever so slightly. "Stand up, Mr. Sworn, and step back from the table."

I obeyed while the old man stood and walked over to me.

"You're willing to believe, I need you to remain accepting and focused." He paced around me in clockwise circles. "I can weave the spell but you need to keep it alive, feed it with your will."

My heart quickened and an eerie silvery mist trailed behind Richard, circling me in stringy lines of smoke.

"Use the drive and determination you feel to help your friend. Use that power." The man's voice grew sleepy, hypnotic and had a mystical chime to it. "Understand. You will move unnoticed, practically unseen. You'll be a shadow in a dark room. Close your eyes."

I did so and for the next several minutes Richard continued to walk circles around me, muttering under his breath. I felt like was on a cloud, floating about, weightless. Finally, he stopped.

"Alright, Jason. Open your eyes."

I stared at the man in silence for a few beats, feeling like I'd been abruptly woken up while in the middle of a dream. My eyes blinked the bright light away. "Did it work?"

"Hmm," Sean said. "I don't see any difference."

Richard smirked and looked at the young man. "Of course. You were in the room with us. You know this is Jason Sworn." He looked at me and winked. "I'm not *that* good. Not good enough to fool people who so openly know the truth." He laughed. "*Truth* is one of the most powerful forces in nature."

"But it worked?" I asked again.

Just then, Chris entered the room, quickly scanning for Michael. "Sir! Everiel exploded!"

Confused, I turned to Vistaer. He visibly perked up and pushed off the wall. "What? Exploded? How?"

"We're not sure." Chris shook his head, speaking fast. "But the place is wasted. Everyone there is believed dead. The news just got out even though it looks like everything went to hell a couple days ago."

"What's Everiel?" I asked, not sure why, given everything that was going on, I was so intrigued.

Richard spoke. "It's an island off the coast of Mexico owned and run by the controller Steven Ark." He paused as I turned to him. "Think of it as a twisted Aswain."

"What the hell?" Chris said, suddenly noticing me.

I turned to look at him. He was looking back and forth from Sean and me.

Olivia chuckled and clapped her hands. "You see two of my baby?" She grinned, happily showing off her sharp teeth while her red eyes glinted. "As nice as that would be, that one," she pointed at me, "is Jason." She looked at me and gave a cute, little wink. "See, I told you Rick was the best. The spell works great."

"Normally you wouldn't even have been noticed but Mr. Fuller is an especially astute man." Richard said, giving Chris a little nod.

"Alright, shush!" Michael interrupted, aggressively shoving his big frame right into my personal space. His attention was solely on Chris. "We need to contact Cross. See what he knows." On his way out of the room he turned back to me and squinted his eyes. "So long, Sworn."

I watched him go, unsure what to make of him. Hell, maybe he was right. Maybe it was hopeless and I was heading off to get myself killed or tortured... No, now wasn't the time for doubt.

"We have to go!" Sean said, suddenly sounding frantic. "My shift starts in a half hour. Jason needs to check in."

Olivia gripped my arm and pulled. "Grab the gloves and your gun and let's go."

I did so then followed behind the young, unlikely couple.

"Jason." Richard called. I turned. "Believe, stay focused and you'll be fine."

I let out a deep breath. "Right."

"And Jason." Richard called again. "Brace yourself for whatever the truth may be. You're here, you're trying, you're doing the best you can. Don't despair over things that are out of your control."

Unsure what to say, I nodded and turned back around to follow Sean and Olivia. On the way I passed Lilly. Her large eyes were planted on me as she bit her thumbnail, nervously.

"Be careful." She said in her soft, sweet voice.

I swallowed. Part of me wanted to worry, to be afraid. But above it all, I felt alive, like I had when I helped kill the osilea. Finally, I was off to help my friend.

-

The asylum was as bland, white, sterile and putrid as ever. The fluorescent lights gave me an instant headache and the smell made me want to throw up. There weren't any signs of the carnage from the day David and I escaped. Everything was scrubbed, cleaned and painted to perfectly match the hell I remembered. If I could have one wish, other than finding David and getting him to safety, it would be to see this place leveled to the ground without a trace remaining. I hated it with all my being.

Olivia and Sean dropped me off a block away from the front gates so I could walk in on my own. The kid gave me a rundown on where to go, what to do and how to behave. The keepers were a smug group, drunk with petty power from their positions and not at all friendly with each other. That worked to my advantage. The last thing I wanted was to be dragged into small talk or team banter. No, the keepers didn't like each other and were always looking to get ahead of the rest so they'd move up in rank. Greedy, selfish, twisted, untrusting power seekers, all of them.

Denver, like all super cities in the Union, held a strict curfew over the millions of people stuck there. No one was to be out after sunset unless they were going to or from work, were on specific tasks from a controller or were one of their officers. So, the streets were quiet as I marched toward the asylum entrance.

Getting through security was a hundred times easier than I thought it'd be and was testament to Richard's enchantment. Hardly anyone even looked at me. I flashed and scanned my card three times and the metal detectors made no notice of my pistol. The electronic and metallic frame of the shock gloves shielded it well.

For the next two and half hours, as directed by Sean, I took on his duties patrolling the asylum, pacing up and down all the wings of the place. His position was primarily to alert others if things got out of hand. That helped improve my opinion of the guy. At least he wasn't one of the bastard keepers assigned to specific pods of inmates. Those were the real monsters. Apparently, Lee wasn't wicked enough for that assignment. Good.

I kept my eyes and ears open the whole time for any sign or whisper of David. There were several computer terminals set up along various halls but it was hard finding the time to access any of them. At one point I had an entire hallway to myself and managed to punch David Holt into the search engine. Nothing came up. I was eventually interrupted and had to move on before investigating further.

Every now and then I passed keepers who were dragging, tugging or pushing inmates from one point to another. None of them even so much as looked at me. It took a considerable amount of restraint to keep from bashing the guards' heads against the wall. I knew the pain and fear the inmates were going through. None of the prisoners deserved the abuse and seeing it all filled me with anger.

I felt like a ghost, gliding through the bland, white hallways. It was almost surreal, walking by groups of people without receiving the slightest acknowledgment of my existence. That's not to say the reality of the situation wasn't tossing and turning in my gut the whole time. Fear, doubt and despair each took their turns tormenting me, forcing me to shut my thoughts down long enough to take several deep, head clearing breaths. I'd made it this far. David had to be around here, somewhere, but the longer the night went on with no sign of him, the harder it was to remain even slightly optimistic.

Where the hell was he? Forrest said David was sent 'home' and Cross confirmed he was here. So where? The puzzle played on in my head as I passed the asylum's surgery room. It was the room where David and I killed Forate. I shivered and quickened my pace.

As I rounded another corner, one that led to a series of pod sleep quarters, I saw a group of six keepers huddled together. After a quick count, I saw they were bullying twelve inmates.

"Shut up!" One of the keepers, a captain I quickly observed spat on the nearest inmate after speaking. "Don't move or you're effed, I swear! Bunch of animals, all of you!"

A couple other keepers laughed and punched several patients in their stomachs. The victims fell to the floor. From there, the keepers began kicking them.

Rage flared inside me, making it nearly impossible to think clearly. I slowed my pace but had to keep walking. To suddenly stop would be suspicious, even with Richard's spell. I considered shooting the keepers right there but that wouldn't help David any. Eff...

I inhaled deeply before blowing the breath out with force. It was best to keep to myself and just waltz by unnoticed. I scanned the faces of the inmates to confirm David wasn't one of them.

"YOU!" The captain shouted, aiming an index finger at me. "Come here."

My heart felt like it was going to pound itself right through my ribcage. Unsure what else to do, I obeyed and stepped up to the pig.

The keeper looked at me, studying my face before speaking. "Help keep watch on these." He gestured the inmates. "I'm leading Doctor Morbal's escort home and can't waste my time here."

I surveyed the group, thinking... Morbal. He'd know where David was, he had to.

"DO YOU HEAR ME?" The captain yelled.

My eyes met his and I nodded my head.

"Then effing answer me when I talk to you!" The man gritted his teeth as he spoke and I wanted to knock every one of them out of his stupid mouth.

I cooled off as best I could and slightly bowed my head. "Sorry, sir. When does the doctor leave?"

"What the eff do you care, *hall monitor*?" He almost laughed. "The cleaning crew will be here soon." He turned and addressed all the keepers present. "Get these sacks of trash back into their beds as soon as the crew is done. You two!" He pointed at two of the keepers. "Come with me."

With that, the man power walked off, down the hallway, followed by the two others. I turned to nearest keeper who was smiling, giddily, leering at the downtrodden group of inmates.

"Alright boys, the cat's away, time for the men to play." The keeper furthest from me spoke in a lusty, mischievous tone I didn't like one bit.

"What happened in the room?" I asked, hoping to sidetrack whatever devilish plans were brewing inside their sick heads.

"One of these slobs got sick." The guard next to me said. "Crapped and puked all over the place. God they're so... I don't even know." He laughed.

"Line em up." The furthest keeper spoke again. He was a good size man, head shaved bald with manic, dark, soulless eyes. He looked at me. "We're going to teach these effers what happens when they make a mess."

"And what happens when they make us work overtime!" Another keeper, who was much smaller than the last, said while looking down on the inmates.

My heart raced. They were going to beat and torture the defenseless men. I couldn't allow it. My heart raced and my adrenaline surged, making my muscles shake. "What about the cleaning crew? They'll show up any time." I tried to stall them one more time.

The third of the keepers, who already had his shock gloves on, spoke. "Hell, they can join in. They're the ones who have to clean the mess. My mom's a janitor, that effing bitch."

When the guard closest to me began charging up his gloves I snapped. My right hand clasped down on the man's left wrist with speed and strength, twisted it as far as it would go. I swung my left fist and landed it flat against his nose. The man's face exploded in a splatter of blood. He staggered back and dropped to the floor, groaning and cursing.

Before the second could react, I rammed my right fist into his gut. He crouched over, bent forward. I grabbed the back of his head with both hands, pulled it down and brought my right knee up, smashing his face as well.

Now the third and largest of the men had his full attention on me. "What the eff are you doing?" He hissed before lashing out at me. I ducked under his swing, dropped down and plowed my right elbow against the side of his left knee. I heard a satisfying crunch of bone. Being a large man, his own weight worked against him and he fell to the tiles. I was instantly on top of him, raining a quick series of lefts and rights against his face. Still conscious, I grabbed his head and rocked it hard against the floor until he stopped moving.

By then, the first, bloody faced keeper was up and coming at me. I snarled and charged him. Either it was due to my rage or hailiorum strength, but I easily overpowered the man, grabbing him, spinning his body around and slammed his head against the far wall. He dropped.

"Jason?"

I quickly turned toward the voice, wide eyed and shaking with adrenaline. I recognized the old man even though he wasn't wearing the thick glasses I remembered. "Tom?"

He grunted as he stood up. "It is you!" He spoke excitedly before lowering his voice. "What're you doing here? Is it another breakout?"

Guilt ran through my brain. The last time I'd seen the man I beat the living daylights out of him. "Um, no." I paused trying to gather my wits. "How can you see me?"

"You've changed." He sounded amazed. "You looked different a couple moments ago. I can't see very well since my spectacles broke but I can see you. I," he looked at the guards sprawled on the floor. "Thank you." His eyes were back on me. "So you've finally seen what I told you. The world is bigger than you knew."

I swore, realizing I must've lost my focus during the fight. I tried to get it back, telling myself Richard's enchants still worked. I hoped I knew what I was doing. The cloak *had* to work again.

"Listen." I started, "I'm here to get David. Have you seen him?"

He squinted as the other inmates got to their feet, nervously surveying the scene. "David Holt?" Tom shook his head. "No. He's here?"

"HEY!"

I turned to see the cleaning crew, a group of three men, heading toward me.

One of them quickened his pace. "What's going on here?"

My right hand automatically dug into one of the gloves hanging from my belt. It gripped the handle of my etherpistol and pulled the weapon out. The small group of janitors stopped in place. I wasn't sure of their intentions but couldn't take any chances. Thumbing the level down to a stun setting, about half power, I aimed and sent out two quick shots. Two of the three men fell to the ground. The third dropped his cleaning supplies, turned and tried to run. I set my jaw, let out a deep breath, aimed and fired, tagging the man in the middle of his back. He flew forward, hit the floor, slid then stayed still.

I turned back to Tom. His mouth was hanging open gazing at the men I'd just knocked out. "They're just stunned." I said. He looked at me before I continued speaking. "Morbal. What exit does he leave from?"

The old man shook his head. "I, I don't know."

Urgency tugged at me, telling me to run. My efforts were in serious jeopardy now. But, I didn't feel right leaving Tom behind or the others for that matter. It was amazing how much internal debating my brain managed in the span of a couple seconds.

I huffed. "Let's get out of here."

Tom smiled and the faces on most of the others turned white as sheets. "No, Jason. If you're alone, you'll never make it out with us limping behind you." He slumped his shoulders. "Get out of here while you still can."

I ran my eyes over the others. Some looked drugged and the rest looked frightened. My focus drifted back to Tom. He was right. I couldn't help any of them right now. If I tried, we'd all get caught. Reluctantly, I surrendered, "Ok. Sorry."

A moan came from one of the beat up keepers, lying at my feet. I gritted my teeth, grabbed him and rolled him upright so I could see his face. "YOU! What exit does Morbal leave from each night?"

"Who are you?" He asked through bloody, broken teeth.

I aimed my weapon at his face. "There's no time. WHERE?"

"I don't know!" He cried.

Tom grunted. "He's lying."

After a brief glance at the old man I turned back to the keeper. My left eye twitched and I squeezed the gun's handle tighter. "Last chance. Where?"

The man was visibly terrified now. "West exit. West, west, WEST! Don't kill me, please!"

I stood, lowered the weapon's power setting a notch and shot him in his chest. I turned to Tom. "Thanks. Sorry for that time I attacked you."

He shook his head and smiled. "You better go."

My footsteps echoed as I sprinted down the hallway, heading the same way the captain went moments before. A keeper exited an office, turned his head and looked at me. "FREEZE!"

I raised my weapon and fired while running. The guard was out cold in a flash. I ran harder, unsure how many others might have been in the room with him. My heart pounded, my brain was spinning and I wondered how and the hell I was going to get into Morbal's escort party. Christ, it might've already been too late.

All the while, I heard Richard's voice in my head. *Calm, Jason. Focus.* It were as though he was right next to me and I could actually hear him. I hoped the voice was just my imagination.

-

Either fortune, which I didn't believe in, smiled on me or Richard's skills were unbelievably powerful. Whatever it was, I was able to slip in with a small group of guards that made up the third of five vehicles in Morbal's motorcade. No one spoke to me and hardly anyone even looked at me. I felt invisible again, half expecting one of the guards to try to sit on my lap.

I searched all over the asylum without finding any shred of David. The sick, rat-faced controller had to have answers. Now all I had to do was get to him. I nearly laughed at my situation. Nothing was ever easy.

Things being what they were, though, I felt bold and confident. I'd made it this far and the magic Richard Sands weaved was working perfectly. My situation could've been a lot worse.

The line of cars eventually pulled up in front of a huge, exquisite mansion. A well lit driveway, with massive, creepy, odd gargoyles planted at its base near the road, led to a large, solid, heavy duty looking gate. I saw two guards posted there, waiting for the doctor to exit his vehicle. He strode, cockily toward them, with other guards marching in his wake to his right and left. He didn't acknowledge the sentries as they bowed. The gate opened and closed as soon as the controller and his escorts were through it.

I bit my lip, clueless how to get through. I saw the lead car start to move out of the corner of my eye and knew I had to act. Now or never.

I waited for my vehicle to start moving then opened the door as quietly and nonchalantly as I could. No one seemed to notice. Unbelievable. We started picking up speed and by the time I slipped out onto the road we were moving fast enough for the impact to sting. I rolled out of the road and felt bruises pop up on my knees, right shoulder and across my back. Thankfully, there was a patch of grass beyond the curb that helped smooth things out at the end. I planted myself flat against the damp, cool ground as the rest of the parade moved off down the street.

Damn. I could only wish for a plan, something that would get me through the gate and into the mansion. There was no way I could've prepared for this. My aim was to find David in the asylum, not follow Morbal home. I gritted my teeth, both frustrated and flustered, almost able to hear Michael Vistaer's mocking voice say 'I told you.'

I tried to think. The best I could come up with was to attack the men at the gate, get them to open it and head inside. The plan was simple, stupid and likely to fail. I swore under my breath.

I reached for the pistol resting in my pocket, ready to strike. Then I felt something cold and solid press against the back of my head. Oh oh.

"Don't effing move."

A string of curses ran through my head.

"Get on your knees and turn around slowly. Hands up."

I obeyed and turned to see one of Morbal's guards holding a gun two inches from my nose. In the dim light it was hard to see his face but it looked like he was smiling.

"Who are you? What are you doing here?"

My brain raced, making it was hard to speak. "I, um… fell out of the car."

"Bull." My senses were on full alert and I could hear the guard's grip tighten on his weapon. "Name."

I debated making up a name, using my fake name Aaron Waters or giving him Sean Lee's name. Not that it really mattered, I was effed any way you cut it.

"I'm ah…" Before I could finish several quiet, high pitched sounds wisped through the air and the guard's shoulders slumped. His face relaxed and his body fell, crashing down right on top of me. I threw him off quickly but not before feeling warm liquid leaking down on me. The guard was dead and the faint sounds I heard were gunshots drowned out by silencers.

"You must be the dumbest assassin in the whole god damned world." A voice whispered from somewhere in the shadows. I turned to see three figures emerge from a thick patch of bushes resting against the wall surrounding Morbal's palace.

One of the shapes spoke, quietly like the first. "Better he does it than us."

"Get out of the light, idiot." A different voice beckoned. I stayed low to the ground and crept toward them. When I was close enough I saw three men dressed in black with masks covering their faces.

"Thanks." I whispered.

All three men faced me. One of them said, "Eff you."

"Fair enough." I almost laughed. "Who're you?"

"C'mon, you think this moron can actually kill Morbal?" The man at the center of the three asked.

I pried a little since they seemed unlikely to answer my question. "What makes you think I'm here for Morbal?"

The man to my right pressed his weapon against my cheek. "If you're not, then you're of no use. Why are you here?"

"To kill Morbal." I lied, quickly.

He removed the gun from my face and spoke with authority, "Good. We'll clear the way for you up to the house."

House? The place was the size of a hotel.

"Then you find him and drop him." He pulled something flat and rectangular out of his pocket that lit up after his thumb tapped one of the corners. A screen showed what looked like blueprints. The masked man showed it to me. "See the dot? That's the doctor, he'll be in his main living room or his study. Third floor, in the southwest wing."

I looked at the blank, dark face. "Ok."

"Wait here and shut up."

Over the next couple minutes I could only hold still and listen. I heard more silenced gunfire, grunts and bumps that sounded like heavy sacks dropping to the ground and then finally, the sound of the gate opening. I wondered who the masked men were and why, since they seemed to have things wrapped up so well, they thought they even needed me.

One of the men showed himself and waved me over to him. I got over to him before he spoke. "Politics."

I furrowed my brow. "What?"

"We'll get rid of the bodies, you kill Morbal." His head nodded. "No connections to Ark."

The commanding voice from before added, "And if you fail you'd better die trying, or we're coming for you and your loved ones."

Even though the guy and his dark clothed buddies were helping me, I didn't like them at all. The thought of blasting them with full charges from my etherpistol popped in my head. But no, I had other matters to deal with.

I nodded and played along. "Right. He's a dead man."

With that, I bolted from the men, breezed past a stack of six or seven dead bodies, moved through the gate and sprinted up to the front door which, to the assassins' credit was unlocked and slightly ajar. Even the alarm had been disabled. Whoever they were, the bastards were good at their jobs and efficient. I decided it was most beneficial I didn't attack them.

Inside, Morbal's home was still and quiet as a tomb. The artwork was just as comforting. Every wall was lined with disturbing pictures and paintings of death, body parts, carnage, skulls and blood. Even the uncovered walls and the furniture were all colored deep, blood red. The air smelled of roses and incense and the sparkling clean hard wood floors were covered in places with red, expensive looking area rugs. I quickly moved through the spacious rooms. The air felt evil and made the hair on the back of my neck stand up while chills ran through my body.

I figured it was my imagination but I actually saw quick flashes of people being tortured, twisted and massacred within the walls around me. Yes, I figured it was all in my head until I remembered old man Richard talking about how my *mind* was opening up. I shivered and rushed up two flights of red carpeted, beautiful, spiraled stairs. When I reached the top I heard noise coming from one of the rooms to my left. I headed down a large, spooky hallway that could very easily serve as a room itself. Dark red leather couches lined the walls and black glass tables, decorated with red candles on gold candleholders, were placed between them. Lamps hung off the walls, giving off a soft orange glow that flooded through the mansion.

I cat walked, ever so silently up to the door, pulling out my weapon on the way. My ears perked up when I heard what sounded like liquid being poured into a glass. I swallowed and darted into the room that held a royal looking desk with an actual throne behind it. The walls were lined with books and more orange light flickered out from a lit fireplace in the center of the wall opposite the desk. There, by the fireplace stood a large man who stared at me.

My weapon was on the figure in an instant but I nearly screamed once I recognized who I was looking at. Forate. He was here, standing by the fireplace, looking at me. He didn't move. Why..?

"Who the hell are you?"

I whirled my gun around to aim it at the voice I knew all too well. Morbal had entered the room from another doorway and stood looking at me with his slicked, jet black hair, large, beaky nose and small dark eyes. He wore a matching robe and slippers and held a glass with ice cubes and what I guessed was some sort of liquor.

"Don't even think of moving." I hissed, darting my eyes back and forth from the doctor to Forate. Every now and then decisions come to me that require very little second thought. This was one of those times. "You know what? Eff it."

I speedily set my gun to full power, aimed it at Forate and fired twice. The first blast hit him square in the chest and the second burned his face away as his body fell backward. It slammed into the wall and then toppled onto the floor. For whatever reason, the rest of him didn't budge. His legs stayed straight and there wasn't a peep out of him. Confused, but satisfied, my full attention was back on Morbal.

He just stared at me for a moment before his beady eyes opened up as wide as they could go. "Jason?" The weasel of a man studied me, addressing the blood that covered my shirt. "You look well."

I wasn't sure how he could see me through Richard's enchantment but, at that moment, I didn't care. I hissed, restraining the strong desire to immediately kill the sick doctor. "Where's David?"

The bastard blinked then gestured Forate. "I don't know if I'll be able to get him like he was. Do you enjoy destroying artwork? We never discussed art in our sessions together."

"What?"

"Forate's body. The taxidermist had him perfect after you killed him." He chuckled. "Ironic that you'd destroy him again."

I almost felt sick to my stomach. "You disgusting son of a bitch! You had that effing thing stuffed?"

"Thing?" Morbal raised his eyebrows. "Forate was one of my greatest accomplishments." He smiled, wickedly. "You could've been greater but David has sufficed just fine."

"WHERE IS HE?" I roared, ready to shoot all over again.

Morbal coolly took a drink from his glass. "Jason, Jason, Jason." He sighed. "As impulsive as ever, I see. It's not too late. I can still help you with that."

I actually growled. "Oh my god, tell me now or I'm going to fry your mother effing brains out."

"Easy Mr. Sworn." The doctor soothed, jingling the ice cubes in his glass. "I'm not stupid. I know the instant I tell you where David is you're going to kill me."

I nodded unintentionally.

"So it was you who attacked the men at my rehabilitation center wasn't it?" He studied me and sniffed the air. "Working with Vistaer's team now? The scent of Sands's enchant is all over you."

I stirred and shifted my weight from one foot to the other.

"Oh yes. I know all about those terrorists. You're a killer, through and through, aren't you? A murderer, an assassin, a hired gun." He paused. "How does that make you feel?"

I squinted and actually smiled. "I'm not stupid either, *doctor*. I'm not going to let you mind rape me like you used to so don't even try." I stepped closer. "If your next words don't tell me where David is, I promise I'll kill you and go off on my own."

"David was sent on an errand that required he visit Everiel." Morbal gestured the chair behind his desk. "May I sit?"

I considered the request while studying the lavish seat. "Sure." I squeezed the trigger on my gun three times and reduced the fancy chair to rubble. "But not there, not like you're some sort of effing king. Sit over there." I motioned an expensive looking but simple chair by the fireplace.

Morbal was visibly upset. "Fine." He spat. "You're brief stay with," he grunted, "August Cross has really had an effect on you, hasn't it?"

I ignored him. "Wait a minute. Everiel? The island that just suddenly blew up?"

Morbal nodded. "Yes. My rival, Steven Ark owns it. He's trying to attain power which I rightfully deserve."

"YOU SENT HIM THERE?" I fumed. "Is he dead?"

"No."

It was hard to even try to believe the psychopath but I focused on calming myself. "How do you know?"

The doctor sat down and crossed his legs. "Because I spoke with him today." He took another drink.

"Where's he now?"

He swallowed. "David went to Los Angeles on another little task, then, as a reward, I'm letting him visit his mother and sisters outside Phoenix."

"You're letting him?" I squinted, extremely skeptical. "And what makes you think he'll ever come back."

To that, the doctor smiled, showing off too many of his perfectly straight, gleaming white teeth. "Because he's *mine*."

The words stung me, taking the air out of my lungs. It felt like I'd been punched in the gut. I quickly regained my composure, smirked and aimed my gun at the Morbal's head. "Not for long."

"I always liked you, Jason. You're a most intriguing man. You have no idea the power and potential that resides within you." He gave me a little salute. "If I'm to die here, so be it.

What a shame. Especially when I'm so close to having all of North America." He stared off into empty space. "I suppose I became too overconfident, lazy, sloppy."

I gritted my teeth. "You prick. You used my pain and fear for your own effed up enjoyment and to create that drug. Don't BS me. You wanted to shatter me so you'd control me like you did Forate and like that bitch Samantha Forrest did to Kara and tried to do to David."

"Tried?" Morbal raised his eyebrows. "Oh, my dear man. David is shattered further than Forate ever was." He looked over at a file cabinet not far from his desk. "You should see it. All the files and session videos are there. A documentation of David's progress." He turned back to me with an evil glare. "His liberation."

"No." I said from the back of my throat.

The doctor nodded. "Yes, and his conversion was sharply solidified when you killed the lovely Ms. Forrest." He trialed off at the end. "She was special. I miss her."

I wanted to protest that what the maniac said wasn't true. I didn't kill Forrest, her osilea master did. I merely watched. I also wanted to confront Morbal on his demonic allegiance, tag him for what he was. But instead, I focused on the present. "ENOUGH! Give me David's family's location, now!"

The man studied me for a few seconds and I could see his brain working. "You really love him like a brother don't you? What a tragedy. You're impulses will destroy you but," he stood and made a dismissal gesture, "as the Master wills, let it be done."

"What master?" I asked, keeping my weapon aimed directly at the doctor's face. "And who said you could get up?"

Morbal pointed to his desk. "I need to print out that address and map as you requested."

"Fine." I moved closer, watching the doctor work his computer, keeping the barrel of my weapon aimed at his head.

"For all you've learned, seen and heard, Jason, you still know nothing." He spoke while pulling up and printing the information before handing the sheet of paper over to me. I snatched it out of his hand. "You can't win if you continue down your present course. The master is with us now and the world will be cleansed of the delusions you and others like you so desperately cling to."

My eyes glanced at the sheet before I tucked it in my pocket. "The only delusions here are yours, you bastard." I aimed my weapon square against Morbal's head. "There is no Master. It's almost a pity you won't be around to see just how wrong you were."

To my surprise, the doctor smiled. "So ignorant. You know so little."

I exhaled and started to squeeze the trigger... then a powerful hand gripped my right wrist and yanked my arm, pulling my aim away from Morbal. I quickly turned to see the owner of the hand. The man's green-gold eyes and caramel skin shook me with surprise. Michael Vistaer.

I was speechless. The big man tore the etherpistol out of my hand then tossed three small, rubbery objects on Morbal's desk. A deeper look showed they were human thumbs.

"The assassins that helped Jason get in." Vistaer said in a deep, cold, monotone voice. "Steven Ark says hi."

Chapter 7

I couldn't speak the whole time Vistaer marched me, at sword point, out of the mansion and into the back of a rickety, beat up van. I numbly obeyed, feeling completely deflated, like my insides had been ripped out. Drew Olsen sat behind the wheel and took us down a dark, damp alley where I figured the men were going to kill me and dump my body. I would've wondered why they were even going through the motions of killing me in a secluded place but it didn't matter. I was dead, Morbal survived and David was lost. It was over.

Oddly enough, my fears turned out to be quite inaccurate. Instead of murdering me, Vistaer pulled out the teleporter device and opened a doorway that led back to the toy factory. From there, I was led into a small, brightly lit office and sat down in a seat across from Michael. A cheap desk made of fake wood separated us.

We weren't alone. Chickadis sat next to me, watching me as intently and closely as ever. I absentmindedly studied the dog's scruffy face, unable to look the traitor in his eyes. I wondered why I was still alive or why I wasn't locked back up in Morbal's asylum. A thick, heavy silence hung in the air for a while until I finally found my tongue.

"Traitor." I stared directly into Vistaer's green-brown-gold eyes, wanting to rip them out of his skull.

He raised his eyebrows. "I guess that's true. I am a traitor. The entire resistance is betraying Tehlasrin."

My eyes narrowed, wondering what he was getting at. He wasn't part of the resistance, he saved Morbal's life. "But not you. You serve the -"

"NO." He interrupted. "No, I absolutely do not. I serve life. I serve God. I serve freedom. I follow these." He tossed two books on top of his desk.

Unmoved, my eyes dropped down to see his small copy of the US Constitution and a thicker book titled The Holy Bible. Both were beat up, worn, scratched and folded; well used. I shook my head, looking again into Michael's eyes. "You're lying."

He set his jaw, eyes blazing back at me. "I don't lie."

"Then why did you stop me? How could you let him live?" My voice was a blend of confusion and anger.

The big man thought. "Because killing him wouldn't be good right now."

"Was it right to put a bullet through Brenner's defenseless head?" My voice raised and echoed through the small office. The dog beside me made a low, gruff sound.

"She can sense your frustration." Michael gestured Chickadis, speaking in a calm tone. "It upsets her. She likes you, she trusts you. Like Fier."

"I don't care what *the dog* thinks of me." I spoke boldly, getting hotter and angrier with each breath.

Michael leaned back in his chair. "But I do. And with that being the case, I like and trust you too."

"Just shut up!" I almost shouted. "No more games. Admit you work for Morbal."

The man blinked slowly and he smirked. He seemed to be enjoying my frustration. "But I don't. You just fail to see the significance of his survival… For now."

"The significance? For now? What are you saying? Are you completely mad?" I spat the words, then I thought for a moment. 'For now.' Did that mean he planned to kill Morbal someday? I hoped that was the case and I hoped Vistaer wasn't really a traitor.

I'll be damned, it was at that time I realized I'd become emotionally invested in the resistance. Of course I hated the Union but I never really felt strongly about anything else. Aswain was beautiful but the rebellion, specifically Vistaer's group, had grown on me in just a couple days. It felt... right. And now, after the man saved Morbal, I was wounded and felt betrayed.

"Perhaps I am mad." Michael said with a laugh. "But you're ignorant. Let me explain things to you. Those men that helped you into Morbal's house worked for the controller, Steven Ark. They were sent to exact revenge against the doctor for his role in destroying Ark's island, Everiel." He paused, mentally putting his words together before speaking. "Now the two will really be at each other's throats. An assassination attempt using highly skilled and decorated killers won't sit well with the psychotic, high and mighty doctor. Ark's men wiped out about thirteen of Morbal's guards. I predict this'll lead to outright war between them."

"So what?" I shot out. "You don't know what the effer did to me, what he did to David and is still doing to thousands of others."

Michael blew a gust of air out of his nose. "I know exactly what he's done." He squinted. "So what you ask? What do you think will happen when two of the largest Tehlasrin forces on the continent are at war?"

I remembered the word the assassin said to me. "Politics."

"Yes." Michael smiled. "With the third most powerful controller, Erica, on our side, the resistance has just taken an enormous leap forward."

I exhaled sharply, now seeing where Vistaer was going.

"Let them waste each other." He said. "Then we'll be in a much better situation. I suspect soldiers on both sides will finally find the courage to join us."

I nodded, unsure what to say.

"Our moment has come, Jason." He spoke in a dream like tone. "Finally. Morbal needs to survive long enough to ensure the end of the Union here."

"I see." I still didn't completely trust him but, for the moment, I gave Vistaer the benefit of the doubt. "What about David?"

The man looked surprised by my question. "You never give up, do you?"

"Never."

"I respect that." He nodded and gave me a little two finger salute. "I waited outside during your time with Morbal. Waited for you to get the information you needed."

"You were there the whole time?" I asked, shocked.

Michael shook his head. "Not the whole time but most of it." He cleared his throat and leaned forward. "Jason, I'll be honest, again. I don't think you can help your friend. He's shattered."

"So you followed me the whole time?" I asked with a spiteful edge. "You know, Chief had me followed too. I'm getting sick of being watched."

"No, I wasn't following you." Michael said with a shake of his head. "Richard was keeping a mental tab on you and when he learned you planned on getting to Morbal I headed out. Honestly, I was angry with you when you left. I didn't want to see you throw your life away."

I folded my arms. Vistaer took the non verbal expression and changed course. "But I was wrong to think that, I'm sorry. I stayed angry until I remembered I swore to August that I'd help you." A pause. "He's in Los Angeles, David that is."

"That's what Morbal said." I confirmed.

"And then plans to head to Phoenix."

I reached down and made sure the map was still in my pocket. It was there and for the moment, my nerves calmed themselves.

"Very well." Michael said before standing. "We'll head out by teleporter to Erica's home tomorrow afternoon."

I stood up too. "Why wait?"

The man let out a hearty laugh. "Because you're exhausted and I need to inform Brass and the others on what's transpired."

I folded quickly, realizing how tired I was. "Ok."

Michael walked around the table to stand next to Chickadis and put a sturdy hand on my shoulder. "Here." He handed me back my pistol. I took it quickly. "In the morning I want you to use the time to talk with my team. Ask questions. None of us have all the answers but we know more than you. Learn. Then we'll head out."

My eyes glanced around the room then zeroed in on Vistaer's. "Alright."

Michael opened the door and Lilly was standing right outside it. Her eyes were filled with tears. "What's wrong?" He asked.

"The dark is getting closer." She quivered. "I'm afraid."

He shook my shoulder, pulling my gaze from Lilly. "Go. Get some rest." He looked at the young woman. "Come inside, dear."

My head spun as I shuffled my way to the bed I woke up in that morning. After ripping off Sean's bloody, sweaty uniform, I slid under the covers. Chickadis sprawled out on the floor next to me.

-

I woke early, immediately plagued with questions and concerns on everything that transpired the night before. The twisted image of Morbal's wicked smile as he said the words 'Because he's mine' burned itself into the forefront of my thoughts. The doctor was sick and conceited, brimming with a hyper charged arrogance and a warped sense of entitlement. I knew better than to put much stock in his delusions but there was something in the way he said the words that felt true.

I ran through a quick workout of pushups, sit-ups and pull-ups using a thick pipe that ran along the back of the warehouse. The goal was to clear my mind a bit, but while I cleaned up, shaved, brushed my teeth and washed myself all over as best I could with only a sink, a towel and a bar of soap, I thought of Kara Childers. She'd been turned into Forrest's devoted slave. I remembered Forate. The demonic bull-like man served Morbal unquestionably. Warnings rang through my head. Sad, remorseful words from August Cross, the five old codgers who made up the Golden Cup, Michael Vistaer and others that told me my friend was shattered beyond repair. Fier Wren believed David was lost too, oh man, Fier…

I still felt sick from betraying her. I hoped to get over the feelings with time, but no. Granted, it had only been a few days but when I thought about it I felt even worse than before.

Enough time passed with me standing there in my boxer shorts, trapped in my thoughts, for steam from the hot running water to cover the small mirror plastered to the wall in front of me. I exhaled slow and deep. Morbid thoughts, regret, worry. I hated all that crap. I was a man of action. Dwelling on theories and warnings didn't do me any good. It wasn't my style.

With renewed resolve, I reached up to wipe the steam off the mirror. After the squeak from my palm rubbing against the glass I was amazed to see foggy, misty images of two people inside the glass. It was like looking into a telescreen only things darker and difficult to make out. The people were far away and looked small but somehow, not sure how, I thought David was one of them.

He was naked, on top of a woman, doing what he loved most. Only… something wasn't right. Straining my eyes and ears, I witnessed the woman screaming, pushing, fighting and scratching. Rape? That couldn't be David. He was a tomcat and a bit of a womanizer but not a rapist. It couldn't be. I was so disturbed and baffled by the hazy exhibition it didn't even dawn on me that I was most likely imagining the whole thing.

The scene changed. The man who resembled David held the attractive body of the woman he'd been with seconds before face down while he straddled her back. I saw a needle and a syringe filled with a strange liquid. The contents looked dark red and thick like a blend of ketchup and grape juice. What was he doing? With a roar of success from the man, Christ it couldn't be David, he drove the point straight into the woman's spine and plunged the contents into her.

The woman's scream echoed through my head until I noticed the mirror was covered with steam again. I turned the water off and panted for good piece of time. What the eff was that all about?

"Hey, almost done in there?"

The voice came from the other side of the bathroom door followed by a light knock. It sounded like Chin. I cleared my throat, "Um, yea, sorry. Just a second." I quickly threw on some of the clothes I'd brought from Aswain; new pair of blue jeans, a black belt and a comfortable, long sleeve shirt that was white over the chest and back with navy blue sleeves. I wasn't completely dry so the shirt clung, uncomfortably to my skin. I grabbed my wallet and a pair of socks along with my shoes then padded out of the restroom. Chin nodded as we passed each other.

"Morning."

The voice drew my gaze and I saw Mike Taft leaning against a wall a little ways from the restroom. His young, brown face smiled at me behind his thick glasses. "Hey." I said before stopping next to him so I could finish getting dressed.

"Nice shoes." Mike said. "Man, new jeans, shirt… I've got to head back to Aswain some day. All they have around here are beat up hand-me-downs."

I stood up after tying my laces. "Yea. You'd still need money though, things aren't free in Aswain."

To that, the young man laughed. "Oh I know. I suppose it's better to blend in anyways." Next, his voice carried an almost cocky edge. "I've know Cross a lot longer than you.

I've worked with him a ton over the years and I've got a good chunk of money stored up on Aswain."

"Ah right, I forgot." I tried to pay attention and be courteous but my head was awash with the disturbing events from the night before and the things I'd seen in the mirror.

"Some people wonder what I'm even doing here when I could be snug and happy on Aswain." Mike went on. He smiled again. "But not you, you're in the same boat. You're here for a purpose too."

My thoughts carried me away and I couldn't help but ignore Taft. Was that really David? What was he doing to that woman? Who was she? No, I must have imagined it.

"Are you ok?" Mike asked, finally gaining my attention. "You look pale. Spaced out."

I raised my eyebrows. "Rough night."

"Oh right, you went to Morbal's. Damn." He shook his head. "Hey, Michael told me help to you with any questions you may have. I made a list of stuff."

A smile sprouted on my face as I watched the young guy pull a wadded piece of paper out of his pocket. He licked his lips after smoothing it out as best he could, then looked at me. "But you know what? I'm hungry. Let's get some breakfast."

I followed him back toward the kitchen suddenly aware of the smell of coffee and eggs in the air. "Where's Michael?"

Mike shrugged. "In his office, I think. He said something about him and Richard contacting the other leaders. Whenever that happens, he's usually tied up for hours."

I thought about Vistaer's promise to take me to Los Angeles. David wasn't at the asylum so now my search was even more desperate and unpredictable. Having the help of people like Michael and his contacts could prove useful. That is, if Michael was even being honest. Hard as I tried, I still didn't trust him... Morbal was finished, I had him. Damn.

I physically shook my head, trying to clear it out. The sooner I found and rescued my friend the better. The stress, uncertainty, weird dreams and visions were driving me crazy. Maybe even literally. What a mess.

Mike looked uncomfortable, almost nervous as we walked so I threw some questions his way. "So who outfits you guys? Where do you get your weapons, clothes, food and everything else?"

He raised his eyebrows. "Lots of places." The man seemed happy to be talking. "We get some stuff from local contacts. Liv is dating a guy whose dad runs a supercenter store. That helps with food and supplies. Weapons mostly come from Brass and the other rebellion leaders."

Oh yea, Rigel Brass, I'd nearly forgotten about him. The guy was hard to read during the short time in Seattle. The other leaders seemed to show him respect and accepted him as their leader. I trusted him even less than I trusted Vistaer. I chuckled a little and wondered if I really trusted *anyone*. Even trusting myself was getting difficult, especially after seeing bizarre images in a damn bathroom mirror. Cross maybe? He still seemed loaded with secrets. Mark was trustworthy but he's dead. There was Fier but I doubted she wanted anything to do with me after I stole from her and ran off.

David. Yes. That was it. I trusted David.

"We also get energy and other things smuggled in from Aswain by teleporter." Taft went on as we rounded a corner that led to the kitchen. The room was fuller than the last time I'd been there.

The tall, long, black haired man, Drew sat at one table with a Hispanic looking man I'd seen around a few times. I'd been given his name before but couldn't remember it. Drew cut his eyes around to meet mine as I entered the room. His look wasn't pleasant and neither was the one I returned.

Olivia sat at another table and ate with the woman, Marie Dubois, who'd been the now dead Sally's girlfriend. I learned the day before that Marie was an extremely skilled hailiorum healer. She'd been hurt more than anyone else after Sally's death.

Chris threw a tennis ball that whizzed by me, bounced off a wall and was then smothered by the tail wagging Chickadis. The dog chewed on the ball for a few seconds before returning it to the man so he could start the game all over again.

"Have a seat." Mike said, calling back my attention. I sort of felt sorry for the young man since I kept tuning out; almost forgetting he was even there. He gestured an open chair at an unoccupied table. "I'll grab us some food." He raised an eyebrow. "Coffee?"

"Please." I nodded then sat down, glancing at the walls and all the clippings tacked against it. My eyes moved on, again observing the men and woman, and dog that shared the space with me. They seemed so, I don't know, content and comfortable with each other. Drew always had a scornful look on his face and Marie looked sad but all in all they seemed rather carefree, not at all like a group of freedom fighters engaged in a war against an oppressive, murdering empire.

"Here you go." Mike set a hot cup of black coffee in front of me. "Sorry, no cream or sugar right now."

I was about to say 'no problem' when Drew blurted, "You're not his damn servant, Mike. Let him get his own breakfast!"

"Ignore him." Mike said, cautiously turning to look at the bigger man. "I don't mind, this once." He headed back to the sink area.

I took a sip of my drink deciding whether to let my mind dwell on how much of a dick Drew was or how I was going to find and help David. Neither seemed especially pleasant at the moment. Chickadis bounded past me again, grabbed the tennis ball and returned it to Chris.

The man saw me watching and tossed the ball my way. I caught it, mildly disgusted by the amount of dog spit now on my hand. Chickadis was right by me, anxiously staring, wagging her tail, waiting for me to lob the ball away.

"Go ahead," Chris said, "toss it. She'll love you for it."

I laughed and threw the ball. The dog was on it in a heartbeat and was on her way to bring it back to me when Chris made a little kissy sound that told Chickadis to come his way. He spoke to the dog while rubbing her ears. "That's enough dog time for him, I think."

"So what do you guys really *do* here?" I asked, mostly speaking to Chris.

"Jesus." Drew stirred in his seat. "What the hell are *you* doing here?"

"We know why Jason's here, you dope." Olivia said with her mouth full of food. "He's here to help his buddy."

Chris eyed Drew and Olivia a bit before speaking. "What do we do? It's obvious, Jason." He smiled. "We cause as much disruption for Tehlasrin as we can and help the rebellion along the way. Most of us are usually on assignment but after the fiasco in Seattle, Michael's given us a little time to cool off."

"Hmm, Ok." I said as Mike set a hot plate of eggs, mixed vegetables, toast and a protein bar in front of me. I looked at him. "Thanks, Mike."

"Denver is a hub of Union activity." Chris went on. "We're plugged in so to speak, gathering intelligence and sending it to our friends."

The Hispanic man let out a little grunt and nodded when I looked at him. "You thought for a moment that all we did was sit around here and eat eggs?"

Olivia laughed.

"No." I shook my head. "I just wondered."

"For example." Chris continued. "Michael verified the location of several plants where Tehlasrin creates chemicals that poison our food, packaging, water, air and other material." I remembered the subject coming up before the controller, Brenner, had his head blown off. "Right now, those plants are being demolished."

I let out a small chuckle. "Good."

"In short," Chris summed up, "we do a lot. It's no cake walk here."

"Eat up. The eggs will get cold and that's just gross."
Mike spoke as he dug into his own pile of mixed vegetables.

All that talk about poisoned food made me think twice.
But I was too hungry to care. "Vegetables, huh? They were
hard to come by back in my military days."

"Yea," Mike smacked his lips, "from that contact at the
supercenter I told you about. Good, clean veggies. We need
the vitamins."

"My baby's dad helps us out!" Olivia said happily.

I ate, quickly.

"So, let's see here." Mike studied over his wrinkled piece
of paper as Chin entered the room, filled himself a cup of
coffee and then sat next to Chris. "I mentioned the teleporter a
little bit ago. Might as well start with that."

Despite everything going through my head, I was
interested. The technology was amazing. "Ok. How does it
work?"

Mike laughed. "No offense but you wouldn't understand
the specifics." He looked around the room. "None of you
would." Then focused back on me. "We're all hailiorea, each
with his or her own special flare. Some are warriors and every
one of you, including Chickadis could clean my clock. I'm
what they call a hailiorum alchemist. In the old days
alchemists worked with plants, herbs and other organic solids
and liquids. These days we're more about science, technology,
electricity and ether. Technology is merely the mind's
understanding of the cosmos."

The kid spoke so fast it was hard to keep up. Since none
of what he'd just said had anything to do with the teleporter I
simply nodded. "Right."

"So, while I was living on Aswain helping Cross and his
development team create a way to harness and use etherspring,
I designed the teleporter." He smiled, proudly. "Only two
exist, one here and one with Cross."

"Ah." I said in a 'now I get it' kind of way. "I bet that's how Cross got to Ravenfall so fast the night we stopped that osilea."

"Um, ok. Maybe." Mike said. "Anyways, the teleporter opens doorways to anywhere on the Earth. Actually anywhere around Earth up to half way between us and the Moon. It creates a type of wormhole that travels through the ether, the bloodstream, the spirit of the planet."

"What?" I asked, brow furrowing.

Olivia giggled. "I love it when Mike talks science stuff. Look how excited he is!"

"Yes, very cute." Marie finally spoke in a soft, gentle tone.

Mike blushed a little. "The Earth is a living thing. I believe it has a consciousness of its own. With the right tools we can hear the Earth's hum song, sort of like its heartbeat." He could see I was lost. "Ok, ok. The teleporter is either powered by etherspring, a *lot* of electricity or even our own hailiorea brainwaves. The portal navigation is mapped out with the help of satellites around the planet. It's how the portal precisely pinpoints locations."

I wasn't very knowledgeable in the schools of science but the whole thing intrigued me. I listened and ate more of my food. Finally I asked, "Do the doorways go both ways?"

"You mean, from here could I open a portal in New York and let them come through to our location?" He said, nodding his head. "Yep, sure can."

I thought for a second. "Then why did we have to travel from the Tehlasrin port up to Seattle?"

Mike laughed and it looked like his face flushed a bit. "Ah. A little hiccup on my end. The darn teleporter was acting up and I didn't have it fixed until after you guys arrived."

"Those 'hiccups' happen more than he'd like to admit." Chris said with a smile.

Mike gave the man a hurt look then turned back to me. "Besides, Michael wanted to get a good read on you before letting you close to the rebel leaders."

I considered that. "Makes sense. Interesting device nonetheless, that teleporter."

"Yea, cool stuff." Mike said. "I supposed the Blue Targe is just as impressive."

I looked at the man. The targe. "Yea, what is that? Some sort of anti missile system?"

"Missiles, airplanes, helicopters, boats, anything." Mike said after swallowing a bite of his protein bar. "There are several, very secret points scattered around North America that link together to create a type of bubble, or *shield* surrounding the continent and Pacificus, er, Aswain."

I sat and listened, amazed something like that could exist without the GU knowing all about it.

"The targe is powered by etherspring too." He paused. "The stuff is amazing, Jason, almost magical. The shield's main control base is deep below Ravenfall. Funny how you just mentioned the city."

"Yea, really." I furrowed my brow. "So Cross controls the targe?"

"Yea, you could say that." Mike shrugged. "He funded it and the main control is on his property. The system is lightning fast and can detect threats within seconds. It uses extremely high powered energy beams that incinerate anything it blasts. The beams are as hot as the Sun."

"It's one of our key tools that'll keep Tehlasrin at bay after we take back North America." Chris stated with authority, his southern accent ringing through the kitchen.

"So, hmm." Mike muttered while looking over his sheet of paper. "The teleporter, who we are, what we do, the targe, who I am and my talents." He looked up at me. "Anything else you've been wondering about?"

I set my fork down, done with my food and took a sip of coffee. "Mostly just David. I've been having some strange dreams and I saw something odd a little while ago. I don't know."

"Richard would be the man to ask about the dreams." Chin said.

Marie hummed. "Indeed, a wonderful man, very wise and powerful. He's busy with Michael right now, though." I looked at her. "Claire, I'm sorry, Lilly might be able to help as well."

I felt my blood start to flow at the mention of the young woman. "You think? Where is she?"

"Alone in her room." Chris said. "Something scared her last night."

I squinted, curious. "What's her story? Why does she seem so sad sometimes?"

Drew fumed and crossed his arms. The rest of the group grew quiet except for Olivia, who laughed again. I wondered why she laughed so much.

Chris spoke again. "We like you, Jason, but we love Lilly. She's family. We're all family now. If you want private information on her you can ask her yourself."

"Fair enough." I glanced around at everyone. "Sorry."

"Don't worry about it." The Hispanic man, what the hell was his name, said. "It's natural you'd be curious. She's very kind and beautiful. I can sense your feelings for her. That's one of my little gifts… or curses. I pick up on other people's feelings and emotions." He chuckled. "It can be quite overwhelming."

"Yes," Marie started, "poor Andres had to keep a good distance from me the last couple days." She looked at him and I finally had his name. "Sorry, dear."

"Don't worry about me, love." Andres said.

The room was quiet for a moment until Chris got up to leave. "Gotta check in with the Bossman and keep watch on the perimeter. Sworn." I looked at him. "Catch." He threw me Chickadis's ball. The dog was right on me, staring. I threw it again for her.

"What about me?" Olivia blurted. "Don't you want to know about me?"

I turned from watching the dog chew on her ball to the young woman. She was sitting on the edge of her chair staring at me, expectantly. Her right knee anxiously bounced up and down.

"Um," I looked at Mike when I heard him snort out a laugh, then focused back on Olivia. "I don't want to pry into everyone's personal lives."

"Oh whatever!" She said with a dismissive wave of her hand. "Everyone in this room has an interesting story. Some are all private about it. Not me. Come on."

I swallowed, not sure where to even start. I remembered a thought I'd recently had. "Ok fine. Why do you laugh so much?"

"Oh that's lame." Olivia said. "I laugh when things are funny. Come on, don't you want to ask about my eyes?" She blinked several times, very quickly. "Or my teeth, or my skills?"

The others in the room weren't paying much attention and even Chickadis seemed uninterested. She was spread out on the floor with her head down and the tennis ball tucked in against her chest. "Why don't you tell me?" I said flatly.

The woman looked a little annoyed with my tone. "I'm not just a hailiorum, I'm part osilea."

"What?" Now she had my attention. Surprised, my eyes hurriedly looked around the room. Only Marie was looking back and forth at Olivia and me. "How is that even possible?"

"Ah, there you go. Good question." Olivia nodded. "My great grandmother, my dad's, dad's mom was raped by a man who was possessed by an osilea. Others in my family had some strong hailiorea blood and now here I am."

I shook my head. "They, the osilea can actually have children with us?"

"It's very rare," Marie said in a soft but strong, scholarly voice, "but possible."

"How?" I asked.

Olivia blurted out. "So that's why I look the way I do. Badass and beautiful!" She smiled, happily showing her sharp teeth again. "You know my eyes glow when I'm fighting, in the heat of battle?"

I nodded. "Yea, I saw them do that the other night at the checkpoint and then again in Seattle. But about the possession thing -"

"Speaking of heat," She interrupted again, "I can make things get hotter, burn longer. Other than my hailiorum warrior abilities, that's my gift."

I put a finger up, nonverbally asking her to slow down. "Ok, but the -"

"I get the molecules and atoms that make up matter to vibrate and move faster, creating friction and heat." She carried on. "If I really wanted to and you stayed still, I could eventually burn you up." Her red-orange eyes looked up to her left, showing she was thinking. "Ever hear of spontaneous combustion? Yea, sorta like that I guess."

"Marie," I raised my voice a little, "how can a possessed person actually breed or whatever, pass on osilea genes with a human?"

The woman smiled even though the sadness she'd been through was still heavy on her face. "We're not sure. It has something to do with the blood and DNA mutation or manipulation. I think the Golden Cup has been looking into that one for a while now. All we know is it can happen."

"And I'm the proof!" Olivia said with excitement.

I blinked while gathering my thoughts then remembered the whole bonding thing Lilly told me about. "Interesting. What about bonding? How does that work?"

Before anyone answered I saw Marie, Andres, Drew and Chin suddenly perk up, looking at something behind me. I turned to see Michael Vistaer standing in the doorway, nearly taking up the whole space. An odd little smile was on his face.

"Jason. I promised to take you to Los Angeles. Get ready, we'll head out in a couple hours."

I let out a sigh of relief. Good, I'd be continuing my search soon.

"Chin, Andres." Michael called. "You're coming too."

Olivia stood up. "Boss. What's up?"

The little smile changed into a wolfish grin. "Our predictable, impulsive controller, Dr. Morbal Maledro has mobilized his forces. He's attacking Ark. The war," he said coolly, "has begun."

Chapter 8

"Put this on under your shirt." Michael tossed a Kevlar vest at me then strode over toward Chris. The other man was sitting behind a computer terminal, washed in the soft light of several monitors. A row of wet clothes hung off a line an arm span from the technological setup and the smell of laundry was heavier than usual.

Chickadis, who'd been lying down on the ground next to me, sat up after I caught the vest. I guessed she thought it was something else to play with. Ever since that morning, since I'd been passed her coveted tennis ball, the dog was on me like a hawk; shadowing me even more than before.

I furrowed my brow and spoke to the back of Michael's head. "What for? I thought Erica was on our side."

He stopped and turned to me. "She is, but something's wrong. Rigel and I haven't been able to get a hold of her. Neither have any of the other leaders."

"She's in trouble." Lilly said in a haunting, distant voice. She was standing next to Andres and Chin with a worried expression. I studied her face and felt my heart pound against my ribs. She looked so innocent, vulnerable and beautiful, standing there in a pair of blue jeans, white sneakers and a cozy looking white sweatshirt that again fit her very well. The somewhat dim fluorescent light in the spacious back room bounced off her golden-white hair as she gazed at me with her large, dreamy blue eyes.

I tried to collect myself as Michael and Chris spoke with each other. They were too far away and too quiet for me to make out any words. After setting the vest down, I checked both etherpistols, making sure they were loaded properly. Mike had returned the gun I gave him back in Seattle, thanking me again for the help and complimenting me on my, what he called, 'moment of genius.'

The young man was in the space with us, fidgeting over the teleporter, getting it ready to send us to Los Angeles. After breakfast, he and I walked all around the makeshift base as he prattled on about the security systems he helped create and set up. Normally I would've been interested but instead I tried to cope with the adrenaline surge that never seemed to go away. The anticipation of finding David was almost unbearable.

After setting the weapons down, I took my shirt off and reached for the vest. I couldn't help but notice Lilly looking at me and, vainly, I was glad I'd worked out a little that morning.

Andres coughed before speaking while I put the vest on and then my shirt back over it. "What do you mean Lilly? What kind of trouble do you think Erica is in? I can feel your concern. Are *you* ok?"

She removed her eyes from me and turned to the man. "I, I don't know." She shook her head, squinted her eyes and scrunched her face as if she'd been stung by a bee. "Erica's like a big sister to me. She's been all my life. I just know something's wrong. I can feel it." A pause. "And I had a bad dream last night."

I studied the faces on the other men in the room. Andres bit his lip, Chin swallowed and Michael turned away from Chris to look at Lilly. Mike Taft didn't seem to be paying any attention. Vistaer said, "Don't worry, kid. She'll be alright."

"Yes." Andres started. "We'll contact you as soon as we see her."

When Lilly spoke she looked at me. "No need. I'm coming with you."

My eyes boggled and Chris whirled around in his chair, even Mike looked up, a surprised expression on his face. The normally quiet Chin spoke before the rest of us. "What? No. It could be dangerous. You stay here." It was obvious everyone in the group cared for Lilly and looked out for her.

She gave the man a stare that was as cold as the North Pole and as sharp as the blades on Michael's back. "You don't tell me what to do."

Chin huffed and slinked away from the gaze, turning to Michael. "Sir, if we haven't made contact with Erica and there's something wrong… tell her to stay here, where it's safe."

Vistaer stood silent for a moment, looking over everyone in the large room. "Each and every one of us is free to do what he or she wants. I lead the group because I'm the most experienced, strongest and most stubbornly egotistical of us all." He chuckled. "If Lilly wants to come, that's her choice."

The Asian man gave up on any further protests.

Selfishly, I was happy Lilly was coming along. Being around her stirred up all sorts of lusty and dreamy feelings and I couldn't deny they felt good. Dismissively, I tossed the thoughts away and kept my priorities straight. David was the one I was here for, not the young woman or my surging libido.

"Load up, everyone." Vistaer commanded. "Mike, is the portal ready?"

The man nodded behind his glasses. "Yea, just about. You haven't told me where you want the doorway to open so I set it inside Erica's intelligence quarter. It's the same place you ported out from the last time you were there."

Michael sighed. "Good. Open it up as soon as you're ready. You'll stay behind with the porter and open a passageway back home after I contact you. Got it?"

"Got it." Mike said with another nod.

I licked my lips and noticed a clock hanging on the wall over the computers Chris sat in front of. It showed one o'clock. Not that it really mattered but I mentally tallied that I'd been back on Tehlasrin soil for nearly three days. I'd hoped to find David much sooner than this.

There weren't any holsters around for my etherpistols but the front pockets on my jeans were big enough to fit a gun each. I checked the ammo again and the setting, about three quarters power, before tucking them away just as the teleporter worked its magic and created another one of those bizarre doorways through space.

"All set!" Mike said proudly.

"Good luck, see you soon." Chris said and waved.

Vistaer pulled his large trench coat on and moved through first followed by Andres.

I was about to step into the rectangular, swirling vortex when Lilly grabbed my hand. "These things make me nervous." Surprised by the feel of her tender hand, I looked at her and smiled. "Will you go through with me?"

I had trouble finding my tongue. "Ah, sure."

"Christ, move it!" That from Chin.

Hand in hand, Lilly and I walked through and instantly found ourselves in completely new surroundings. We stepped forward and drew closer to Michael before Chin magically appeared behind us. The portal disappeared a couple seconds later.

The new room reminded me of the intelligence base on Aswain. It was large but filled to the brim with desks, cubicles and computer stations. Light came from a few overhead lamps but mostly from the multitude of computer monitors and large telescreens that hung on every wall. The displays showed detailed maps of city streets and buildings. The images were zoomed in to far for me to pinpoint what part of the world they showed but I guessed it was the southwestern territory of North America that Erica controlled.

"HEY!" Someone yelled from behind a computer station. I jumped and Lilly gasped, grabbing my hand even tighter. "Who the hell are you? FREEZE!"

I turned to see a man in a Tehlasrin uniform aiming a gun in our direction. The barrel bounced back and forth between all five of us. Instinctively, I let go of Lilly's hand and reached for my weapons. I had them out when Michael spoke.

"Where friends of Erica Wood." He spoke slowly and calmly, hands up, palms out. The man seemed out of character acting so passive. "Can you contact her, please?"

"Get on the ground! Hands on your heads!" The man was alone and looked like he was panicking. "You're all under arrest!"

Screw this. I was an inch away from opening fire on the soldier when a shot came from behind him. The bullet appeared to have hit him square in his back. He stumbled forward and collapsed, his gun fell from his hand and clattered on the floor.

The shooter quickly came into view, snatched up the fallen weapon then put another bullet in the back of the not quite dead man's head. He looked at Michael with an awfully grim look on his face. I imagined I looked the same. "Jesus, Vistaer!" He exclaimed with a brief smile. "Why the hell didn't you tell us you were coming? This guy is *not* with the resistance!"

"I'm sorry, we tried -" Michael began before being cut off.

"We're not all rebels, you know." The new soldier holstered his weapon and looked the five of us over. "What are you doing here?"

"John," Michael said with his normal tone, I relaxed the grip on my weapons. "We need to talk to Erica. I tried to contact her but never got through."

Andres inhaled sharply. The rest of us looked at him. "What?" Michael asked.

"So much." He said. "So many emotions, confusion, betrayal, pain. Madness." His eyes were tearing up when he looked at the guard. "What's happened here?"

The soldier, John, slumped his shoulders. "I don't know. I'm just a low rung officer. All I know is everything's gone to hell and everyone's fighting."

Vistaer stepped closer to the man. "How so? Why is it so empty here? This place is usually packed."

"Everyone else has been called out, targeting groups and arresting dissidents." He swallowed. "Things were fine, normal up until yesterday morning. Then command mobilized us. We've been sent out in sweeps, cracking down on people, schools, businesses, everything."

I could see Michael was visibly upset and confused. He growled when he spoke. "What do you mean? Where the hell is Erica?"

"Michael." Lilly's voice was tiny amongst the large room and high tension. "Something's happened to her. She's been hurt, badly."

Vistaer turned from Lilly back to John. "Take me to her, now!"

To my surprise, the guard smiled and let out a deep sigh. He looked relieved. "Ok. Ok, this way. Thank God you're here." He started down a hallway that led away from the intel room. "Stay behind me. I don't know if we'll run into more loyalists like…" he swallowed, "Roger."

I filed in with the others behind John, uncomfortable with the place. "Did you know him?" I asked, trying to get a read on the man.

He glanced back at me with a morbid expression. "Of course. He was a good kid but he would've killed you once he learned who you were."

"He would have tried." Vistaer said in a deep, menacing tone. "So, you haven't seen or heard from Erica in over a day? She's always been especially visible and hands on."

John shook his head and spoke once we reached a large set of several elevators. "No, I haven't seen her at all." He sighed again. "I think she's up on the ground level, in her command office." The door in front of him opened. "Get in, quickly."

I stepped in and made sure to position myself between John and Lilly. I didn't trust the guy, something was seriously off. Glancing at the array of buttons on the wall I saw that we were five floors below what was tagged 'Ground Level.' There were several buttons above that. This place was huge.

The ride up was quick and quiet and I could almost feel the stress and fear pouring out of John. Lilly pressed herself against me while Michael stood straight and tall with a serious expression on his stone-like face. Chin took the brief moment to close his eyes, no doubt psyching himself up for any trouble and Andres was sweating, eyes bouncing all around.

A chime rang and then the large doors opened up. Immediately, smells of fresh dirt, grass and flowers poured into the air around us. Stunned, I had to force myself to follow the others off the elevator. Sure enough, the enormous ground level lobby was filled with small trees, surrounded by grass, flowers and rock gardens strategically placed around several indoor fountains. Green was the predominant color but there were splashes of reds, yellows and whites from flowers, some in baskets others on bushes.

The area was bathed in natural sunlight that poured through glass walls which enclosed the entire area. In short, the place was gorgeous. Unfortunately, it only took a few seconds for my eyes to drop from the high, fan filled ceiling, down along the intricate glass walls to the outside beyond. My vision went from heavenly to chaotic.

Fires burned in the distance with plumes of smoke that blackened out parts of the otherwise clear blue sky. Explosions boomed, some a distance away and others much closer. People of all sorts, young, old, men, women, soldiers, civilians ran in panic through the streets. Anyone who got too close to the glass palace was abruptly gunned down.

My heart shriveled at the display. Out of the corner of my eye I saw Michael ball his hands into tight fists. He grabbed John by his shoulder and whipped him around, eyes bulging. "WHAT IS THIS?" He shook the poor man who appeared close to pissing his pants. "WHAT'S HAPPENING?"

"I, I," John bumbled, "I told you, I don't know."

"ERICA!" Michael roared into the air. When he turned to us I noticed we also seemed be alone in this new, huge space. Everyone else, Erica's guards, looked like they were outside, keeping the mobs of frightened, angry people away. "Take cover, all of you! It's not safe here."

I moved, grabbing Lilly's hand with my left and pulling a pistol out with my right, I tugged the young woman over to what appeared to be a reception desk. We ducked down watching more of the ensuing madness outside.

Andres followed Michael into a large nearby office almost directly across from Lilly and me. Chin was nowhere to be found and John just stood where he was, looking dumbfounded.

Vistaer's voice boomed from the office. "Jason! I'm in Erica's office but she's not here. John, for Christ's sake do something! Find out where she is!"

John swallowed and slumped his shoulders. "She must be in -" He was cut off and cut down by gunfire. Three shots, all direct hits, two in his back, one in his neck. I knew he was dead before he hit the floor.

I aimed my weapon in the direction the bullets came from and saw three others, in Tehlasrin uniforms move away from the elevators. My finger had the trigger half way pulled when one of the three, an older man with a sharp mustache, spoke.

"Mr. Vistaer? Come out." His voice was haggard and cracked as he yelled. "The Lady knows you're here and wishes to see you."

My eye twitched. I didn't trust anyone and these three were about the most untrustworthy people I ever met. People were getting killed left and right, I didn't want to be next. A voice of common sense and survival whispered in my head. It told me to shoot all three of the soldiers. I was about to when Michael spoke.

"Jason, Chin, hold your fire." When he spoke next, his voice was a growl. "You three! Drop your weapons! NOW!"

One of the new arrivals, a black woman looked at the old man and protested. "You heard our guest." The leader said. "Weapons on the ground. We must abide the Lady's wishes and escort this party up to her penthouse."

After all three guns were on the floor and slid away by the guards, Michael and Andres exited the office. Chin showed up out of nowhere, almost literally reappearing in thin air. I looked at Lilly, into her sweet, frightened, blue eyes and gave her shoulder a little squeeze while gesturing the group with a nod of my head. "Come on."

Michael hissed as he power strode up to the new group. He looked pissed as all hell. "Why the eff did you kill John?"

The third guard, a young man, furrowed his brow. "Who?"

The old man silenced him with a quick 'Shh' and a scolding look. "*John* was with the Union. A spy. He was leading you to your deaths."

I snorted. "But what about the guy down -"

"JASON!" Michael yelled. "Quiet." His eyes shifted over to the three guards as he shucked off his coat and unsheathed both of his swords. "Andres, get the weapons. Mr. ah, what's the name?"

The old man straightened himself. "I'm Colonel Paul of her Lady's inner guard."

"You know," Michael started, cautiously inching closer to the guards, "I've known Erica a *long* time. She's never been very formal." Everyone was silent for a moment, allowing the sounds of death, fear and destruction from outside fill the air. I moved up behind Vistaer, keeping my aim on the soldiers. "You lead us to her now. Any lies or tricks, and you'll all join my friend. I knew him a long time too."

The old man appeared unfazed and nodded his head ever so slightly to the side. "Perhaps you didn't know him as well as you thought." He glanced at all five of us. "This way please. We must not keep the Lady waiting."

"Hey!" I yelled as the colonel and the two others headed back for the elevators. "What's going on outside? Have you seen David Holt? Is he here?"

The old man stopped and perked his head up. His back was still to me when he spoke. "Please follow us."

Michael and I exchanged glances. The big hailiorum nodded and gripped the handles on his blades tighter. I could hear his grip squeeze the leather.

Chin was more direct and whispered. "We know where Erica is. Let's grease these three. I don't trust them."

I raised my eyebrows and studied the guards as the elevator door opened behind them. If they heard Chin, the comment didn't seem to bother them in the slightest. Odd, especially given the madness and murders going on everywhere. Everything was seriously effed up here.

"No!" Lilly hissed. "No more killing."

Andres gasped. "Yes, please." He leaned close to Michael's ear and spoke softly. I could still hear him though. "These three have been absolutely traumatized, Sir. They're," he swallowed, "minds are nearly gone. Cracked, devastated."

"Please enter the elevator and we'll take you to the top floor." The colonel spoke in a perfectly normal voice.

At the same time I heard a blood curdling scream from a woman outside. It wasn't a scream of physical pain, it was one of loss and sadness. I'd heard it too many times and knew the horrible sound all too well. Andres heard it too, no doubt feeling it much more than I did. His body quivered. He shouldn't be here.

We entered the elevator and kept a close watch on the seemingly unarmed guards. The tip of one of Michael's blades was only an inch away from the young soldier's ear. The man didn't seem to even notice.

"You never answered my questions." I said, breaking the silence.

The Colonel looked at me. Well actually, he looked in my direction, sort of looking through me, not at me. His eyes were glazed over almost like he was hypnotized. "The Lady will answer your questions, I'm sure."

"Jason." Michael spoke as soft as his deep voice would allow. I looked at him and saw deep concern on his face. "We'll find out if she knows anything about David but I want you to keep a watch over Lilly, no matter what happens. You understand?"

I crinkled my brow. "What do you think will happen?"

With that, the elevator doors opened and the eight of us stepped out into an enormous, luxurious penthouse surrounded by windows. Sunlight filled every inch of the floor, making visible expensive, comfortable looking couches, chairs and tables. There was a giant telescreen in the northwest corner with every type of home entertainment gadget known attached to it. The northeast corner had a bar set up that could comfortably seat ten people. Like the lobby, several plants decorated the area and large, beautifully crafted area rugs, deep green in color covered parts of the gleaming clean wooden tile floor.

"Jesus." I said.

Michael grunted and I looked at him, his eyes were darting all over the place. "Erica doesn't give a damn about any of this glitz and glamour." He looked at me. "It's all a show for when other Tehlasrin leaders come around. It's part of her cover."

"Please have a seat." The Colonel said, motioning the matching couch sets. "Lady Wood will be with you shortly."

"We'll stand." Michael growled. He stepped up close to the old man, almost bumping noses. "Where is she?"

"Oh God." Andres said in a shocked but restrained voice.

I followed his line of vision. There were two dead men, naked, lying on the ground in pools of blood. They were surrounded by furniture in the center of the main living area. I'd had enough. I quickly pushed Lilly behind me then aimed both my weapons at the three guards. Chin did the same and Michael squinted.

Before I could fire, Vistaer smashed his elbow into the Colonel's face, grabbed the woman guard and rammed her head into the elevator wall then smacked the young guard's head with the side of the blade in his right hand. He did all this in less than two seconds with that same, incredibly fast, inhuman speed I'd seen in Cross, Forrest and other hailiorea. He looked at Chin then at me and we lowered our weapons. "Watch yourselves."

"Is that the wonderful Michael Vistaer, I hear?" A woman's voice called from behind a mostly closed door along the eastern wall, about four yards from the bar.

I raised my weapon and aimed it toward the door. Michael, still holding both swords, rested his left hand on my arm, wanting me to lower the weapon. He shook his head. "Erica. Yea, it's me."

"Oh, how *lovely*," the last word was said with an unfitting blend of joy, humor and seductiveness. "I'm just getting all pretty for you, I'll be right there. Make yourselves comfortable."

I had it. "Comfortable?" I boomed. "Where? Over on the couch by the two dead, naked guys?"

"Damn it, Jason." Michael lowered his voice. "Let me talk."

"Oh, you're not alone. Who was that?" Erica asked. "Could it possibly be the famous Jason Sworn?" She purred a string of laughs and I just about snapped. She knew who I was. That told me she knew who David was.

I stepped forward, heading for the door when Michael rushed to block my path. "Relax! Something is seriously wrong. Remember what I said. Protect Lilly."

I fumed and turned to look at the young woman. Turned out she was still right on my heels. My face whipped around to look at the door again. "Famous?" I asked. "Where is David? Is he -?"

I was speechless after the woman opened the bathroom door and stepped out. Her face was covered in thick layers of makeup, making her look like an overly glamorous, ridiculous clown. Her lips were smothered with bright red lipstick that ran almost up to her nose and down halfway to the end of her chin. Her cheeks were giant circles of pink and her eyes were covered in sky blue makeup that went all the way up to her eyebrows. She smiled, showing her perfectly white teeth. Her brown hair was wet and pulled back behind her. Amazingly, the makeup was so distracting I noticed that before it dawned on me the woman was completely naked. There was nothing on her but the paint on her face and blood red polish on her finger and toenails.

"Oh, a whole party!" She said happily, looking at us all. Her eyes stopped on Lilly. "Claire! How great to see you."

Lilly didn't bother correcting Erica like she usually did. Instead she grabbed hold of my left arm and squeezed. I swallowed and glanced at her. The young woman's eyes were a blend of fear, confusion and disgust.

Michael placed himself between Erica and the rest of us, looking at the four of us in turn. He spoke softly and slowly. "She's been shattered." He blinked, ever so slowly and collected himself before turning around. "What's going on here, dear?"

"What do you mean?" She sauntered over to the bar in long, graceful strides. The woman's body was in terrific shape but the combination of the makeup and the fact that she was bat crap crazy prevented my brain from registering her physical beauty. "Would you all like a drink?"

"ERICA STOP!" Michael roared, his patience had already eroded away. "People are dying outside! Your team is killing each other. There are two effing dead men in your living room!"

Erica's eyes widened along with her smile. "They couldn't keep up. Neither of them were man enough." She paused long enough to lick her lipstick caked lips. "What about you, Michael? Are you *man* enough to satisfy me?" She giggled and started rubbing the insides of her thighs. Then she turned to me. "Or you? Mmm, you look like you could keep a girl real happy for a long time."

Lilly grabbed my arm even tighter. I took the opening. "Where's David?"

"David, David, David." Erica waved her hand in the air. "Is that all you care about? He was here, then we…" She stared off into empty space, blinking. "He was here. He and I met. He was here." Her voice trialed off.

"WHERE IS HE?" I asked, afraid my friend's body was somewhere in the building lying in his own blood like the two sorry bastards only a few yards from me.

Michael moved closer to Erica. "There are bigger things to worry about than David, damn it. Erica, look at me!"

"David's going home, to see his mother and sister near Phoenix. Isn't that cute?" She smiled again and looked at Michael. "Take your clothes off." Then she looked at the rest of you. "All of you. You too, Claire. Let's have some fun."

"ENOUGH!" Michael roared through clenched teeth.

"She's gone." Andres said in a wobbly voice. "I don't know how but it's true. She's completely twisted."

Suddenly, Erica screamed. I never would have guessed such sound could come from a human body but the pitch and volume of the shriek nearly made me faint. "YOU DON'T KNOW ANYTHING, YOU LITTLE FAIRY!" She railed, now pointing at Andres. "YOU WANT TO KNOW WHAT TWISTED IS? LEARN!"

Something was happening between Erica and Andres but I wasn't sure what. All I know is Andres whimpered then crumpled to the floor. Chin fired his weapon and I quickly saw the three guards had gotten to their feet before being knocked down again, presumably dead this time.

"STOP!" Michael yelled and raced up to Erica while sheathing his swords. He grabbed the woman by her bare shoulders. I aimed my weapon toward her in case she made a move toward Lilly or me. "What have you done? What happened to you? TELL ME!"

Erica laughed, her hands clawed at Michael's belt buckle. "Take this off! I need it. Nothing happened to me! I'm going to be the queen of North America. The resistance isn't needed anymore so I'm having all those dirty, silly rebels put in their place."

On queue, I heard a bomb go off from outside the building and felt the vibrations from the shockwave run up my feet and legs.

"*WHY*?" Michael shook her again, more violently this time. I could tell he was unraveling, filled with confusion and pain all while losing hope. "You're part of the resistance! You believe in liberty, in freedom! You're not a damned queen. What in God's name are you thinking?"

"Poor, Michael," she soothed. "You don't understand. I've been freed, reborn. I know who I always should've been. Who I was born to be." Her voice gained strength as she spoke. "I am becoming that woman. He set me free. He showed me the truth!"

"No! Erica!" It was Lilly, screaming and crying. "Don't!"

I could only watch. Michael looked from Erica to Lilly and back to Erica. "Who? Who set you free?"

"The darkness, the sweet splendor of true power. It's coming. Part of it's already here." With that she flailed her arms and broke Vistaer's grip. The man was stunned giving Erica the opportunity to plant both hands, palms out against his chest, pushing him away, through the air before his big body crashed to the floor, landing on his back.

Erica laughed.

Vistaer jumped back to his feet, tugging out his weapons as he did so. His lip was curled and rage poured from him. I could feel the man's determination and drive. Somehow it filled me as well. I nearly pulled the trigger on my weapon right then and there. The woman was insane and reminded me, uncomfortably of a blend of Kara Childers and the bitch Samantha Forrest. Erica was a serious threat and dangerous. Michael knew that to. She had to die.

"Just stop!" Lilly cried. "Don't hurt her!"

Erica turned to Lilly and laughed. "You silly, weak little slut. Even with your mother bonded to you, you're still a pathetic, manipulative brat who uses people to get what you want." Erica looked at Michael, then Chin and me. "They can't hurt me. They can't stop what's coming." Next she spoke in an eerie whisper. "They can't stop the coming power and wrath of Xolzv."

I gritted my teeth. "Don't talk that way about Lilly, you psychotic bitch!"

"Lilly?" Erica looked straight at the young woman. A wicked smile sprung up on her heavily, disgustingly decorated face. "Oh. Oh I see. She always liked the name Lilly."

Michael hummed something under his breath and crossed his blades in front of him, close to his chest. The gesture made for an odd pose. He spoke softly. "Erica. I love you as a sister and a great comrade in arms. We've bled and fought together for years. We wanted to bring hope back for others, for us all."

"Blah, blah, blah." She laughed. "Enough talk. Either strip and let me take you, leave or kill yourself. I don't care." The woman looked at me with a suddenly grim and almost horrified look on her face. Something about the expression was painfully familiar and the images I saw in the mirror that morning. "You want D…" She shivered then regained her composure. "David? Fine, take one of the cars in my garage. Leave. I don't care."

Lilly cried at my side. "Erica, this isn't you. It's not too late." She pleaded. "Tell us what happened, maybe we can help you. Richard and I together -"

"YOU'RE A DISGRACE TO YOUR MOTHER!" Erica railed at Lilly, making my anger burn even hotter and driving the haunting pictures out of my head. "I know what you're after. You don't fool me like the morons you surround yourself with."

"I tried to save a shattered friend once." Michael said to Erica in an even tone. "You know what happened?" She turned back to him and raised her eyebrows. "The bastard killed my sister, beat her and killed her."

I swallowed and saw Vistaer's lip curl. "I'll NEVER make that mistake again. I love you, Erica. But you're beyond saving. In the name of God, I'm sorry." With that he roared and lunged at the woman, bringing both blades down on her.

She swiftly sidestepped, dodging both of the swords, and leapt over the bar, ducking for cover under a flurry of Michael's swings.

Lilly screamed again. "ERICA!"

Chin bolted over several couches and chairs to get a better angle on Erica. Between him, Michael and me, we formed a triangle with Vistaer at the point, merely a few feet from the shattered hailiorum. The Asian man sent out a couple shots that missed the woman's head, exploding expensive bottles of liquor. Glass and liquid splashed wildly behind the bar.

Then, to my shock, Erica jumped, almost flew, out from behind the bar armed with two deadly and medieval looking flails, one in each hand. The weapons had handles that were about a foot long with spiked chains coming out of the tops that were then capped with wicked metal balls the size of large grapefruits. Those were covered in pointy metal spikes.

With seemingly ease, Erica dodged every shot I sent her way as she spun toward Chin. The man ducked under her whirlwind blows but still caught a nasty blast to the back of his head. He fell and stopped moving. I wasn't sure if he was dead or not.

I aimed my weapon at Erica again and was about to shoot when Michael charged the naked woman. He rammed his massive shoulder into her side sending her much smaller mass flying. Her body crashed into the large telescreen, bringing the thing crashing down off the wall.

"GET CHIN!" Vistaer hollered at me, again charging Erica. "Protect him and the others!"

I looked at Lilly, "Stay with me!" and darted over to Chin. Miraculously, I didn't see any blood and quickly yanked his body up, tucking my head under his left arm before hurrying over to where Andres had fallen.

All the while, Erica was back on her feet, dueling Michael. The two were ducking, weaving and swinging in a mad dance to the death. I set Chin flush against his comrade and pulled Lilly's little frame behind me. It was the best I could do as far as protection. Now, I had both weapons out, set to full strength, aimed at Erica's ever changing positions, hoping for an opening.

Finally, Erica managed to whip the chains around Michael's swords so all four weapons were tied up good and tight. The two pulled into each other so close it looked like they were about to kiss.

Erica growled. "You've no idea the pain I've been through!"

"You're only creating more pain!" Michael shot back. "Let's end it! Quick and easy." He grunted, muscles bulging against Erica's inhuman strength. "I don't want you to suffer any more!"

"Never!" She spat right into his eyes. I could see the strain on Erica's face and wondered how someone as small in comparison to Michael could match his raw power. She spoke through clenched teeth. "You're a coward. You think you fight for justice?" The two grunted more and fought to overpower each other. "Those you fight for and with will betray you! I know it! You'll die as you lived, a fool! I will rule for Xolzv. It'll end it all! True freedom."

A savage roar bellowed from the recesses within Michael Vistaer as he hammered his forehead down on the bridge of Erica's nose. The woman's face was now covered in red that wasn't makeup. She backpedaled, staggered and released the grips on her weapons.

The opening was there, I was about to shoot when I caught a glimpse of Erica's back. The direct center was covered with a large, black circle, right where the needle entered the woman's spine in my vision. My mouth dropped open. "What…" I mumbled. "How?"

"Oh, Jason." Lilly hugged me and buried her face in my chest making me *feel* the entire tragedy of Erica Wood. The feelings were overwhelming and filled the entire room. Each breath of air I took in flooded my insides with sympathy. Something or someone had destroyed everything that was once honorable and kind in her. I didn't have the will to shoot, pity forced me to lower my weapons.

Michael was watching everything. He nodded and shrugged the flails off his blades. "It's ok, Jason." He stepped toward Erica who was now on her knees, crying. "Erica, honey. I'm sorry." Tears welled in the big man's eyes.

She looked up at him. "What happened, Mikey? I didn't want this." I heard her let out a light chuckle. "We used to play as kids, remember? Always saving people from evil monsters. What happened? How did I become a monster?"

"You're not a monster." Michael looked down on her. "You've been hurt and damaged. I need to kill you. Do you understand? I need to free your soul. I have to before you do more harm to others."

Erica drew in a deep breath and stared into Michael's eyes. "Are you sure it can be freed?" She shook her head. "Are you sure there even is such a thing as a soul?"

"With everything we've seen?" Michael raised his eyebrows. "Yes. I'm armed with experience and faith." A pause. "And so are you. If you live, you'll cause more pain and destruction. I need to fix the mess you made."

"Start with the detention camps." Erica shook her head. "They're good people." The woman began a soft wailing and spoke through her cries. "I betrayed the resistance. I betrayed the hailiorea, you, Hannah, August, everyone."

"No." Vistaer said boldly. "You helped the rebellion. We're going to win and couldn't have done it without your bravery, sacrifice and compassion." The big man drew in a deep breath and nodded. "The Union and the osilea will fail."

At that moment, there was a changing feeling in the air. Danger replaced remorse. Madness replaced sorrow. Hatred replaced pity. What the eff was going on?

"No!" Erica bolted up. "I won't allow you to end my blessed life. I'M THE QUEEN! Kneel to me! Worship at my feet!" She laughed. "I know, deep down, *Mikey*, that you desire to surrender and serve. You crave the sweet release of slavery. All men do. Love me. Yes."

Without another word, Michael drove both blades through the woman's body and pulled up, creating two massive, mortal gashes. Her body dropped. Then, to my horror, the big man cleaved the woman's head clean off her neck. Silence hung in the air for several heartbeats. Lilly stared at her feet, crying as tears dropped on her shoes. Andres had woken up and was checking on Chin. Michael put his blades in their homes behind his back and walked up to Lilly.

"You tried, kid. You tried." He hugged her. "I'm sorry."

I held on to my etherpistols and furrowed my brow. "Tried what?"

Andres spoke and I turned to him. "She tried to inspire hope and love… and pity" He choked back his tears. "It only worked a little."

Lilly's face was flush against Michael's chest and her voice was muffled when she spoke. "I'm not strong enough."

"Hush." Vistaer said, petting the girl's head in a fatherly way. "Chin, are you alright?" He let go of Lilly.

The man nodded. "Yea, sorry. She had a lead on me and I had to tuck in. I focused every shred of energy I had into a quick shield." He ran his right hand through his short, black hair. "My head's still in one piece. Seems it worked."

Michael nodded. "Let's head back down to Erica's office. See if we can help undo some of the chaos here."

Chapter 9

"All outside communications have been shut down. Everything." Michael spoke in his deep voice. "Only internal command channels are still open. Damn."

He was seated behind Erica's elaborate desk positioned in the back corner of her large office. Chin was leaning over his shoulder, eyes fixed on the large dual monitors set in the middle of the desktop.

The sounds of gunfire from outside continued to fill the air while I watched Michael pull his mobile phone out of his pocket. He thumbed several buttons. "Nothing, no signal." He glanced up at Chin. "We won't be able to contact Mike for a portal home."

I was sitting on a very comfortable couch that looked and smelled brand new with my arm around Lilly. The woman was still extremely shaken. "Are we leaving then?" She asked.

Vistaer looked at Lilly, then Andres and then me. "I'm not, not yet. But you are. Get Lilly out of here."

I shook my head, about to speak. I had no intention of heading back to Denver. Michael spoke first. "She can show you to Erica's garage. Load one of her cars up with etherspring and get the hell out of here. It's not safe."

"Michael." Chin started, his voice filled with doubt. "What are they going to do? Just take a nice, little drive down

Main Street, ignoring by all the shootings, bombings and arrests?"

The big man showed fatigue for the first time. He closed his eyes, blew out a deep breath and rubbed his temples with his left hand. He spoke calmly, eyes still closed. "Richard's enchant on Jason is still strong. If he can focus and Lilly can manage to bolster the spell, they should be fine on their way home."

Chin shook his head. "And if they can't? Will they be fine?" He lowered his voice and leaned in close to Michael's ear. I only heard the name Lilly whispered. Both men's eyes darted over to the young woman. Everything else was too quiet to make out.

I was done playing the 'say nothing bystander.' I started loud and clear. "I'm not going back -"

Michael interrupted. "Chin, Andres and I are staying behind. Jason and Lilly are leaving. That's all there is to it."

"What are we going to do? What can we do?" Andres asked. He was seated in a chair across from Michael and Chin.

Vistaer grunted. "First, I'm going to use Erica's executive command code to order all the prisoners released from the internment camps and prisons. Then... oh eff."

"What now?" I asked. I wanted to tell the man that I planned to head to Phoenix and checked to make sure the map to David's family was still in my pocket. But, as usual, curiosity got the better of me.

"Samuel Rice." Vistaer began. "A controller running a small district north of here has moved his troops into the area. The bastard is looking to take the whole sector over."

"So what does that mean?" Lilly asked in a soft, shaky voice. I looked at her then back at Michael.

The man blinked. "It means not only do we have to sort through Erica's people, those who are with the GU or with the resistance, but we also have a small army to fight." He shook his head. "This just keeps getting worse and worse."

"I think we'd better all get out of here." I said.

Michael slumped his shoulders and looked at me with droopy eyes, shaking his head. "You don't understand, Jason. We fled Seattle in the midst of war because I knew Hannah was there to pick up the pieces." He grunted. "There's no one here I trust to do the job and the people are in trouble. I can't turn my back on them."

I let out a deep breath. "I understand that, but I -"

"Need to find David." Michael finished. "I know." He paused, studying my face. "I like you, Sworn. But you know damn well David will be just like Erica."

It felt like shards of ice ran through my body. I didn't know what to say but managed to mumble, "I have to try."

Michael nodded. "We all have to do what we have to do. I have to help bring stability and freedom here, you have to find your brother." I swallowed and nodded. David wasn't my brother but he was damn close to it. Vistaer's eyes turned to Lilly. "Do you have your phone?"

"Yes." She said quietly.

"Good." He looked back at me. "Get a car, get past the area's limits, out of the blackout zone. As soon as you're able to contact Mike, have him open a portal so Lilly can go back home."

I stood up, suddenly uncomfortable with the thought of driving through a war zone. Still, Michael's plan was better than anything I could come up with. I hoped Richard's voodoo still worked. "Alright."

"From there, you're free to do and go where you want." Michael sighed. "Give me a little time before you head out of the garage. I need to input these commands then try to contact some of the surviving leaders I trust."

"What for?" I asked, furrowing my brow. "Why wait?"

"Look at it out there." Michael made a slight gesture toward the world outside the windows behind him. "You'll need a distraction. We can give you one."

I reached a hand out to Lilly. She took it and pulled herself to her feet. I acknowledged Michael and the others. "Ok. Good luck. Be careful."

To that, Vistaer let out one of his hearty laughs. "I've never been careful my whole life. You just stay low, out of the way and don't do anything stupid."

I chuckled. "Stupid? Me?"

"You're a good man and you're a survivor. You'll be ok. I'm trusting you to help Lilly." He looked at her. "I love you, girl. Just like I love my daughters." Michael shifted his gaze and focused on the computer screens, typing away on the keyboard in front of him. "Take care of yourself, Jason. I hope you find David, unharmed and undamaged."

"Thanks."

With that, Lilly led me out of the office and back to the elevators. On the way, my brain was a blended mess of distracted thoughts. The sights, sounds and smells around us worked their way to the back of my brain, far behind the thoughts of saving my friend.

-

Erica Wood's garage was more like a parking lot. She had vehicles of all sorts, perfectly lined up in rows five deep and eight across. The ceiling was lined with large, rectangular lights that bounced their soft yellow-orange glow off the fresh, gleaming paint on the cars. They ranged in sizes and type. Some were sporty two-seaters and others were larger utility vehicles and trucks. I shook my head in wonder. Why and the hell would anyone ever need so many cars?

Lilly was snaking her way through the selection, examining them, looking for the right one. I preferred the fastest of the bunch. The quicker I could catch up to David the better. But no, Lilly was more interested in some of the huskier utility vehicles. It made sense, given the carnage and chaos going on outside.

The woman was gaining her spirit back at an odd and almost alarmingly rapid pace. Ten minutes ago she was a shaken mess, mourning the death of her friend. Now, her eyes were wide and alert, happily glancing over the cars like a child in a toy shop.

She stopped in front of a dark green vehicle that wasn't the biggest but larger than most. I wasn't sure on the make and had actually never seen or taken notice of the model before. Hell, most of the cars on the road, which only a few people were able to afford, were rusty, broken down and unreliable. Only the rich, make that the very rich controllers ever owned new automobiles.

She looked at me, smirked and raised an eyebrow. "Well, Mr. Protector. I trust you can drive, right?"

The provocative look she gave made me instinctively puff my chest up and out. "Of course." It wasn't a lie but in truth, I'd hardly driven at all my whole life and I was by no means an expert.

"Good, because I can't." She laughed and turned to look back at the half truck-half van parked next to her. She slapped her hand on its hood. "It'd be unbelievably funny and horrible if it turned out you couldn't drive. This one will do. It's quick and sturdy."

The 'quick' part sold me. "Ok. Are the keys inside?"

"Oh?" She turned back to me and sauntered toward me. "Ready to go so soon?"

I watched her walk and felt my heart quicken. My brain went on a lusty field trip, imaging every curve of the young woman's body without the obstacles of clothing. I thought of her soft skin, warm breath, shining hair. For the first time in days, I had to rub the back of my neck. Lilly and I smiled at the same time. "You have to stop that."

"Stop what?" She asked, smiling even cuter and hotter than before.

The reality of the situation washed over me. "Listen, we're basically stealing this thing and I don't want any trouble with more of Erica's people." I moved close to the driver's side door. "Yea, let's go."

"Not yet." Lilly shook her head. "We need to fuel this guy up all the way and tuck away some extra energy. It's about five hours to Phoenix and we won't want to have to stop anywhere public, will we?"

I smiled, wolfishly. "We? Sorry, darling but you're headed back to Denver as soon as we can call Mike. That's what we promised Michael."

"I didn't promise anything." She placed her right hand on her chest, gesturing herself and half closed her eyes in a snobby way. "But you're right."

"Right." I nodded and looked around the garage. "Let's fill up. The energy station is over there."

Lilly walked over to the etherspring tanks while I started the car and rolled it over to them. Embarrassingly, the accelerator was much more powerful than I anticipated and the brakes were especially more sensitive than I planned. I stopped and went like a complete rookie, almost bumping several other cars along the short way. We started filling the vehicles energy tank when the young woman poked me in my side, just under my ribs. The touch tickled like crazy. "You sure you can drive?"

I bent my body away from her delicate, beautiful little index finger which was ready for another jab. "Don't worry." I blinked. "I'm just a little rusty."

"Been a while, huh?" She bit her lip and gave me a look, I don't know how women do it, that made my brain and body tingle all over.

I snorted and headed over to the reserve energy tanks, filling them up as well. I figured one would be enough so I planned on filling two. Hell the stuff was free and it was better to be safe than sorry.

"Oh, all serious now?" Lilly asked with a little laugh.

I looked at her after setting the second tank in the spacious back compartment of our soon to be stolen vehicle. "What's with you?"

She shook her head and blinked, looking dumbfounded. "What do you mean?"

"I mean we're in the middle of a warzone, we could get captured or shot any second, Michael and the others are putting themselves in danger and your friend went insane and had to be killed." I grimaced. "You were devastated a few moments ago but now... now your -"

"I know. I know." She said, eyes drifting down to study her shoes. "I loved Erica but she was hurt by, I don't know, by something." Lilly's big, beautiful eyes looked back up at me. "But she's free now, Jason. She's free from pain and we have a job to do."

"Ok then." I felt like an ass for even mildly lecturing her. "I'm sorry, you just seem, happy."

Another laugh. "Do I? Good." She closed the back door to the vehicle once I'd stepped away. "That means I'm getting better. I told you my gift is inspiration. Well, I'm working real hard to build that up."

I furrowed my brow. "Why?" After a shake of my head I said, "I mean, I'm glad you're feeling better but... Oh I don't know." I was rambling now. Nice. "You can just... turn your emotions on and off like that? Make yourself feel better so quickly?"

"I used to always be happy." She said. "I was able to see the good in all types of situations. There was always hope." A pause. "Richard is helping me get back to who I was. So I guess the answer is yes. I can, sometimes, just make myself happy." She raised an eyebrow. "Can't you?"

I almost rolled my eyes. "That's not what I mean and you know it."

"Look," she started, "our only chance past the mobs, the soldiers, the fighting, the surveillance cameras, the patrols and the checkpoints is with Richard's enchant." She could tell I was feeling odd, unsure what to say and reached out to grab hold of both my hands. "I need to inspire that focus and strength in you, Jason. In short, you're our only chance out of here."

"I'm confused." I admitted. "Is this all an act then?"

Lilly smiled and lightly shook her head before drawing in and wrapping her arms around my back. I instinctively hugged her sweet body back. "No, it's not an act. I'm working on becoming who I really am, who I was before my bond with my mother. Somehow, you help me with that."

"How?" I asked with a whisper. It was hard to even talk having the woman in my arms. The feeling was sheer delight and I think I moaned.

Lilly ran her hands up and down my back. "I'm not totally sure but it's working. Let go and relax. We have to wait a little while for Michael to get things set on his end."

I brushed my cheek and lips against Lilly's soft, golden hair. "Ok."

"We'll use the time to help the magic grow. Focus on Richard's spell, let it get stronger." She was whispering now too. The last thing in the world I wanted to think about was Richard but somehow, no doubt more of that crazy hailiorea stuff, it felt like a large, soft, dark cloak suddenly surrounded us. Whatever she was doing was working.

I couldn't keep from kissing the top of her head or stop myself from dropping my lips down to her delicate cheek. I kissed that too and inched closer to her mouth.

"This way." She said abruptly, pulling me closer to the van. "Get inside." She was still speaking softly but also had a sense of urgency in her tone. "We need to create a bubble around the car."

I obeyed, pulled along by the woman like she had a rope around my waist. I absentmindedly sat behind the steering wheel and Lilly quickly darted over to the other side, opened the passenger door, hopped in and cupped my right hand in both of hers.

I looked at her and felt my eyes droop to a near close. Without thinking, I leaned over to kiss her, Lilly, the most beautiful person in the whole twisted, effed up world. She closed her eyes and leaned toward me but didn't meet my lips with hers. Instead my kiss planted itself on her forehead.

"Good, Jason." She purred softly. "I'm sorry for being so flirty but it's part of my essence. I'm strengthened by life, love, creation, affection, everything in the world that makes living wonderful. It helps me inspire people, especially you."

I sighed in delight still hardly able to speak. "It's ok."

"Not that I don't care about you." She said to my approval. "You're special. You're a good, strong man here to help a friend. Close your eyes and tell your difficult, skeptical, wonderful brain to remember Richard's spell."

My eyes shut on command, my ears were filled with Lilly's voice and my nose was filled with the smell of her hair, skin and clothes.

She was whispering again, right into my left ear, tickling me with every word. "Let the cloak wash over us and out over the vehicle. Let it out. Believe. Remember its success at the asylum. Trust yourself, your strength. Trust me."

"I trust you." I said. And then I was asleep.

-

An explosion startled me awake. I jumped and quickly aligned myself. Somehow I was lying on a couch that made up the mid section of the large vehicle. Lilly was in my arms, also stirring.

I shook my head, casting off my sleepiness and drew in a quick, deep breath. "What happened? How did I get back here? How long were we asleep?"

"I wasn't asleep." Lilly said. "You climbed back here yourself. I'd hardly be able to move you."

"Yea." I started to get up and waited for Lilly to brace herself before pulling my right arm out from under her. I studied her face. "So, how long?"

She shook her head and pursed her lips. "Not long, about thirty minutes."

"Ok," I rubbed my face and let out a little grunt before opening the rear passenger side door and stepping out. "I think it's time we hit the road."

"Exactly." Lilly agreed. "We're ready and I imagine Michael is too."

By the time I sat myself down behind the wheel, Lilly had squeezed through the two front seats and parked herself on the passenger side. I smiled at her, feeling incredibly relaxed and confident. In fact, I hadn't felt this good since the night I helped destroy the osilea on Ravenfall. Damn, these hailiorea tricks were something else.

Without another word, I turned the key and started out of the garage. Lilly navigated, letting me know how to get out of the place. We drove up a small ramp that led to sunlight. Sunlight and destruction. The gate separating the garage from the outside opened as we neared and my eyes took in the curiously empty sentry booths positioned on all sides, right and left, before and after the gate.

"Just drive." Lilly said through tight lips. Her eyes were darting over the people, rushing, crying, screaming and fighting all over the place. "Straight as you can. Don't stop."

I swallowed. "You don't have to tell me." I pulled out onto the road and accelerated, cruising past fires, makeshift barricades and running people. I saw several frantic men and woman rushing for safety, some holding looted items from burning, torn up superstores. Others huddled down holding each other, men, women and children in their arms, terror showing on their faces. Surveillance cameras and megaphone speakers were busted, knocked down and shattered, littering the road.

"How the hell is Michael going to make any order out of this?" I asked, noting we were moving about forty clicks an hour.

Lilly grabbed and squeezed my hand, her voice filled with excitement and worry. "There he is!" I spared a glance out her window. "Oh my god, he's in front of a line of soldiers!"

"WHAT?" I couldn't see what she was looking at, too busy trying to keep from running anyone over. It was as if none of the people even saw my car, like it was invisible. Several men and woman darted right in front of me, forcing me to give the extra sensitive breaks a good workout. "Is he trapped? Are they going to k -"

She shook her head. "It looks like he's talking. Keep driving!" She looked at me with a frightened expression, knowing I was thinking of turning around to rescue the man. "Don't stop!"

"But Michael…"

"Jason, he wanted us to go." She turned to look back out her window. "He's got several armed people with him. It looks like a stand off."

I stepped on the gas and nearly doubled our speed. "The man *is* insane." I decided, with Lilly's encouragement, that Michael could take care of himself. My responsibilities were to get Lilly to safety and to find David.

Gaining ever more confident driving, I sped up close to one hundred clicks per hour, zig-zagging around a chaotic array of obstacles littering the street.

"God damn!" Lilly said with a hint of excitement.

I smiled, cockily and glanced at the woman out of the corner of my eye. She was quickly fastening her seat belt, bracing herself, staring at the whirl of activity flying by her window.

"I told you," I started before slamming on the breaks, letting a small boy race across the street then flooring the gas again, "I can drive." Truthfully, I was amazed myself but every now and then even my life had its pleasant surprises.

Turns out, whether it was my hailiorum talent, desperate skill or dumb luck, I was a pro behind the wheel. Hell, I almost felt like part of the car now.

"Actually, you can't." Lilly said, smugly. "It's the car. These new models run on autopilot." She laughed.

"WHAT?" I said again, my eyes racing over the dashboard for the autopilot interface before realizing Lilly was teasing me. I smiled and spared another glance. It seemed she wasn't going to let me gloat without a little zing. "Shut up!"

Lilly laughed again. "You got it, racer man. Just get us out of the city."

Hell yea.

-

Two hours later and we were well past the densely populated areas, rolling through three abandoned checkpoint stations in that time. The places looked like they'd been left in a hurry; doors were wide open and random equipment littered the ground. No doubt the men and women, soldiers stationed there, had been called into the city to help bring order. Or maybe they simply left their posts, giving up on their duties.

Lilly had fallen asleep after passing the last empty security point. She was out for about a half hour and insisted I woke her up if we came across another checkpoint. I guessed she was exhausted after everything she'd been through. The work she put into bolstering Richard's magic probably took a toll too.

We were cruising down another long stretch of road when I remembered Michael's instructions. I reluctantly pulled over to the side of the eerily empty freeway, put the car in park and gently nudged Lilly's shoulder.

"Lilly, wake up." I said softly. She moaned and moved a little after my touch before finally opening her eyes. I sighed, not really wanting to say what had to be said. "We're probably clear now. Check your phone."

Without a word, Lilly sat up, unbuckled her seatbelt, opened the door and stepped out of the vehicle. I did the same and walked over to her, stretching my legs and inhaling the warm air.

She reached into her pocket and pulled out her phone, looking at me with an odd, unreadable expression.

"Well?" I asked. "Do you have a signal?"

I nearly jumped when a speaker posted atop a tall pole near a streetlight about twenty meters down the road started speaking. "Tehlasrin is in a state of emergency. Report immediately to the nearest security station. This is an order from Global Union Command."

My eyes squinted, studying the speaker. I wondered if it was just an emergency recording or if there was actually someone speaking in real time, watching us from the camera planted next to the speaker. The thing started all over again, the same voice, the same tone.

I snorted, pulled out one of my etherpistols, aimed it at the camera and speaker and fired, full power. The thing exploded in a satisfying shower of sparks. The area was silent again and I turned back to Lilly.

She swallowed and gripped the phone with as much force as she could muster, showing white knuckles and straining tendons in her hand. "Yes, there's a signal."

I nodded. "Ok, call Mike."

Without a word, Lilly threw the phone down, as hard as she could against the pavement near her feet. The tiny phone broke in two. Then she lifted her right foot and slammed her heel down on the larger of the two pieces, smashing it even more.

My mouth dropped open. "What the hell are you -?"

"I'm not going back yet." She looked up at me with intense eyes, her mouth locked in an aggressive snarl. "I'm helping you."

My left hand covered my mouth and squeezed before pulling my lips out a bit and then forcefully sliding down my chin. I sighed again. "Do you know the number? Maybe we can find a payphone or something."

"No." Lilly shook her head. "I don't have his number memorized."

I looked at the sky the way people do when pretending to look for help. "Christ."

"Yea, pray if you want." She said with attitude. "But I've made my decision. It's my life."

I couldn't stop the smile that formed on my face. Lilly's determination and spirit impressed me and I was selfishly glad to hear she wanted to stay with me. But, I was headed into danger and didn't look forward to the added responsibility and headache of keeping her safe. "Come on. This is crazy. You must know Mike's number. We'll find another phone."

"Crazy?" She laughed. "You're headed out alone through a damn prison planet to find and help your friend. The odds of making it are stupidly slim. You're telling me *I'm* crazy?"

I studied her face, thinking. "Yes, it's crazy but it's why I'm here. David isn't your concern."

"Don't tell me what is and isn't my concern." Lilly said, sternly.

I cursed. "Michael's going to kill me."

"Stop worrying." She stepped up to me, grabbed my shirt, tugged a little, stretched to the tips of her toes and kissed me, gently on my lips. "It's my choice, ok?"

My tongue, seemingly having grown a mind of its own, licked my lips after the small kiss, tasting Lilly. I shook my head, amazed and amused. "Who the hell are you?"

"I'm your friend." Her eyes glossed over, filling with fresh tears that threatened to rain down her cheeks.

I've never been an emotional man but only a stone cold son of a bitch wouldn't be moved by the display. "Ok." I smiled. "Together then."

We got back into our respective seats and strapped in. Before continuing, I looked at Lilly and reached into my pocket. "Here, take this," and handed her my spare etherpistol. "Just incase. It's best you be armed."

Lilly winked at me. "Thanks."

I looked forward, about ready to move on. "It's going to get dicey up ahead. I think we have about two and half hours before we reach," I looked at the map Morbal printed for me, "Spring Creek. What do we do at any checkpoints between here and there?"

"Our illusion shield should help but there's also this," Lilly tugged a few sheets of what looked like legal papers out of her pocket. At a glance I saw what looked like hand printed signatures and official Tehlasrin labels. "Back in the garage, while you slept, I used Erica's computer to print ourselves some *official* orders."

My eye twitched. "What the hell? You're a genius."

"I know." Lilly cleared her throat and sat up straight before reading aloud. "By order of Her Lady, Erica Wood, these two, Aaron Waters and Lilly White, are to meet with His Lordship Alex Bloom of the Phoenix district with confidential information, property of Tehlasrin command. It is of the utmost priority this message be delivered. Failure to allow delivery of this message will result in immediate detention of all involved." She looked at me, her face filled with pride. "Signed, Erica J. Wood, Governess of Tehlasrin North American district seven."

"What the hell." I said with a sarcastic edge. "The bastards are just openly calling themselves 'Lord' and 'Lady' now. What an effing joke."

"Whatever." Lilly said, tucking the letter away. "It'll work. Drive."

I shifted the car into drive and spared another glance at Lilly. "You planned this all along, didn't you?"

"Move it, Sworn!" She said while pointing a bossy finger forward.

Another hour and a half later and Lilly's forged document helped us breeze through two more checkpoints. The stations were manned but by only half the usual number of soldiers. Being one of the only vehicles on the road, the interrogations were quick and surprisingly painless.

Both times, the Tehlasrin guards started their questions with the usual cocky, arrogant, predatory demeanor. After reading and verifying the document, their attitudes quickly changed. Suddenly, they were all roses, politely handing back the orders and even wishing us a good, safe trip. Bastards.

Overall, the entirety of the trip was mostly silent. I could tell Lilly's brain was just as busy with thoughts, doubts and fears as mine. She mostly stared out her window, into the south, observing the desert landscape and vast horizon. The Sun was directly overhead now and the clock on our vehicle's dashboard said it was two-thirty. I didn't know if it was showing the correct time zone or not but didn't really care.

The liberating feelings I'd had when leaving Los Angeles were still there but somewhat diminished. Anxiety grew along with giddy anticipation of finding my friend. Part of me doubted he was even at his mother's home but I told myself Morbal had been right about David visiting the city now hours behind us. I tried to convince myself the doctor was truthful about Phoenix.

A sour taste filled my mouth. I was taking the word of a sick, evil, conniving, control freak who tortured people for his own pleasure. Yea, solid testimonial.

At one point, I asked Lilly about the horrible things Erica had said about her back in her penthouse. In hindsight it was probably a stupid and rude thing to do but I was uncomfortable in the lingering silence with nothing but my own determination, hopes and second guessing filling my head.

Lilly was ok with it though and shrugged Erica's remarks off. She noted that the woman was in horrible anguish and had lost most of her mind. Then she said she forgave her now deceased friend. I accepted that and continued down the road.

It wasn't long before we were coming up on another damn checkpoint. I gritted my teeth, there were just so many of the things, both occupied and abandoned. Had it not been for the chaos in LA, they would have all been bustling full of ego maniacs on power trips with their little badges and delusions of power.

I wondered how and why the masses even put up with it all. One would think eventually enough would be enough and people would openly rebel everywhere. The very existence of the police state grid proved otherwise. Most people were still in shock from the recent major string of wars, I guessed. The destructive period tore sovereignty and everyone's freedoms to shreds. Most were trapped in fear with their spirits completely crushed. It seemed many just didn't have the will to fight back and simply gave up, rolling over into near slavery.

Michael's rebellion meant a lot more to me at that moment. He and the thousands or millions of others fighting for freedom, privacy, hell even just for a little dignity, could only be called heroes. For a moment, I almost found it funny how concerned I was with one man's, that being David's, freedom and safety. One person hardly seemed significant given the greater scheme of things. But then again, maybe helping one person at a time was all anyone could really do.

"Whoa." Lilly said, pulling me from my thoughts. "What the hell is going on up there?"

"Huh?" I asked, locked in tunnel vision, staring straight ahead at the checkpoint a quarter mile down the road. I caught Lilly's line of vision and followed it, aiming out, beyond the gated station. "Oh wow. Eff."

We saw a convoy of military vehicles, jeeps, trucks and cargo carriers positioned along the freeway all the way up an entrance ramp. I slowed down a bit and visually followed the row of machinery, each flying the sick Tehlasrin flag. The line went all the way back to what looked like a small town. Perhaps they stopped there for supplies? Whatever it was, the cluster moved slowly, rolling onto the freeway heading eastward. Curious, I would have thought they'd go west, toward Los Angeles…

I spared a glance at Lilly. Her pretty blue eyes were wide open, taking in everything. I could almost see her brain working. Sensing my gaze, she looked at me and licked her lips. "Calm, stay calm. We have to stay calm. They're not here for us"

I nodded in agreement. "It looks like a supply line. A heavy group usually used to feed and equip forces as much and as quickly as possibly."

"They're hardly moving. Quickly isn't a word I'd use to describe them." Lilly said with a disappointed tone.

I huffed. "Yea."

"What are we going to do?" She asked, raising her hands, palms up in the air and shrugging her shoulders. "They're taking up the whole freeway and most of the side streets. We can't pass them and we don't want to get caught up in their mess. Richard's enchant isn't all powerful."

"I know, I know." I spoke quickly, a little annoyed with Lilly but mostly flustered by the new predicament. This was going to slow things down and put a serious damper on reaching David sooner than later. I swore under my breath. "Let's just get past the effing checkpoint first, ok?"

We rolled up to the first stop sign and since we were the only travelers at the station, a group of three security soldiers were at my window in seconds. Lilly had the forged document sitting on her lap, ready as could be.

Surprisingly it was the youngest looking of the three that spoke. "What are you doing on the road?" Christ, he didn't appear a day older than eighteen but his eyes looked menacing, cruel and dangerous with dark circles around them. "We're in a state of emergency, idiots! Pull over there and turn your vehicle off." He pointed to a section away from the arm bar gate similar to ones we'd passed through several times on our trip.

I played it cool and strong. "Sorry, we can't do that. We're on -"

The man's eyes bugged out before I could finish. "What did you say?"

"C'mon Joey!" An older guard said from behind him. "We don't have time for this. Just let them go."

"SHUT UP!" The young man, Joey, yelled. He curled his lip at me. "PULL OVER NOW!"

I'd had enough. "We're on orders from Erica Wood!" I grabbed the orders and shoved them in the young man's face. "Now clear aside and let us pass!"

The man read the letter as the other two stepped up to peer over his shoulder at the papers. Joey squinted. "What's this supposed to mean? I don't care who you are or who Erica Wood is. This is my base and you'll follow *my* orders, got it?" He wadded up the letter and threw it at my face. The papers bounced off my nose and landed by my feet.

I gripped the steering wheel as hard as I could, trying to vent my frustration, and turned to look at Lilly. She didn't look frightened in the slightest. Instead she was looking out through the windshield. I looked too.

Men and women in Tehlasrin uniforms were hurrying about in an urgent way with worried expressions. Joey was about to shout again when he also turned to the others. "HEY, WHAT THE HELL ARE YOU DOING? GET BACK TO YOUR POSTS!"

"Eff you, Joe." One of the few women guards said. "The troops are moving out. We're gone."

"YOU'LL ALL BE ARRESTED FOR THIS!" Joey's face was beet red now and he actually stamped his feet like a spoiled child. "I'M REPORTING ALL OF YOU!"

"Like hell." The older guard said in Joey's ear. The man, who was much bigger than the young guard grabbed Joey by his neck and slammed his head against the rear driver's side door. The boy fell down to the ground with a thud.

I studied the older guard. "What's going on here? Where are those troops going?"

"Are you kidding? Don't you listen to the broadcasts?" The man looked at me like I'd sprouted antlers. "They're off to play wargames or something. Morbal and Ark. The whole thing is effed up and the god damned terrorist rebels could strike at any time."

The third man, who'd been silent until now finally spoke. "They're *not* terrorists, you effing moron!"

The older guard spun around. "What? Of course they are."

"I've had it with you, you pig!" The third guard pulled out his pistol and fired a bullet right into the other's gut. He shouted. "LONG LIVE THE RESISTANCE. FOR FREEDOM!"

Now the group of men and women in front of the vehicle started fighting each other. The groups looked about even and it was obvious some were with the rebellion and some were with Tehlasrin.

I heard another shot nearby and quickly turned to see the older guard had managed to pull his own weapon out, fired it and hit the third guard in his cheek. Blood splattered everywhere.

I swore and pulled out my own weapon, ready to fight.

"NO!" Lilly hollered. "Let's go! Get the hell out of here!"

I wanted to fight, I wanted to help the men and women with the resistance but it was impossible to tell who was with who. I obeyed without a word, shifting into drive and stomping on the accelerator. We blew past the fighting group, plowed through the gate and sped away from the station in seconds.

I yelled as wind whipped past my face. "We can't stay on the freeway with those bastards ahead of us, we'll have to go around or wait them out!"

"Get off the freeway!" Lilly shouted. "Find somewhere out of the way to park."

We did just that, eventually finding a parking lot filled with what looked like broken down, abandoned cars. The cluster of vehicles rested along side a building that was basically just a large, two story, brown rectangle with very few windows. The sign said "Tehlasrin Education Center."

Beyond the building the motorcade continued to slowly roll onto the freeway and off to the east. I took a moment to slow my breathing and heart rate. I looked at Lilly. She shook her head, looking both shocked and disappointed.

Damn, the whole place, everywhere was a war zone. Once again, I had to wonder if all the madness and death was worth the price. Lilly grabbed hold of my hand. I squeezed back and pet the top of her hand with my thumb. Her warmth poured from her skin into mine. It felt good, alive and strong, reminding me of the things that were worth fighting for.

Yea. Yes, it was worth it. I wasn't sure who coined the phrase 'give me liberty or give me death' but right then and there, it made perfect sense.

Chapter 10

Another hour. It took another, effing hour for the last vehicle of the supply motorcade to lumber itself onto the freeway. Sixty minutes doesn't really sound like that much when you say it. Hell, a minute passes quickly. But when you're stranded, angry, frustrated and anxious, every second is an irritating pain in the neck.

Lilly sighed. "Thank god. Now we just have to let them get a good lead on us." She sank into her seat and rubbed her eyes, groaning a little. "It looks like they're picking up speed now that they're all set. I say we give them another hour or so."

I nodded, noticed her eyes were closed then said, "Right." I was angry at having to wait another hour but somehow just hearing Lilly's voice made me feel better. I watched her relax, her chest moving up and down with each breath. It was the same thing I did for the forty-five odd minutes she'd slept since we parked. It was a lot more fun gazing at the beautiful woman than thinking about how pissed off and impatient I felt. "Sleeping some more?"

Her eyes opened and she smiled. "No, just easing awake." Her left hand reached over and poked me in my right shoulder. "Why don't you get some sleep?"

I looked at her and chuckled. "I can't sleep. Not out in the middle of nowhere, surrounded by the Union's troops."

"They're gone now but suit yourself." With that, Lilly pushed herself out of her seat, climbed over the compartment separating our seats and bounded into the back. "Hungry. Want anything?"

I stared off at the back of the last military vehicle creeping away. Lilly was right, they were picking up speed. Good. I hit the clock button on the vehicle's dash, three thirty-five. My brain quickly tallied up some numbers. Another hour waiting put us at four thirty, then another hour and a half driving. If things went well, we'd be at David's mom's house around six o'clock.

"Here." Lilly dropped two bars in my lap, ending my thoughts. I looked down, a protein bar and a vitamin packed energy bar. "Eat up, if you're not going to sleep at least get some energy back."

I tore open the protein bar and took a bite. "Thanks." I said while chewing. "Speaking of energy, I should fill up the tank while we're here."

"You ok?" Lilly asked, sounding concerned.

I looked at her, furrowing my brow. "I guess, why?"

"I don't know." She shrugged. "You just seem so distant, detached."

I took another bite and chewed while thinking. After swallowing I said, "Sorry. Just a bunch on my mind. Rebellion, death, pain, freedom, Michael, David…" I looked at Lilly. "And then there's you."

She smirked, raising an eyebrow. "Me?"

I nearly laughed. "Yea. And that whole Erica thing. Jesus, what a mess." I saw Lilly's expression change the moment I said her friend's name. "Oh damn, I'm sorry."

"Why do you keep bringing her up?" Lilly asked, staring deeply into my eyes.

I felt like a complete ass at that moment. "I don't know." I sighed and leaned back, hard against my seat, throwing the last third of the protein bar out my window. "Because I'm an idiot, I guess."

"It just hurts, you know?" Lilly said in her usual, dreamy, soft voice. "I'm trying to keep a positive head here." I looked at her. She gestured the empty air around her. "It helps keep the illusion strong."

"That's right." I shook my head. "I keep forgetting about the cloak thing."

She nodded. "You remember, unconsciously. That's good enough." I almost rolled my eyes. "But you're right. Erica was unexpected. I knew, actually I felt something was wrong but I couldn't have guessed it was so bad."

I strained my brain, thinking. "What the hell happened to her? I mean, Michael said she was shattered, which was pretty obvious. But how?"

"I wish I knew." Lilly frowned. "Someone or *something* got to her. People, hailiorea don't just shatter suddenly for no good reason." She studied my face. "What do you think happened?"

"Hey, I thought we weren't talking about her." I said, now focused on opening my energy bar.

"Jason." Lilly called my name, somehow forcing me to look at her. "I'm sorry for scolding you. It's not your fault. You can ask me more about Erica if you want."

Oh lord, something in her soft voice, the loveliness of her tone and the beauty of her mouth made my head feel like it was in the clouds. The girl was so strong and vulnerable at the same time. I just wanted to grab her and never let go. Part of me wanted to give it all up. My brain considered the possibility of quitting the search for David, taking Lilly back to Aswain and living the rest of my life with her.

Then Fier Wren popped into my head. Oh eff. It dawned on me that the feelings I've been having for Lilly were similar to the ones I had for Fier. They'd always been there, from the time, that night, I ran into the spunky woman at that bar. The night she dealt with me, annoyed as all hell, and told me to rub the back of my neck. Only now, recently have I been able to acknowledge those feelings. I had no idea why or how, but it was like retrieving long lost memories. But now, the thoughts and emotions were so vivid it almost seemed impossible that I'd never known they existed. What the hell?

"Hey." Lilly said, quietly. "You awake?"

I blinked. "Yea, sorry. My brain was wandering." I reached out and grabbed Lilly's hand, mildly startling her. "Do you know why I've been, I don't know, *feeling* more lately?"

She swallowed a bite from one of her bars. "Feeling?"

I snorted, unable to find the right words. "Yea, I, ah. I can't explain. It's like I used to not, like, pay attention as much. To others or I guess to myself." I hoped a speck of this made sense to Lilly because it sure as hell didn't to me. "I've always been so reaction oriented, sort of unaware of others' feelings or thoughts. But now..."

"Well of course." Lilly said, nonchalantly. "Richard read you. He opened your mind." She shrugged. "Obviously, you're going to be more in touch with the world."

I'll be damned. "Richard, huh? I remember him saying something about 'opening my consciousness.' That must be it."

"What makes you ask, anyways?" Lilly asked, neatly folding up her empty wrapper and tucking it away in a side compartment nestled against the passenger door.

I was beginning to feel uncomfortable, too open. I think I blushed. "I'm just remembering or noticing feelings I've had in the past. Feelings I must have ignored or blocked out before."

"About your parents? Your brother, about David?" Lilly asked, nodding. "About Fier Wren?"

Lilly's mention of Fier sent a cold jolt up my spine that went straight through my head into the tips of my hair. She could tell.

"Do you love her?" She asked. "I've known her a little while. We've never been real close but she seems like she's your type." Lilly smiled and blinked, her brain considering. "She's beautiful too."

Not as beautiful as you. I thought instantly. But a moment's consideration made me wonder if that were even true. Christ, I didn't know what to say or think. The truth was, I was just now finding out, I did love Fier. Somehow, it was true and it pissed me off to no end. The other truth was that Lilly was the sexiest, sweetest, kindest woman I ever knew. Just four days ago I would've never believed someone like her really existed in the world. Fier most likely hated me and Lilly was right here.

And out there, less than two hours away is your friend who you owe your life too. I laughed, suddenly finding humor in my stupid situation. I was here for David. The other stuff could be sorted out later. I shook my head, smiling.

"You're just having a great time over there, aren't you?" Lilly asked, seeming amused. "Mind filling me in?"

I waved my hand in the air, dismissively. "Don't worry about it. I'm just laughing at how dumb I am." I reached out and gently rubbed Lilly's cheek with my thumb, resting the palm of my hand against the side her neck just under her jaw. "Thanks for helping me. I mean it."

She pressed her own hand against mine. "Of course." Her expression changed, suddenly more serious. "While we're being more open and we'd brought up Erica, I need to ask you. Do you know who or what Xolzv is?"

"Xolzv?" I had trouble even saying the name. It was familiar but I had no idea where I'd heard it before.

"Yea." Lilly started. "Erica mentioned it." She sighed. "I just wondered if it meant anything to you. When I heard the name, I remembered nightmares I'd been having about a dark, evil... something coming toward us, toward me."

I thought back to the quick, deadly fight between Erica and Michael then remembered her shouting the odd name. In that second, I remembered seeing something back on that security van leaving the port with Michael and Richard. David was in my thoughts. He was with something dark and ungodly sinister. Why would this Xolzv name bring back that memory? That was all just in my head though, my imagination.

"I don't know." I said finally. "It makes me think of something evil and dangerous. It makes me think of that osilea I helped kill." Lilly and I studied each other for a moment. "What did Erica say? That Xolzv was coming to take over or something?"

"Something like that." Lilly bit her lip then scrunched her face, trying to remember. "It's hard to think. I was such a mess back there."

"Well let's just hope it was all crazy talk." I thought of apologizing for calling Erica crazy but I was suddenly sick of being apologetic. "Stay here, I'm going to fill the energy tank up."

It only took a few minutes to pull one of the reserve tanks out from the back of our vehicle, attach the cables and let the etherspring transfer into the car. I took the time to cool off, letting everything slip from my mind other than the task of finding David.

The Sun wasn't near ready to set but it was headed down to the western horizon. It was still spring, only April and the desert air was dry and warm but not yet hot. I'd never been in the old US southwest during the middle of summer but from what I'd heard of the heat, that was just fine with me.

Judging by the rust, the chipped paint and the many flat tires, I guessed the cars surrounding ours had been sitting here for some time. It was curious why so many vehicles were left here. I sighed. It seemed the whole continent had gone to hell. Beat up, run down and falling apart. That happened when people had nothing to aspire to. There wasn't any drive to clean the environment up. Most were locked in super cities scattered about or trapped as serfs on controller owned mega farms.

That didn't mean there weren't still people scattered about but most of the old suburbs and rural communities were ghost towns now. I looked at the building again. It was a school. I wondered if it was even still in use. Nothing showed through the few windows along the base level.

On queue, someone near the building blew a whistle, startling me to full awareness. Lilly rounded the passenger side back of the vehicle, eyes wide. "Jason! Get inside, quick!"

With speed, I unhooked the cable going from the tank to our car, picked it up, tossed it into the back and quietly shut down the hatch. Then I crept along and slid into my seat behind the driver's wheel. Lilly was already back in her seat.

"The spell might not work outside the car anymore." She said, staring forward.

I watched, finally seeing the person who'd blown the whistle. She was an older woman in a dull gray skirt that fell all the way to her ankles. Her plain, white blouse almost glowed in the sunlight. Her drab hair was done up in an unflattering bun on the back of head and her eyes looked like those found on a hungry eagle, skimming the ground for its next kill.

Then children, boys and girls aged between six and sixteen marched out of the building followed by more adults. The line of about forty or so people headed off into the fenced in dirt covered lot behind the building.

No one spoke. The group just marched around the lot counterclockwise. The kids looked drugged, no spirit, no laughing and no smiles. They walked, mostly staring down at their feet, overshadowed by adults strictly observing their every move.

I shook my head and almost swore. "It's a god damned prison."

"Not much difference between schools and prisons." Lilly said, in a matter of fact tone. "Whatever I may say or think about my parents, at least they kept me out of these places." She looked at me. "Did you go through school like this?"

I spoke without taking my eyes off the sorry display of depressed, lifeless children. "No. No, I was a kid before the Union was even around."

A slap on my shoulder made me turn to look at the young woman. "Yea, so was I. The GU's only been around for eight years but schools, especially public schools had been like this for years before." Lilly pouted her lips in a sassy way. "Sorry for hitting you."

I pretended to be in pain, rubbing my shoulder. "I may need a doctor." Lilly smiled and I continued. "My school sucked. It was just your run of the mill indoctrination, fear based, controlling institution but it wasn't like this." I thought. "At least I had Mark there with me. He helped keep the thugs off my back and kept me from getting into even more trouble than I did."

"This is just so *sad*." Lilly said, again watching the students.

"It's effing pathetic." I added quickly.

"Their days go from about seven in the morning to eight at night in most schools. Others keep them twenty-four hours." Lilly narrated. I wasn't up to speed on the latest atrocities that came from Tehlasrin's education system having been locked up in the asylum for a year and a half. "For most, the family has been completely destroyed and so many don't even seem to care..." Her voice trailed off.

"My parents didn't care about Mark and me." I spoke in a hazy, dreamlike voice. "I imagine they would've been happy to tuck us away in a place like this."

The group made three laps around the lot before the frumpy woman with the whistle gave two sharp blows. Without a word, the mindless looking little robots marched back into the prison like school.

"You don't know that." Lilly said. "They must have done something right. You turned out good."

I laughed.

"And it sounds like Mark was a fine man." She said, ignoring my reaction.

I nodded, looking at her. "He was the best man I ever knew." A lump grew in my throat. "David is a close second if not tied."

With speed only hailiorea could manage, Lilly moved over and kissed me on my cheek. I couldn't help it. I reached my hand behind her sweet head, feeling her soft hair brush through my fingers, nudged her closer to me and kissed her full on the lips. Our tongues gently danced, exploring the insides and outsides of each others' mouths.

My heart sped up as Lilly slid her left hand under my shirt, running it across my stomach, my side and my back. Her right hand glided up my chest and over my neck before resting on top of my shoulder. My hands were just as busy. My right stayed on her neck, massaging and rubbing, not allowing her to escape and my left swooped around her, gently squeezing her ass.

Then, a loud, obnoxious horn went off from the school, jolting the two of us apart. My eyes raced over every inch of the building and the grounds around it. Nothing. I thought for sure we'd been found.

Lilly panted, now back in her seat an arm span from me. "We need to stay alert, damn." She looked at me, raised an eyebrow and bit her lip.

"Yea." I said while my heart continued to pound. I chuckled. "Only fools like us would make out in broad daylight surrounded by a world that wants us dead."

She smiled. "Meh, worth it though, I think."

As it turned out, the horn seemed to signify it was time for the lot and school to be completely shut in. Lilly and I watched several electronic gates close shut then we heard what sounded like generators powering up. I was willing to bet a hundred gems to a wad of spit the fences were now charged with powerful electric currents for any unfortunate enough to touch them. The effing union seemed to love shocking people.

"Unbelievable." Lilly said, her face was as angry and disgusted as I've ever seen it. The sight seemed wrong. "Those guards back at that last checkpoint, well some of them at least, see the resistance as a group of bloodthirsty, murdering, terrorists. Anarchists. To think that they'd just bail on people, schools, children." She sighed. "They just don't give a damn about anything."

"Feel lucky they did." I said flatly. "Who knows how well we'd fair with the usual surveillance grid and troop patrols all around us."

She shrugged. "Yea, you're right. It just amazes me."

I squinted. "I wonder, even if Michael and the others win this war, even if we get back our freedoms... how can kids like these ever shake this off? I hope people will be able to function in a free world."

"Time is a magical thing." Lilly said boldly, her face now relaxed, calm and beautiful. "Give it a generation tops, time and freedom will cure the Union's evils."

"Speaking of time." I started. "Let's wait another thirty minutes then hit the road. That damn convoy's had enough time and I can't look at this building anymore."

"Ok." Lilly said, a hint of nervousness in her voice.

I reached over and tapped her left thigh, smiling. "Don't worry. We'll be alright."

She gazed at me then ran a finger along the scar on my neck, smiling back. Her next "Ok" sounded more confident.

Chapter 11

Judging by the Sun's position, I guessed we had about an hour of daylight left by the time we finally reached Spring Creek. The city, or town, or whatever it was, rested about twenty miles north of the Phoenix mega city and was sparsely populated.

I was glad to be off the hauntingly odd, abandoned freeway. But now, traveling down a mostly empty road called Strong Drive, I still felt exposed. Again, I had to put faith I didn't really feel comfortable with into Richard's enchant. I hoped the thing was still working right.

In the distance, small to mid-sized reddish-brown mountains surrounded the entire area. Here, in the seemingly small town, there were lots of open, empty fields filled with dirt, rocks, shrubs and tall saguaro cactuses, some reaching well over fifteen feet in height.

Remnants of civilization popped up here and there, found in old, broken down gas stations, abandoned strip malls, closed up restaurants and beaten down, burned out subdivisions. The only real sign of life we passed was a large super center that had a good number of people filing in and out of it. An enormous Tehlasrin flag, dark blue with a series of interlocking white loops on it, flapped in the warm breeze. It looked pretty and peaceful with the clear blue sky backdrop but the symbol represented pain, fear, corruption and injustice. I winced.

We moved further north on the road at a steady fifty clicks per hour. I kept my eyes open of trouble like cameras, microphones and security but so far the stretch was clear. I spoke without turning, taking note of every street sign we passed, glad there was still enough sunlight to help see. "What's the map say? Where do we turn?"

"Um," Lilly was studying the small and rather crude map Morbal had given me that night in his dementedly decorated mansion. "It looks like we'll need to turn right onto Vista road." She paused and I saw her looking around out of the corner of my eye. "Should be a couple streets ahead. Maybe at that cluster of houses over there."

I followed her gaze and sure enough, ahead a half mile or so and off to the right was what appeared to be a neighborhood. It looked packed with good sized houses; all colored a blend of tan and brown. The homes were a little bit off the main road and after turning onto Vista I had to snake through several winding roads and roundabouts before we found the address that was supposed to be where David's family lived.

I parked our vehicle on the street and took in the surroundings. The place looked dead. Rotting cars lined the street, garbage cans and other debris sat around on front yards or had rolled into the middle of the road. The windows on several houses, homes which had no doubt once been beautiful, were shattered and doors looked knocked off their hinges. Other houses looked like they'd been set on fire. No, the place didn't just look dead, it looked like a war had rolled through.

"Damn." Lilly said. I looked at her and noticed she was gripping the weapon I'd given her. Good idea given the environment. "What a shame. God, I hate the Union."

I nodded and instinctively put a finger to my lips. "Shh." I spoke quietly, making sure the address on the house we were in front of matched what was on my sheet. "Tehlasrin might be listening. I wonder if they even care or have the resources anymore."

"Who knows?" Lilly said in an upset, defiant tone. "The bastards let good neighborhoods like this go to hell. All so they can control people better. They killed comfort, privacy and prosperity just like they killed off billions of people. Poisonous sons of bitches."

I leaned over, twisting my body a bit and gently grabbed her shoulders. "Hey, hey. Calm down. With luck all this crap will get turned around." I nodded at the house. "We're here. Let's go say hi."

"You're right, sorry." She sighed. "It's just the waste of it all." She gestured the world outside our vehicle. "It sets me off. I can't help it."

I smiled despite the butterflies in my stomach, admiring Lilly's spirit. Looking past her golden white hair, I saw the house, David's house, looked better than most. The windows were still in place and the door was in tact. Overgrown weeds, some dead, covered the front yard which was filled in with small rocks and a few small sickly looking trees.

After giving her shoulders one more little squeeze, I pulled back, drew in a deep breath, grabbed hold of my weapon, opened my door and stepped out. I rounded the front of the vehicle and stood side by side with Lilly, collecting myself. From there we walked up the short, paved, yet degrading walkway that led to the front door. I knocked.

There wasn't a response for a piece of time with only the sounds of Lilly and I breathing in the air. I knocked again. An answer came this time only it wasn't at all what I expected. The door slowly creaked open, sounding like it hadn't been opened in ages. A child's eyes blinked at me from the cracked opening.

I furrowed my brow and swallowed. "Hello? Is this the Holt residence?"

No answer. The kid, a young boy now that I could tell, only shifted his weight from one foot to the other.

"I'm looking for my friend, David Holt." I spoke slowly and as non-threateningly as I could muster. "Is he here?"

The boy's eyes cut around to examine Lilly. Something about the move seemed more grown up than it should have, almost calculating, studying. She smiled and spoke in a much kinder voice than I could manage. "Hey there. Are your parents home, sweetie? It's ok, we're not going to hurt you or take anything."

That got a response, finally. The boy backed up from the door and called out, "Mom!"

Five seconds later a woman was at the door, eyeing us intently. She looked to be in her late twenties or early thirties. Her blonde hair was long and disheveled, her eyes hallow and her clothes, grey sweatpants and a large, baggy, faded pink T-shirt, were wrinkled. "What do you want?" It was almost a mumble, the way people talk right after waking up.

I swallowed. "My name is Jason, I'm David's friend." The woman's eyes squinted and her mouth dropped open a little. "I was told he was here."

"Who're you?" She asked Lilly in a neutral tone.

The young woman managed a pleasant smile. "My name's Lilly." She nudged me with her elbow. "I'm his friend, his travel buddy."

Quiet hung in the air for an uncomfortable time until the woman spoke again, cold and direct. "Go away."

"Please." I blurted, battling my brewing impatience. "It's important. David and I have been through a lot together. I'm here to help him."

"For Christ's sake, let them in!" Another woman's voice said from inside the house. Her tone was strong and bossy, almost bitchy.

With seemingly regret and disappointment, the sleepy looking woman opened the door all the way for us, turned and shuffled away. I closed the door after Lilly came through behind me. We walked through a short hallway with several framed photographs hanging on the wall. To my delight, several of the pictures had David, at various ages, in them. It was hard to see since the light was so dim but I recognized my friend.

The hallway eventually led into the kitchen where I saw the other woman we'd heard. Where the first had sleepy, tired eyes, this one, had a piercing look that meant business. Her blonde hair was short, crudely lopped off to form a short bowl around her forehead and ears. She wore a beat up looking black T-shirt and well worn blue jeans with holes in the knees. It was still close to dark in the rest of the house since all the blinds were more than half closed. But a ray of sunlight came in through a dining room window that glinted off a very shiny and very large knife in her hand.

My eyes casually drifted away from the weapon, trying not to dwell on it since the woman was studying me so intently. I gazed around the kitchen. Dirty dishes filled the sink and the counters were covered with wrappers and boxes. The dining room was off the west of the kitchen and the other direction led into a family room. It was rather large but cluttered, dirty looking and dusty. Mismatched furniture, two couches and a chair filled a lot of the space, circling a round coffee table. Beyond that was a glass door wall that no doubt led to the backyard.

The place carried an odd blend of smells. My nose picked up the scent of candles, incense, stale cigarette smoke and a faint stench that resembled old cheese. The air had a damp feel to it and there was something else… A weird sensation that squeezed the sides of my head, an odd pressure on my temples I didn't feel until stepping into the kitchen.

The second woman sucked on her teeth, looking at us. "Hell, you look harmless enough." She turned to the other woman. "If they were more of those damn junkies they'd have made a move by now." Her eyes were back on me. "Looking for David?"

"Yes." I said quickly. "Is he here?"

The woman pointed the tip of her knife at me. "Jason?" The blade's tip shifted to Lilly. "Lilly was it? My name is Jamie, this is my sister Franny."

I smiled despite the overall uncomfortable atmosphere. The names were familiar. "Yes, David told me about you two. You're his sisters, right?"

"How the hell did you get here?" Jamie asked, ignoring my questions.

I spared a glance at Lilly whose eyes were locked on the blade in Jamie's hand. "We drove. Drove in from Los Angeles."

"God damn, piece of crap Union." Jamie said, now looking at her sister. "The whole thing is falling apart. These two dummies just rode right through." She sighed, sizing me up again. "David was right."

Oh man, I was about to lose my mind. "Where is David?"

"He went out." Franny mumbled, meekly.

Jamie spat. "Yea, he *should* be back. Unless he got himself arrested again."

I heard Lilly let out a relieved breath. I wasn't sure why she seemed so eager to see David, must've been for my sake. "Great." I said with a nod. "When did he get here?"

"Two days ago." Jamie said with an edge of spite in her voice. "He was here for less than half a day, brought us some groceries then headed out, said he'd be back." She set her jaw, looking pissed. "Haven't seen him since."

The hope and excitement I'd had a few moments ago quickly started to drain away. "What? Where did he say he was going?"

"You know, I'm sick of answering your questions." Jamie spat. "What the hell do you care anyways?"

Why did I care? The question sounded so stupid in my head I didn't even know where to begin. When I finally spoke, my tone was much stronger than anticipated. "I care because he's saved my life more than once. I care because the last time

I saw him, he was in pain. He was delivered to a psychotic, murdering madman and I can't sit by and do nothing. Why do I care? Because he's my friend."

"Friend?" Jamie rolled her eyes. "The world doesn't allow for friends anymore, fool. They'll either end up dead or they'll cheat you, hurt you or steal from you."

I was about to retort, feeling my blood pressure rise, when a third woman's voice, an older sounding one, called from the family room. "Hush, girl! Is that Davey? Is he back?"

I answered before Jamie could spin her side of things, turning my head and sending my voice in the other room's direction. "No. I'm David's friend. I've been looking for him."

"Oh, lord. You must be Jason, then." The third voice said. "Davey said you might show up. Come make yourselves comfortable and Jamie! Put that damn knife away."

I looked at Lilly, confused. Her expression was cool and expectant. She seemed to know something and I would've given a million gems for the ability to read her thoughts like some hailiorea could.

The four of us filed into the family room. Jamie and Franny sat on one couch, Lilly and I sat in the other. I moved several small pillows out of the way. They looked hand made with the names David, Franny, Jamie and Alan stitched on them.

The third woman, older than the others, sat in the chair. She had silver hair, done up in a bun, and an aged face which would have looked like any other sixty-something woman except she had two bruised black eyes and a large cut on her cheek. She smiled at us while lighting up a cigarette.

My instinct wanted to ask what the hell happened to her face but Lilly spoke first, diplomatically. "Thank you, Ms. ah?"

"Oh, my name's Helen. I'm Davey's mamma." She brought a shaking hand up to her lips and took a puff. "He should be back any moment. So lucky of him to have friends that care for him." After exhaling, she raised her eyebrows. "Would you like a cigarette? Something to drink?"

Both Lilly and I said "No thanks" at the same time. The older woman smiled and leaned back into her chair.

I glanced at the three women, David's mother and two sisters. Franny stared off into space and Jamie looked bored, pissed and annoyed all at the same time. The boy who'd answered the door was half hidden behind a wall, spying on us and doing a poor job of it. I spoke. "We've known each other for almost a couple years. David and me."

Jamie snorted. "You meet him in prison then?"

I was about to answer but Helen spoke first. "Shut up!" Her kind, gentle voice from before quickly shifted to intense and demanding, almost demeaning. The look she gave Jamie was menacing and dangerous. "Be nice." When she turned to me, she was all sweet again. "Good. He's such a sweet boy. Brought us some well needed groceries. We don't go out much, too dangerous."

"Thieves, druggies, renegades, effing guards." Jamie sneered. "God damned war zone out there."

"Excuse me." Lilly's voice was especially sweet given the present company. "How have you managed to stay here? Must be hard, especially with all the centralizing the Union's been doing over the years."

"Miss, I *own* this house." Helen said with pride. "I've owned it for years. My late husband, Mr. Holt, made sure his family was set up before his passing."

I fought to keep calm and quiet. I was so close and desperate to find my friend all this small talk was driving me insane. Lilly carried on. "Oh, I'm so sorry to hear that, Helen."

"It's alright, dear." The old woman said between hits of her cigarette. "Everyone dies. I think of it as a welcome freedom from this world." A strange look, both yearning and maniacal, covered her face. "Do you want to die with us?"

"Mom, Jesus." Franny said, finally showing some emotion.

I bit my tongue. I wanted to speak but thought better of it since I'd only end up insulting the old woman. No, David was my priority, not his strange family.

Lilly spoke. "No. I don't want to die." She gestured me. "We're working to help the world, to make life better."

Jamie laughed out loud. "Christ. Give me one of those smokes, mom."

"YOU SAY PLEASE!" Helen shouted, suddenly sitting up straight. "I'll not allow you to disrespect me anymore. Things are different now. I have the power, not you, you little brat! Don't make me punish you again!"

The tension in the air made it hard to breath. I watched the show carry on, too confused and uncomfortable to dwell on the fact that David wasn't here and might not be coming back. Jamie's face turned white as a ghost and Franny closed her eyes while tears ran down her cheeks. The boy from before hurried around the corner and crawled into the woman's, his mother I guessed, lap.

Again, the old woman's tone and attitude completely shifted when she turned to us. "That's so sweet to hear. You're so young and idealistic. I used to wish for things to get better. My money won't last much longer, damn bills and taxes. Water, electricity, suburban security patrols." She smashed her cigarette down into a very full ashtray, snuffing it out. "Oh well, when the money's gone that's my queue to die." She smiled.

My eyes went from Lilly, who somehow kept a neutral face, to the boy. Now he was crying too. Then I looked at Jamie who bit her lip, blinking, staring down at her feet. Finally my gaze shifted back to Helen. She was looking at my face, seemingly expecting me to say something. I swallowed. The best I had was, "That sucks."

"Maybe we can help." Lilly said in her soft, dreamy voice, obviously a much more caring person than I'd ever be. Her eyes cut around to me then back to Helen. "We might be able to send you some money?"

"That's sweet but we're not looking for charity, nor would we accept it. We're too proud." Helen studied her daughters then looked down at her lap. "Let's see what's happening in the world while we wait for David to get home." And again she spoke in a pleasant, happy tone while pressing a button on a remote control that had been sitting between her legs. A small telescreen on the wall opposite her came to life. "It costs a lot too, the broadcasts I mean, but a little here and there is ok."

I studied the screen, thinking how just seconds ago the woman basically said she was going to kill herself once all her money was gone. Private television wasn't cheap and was a luxury for the rich and the controllers. Every second cost a good amount, every second shortened Helen's life.

It was all a huge waste, television. I never liked it when I was a kid, back when my parents were able to afford it. Those were pre GU days. It felt like a tool to control and lecture me or treat me like a stupid child. It was boring. I'd watched a little during my time on Aswain but it was just background noise; a distraction to keep my thoughts busy, away from whatever was troubling me at the time.

The screen showed an attractive woman's face, no doubt reading a teleprompter, giving the daily propaganda report. The media and press were *supposed* to remain free and independent of the government but only the extremely blind and gullible believed that. No, the news told the masses exactly what the sick, murdering, raping, controlling Union wanted. The more the woman spoke the angrier I got. It didn't take long for me to seriously consider slamming my fist through the little screen.

"In breaking news," the woman on the telescreen said, "we've received reports of a shocking string of violent activity covering the Los Angeles area. Wanted criminal and known terrorist, Michael Vistaer, seen here," a headshot of Michael filled the screen and I wondered where they got the picture from, "tried, unsuccessfully to lead an uprising against peacekeeping Union officials."

I turned, slowly to look at Lilly. Her eyes were glued to the screen, visibly filled with concern and fear. The voice called my attention back. "Authorities are continuing to settle the area and expect to regain order along with the capture of the terrorist Vistaer in the coming hours. Local magistrate, Lady Erica Wood was not available for comment."

I shook my head, blurting the word, "Lies."

"What's that, Hun?" Helen asked.

I turned to her and shook my head again. "Nothing."

"No, they're liars, all of them!" Jamie said, regaining her spunk. "Everything those mothereffers feed us, in the news and in our food, is poison and trash." She nodded at me in an odd, little salute. "You're right, they're effing liars!"

"Across the nation," the telescreen woman started again in a joyous tone, "military forces of Lord Maledro Morbal and Lord Steven Ark are engaged in combat simulations, honing their preparedness for other such terrorist insurrections. Both Lords Morbal and Ark have assured us that their wargame campaigns are designed to be as real as possible but that no one will actually be harmed. Everyone is instructed to ignore any concern for the very real looking activities should they come to your city or neighborhood."

I couldn't help it, I laughed, calling all eyes onto me. I looked at David's family in turn. "They're not wargames, they're trying to kill each other off. Both of those bastards want to rule the continent." I closed my eyes and rubbed my now throbbing head. "What a joke."

The next thirty or forty minutes passed rather quickly. It was hard to tell exactly how much time since I didn't see any clocks around. Time didn't matter much to David's family it seemed. We sat in silence except for the continued droning of Tehlasrin news feeds. Normally the unproductive period would have driven me up the wall but there was something about the place that weighed heavily on me. Something about the room, the house, the air… it just wasn't right. I glanced at Lilly, she looked tired, almost ready to fall asleep.

The Sun had nearly completely set and Helen told Jamie to light a slew of candles scattered about the house. The dim light didn't help my own tiredness and when I was able to actually think, I debated how long Lilly and I should remain here. My hopes of David coming back were all but evaporated. Now, being here was just a waste of time and an odd one at that.

After the last segment of news ended, Helen turned the telescreen off and spoke. Her voice oozed through the dimly lit, otherwise silent air. "It's so nice having you two here." She smiled at us then turned to Jamie. "I have to pee."

With a sigh, Jamie stood and moved over to her mother, helping her out of her chair. From there she helped her out of the family room and into the bathroom, I guessed. That just left Lilly, Franny, the boy and me.

Lilly spoke, quietly. "At least we know Michael wasn't captured. The news would've bragged all about it had they gotten him."

"I don't think David's coming." I said in a defeated tone, not really concerned with Michael Vistaer at the moment. "We should go."

"He's not the same." Franny said in a hushed voice. She didn't look at us, instead she seemed to be hypnotized, just staring blankly at the carpeted floor. "He… he's not the same." With one hand she rubbed the boy's back and with the other she massaged her own side, groaning in pain a little. "It hurts."

I furrowed my brow as alertness slowly crept back into my brain. "What do you mean? What's he like?"

"Uncle Divad has gone home." The boy said, positioning his head to look at me.

I gazed at him, quizzically. Did he say 'Divad?' "Home?"

"What's your name, sweetie?" Lilly asked with an incredibly gentle tone.

The boy looked at her. "Allen." Then he turned back to me. "Yes, home."

"Where's home?" I asked, afraid to hear the answer.

The kid made a face that equaled an eye roll. "Denver."

Because he's mine. Morbal had said. God damn. I cursed under my breath, gritting my teeth and stood up. "What a waste of time." I was beyond pissed, staring at Allen. "You're positive? Don't lie to me."

The boy's eye twitched. "Yes, he's back in Denver. I *know*."

I shook my head, turning to Lilly. "Let's go."

"Go?" Helen asked as she was being helped back into the family room. I hadn't heard any toilet flush. "You can't leave. You're going to protect us."

I snorted, not in the mood to upset the old woman. "I'm sorry but David is the reason we're here. We need to go."

"NO!" Helen roared.

Jamie turned to her mother. "Let them go, they're no use to us."

"How *dare* you?" Helen scolded her daughter. "I say who comes and goes in my house!"

Franny abruptly stood up and grabbed Allen by his hand. "Come." There was urgency in her voice and she led her son out of the room. A second later I heard a door close.

"Mom!" Jamie protested in what sounded like a pleading tone. "They can leave if they want to."

The old woman screamed and flailed her arms out sending Jamie reeling back, slamming into a wall behind them. "HEY!" I yelled and Lilly got to her feet.

"You won't leave!" Helen, now standing just fine on her own, clenched her hands into fists. Then something heavy flew from the kitchen and slammed into the side of my head. I saw stars and fell backward into a sitting position back on the couch. Before I could react, the coffee table lifted itself off the ground and whizzed at me. I had just enough time to shove Lilly out of the way, leaving the full force of the table's weight to ram into my chest. I heard something crack and guessed the thing had broken a couple of my ribs. Warm blood ran down the side of my face and into my left eye.

"STOP IT!" Lilly screamed, reaching for the etherpistol I'd given her. I was busy trying to shove off the table. It was pressing down heavier on my lap but no matter how hard I pushed the damn thing wouldn't budge.

Helen shifted her attention to the young woman and made a strange sound that came from somewhere deep in her chest and resonated out through her mouth. I saw Lilly fly backward, crashing her hip into the armrest of Helen's chair.

The distraction lightened the table and I was able to finally pull out from under it. I was on Helen in a heartbeat, shoving the old woman against the wall over Jamie who was lying on the floor. My own pistol was in my right hand with its barrel flat against the crazy woman's neck. I thought of shooting, angry as all hell at her lies, her trying to keep us captive, hurting me and hurting Lilly. But no, I couldn't. The blast would most likely kill her.

Lilly stood back up. "She's telekinetic!" I didn't flinch and kept my focus on Helen. "Either kill her or let's go, right now."

I roared and grabbed Helen's shoulder with my left hand, throwing her to the ground. She flailed her arms again as she fell, knocking several candles off a cheap shelf that hung on the wall. "MOVE!" I roared, sending waves of stinging through my chest. Moving was easier said than done. My momentary adrenaline rush had passed and was replaced with horrible pain from my head and ribs.

Lilly was at my side in a flash, helping me limp toward the door. The world spun and my eyes wanted to close but I resisted. Debris, dishes, vases, forks, knives, knickknacks, all sorts of things flew at our heads, barely missing and crashing against the wall. Helen, who as far as I could tell was still on the floor, was giving it her all. We drew closer to the door and

Lilly fired her weapon, full blast, blowing the thing outward off its hinges.

Helen screamed from inside the house as we stumbled to our vehicle. I fished the keys out of my pocket, fell into the driver's seat, started it up and sped off, nearly hitting every obstacle in our path.

"JESUS!" Lilly called. "Can you drive ok?"

I panted then groaned. "Not much choice." We got back onto Strong Drive and then about a mile down the road before I finally caved. I found what looked like an abandoned house, a lonely, burnt out structure surrounded by nothing but dead trees. After pulling around behind it I shut the car off and clenched my eyes shut. "I can't go anymore. Eff!" The pain was miserable, like blades of lightning repeatedly jabbing my insides.

"Oh, Jason." Lilly unbuckled her belt and then mine which I didn't even realize I'd put on. "Try to get in back so you can lie down."

I fought to speak, wincing as I glanced back at the large couch that made up most of the vehicle's mid section. "Why?"

"So I can heal you."

Chapter 12

"Effing waste of time." I grunted while trying to ignore the pain in my chest. "A giant, god damned circle…"

"Shut up and try to relax!" Lilly snapped while gently gliding her soft hands over my chest. She helped get my shirt off and was now on her knees, leaning over me as I sprawled out on the van's couch. "I need to focus."

Relax? It seemed impossible given the broken ribs, my throbbing, bleeding head and the utter disappointment I felt. Still, Lilly kept trying to heal me, whispering 'shh'es' every so often.

"Close your eyes. Close them." Lilly's voice rang though my head, emptying it, making her words echo between my ears. "Just focus on my voice."

She went on and on for what felt a long time and soon, I'll be damned, I started to feel numb. I held still and some of the pain went away. I could feel the warmth of her hands on my bare chest even though they hardly made contact with my skin. Her light touch tickled.

I tried to shut down my brain and go blank but couldn't completely. I opened my eyes, seeing the focus and strain on Lilly's face as she worked in the dim light. It felt like the bones of my ribcage were sliding, moving back into their proper place. It was painful and strange at the same time.

She put her right hand over the wound on my head and the sting made me wince. Soon though, the soothing feelings drew my eyes back to a close. A soft, warm heat bathed my head and for a brief moment, I felt pretty damn good. Briefly.

"That's it. The best I can do." Lilly said with a heavy sigh. She was nearly out of breath as she wiped her hands on the vehicle's carpeted floor. "Now we let it heal."

"What's wrong?" I asked, fighting to ignore the sharp, lingering pain.

She let out a little snort. "Nothing. I'm just no good at healing. I'm half assed at everything, not good at anything."

I reached out and gently stroked her shoulder. "Don't be stupid. Hell, I feel a lot better. You did great."

Lilly smiled. "Thanks, but some of those ribs are still busted and the wound on your head is just barely closed. Marie would've had you all fixed up by now." She huffed, a labored, tired sound that was almost a growl. She was frustrated.

"Now why don't *you* relax a bit?" I recommended. "Take a break then give it another go if you want. We'll get back on the road once I'm better."

She smirked at me shook her head. "You won't be able to drive anytime soon. Sitting up there, driving with all the bumps in the road would rip you up."

I considered Lilly and all the different sides of her I'd seen the past few days. Strong, sad, scared, playful, happy, angry, flirty. I couldn't help but compare her with Fier. Fier was generally the same all the time; cool, tough and honest. Lilly was everything else. That and she was a bit of a mystery.

I swallowed, remembering the way Lilly looked the night I'd confronted Morbal. She was crying her eyes out and terrified of something. I wondered. "What did you mean the other night when you said something to Michael about the darkness getting closer?"

"You always bring up the nicest topics, don't you?" The look on her face was steady, unreadable.

I squinted and pulled my hand back, unsatisfied. "Yea, I guess I do."

Lilly was quiet for a few seconds. "I don't know, just a feeling, or maybe a premonition." She looked around the inside of the vehicle then turned back to me. "Look at the trail we've left behind us. Madness and destruction everywhere."

"And it's everywhere David's been." I said, strongly, the point being one I'd thought about but hadn't dwelled on. "I wonder what it means."

Lilly blinked and I realized how much my eyes had adjusted to the limited light. Seeing was helped by the full Moon that had slowly risen and now hung low in the eastern sky. "I think it means he's connected to it all." She paused after seeing what felt like an odd expression on my face. "I don't know how, but you have to find him."

"Damn straight."

She nodded. "I have to, too."

"Why?" I asked. The woman's interest in my friend didn't make sense.

"Because it's the right thing to do and it's important. I'm a hailiorum like you, we have to help others. Everything is connected, I can sense it." Her voice grew bold and poignant. "If the darkness is coming I'm going to fight it. This thing wants to destroy everything good; hope, happiness, life itself. It has to be stopped."

"The osilea, right?" I asked. "Is that what it is?"

Lilly nodded. "I think so, only it's gaining strength." She licked her lips. "It's like all this carnage we've been seeing is feeding it." Her eyes pierced mine. "Michael and the others don't really understand, they're too focused on the rebellion."

Something about the girl's tone, the way she spoke, the look on her face and her resolve was really turning me on. I was growing more excited than my beat up body should allow. I wanted her bad and took a moment to pause and maintain my composure. "You believe in the resistance, don't you?"

"Of course I do!" Lilly exclaimed, inching closer to me and again running her sweet, sexy hands over my chest. "Only, it's just part of it. Tehlasrin is a symptom of the cancer, not the actual source."

I breathed loudly through my mouth, almost panting. The healing was an odd, intoxicating blend of pain and pleasure. I cut my eyes around to stare at Lilly's face while she worked on my body. God. She was like an angel, a luscious piece of candy wrapped in a sweet smelling, beautiful wrapper.

Somewhat involuntarily, blood rushed to various parts of my body, some more noticeable than others. My teeth clamped shut and my lip curled. My heart was beating like a rabbit.

Lilly ran her eyes over my body, halting her glance for the briefest of seconds just below my waist. She smirked. "Oh." Then she winked at me.

That was it. I tossed aside all restraint, not caring one bit about the pain or any other consequences. I grabbed her right hand with my left then pulled it to my lips, kissing its soft skin. Lilly stopped moving, studying me, no doubt wondering where I was going.

I knew exactly where I was going. I reached over with my right arm and slid my hand behind her left shoulder, nudging her down to me. To my approval, she took the invitation and brought her face down to mine. Our lips locked, our tongues danced and soon our hands were exploring, running all over each others' bodies. Still mindful of my damaged ribs, we managed to pet and rub each other while our lips peppered each other with kisses in all sorts of places.

By now, it was beyond obvious that Lilly's passions were just as flared up as mine and before I knew it, our clothes were nothing but a forgotten obstacle. Given my current situation, I remained on my back while Lilly straddled my waist, taking me inside her. Lord, it felt like I'd melt from the warm, oozing pleasure, like I'd be reduced to a happy warm puddle of ecstasy. We continued our dance.

To Lilly's credit, the woman worked her magic on me without causing a shred of additional pain to my chest. My hands cupped her breasts, gently squeezing and playing while the young woman moved her hips up and down, moaning in delight. I growled like an animal, thrusting upward as best I could over and over.

Time is a funny thing. Quick when having fun and slow when bored. Here, time just seemed to vanish. All I know is after two runs around the block, so to speak, we were both completely spent.

For several lovely moments, I thought I'd died and gone to heaven. Christ, I didn't even believe in heaven but if there was such a place, how could it feel better than this? Lilly gently rested her head on my chest, careful to avoid anywhere that would set me down into a screaming fit in pain. I stroked her beautiful golden hair, breathing in her smell and closed my eyes. I was beyond content.

Then Lilly purred one word, one name in a voice heavy with satisfaction and complete fulfillment. "David…"

"What?" I blurted with a sharp exhale. "David?"

Lilly bolted upright, sending a blur of pain through my chest, hopped off me and quickly put her shirt on. I watched her, my mouth gaping open, searching for some clue, some reason why a woman I'd just had sex with would moan my best friend's name.

It was dark but the moonlight allowed me to see the guilty, shameful look on her face. I wished I couldn't see her expression and damned the Earth's natural satellite. Lilly quickly worked at getting her pants on. I stopped her. "Hey!" She looked at me. "What the hell..?"

"Jason." Lilly mumbled. "I, I don't want to hurt you."

"Do you know David?" I asked, beyond confused. "Have you two met?"

She shook her head. "No, not really."

"Not really?" I raised my eyebrows. "What the hell does that mean? Hey! Look at me!" She'd focused back on her pants before stopping and closing her eyes.

I'm not sure how, but next I suddenly felt like I was inside Lilly's head. It was a strange, hazy and confusing feeling, like being dropped in the middle of a maze with no idea where to go. Somehow, though, through it all I felt how important David was to her, how important he'd been to her for a long time. She wanted him, not really sexually or even emotionally but somehow… like she wanted to control him.

I shook my head, pulling my brain back to the world outside Lilly's mind. "What the eff is going on?"

"I don't want to hurt you." Lilly repeated. "But I can't help it. He's important. I have to find him. I'm not going to apologize."

"David?" I asked, dumbly. Nothing made sense. One thing dawned on me though, I wasn't really upset. Granted it felt like Lilly had been lying to me but the rational part of my brain told me there was no harm done. I didn't feel betrayed. Hell, I was the one who started our little romp. Then I reminded myself that I didn't love Lilly and she didn't love me. Fine. We were two young people who were attracted to each other. So, big deal. I bet stuff like this happened all time.

Now, all that aside, I felt more curious than anything. Perhaps I just didn't have the mental strength to care. Not surprising given everything I'd been through, my injuries, our recent struggles, the war, the fighting, frustration and then the physical euphoria of sex. Finally I asked, one word, "Why?"

Lilly sniffled and I guessed she was close to crying, great. It was hard to tell in the dark. "It's my mother's fault." Now she buried her face in her hands. "Damn her."

"Your mother?" This just kept getting stranger and stranger. "What does she have to do with it?"

She pulled her hands away and looked at me. "Remember the bond I found out I had with my mother after she died? That's when it happened."

"Ok." I drew in a deep breath and cursed myself after a jolt of pain lit my nerves up. My head was beginning to hurt now. "Why then?"

Lilly's face was as grim as Death itself, easily noticeable in the soft dark. She sucked on her bottom lip for a moment before speaking. "Because my mother was the one who shattered him."

Wham.

Talk about a slap to the face… The hairs on the back of my neck stood up. "FORREST? Samantha Forrest was your mother?"

Lilly didn't speak. She didn't have too.

"The woman who tried to seduce me and make me her slave like she did with Kara and all those others? With David?" I swore, turning to look up at the vehicle's ceiling while bringing my right hand around to rub the top of my now throbbing head. "And you waited to tell me until now?"

"I was afraid you wouldn't trust me." Lilly said in a pleading tone.

I looked at her and chuckled a little. "You're probably right. Forrest was a murdering, psychotic bitch who kidnapped and effed up my best friend. She twisted and tormented a bunch of other people, nearly destroyed Aswain and served an osilea. And now, part of her *spirit*, or whatever, is in you?" I closed my eyes. "Yea, not real trustworthy material."

"Jason." Lilly reached over and grabbed my left hand, gently squeezing it.

I thought of pulling away but I was too tired. "Save it." I looked at her. "You didn't hurt me. You were just helping me look for David. I just don't get why you want to find him. What? Is it the part of your mom that still wants him as her slave or servant or whatever?"

"No, not exactly." She said in a low, ashamed tone.

"Not exactly?!" I wanted to roar with frustration. "Why did you have sex with me then? Be honest."

"Alright." Lilly said, finally gathering back some of her strength. "Because you and David are connected, bonded by friendship, brotherhood and warrior companionship. I can feel him through you."

"Great. Just effing great." My brain tried to figure out how to get back to Denver as quickly as possible. I didn't feel comfortable around Lilly anymore. Hell, I might've been trapped with Samantha Forrest for all I knew. Maybe she'd completely taken over her daughter's mind. I couldn't believe I accepted any of this stuff...

"But also," Lilly went on after swallowing, "because I do like you, Jason. You're a good man and unbelievably sexy."

I scoffed. "Yea, I'm a real heartthrob." I looked at her, hearing David's voice in my head telling me, *don't be a dick*. "Seems we're both really just here for my friend. Come on, what do you want with him? Tell me."

"I don't know." Lilly's non answer irked me above everything else.

I raised my voice. "Look, enough bull crap! What do you want? Are you going to try to kill me? If so, you better do it now while I'm weak. Either that or let me get some god damned sleep. I'm sore as hell, tired and sick of this runaround."

Now Lilly was outright crying. I wanted to turn away but couldn't. "I'm not a killer. I like you, you're my friend." She bowed and pressed her forehead against my shoulder. "I'd never hurt you. I'm not evil."

Ugh, I was such a sucker, so weak when it came to crying, pretty women. Even now, as angry and confused as I was, I caved. "Sorry." I squeezed her hand and smirked. "Hey."

"Yes?" She looked up at me with tear filled eyes.

"Sorry for being a prick. I still trust you." A load of guilt wash away from Lilly's face. "Sort of." Then we both laughed.

With a sigh, I marked this one as yet another failed, effed up, albeit brief, romantic relationship. It'd been a long time but some things never changed.

"You should get some sleep, Jason." Lilly sounded better. "Things will be ok."

I agreed and closed my eyes. Well, Lilly *could* be a monster that might slit my throat the second I closed my eyes but at that moment I didn't care. Eff it. Whatever happened, happened. I was just so sick of thinking. So much had happened and changed in such a short time. It was nuts.

But that's how things were. The world was awash in revolution both internally and externally. Nothing could be taken for granted and I knew whatever was going to happen, whatever the future brought would be unexpected.

-

I woke suddenly, startled by something. I didn't know if it was a sound from outside or another dream but whatever it was, it tore me awake and my heart was racing. Jerking my head around as best I could to examine the inside of the vehicle, it quickly became clear that I was alone. The reality of the situation cleared the sleepiness from my head. God damn it, she left me.

I didn't know whether to be angry, relieved, scared or concerned for the woman's safety. She took off either out of guilt for tricking me, thinking I was of no more use to her, or with hopes that I'd get killed being on my own so others wouldn't know her true aims. A tangled mess of thoughts tied up my head. Lilly was stupid heading off somewhere, alone in dangerous territory.

With an extreme effort, I managed to get myself dressed. Pulling on my blue and white, long sleeve shirt was especially hard and getting my shoes on wasn't any easier. Anything that required leaning or stretching was absolute hell. Pain existed for a reason, I knew, but I cursed every jolt, every sting, wishing for whatever power or force that might be out there to make the hurting stop.

Now dressed, I searched for the vehicle's keys. They were gone too. What the hell? Luckily, my etherpistol was still in the car.

I sat in the dark, thinking, trying to plan my next move. Maybe I'd be able to find another vehicle or some other way back to Denver. I numbly ran my thumb over the weapon wondering if I even had the strength to head out. A rumbling in my stomach told me I was hungry.

I reached for one of the passenger door handles, gave it a pull and found it was locked. At least Lilly had locked the doors for me. The girl, sexy and deceptively sweet as she was, was a complete mystery. After finding the lock, I gave the handle another pull and pushed the door open, feeling the strain and a burning pain race through my chest. I stepped out and heard the crunch of dried dirt crumble under my feet. Standing now, my head protested; banging and spinning. What a crappy situation to be stuck in. I thought about climbing back into the vehicle and sleeping some more but couldn't do it. I was too alert, lost and threatened.

The abandoned house stood eerily over me, casting a long shadow across the dry desert ground. It was surrounded by a few large, dead trees. I hobbled up onto an old deck made of rotting wood that led to the back door which barely held in place. Peeking inside, I only saw darkness. Maybe Lilly was inside.

"Hello?" My voice echoed through the black space. There wasn't an answer. I thought of heading inside to investigate for anything of use but then thought better of it. Knowing my luck, I'd probably trip and break my neck.

I headed back down the few steps, nearly falling a couple times. After making it back to the vehicle, I leaned on its hood, panted through the pain in my head and chest and then crashed to the ground. Yep, I was stuck. Stranded and busted up.

Attempting to go anywhere was stupid, just like my entire endeavor to find David. It'd been days and I'd found nothing but a death, madness, a country tearing itself apart, a group of foolishly hopeful freedom fighters and a woman who lied and abandoned me.

"What a effing moron." I whispered to myself. My feet slid outward and I eased down to sit on the dusty, dirty, rocky ground in front of the vehicle. After remaining quiet for a piece of time, I became aware of the sounds of various desert creatures; toads, crickets and yipping of what I guessed were coyotes or wolves in the distance.

That would be a riot, I thought, traveling all this way just to get eaten or stung by wild animals in the middle of nowhere. My eyes dropped to a close and sleep nearly had me back under its spell until the sound of footsteps pulled me back.

I swallowed and gripped my weapon, straining my ears to pinpoint which location the sound was coming from. It was behind me and to my left, coming from the road. I scooted over near the front, driver's side tire and aimed my weapon, blinking my eyes in dumb hopes it would help me see better in the dark.

A lone, short figure was coming. I aimed my weapon and thought of firing rather than asking any questions until a glint of Moonlight bounced off the person's hair… golden hair.

"Lilly?" I said, both quietly and hopefully.

The figure sped up toward me, making my heart skip a beat. "Jason?" Lilly's voice called. "What the hell are you doing out of the vehicle?"

"I was going to ask you the same thing." I spoke with a grunt, biting my lip which somehow helped with the pain. A few seconds later Lilly was at my side, crouching down to help me stand. "I thought you left me."

"I did." She said flatly. "I had to find a phone."

"A phone?" My brain tried to make sense of things but every word and thought sent a bolt of pain through my body.

"You are crazy." I was standing now, leaning on the car again with one arm around Lilly's shoulders.

"No." She said with a shake of her head. "It was the only thing I could think of. I can't heal you well enough. You can't drive or even walk. I had to call Mike."

Lilly could no doubt see the expression on my face and I wondered if the look showed just how stupid I thought she was. "You went out there, in Tehlasrin territory, *alone* to find a phone? Jesus." I shook my own head, remembering. "Wait. You said you didn't know Mike's number."

"I lied." Lilly said, flatly.

I sighed, chuckling a little. "This is becoming a real nasty habit of yours."

"Come on." She tugged at me with her left arm gently wrapped around my back and waste. "I couldn't give him our exact location so the portal should be opening around here in a couple minutes. It'll be easy to spot in the night."

I groaned as we started off on foot toward the road. "Right, the thing will light up like a -"

"Where you goin' honey?" A male voice called from about thirty yards down the road. "Come on over here."

Lilly drew in a sharp breath and I turned toward the voice, seeing the shadowy outlines of two people headed our way.

"Who's that with you, sweet thing?" A second voice, also male called. "Looks broken, why don't you toss it and come with us?"

A surge of adrenaline pulsed through my body. These guys were trouble, any fool could see that. Without a word I planted my feet, leaned on Lilly for balance and aimed my weapon. There was no internal debate. The two had to be stopped. The only question was whether I should kill them or stun them. At the last second, I thumbed the gun's power level down to a high stun setting. The men started running toward us and I fired four quick shots. In a flash the two were on their backs, quiet and unmoving.

"Oh god." Lilly hummed. "I'm sorry. I didn't know they were following me."

"YOU BITCH!" Someone yelled from behind me. Something that felt like a pipe smacked hard against my back. I crashed to the ground, dropped my weapon and Lilly stumbled, half trying to catch me and half trying to stay standing. She failed at both.

I managed to roll over, roaring from the pain in my ribs. There he was, another man in dirty, ripped, baggy clothes, standing over me holding a club. "You effer!" He hissed, spraying my face with his spit. "You killed Dwayne and Rick!"

Another man appeared out of the darkness and grabbed Lilly from behind. She struggled for freedom but couldn't break the hold. "Shh, shh." He made the sound in her ear before laughing. "She smells nice."

"No, they're not dead." I growled. "Go see for yourself."

My eyes darted back and forth from the man standing over me to Lilly. She squirmed harder and harder to break free but the bastard behind her wouldn't let go. When he started licking the sides of her face I officially flipped out.

"YOU'RE DEAD!" The man next to me roared, raising his weapon high, ready to bring it down on my skull.

I don't know if it was from my hailiorum skill or the rage that came from the thought of Lilly being assaulted by these guys, but somehow, and rather quickly, I was on my feet and able to dodge the man's swing.

He swore and swung again, then again. I ducked and moved, avoiding all the blows, feeling what strength I had left build up like a volcano ready to erupt. Before the thug could swing another attack, I kicked him square in his chest, driving the bottom of my foot flat against his ribs. He fell back, dropped his weapon and gasped for air. From there, I pounced on top of him and dropped one of the most forceful punches I'd ever managed flush against his face. I was mad, real mad and the son of a bitch under me paid the full price.

The other guy let go of Lilly and came at me. He didn't make it far though. As soon as her hands were free, Lilly pulled the weapon I'd given her from her pocket and blasted the man in his back with a deep, dark blue killing shot. The body dropped hard on its face.

Seeing what she'd done, killing the attacker, brought my spinning, bloodlust filled brain back to its senses. I looked at the young woman as she lowered her weapon and wiped frightened, angry tears off her face. Her expression was strong and cold but somehow... still peaceful. Christ, Lilly was a strange person.

I huffed and puffed for a few moments, trying to settle myself down. Unsure if I could even stand, I remained on my knees, in the dirt with the bloody faced, unconscious or dead attacker under me. Lilly held still, breathing heavily.

Next a light suddenly flickered on about five or six meters behind Lilly. She spun around raising her weapon again.

"Whoa! Whoa, easy!" The newcomer said. "Hold on! I'm not here to fight!" It was another man who looked to be about fifty years old with dirty, scruffy clothes, a big belly and a full beard that almost glowed in the moonlight. A beat up baseball cap sat firmly on his head. He held a lantern in one hand and a shotgun in the other. He spoke in a 'good-old-boy' Texas accent. "What the hell you two doin' out here?"

"Drop your gun!" Lilly ordered. She gestured the fallen men. "Are you with them?"

The man cut his wide, aged, wrinkled eyes between the two of us and then gazed over the fallen hooligans. "Hell no. Looks like you ran into some of those nasty boys that hang around here." He pointed at the dead man Lilly shot, the guy I bashed then at the other two, unconscious men. "They dead?"

"These two are I think." I grunted, finally getting to my feet with Lilly's help. "The other two are just stunned. Lilly, grab my weapon, please." She picked my gun up and then walked over to stand by my side. I looked at the man. "Who're you?"

The guy tensed up at the sight of me being armed. I took the pistol from Lilly's hand and quickly tucked it away in my pocket. He relaxed. "I'm just heading into town for some supplies. I'm with one of the Michael Vistaer freedom groups. You ever hear of him?"

I smiled. "Oh yea, we've heard of him. We're actually heading back to his base."

"No kidding?" The man smiled. "Small world. Crazy, small world. We're all over the place; little freedom groups. The country is changing. We're going to win our freedom back. It's too bad so many of our young ones are acting like rabid dogs." He gestured the four men again. "They'll have to learn sometime." He raised an eyebrow. "You look busted up pretty bad. Need some help?"

I leaned harder on Lilly and shook my head. Having spent the last of my adrenaline, my energy was draining fast. "I'm not as busted up as that guy."

The man walked over to the guy I pummeled. "Yep. You did quite a number on him." He kicked the man's foot, checking for a reaction. There wasn't one. "I was hanging back for a bit after I saw some flashes of light that came from here. Then I saw you go primal on this one."

Primal was the right word. I nodded in the dark. "Right. Thanks anyways, but we've got help on the way."

The portal opened on queue not ten meters away. "Holy shoot!" The man exclaimed. "What's that?"

"Our ticket out of here." I said. "A portal to Denver."

He shook his head. "Damn, futuristic, space age stuff. And those flashes of light… What do you have, laser guns?"

Lilly was helping me hobble toward the rectangular, glowing vortex. As we passed the man, she reached out and grabbed his shoulder. "Something like that." Then she kissed his cheek. It seemed sweet but all I could think of was how much of damn flirt the woman was.

I decided to try and one-up her. "Lilly. Give our friend here the keys to Erica's car."

She obeyed and I studied the man's surprised face. I said, "You'll find a nice, new vehicle behind that house. Take it."

The old man smiled wide under his beard. "You all take care now. For tomorrow's freedom!" He waved and moved off toward the car, taking his light with him leaving us in the dark with only the Moon and the eerie glow of the portal to lead us.

Lilly quickened her pace and I struggled to keep up, nearly tripping. We reached the portal and stumbled through, immediately finding ourselves back in the musty, dimly lit back room of the old toy store.

Mike smiled at us and quickly worked to shut down the portal. His expression changed when he saw the condition I was in. Chickadis howled and was all over Lilly and me, wagging her tail and sniffing our legs. She got more excited with time and actually jumped up on us, jamming her front paws into my gut.

I bit my lip and grunted in pain. "God damn!"

"Chickadis, down!" The dog scurried around behind us, tail between her legs, not jumping anymore. "Help me!" Lilly shouted, calling Chris and Chin over to help pull me along.

Chris spoke in his gentlemanly, southern accent. "Let's get him to his bed." He yelled to someone I couldn't see. "Get Marie, now!"

I panted, finally allowing the pain from my injuries free reign to completely wash over me. I limped along and picked my head up just enough to see Michael Vistaer. His arms were crossed as he stood still, silently watching over everyone like a sentry. His gaze shifted between Lilly and me. He looked pissed but given the situation, I really didn't care.

Chapter 13

Hundreds of oddly cut, jigsaw puzzle like pieces glided through a light blue sky, surrounded by beautiful, fluffy, pink and white clouds. The Sun radiated a heavenly, warm, golden light through space that bounced off the surfaces of the game parts as they merged together, working to form a whole. The things seemed to randomly blow in the wind until they met their interlocking counterparts. When they were all done, the shapes had formed an impressive skyscraper floating between the clouds in front of me.

I eventually realized I was dreaming. When I opened my eyes I saw a pierced ear, some strands of black hair and the side of Marie's face hovering over my eyes. She sensed I was awake and looked at me, blinking her middle aged, brown eyes.

"Hello, Jason." She said with a peculiar accent I couldn't place. Marie turned her head to look toward the doorway. "He's awake. I'm done here I think."

I watched her stand up and stretch before letting out a small groan and a yawn. She patted me on my bare shoulder and smiled. "You're a good patient, very receptive to healing. Made my job easier. You get some rest. You're going to be sore and tender for a while."

I drew in a deep breath which didn't hurt for the first time since David's crazy mother slammed that table into my ribs. "Thanks, Marie." My eyes followed her as she walked out of the small room, passing Michael Vistaer who stood just outside the door holding what looked like a bottle of beer.

"Thanks." He said to Marie in a near whisper. After turning to me he said, "May I come in?"

Oh boy. The guy wasn't wasting any time. I bet he was eager to scold me and yell at me about dragging Lilly around. That was expected but right now I wasn't up to arguing or defending myself. I glanced down at my body, suddenly realizing I wasn't wearing anything but a pair of my boxer shorts. My chest was bruised black and blue, especially over my left pectoral muscle, but other than that, I seemed ok.

I sat up as best I could on the bed and positioned my pillow between my back and the wall that served as a headboard. Again, doing so didn't hurt, proof Marie was a good healer. The room was cold so I pulled the bed's white sheet and quilt over my bare legs and feet. Michael was still waiting. I nodded. "Sure. This is your place, remember?"

The man's broad shoulders barely fit through the doorway. As he entered, Chickadis stood and walked over to lick the Michael's hand. I didn't even realize the dog was in the room until she got up. He smiled at her then addressed me. "You're my guest. I wouldn't come in without permission. Besides, this isn't really *my* place. We're just borrowing it." He sucked on his teeth. "We'll most likely have to find somewhere new soon, unless the Union infighting continues to go the way it is."

He tucked his bottle under his left arm and pulled out a new, unopened beer from a six pack case I hadn't seen in his left hand. He handed it out to me. "Have one, it'll help dumb down the lingering pain."

I took the bottle. "What time is it?"

"Five a.m." Michael said before winking one of his gold-green eyes at me and taking a large swig. He sat down in the chair Marie had been using.

I laughed and twisted the cap off my drink, bringing it to my lips and downing a sip. It may have been early in the morning but damn the beer tasted good. I remembered how long it'd been since I'd eaten.

"It's early I suppose," Michael went on, "actually late for me. I haven't slept and just got back from LA about four hours ago, a couple hours before you and Lilly got back." He shook his head and swore. "It never ends. Brass called me up and screamed at me for about two and a half hours."

"What's his problem now?" I was both curious and at the same time glad I wasn't the topic of conversation.

Michael gave a blend of a laugh and a snort. "His problem is me. He thinks I overreacted in Los Angeles." He looked me in my eyes. "But he didn't give any alternative ideas. He wasn't *there*. I guess he just needed someone to yell at. The kid's overstressed."

I took another drink and grunted, trying to figure out how to feel about the resistance's so called leader. "What wound up happening there after we left?"

"War, fighting, pain, terrific bravery from those who chose freedom and eventual victory." Vistaer chewed on his lip for a couple seconds. "I gathered all the local leaders together, those both inside and outside Tehlasrin who're loyal to the resistance. We mobilized, set the prisoners free, fought off the Union and stabilized things as well as we could." He blinked. "Given the circumstances, I think we did a damn good job. The GU has lost control of nearly the entire west coast."

I considered that, absentmindedly scratching Chickadis behind her ears with my left hand. "Yea, it sounds like it. Why the hell is Brass mad then?"

"Because I reacted without consulting him." Michael let out a light growl and I could feel the dog tense up under my fingers. "He won't admit it but I know that's it. Officially, he says the problem is that our pieces weren't properly in place before all hell broke loose. Just like what happened in Seattle." Now Michael shook his head. "It's all public relations BS. Rigel has an ego on him that's sometimes too damn big."

"Hmm." I made the noise, considering the situation. "Why do you care what he thinks? He seems like a spoiled punk to me, stuck up on a power trip." I looked around the room. "Not much different than any GU controller."

"I don't believe that." Michael said, strongly. "I've known Rigel and his parents a long time. Deep down, he's a good, young man who knows how to lead. The others like him too. He has the largest group of supporters and a massive stockpile of currency and weapons."

"Oh." I said, not sold but not really wanting to argue the point. "Maybe he just needs to grow up some more then."

Michael nodded. "Yes, he does. He wasn't with us when we stopped Erica." His voice broke up a little while saying his dead friend's name. "He doesn't believe in the real dangers out there, the real evils that truly drive the Union." After setting the remaining unopened beers on the floor he looked at me and raised his eyebrows. "There are other contenders out there who'd like to lead after we kick out the GU. From what I've seen, Rigel is the best qualified."

"Why don't you go for the job?" I said, smiling and giving a little salute with my bottle. I'll be darned, I really did feel better. Marie had done a marvelous job.

Michael laughed, loud and hearty. "Who in their right mind would follow a rampaging, madman like me? Sure people like me, but I'm a soldier. If there isn't any fighting to be done, I'm nothing special."

"That makes two of us."

Michael clanged his bottle against mine in a quick toast, sending a satisfying ring through the air. We both took large drinks then Vistaer set his now empty bottle down and opened another. I studied him. "Why are you here, in my room? Why are you telling me all this?"

"I'm just checking up on you, making sure you're alright, not in agony or losing your mind." A pause. "You thought I'd be angry about Lilly?" Michael laughed. "That girl does what she wants. I've tried to keep a watch on her for the better part of twenty years. Pointless."

I exhaled, glad I wasn't going to receive any lectures. "You looked ticked off when I saw you."

Michael yawned. "Bah. I'm always *ticked off*. When you saw me I was stressed and strung out from everything that happened in LA. Well, I was also concerned about you two, same with everyone else on my team." He saw my expression change. "Hey, like it or not, you're part of the team." He took another drink and pointed at my chest. "You're healing up good."

"Yea, Marie knows her stuff." I nodded. "Richard too. That spell of his kept on working just fine."

"We're lucky." Michael said. "We've got some of the most honest and talented people working with us. You're right though, Marie really knows her stuff. You won't even have any scars. Unlike that beauty on your neck."

I instinctively brought my right hand up and rubbed the mark on the right side of my neck. It nearly ran from my chin to my right ear. "Yea, this one's here to stay."

"How'd you get it?" Michael asked. I looked at him and saw the man's expression abruptly change. "Sorry, it's personal. I see."

I considered telling him how I'd gotten the scar, about how I wanted to kill myself, tried to, and failed. But no, there was too much else going on and I didn't want to get into something so deep. So instead I just said, "Long story."

"Hell, we've all got long stories." Michael leaned back in his chair and slapped his lap with his left hand. "Most of us have scars too. Well, we all have emotional scars but physical ones too. Look at this." He leaned forward and bowed his head so I had a clear view of his scalp. His buzzed hair was short enough to where I could see a discolored zig-zag line about five inches long on the top of his head.

"Damn." I said. "How'd you get that?"

Michael laughed and picked his head back up. "Sword. The bastard was good and nearly had my number. His blade probably would've split my noggin in two had I not gotten a quick psych shield up at the last second."

"Christ." I drank the last gulp of my beer and Michael had a fresh on in my hands before I knew what hit me. "How did you learn to use that? That shield thing?"

Vistaer perked up and his deep voice carried a twinge of giddiness. "You wanna learn? Hell, I'll teach you. You already use it, instinctively." He pointed at my chest and the side of my head that had been cracked open. "With a little knowledge, study and practice you can control it, turn it on and off when you really need it."

"Thanks." I said, blurting my next words without really thinking. "You can show me after I save David."

"Jason." Michael said, suddenly rubbing his temples. "After everything you've seen, after what Lilly told me, after what she told you, after your dreams, you're still going after him?"

I squinted. "I don't know what all that means or how you know about my dreams but of course. I'm going to find David and I'm going to save him."

"Ok." Michael said softly, putting his palms out. "Ok, fine."

I couldn't keep myself from spouting the next question either. "What did Lilly tell you? Did you know she was bonded with Samantha Forrest?"

"Of course I knew." Michael said, quickly. "I've known all of them for years, since before Lilly was even born."

"Oh, right." I felt dumb for forgetting.

Michael hummed, drawing my gaze. "You probably don't want my advice."

I kept a neutral face and stayed quiet.

"Lilly's a beautiful woman and I love her like she's one of my own daughters." He stated. "But she's not in the right condition for a relationship right now."

I nodded. "I'm not either. So what's your point?"

Vistaer smiled. "Nothing. I recommend you keep from dwelling to much on Lilly Claire White. Richard told me years ago that she's got some serious work to do so I'll protect her but also stay out of her way. You should do the same."

"I don't have a clue what you're talking about, really." I said with a laugh. The topic was serious but something about it was a little funny.

I was generally enjoying my time with Michael. He wasn't too hard to get along with once you got past his brutish, overbearing and intimidating side. Eff, the same could be said about me.

"So, daughters, eh?" I furrowed my brow. "Are you married?"

Michael's face showed a soft, sad little smile, one that showed longing or something. "Two daughters, yes. One's fifteen and the other's five. They have different mothers. No, I'm not married."

"Oh." I was surprised, suddenly seeing Vistaer as a tomcat.

"My oldest daughter's mother died years ago." Michael looked off into empty space then brought his gaze back to me. "Hannah's my youngest girl's mom."

"Hannah from Seattle?" I asked, dumbly.

He nodded.

"You care for her? Hannah, I mean."

"You bet your ass!" Michael boomed. "I love her with all my heart. I loved Danielle too. The one who died." He clarified. "Eff, I love lots of people."

"How did she die?" I felt nosey asking but I had the impression Michael almost wanted me to pry.

The big man swallowed. "She and I were with the resistance before the Union officially started." He took a sip of his beer. "She went out on a routine assignment, gathering some information, dirt on men and women for August to use. He needed it to blackmail them, all part of our efforts to make the new order not quite as hellish as it could've been." He sighed. "Well, Danielle got caught in the middle of a firefight, a mob war of sorts." He shook his head and pursed his lips momentarily. "She died quickly."

"Damn." I said, sipping my beer.

"I was back on the west coast with our daughter when the news reached me." Michael grunted. "Effing controllers… and their demon masters." He drew in a deep breath and raised his eyebrows. "But now I have a child with Hannah. I don't second guess the past. What's done is done."

I stretched my arms and my chest muscles. They were still a bit sore but felt good. The beer was helping even more. "I wonder how bad the Union could've been."

Michael sat up straight then leaned forward, closer to me. "I saw their plans, the early hellish draft. Cross had a copy. Jesus, it could still get that bad if we're not careful. In any time of change the world can be a breeding ground for freedom or tyranny." He grunted, appearing as though some sort of realization hit him. "Shoot, maybe Rigel's right. We do have to be careful."

I considered what he said and was especially interested. I wasn't sure why, maybe I was hoping to actually feel good about the way the world was rather than always thinking about how bad things were. Or maybe I just wanted to hear about the successes of the men and women who thwarted the Union's original goals.

"Everyone was going to be tagged, chipped and marked." Michael went on, his eyes glossing over as if he were reading his own memories. "Eighty-five percent of the world's population was to be eliminated, quickly. The rest would be outright, blatant slaves. Granted, Tehlasrin still implemented many of their plans, the sterilization, the poison in our food, water and air, the control grid… but what we have now is nothing compared to what they wanted. The lackluster result the Union actually produced allowed the resistance enough of a foothold to get started."

I blew out a gust of air. "Wow. It's all just too much. Everything. I'm just so, I don't know, drained."

"Get some rest." Michael said. "I'm gonna do the same after I sharpen up my swords." His face changed, showing a cold, hard look. "They went through a lot in LA."

I imagined the guy plowing through enemies, cutting them down the way he did during the battle in Seattle. I gestured the remaining bottles of beer. "Let's finish those first, then call it quits. You were right, they do help." I took a sip. "Why do you use swords? Why not guns?"

"I'm not dumb if that's what you're thinking. I know the advantage of a projectile weapon." Michael started with a smile. "But we're hailiorea. We're, in ourselves, stronger than any gun or rifle. Once that bullet, energy blast or whatever leaves our fingertips, it's literally out of our hands, gone. The shot is on its own destiny." He licked his lips and took a drink. "Our bodies and the weapons we hold on to are always under our power. The sword is stronger because we're stronger. We have more control and force. I can drive the tips of my blades through materials greater than most guns can. And I told you in Seattle… blades are quieter."

I laughed. "That almost makes sense."

He laughed too. "To me it does." He paused. "Ok. So you want to go after David again. Do it. I can't, well, I could stop you, but it's not my job. Men and woman are free, thank God."

I was surprised Michael seemed so willing to let me on my way but didn't feel like questioning it. "Alright." I said, lifting my beer for another toast. Vistaer, who suddenly felt like a friend and a mentor, met my bottle with his. "To David."

"To Erica, Sally and all other freedom fighters, living and passed." Michael had a real skill at working his voice to fit the situation. His toast was sad, encouraging, kind and strong all at the same time.

We finished the rest of the beers then I hit the bathroom before falling back into bed, once again pleased I was able to live without the wretched pain in my chest. The smell of coffee hit my nose as my eyes closed. Food sounded good and David was still out there waiting for me but right now I needed rest. I was out in seconds.

-

Yep, when it rains, it pours. That's about the best way I could describe what happened next. I was too surprised and dumbstruck to word it any other way.

I woke up six hours after falling into a hard sleep. Without thinking, I stumbled out of bed, pulled on a pair of jeans, nearly tripped over Chickadis, then shuffled along, like a zombie, to the restroom, relieved myself and quickly washed up. Sweat, dirt and dried blood ran off my skin and hair in sheets and it felt great getting the gunk off. I didn't bother shaving but made sure to brush my teeth to remove the old, stale beer taste from my mouth.

Then it happened. Still groggy, I stepped out of the restroom and almost couldn't believe my eyes. There she was, looking as cool and as sexy, in her own imperfect way, as I remembered. She wore a nice, clean, slightly tight pair of blue jeans and a light, comfortably soft looking, auburn sweater that matched her not too short hair. Her hazel eyes studied me as I stood there, still damp, only wearing a pair of jeans. Her look was intense and her jaw was clenched tight. I knew her brain was racing but I couldn't tell if she was angry, happy or indifferent. The woman was hard to read. Fier Wren.

Despite it all, my uncertainty, leaving her without a word, stealing her contacts list and not knowing just how pissed she was, I smiled then laughed. "Holy hell!"

She raised an eyebrow and slowly crept up to me without a sound. Our eyes locked, she smirked and then she slapped me hard against my left cheek. My skin blazed with heat and I grimaced, immediately rubbing what I knew was a fantastic red handprint on my face. "Nice to see you, too." I said.

"You… ASS!" Then she hugged me.

I swear to whatever god people pray too, women were more confusing than all the inter-workings of Tehlasrin, the hailiorea and the osilea combined. So, unsure what else to do, I hugged her back. It felt nice. I spoke softly in her ear. "What're you doing here?"

"I wanted to make sure you didn't get yourself killed." She said, still hugging me and squeezed tighter. "That and Cross asked me to deliver some information on Everiel. He thinks it's tied to the chaos that happened in Los Angeles and the woman, Erica Wood losing her mind."

We released each other. "That island that blew up?"

"Yea, the island." She eyed my body up and down, seemingly just now realizing the bruises on my chest. She pointed at an especially discolored patch.

I ignored her curious look. "How'd you get here?"

"August sent me through his portal… Jesus, was that from David's mother?"

I looked down. "That old woman was insane. She seemed fine at first, kind even. Then she snapped and everything went crazy." I turned up to face Fier. "How do you know about all that, David's mother and everything?"

"I met with Richard and then Michael woke up a little bit ago." She furrowed her brow as she studied my bruises then locked her eyes onto mine. "Michael's just as tired and out of it as you are. Anyways, they filled me in."

"Yesterday was a hell of a day." I sighed.

"Sucks about Sally." She snorted. "I'm *so sick* of good people dying. You probably didn't get to know her at all."

I shook my head. "No. I hardly talked to her."

Fier showed a sad, pained expression before snapping out of it. "Get dressed and grab some food." She thought for a heartbeat, examining my face. "Coffee too. We're having a meeting in the main room in a little bit."

"Ok." I said before she graced me with a smile. Hmm, maybe she wasn't upset anymore about my leaving her but I still felt like a creep. She started to turn away when I called her. "Fier. Sorry about ducking out on you the way I did."

She squinted. "I was pissed for a couple days. But I cooled off. I should've expected you to go. You all but told everyone you were gonna go after David." She shrugged. "You could've said goodbye though, face to face."

"I know. I'm just, well," I rolled my eyes, "me. I'm a jerk and a coward sometimes. I had to go."

Fier put her hands up, palms out. "Don't sweat it. I said I cooled off. You're still alive and we know David is at Morbal's -"

"We do?" I asked, suddenly.

She nudged her head in the general direction of the large, open space in the toy store's backroom. "Olivia and that guy she's with, they'll fill you in. Anyways," she said in a way that showed she didn't appreciate being interrupted, "I'm not angry anymore."

I raised my eyebrows. "Hey, if you say so, that's good enough for me."

"Still, it was a dick move on your end. And don't give me that smirk." Fier smiled. "Stop trying to be so charming."

Without thinking I leaned down and kissed Fier on her cheek, surprising myself as much as her. I really needed to talk to Richard. My thoughts, dreams, intuitions and emotions were really getting carried away. "It's good to see you."

She winked and headed off while I rubbed the back of my neck.

-

It was all bland, the eggs, the toast and the coffee, but damn it was nice having food in my stomach again. Everyone was assembled in the large open area of the store's backroom. There weren't any wet clothes hanging on any lines so the musty, soapy smell was at a minimum. Florescent lights sent their soft, artificial glow throughout the dank area.

I sat alone, well, not actually, Chickadis was right next to me. I gently stroked the dog's head with my left hand, still trying to completely wake up, holding a hot cup of coffee in my right. The warmth felt nice between my fingers.

Cheap, plastic, rectangular tables were set up in a vague row, each with four flimsy chairs placed around them. I picked a seat at the back, away from the others who were all clustered together. I'd always been a fan of personal space. That was part, a small part, of what made Morbal's asylum so awful.

Sean Lee, the young looking, Asian kid was present and Olivia was sitting on his lap. It was a funny image, especially since she was actually taller than him and most likely weighed more. Now that I saw them, I wanted to ask about David but decided to wait until after the meeting.

Chris was in the far back, monitoring a bunch of computer screens. Michael stood at the head of the group, silently watching everyone.

Fier's laugh caught my attention. She was chatting with Richard who smiled at the woman admiringly. I set my attention on the two, trying to catch what they were saying.

"Well, it's a pleasure having your company, Ms. Wren." Richard spoke in his usual, noble tone. "If I were a few," he coughed, "make that, several years younger I'd be unable to resist any attempt to court so lovely a woman as yourself."

I felt the muscles in my face contort into what had to have been an odd expression. Fier blushed a little then glanced my way. We locked eyes and I smiled before cutting my own sight around to see Lilly. The young woman was seated next to Andres and Marie, gazing back and forth between Fier and me. She caught me looking at her and I quickly looked back at Fier whose face now had a curious look of its own. Oh brother.

Fier looked at Lilly. Lilly smiled and waved, sweetly. Then Fier turned back to me, squinting, before focusing back on Richard who seemed oblivious to the entire exchange, almost mesmerized by the auburn haired woman. "You flatter me, Richard."

The old man's eyebrows perked up. "Not one bit. I'm wholeheartedly honest."

Was he really hitting on Fier? And... was I jealous?

Michael Vistaer abruptly laughed and clapped his hands loudly. "Oh my lord. Can you all just settle down?" He was glancing around at Fier, Richard, Lilly and me, obviously aware of the whole ordeal. "Fier. Let's hear it."

"Right." She snaked her way through the tables and chairs to stand next to Michael then turned around to face the group. She held her gaze on me the longest. "Hi everyone. I arrived this morning on Cross's request to keep you all up to speed on what happened on Everiel."

Chin raised his hand and then spoke before being acknowledged. "Why are you telling us? Shouldn't you report this stuff to Brass and the other leaders?"

"I don't know. I guess so" Fier said, sharply. "August gives me orders and I follow them. You guys are always in the middle of everything big that happens so I guess Cross wants to make sure you're informed."

"Yea, ok" Chin groaned, "but what can we do about it?"

Fier glared at the man. "I'm just here to fill you in."

"I just don't get why an explosion on Everiel is our business." He folded his arms.

"Christ, will you let her talk?" I blurted, feeling my temperature rise. Chickadis licked my hand.

Chin sneered at me. Drew murmured something under his breath and I quickly zeroed in on him. I'd nearly forgotten all about him and the fact he didn't like me for whatever reason.

Michael spoke, sending his voice resonating through the room. "Right. Chin, relax. Let's hold off on the questions for now, ok?"

Fier sighed and nodded to Michael then me. "Thanks. We know the island exploded four nights ago and nearly the entire place was engulfed in flame. We're not sure but we think there may still be some people alive there. But the place is surrounded by ships from the Tehlasrin navy." She raised her eyebrows. "We considered using the teleporter to search for survivors and getting them out of there but there's no guarantee they'd even take our help. Remember, Everiel is, or was Steven Ark's island and he's got heavy ties with the GU."

I watched Fier look over a sheet of paper before continuing. "The design of the island's infrastructure is extremely curious. From what Cross has gathered, it looks like the whole place, every building, every house was linked to where setting off an explosion in the right spot would light everything up."

Half the group gasped and the other half murmured amongst themselves. I could hear some of what was said and it all was to the point of why would anyone design a place like that.

"Right." Fier said, calling back everyone's attention. "I agree. The explosion and all the deaths that resulted, nearly half a million people, appear to be deliberate." The group burst into several quiet conversations all over again. "We all know Ark has been conducting rituals on Everiel for years. We know most controllers worship the osilea. Well, Cross believes the explosion was yet another ritual. A huge sacrifice used to feed some dark entity or energy."

I looked at Lilly, remembering her talking about the darkness getting stronger and closer. David was on Everiel, sent there by Morbal. Did he have a part in all this? I tried to believe none of this was connected but couldn't. Mother effer.

"After all the madness and chaos that occurred in LA, August and others on Aswain believe a powerful osilea force has materialized and may be working its way across the continent." Fier swallowed. "It might be headed for Ark. He's based in New York. At any rate, we should all be extra careful. If this is true and this thing was able to shatter a hailiorum as powerful as Erica that quickly, we're all at risk."

The room was quiet for a while.

"That's it." Fier said. "I know it's a brief report but we couldn't risk sending the message electronically. Who knows what Tehlasrin goons may be listening."

"An evil force may have materialized?" Andres asked no on in particular.

Michael brought his right hand to his chin, thinking. "Erica was hurt and twisted by something dark and powerful. That evidence is clear though we still don't know any specifics. None of the men and women I spoke with who worked for her had any information. She did mention the name Xolzv." He cut his eyes around to look at Lilly. "There's more to all this than we know. Ark and his forces are busily at war with Morbal's army. If Cross's guess is right, this thing may be looking to capitalize on everything. Poor Erica might've been its first target" He stared off into empty space and swore before blinking and turning back to Fier. "Thanks, dear."

She nodded and headed over to me while sending a 'come hither' gesture with her hand to Olivia and Sean. The two young lovers stood and headed my way. The rest of the group talked amongst themselves, no doubt speculating on Fier's report.

The three reached my table at the same time and seated themselves. Chickadis sniffed everyone in turn then wandered off toward her food bowl.

Olivia looked at me and laughed, her red-orange eyes lit up. "Wow! That must have been a stinger!"

"Huh?" I gave the girl a curious look.

Sean spoke, "Geez, it's like a perfect handprint on your face!"

I rolled my eyes and turned to Fier. "Thanks."

The Aswain Captain pointed at the young, baby-faced man, ignoring the conversation. "Sean says the asylum has changed. Things have gotten weird there."

I furrowed my brow, turned to the kid and said, "I was just there two days ago. The place seemed just as sick and twisted as I remembered."

Sean spoke in his usual, nervous way. "Um, yea. I went there last night to pick up my last pay voucher and, god, I couldn't believe it. There weren't any guards at the gates or security points." He shook his head and looked at the three of us. "They were all just hanging around, talking, laughing and even drinking!"

"Who?" I asked.

He exhaled, almost laughing. "The guards, the keepers, all of them. Just hanging out getting drunk, like they were at a big party or something."

I tried to verbalize another question but failed. Instead I just scratched my head.

"Heck," Olivia started, "Morbal may be gone, off to fight his war. Maybe the others are just slacking while the boss is away."

I shook my head. "No. The keepers there aren't the types to party with each other." I looked at Fier. "If this is true, it's messed up."

"Anyways," Sean said, "I heard a bunch of them talking about how cool someone named Divad was and then I remembered you were looking for a guy named David." He bobbed his head. "So I told Liv and she said I should tell you guys."

There was that mispronunciation again, Divad. What the hell was with that? Whatever, it didn't matter. "I'm going. He's there and I'm busting him out."

"Busting him out?" Sean asked. "Didn't you hear me? The place is wide open!"

I ignored him, instead looking at Olivia. "Can you drive me there again?"

The part osilea woman smiled as usual, showing her sharp teeth. "The van belongs to my baby but I bet he'd let us use it again if I asked nicely." It was obvious her hand was busy under the table, rubbing on Sean's thigh and beyond.

Sean gasped. "Ah, sure! Yea, we'll take you."

"You'll take us." Fier said.

I looked at her and slumped my shoulders. "What? You don't have to go."

"I know. I'm going though." Fier folded her arms and gave me a look that said 'don't eff with me.' "Technically, you and David are still citizens of Aswain, part of the intelligence team and under my command."

I smiled. "You're a tad out of your jurisdiction."

"Who cares?" She spat. "I'm going."

"So am I." A soft voice said from behind me. I didn't need to turn around but did anyways. There was Lilly, gazing down on the four of us with a dreamy, peaceful stare. I nearly swore, wondering how someone so sexy, cute and kind looking could actually make me nervous. Then I remember she was Samantha Forrest's daughter.

Fier protested. "Huh? What for? It could be dangerous. You stay here."

I nearly cursed. On top of everything else, now I was going to have the woman I really cared for and the woman I recently had sex with around while entering the very maw of hell looking for my friend. What a nightmare. I turned forward, knowing full well what was coming next and not wanting to be in the middle of it.

"I go where I want, Fier." Lilly said. "And I want to help find David."

Fier looked at me, searching for support. "I know." I said. "I think it's a bad idea too. I think you both should stay here. But we can't really stop Lilly."

"Why not?" Fier asked, coldly. "I can stop her."

"That's not the way we do things here, Hun." Michael's voice boomed. He strode up alongside our table with Richard a step behind him. "We're in danger all the time no matter where we are. So don't play the whole, 'stay where it's safe' thing. You're our guest," he said to Fier, "so I expect you to accept our rules. If you want to go, if Lilly wants to go, you all go and you'll help protect each other."

A giant 'what the eff' siren went off in my brain. I'd heard Michael say things like this before but the fact that he was just going to let Lilly march off into dangerous territory felt strangely out of character. I wasn't Vistaer's responsibility and neither was Fier… but Lilly? Also the guy was all up in arms about me going to Morbal's the last time. Now he didn't even care. Something was off and didn't feel right.

"Also," Richard began, "we have word that much of the city's surveillance isn't being watched. They don't have the manpower anymore since most have run off to war with Ark."

Michael nodded. "And on top of Sean's accounts, we've learned the asylum is in total disarray. It sounds like even the prisoners are free, mixing in with the keepers." He studied everyone in turn. "It makes us wonder why they haven't left, the prisoners I mean." He paused, thinking. "You be extra cautious. The place may truly be a madhouse."

That was it. I stood and grabbed Vistaer by his arm, tugging him away from the group. "Come here a second." I said, under my breath, leading the surprised big man to an isolated corner in the large warehouse space. When I felt confident the others couldn't hear us I said, "What the hell's going on with you? Lilly? She could get killed. We all could."

The man stared at me for a few breaths. "That's true." His shoulders dropped. "But it's not my place. I told you last night; we're all adults, we control our own lives." He gestured in Lilly's direction. "She's not a child anymore. It might be hard to understand, but the whole thing with Erica, LA, then Brass and the other leaders coming down on me taught me something. Our best laid plans aren't always the most wise. I'm not a prophet or a genius. I'm an emotional, reactionary brute." He smiled. "Just like you. I'm fifteen years older than you which might contribute to some of our differences but deep down, you and I are the same. That's why I visited you last night. You're like a younger brother in many ways. It's not the place for men like us to decide the fate of others. All we can do is help."

"So what?" I asked, trying to keep my voice down. "You just toss any responsibility? Are you giving up?"

Michael's face flushed red and I thought for a moment he was going to punch me. "Never!" He exclaimed. "My drive, my entire being is aimed at destroying the Union and helping to bring liberty back. I serve God almighty and I pledged myself to the duty of resurrecting freedom in our world. I live and I'll die with that commitment. Eff, given up..."

"And now you just don't care that I'm heading back into the asylum when just a couple days ago you thought it was the dumbest thing you'd ever heard of." I raised my eyebrows, looking the man square in his eye.

His brow furrowed. "Of course I care but people change, Jason." He huffed. "I'm still trying to deal with Erica, alright? More than anything... It's a horrible thing ending the life of a teammate, a partner, a friend. I hope you never have to face the same challenge."

I studied Michael's face, thinking. "You didn't have to kill her."

"No, I did." He looked me back in the eye and I could see a universe of thought and consideration swirling in his brain. "She was gone. Lilly helped bring out one last moment of Erica's true self but it couldn't last. She was a danger to everyone including herself and her soul." His eyes dropped down to look at his feet. "It was my duty as her friend to set her free. I thank God I had the strength to do it."

I nodded, unsure what to say.

"We all have the gift of free will. Get used to it." Michael said and I felt the tension in the air ease up. Then he actually smiled, bringing his right index finger up to brush against my left cheek. "Nice love-tap there."

I grunted. Love-tap... Yea right. "Don't get me started." With that, Michael headed back toward the table where Fier was seated. I followed behind him and it was impossible to not notice both Fier's and Lilly's eyes were locked on me.

"Why don't you go too, boss?" Olivia asked, happily once he was within arm's reach. "We'll be ready to head out shortly."

Michael looked at her. "I have a war and a country to monitor. I'm busy. Are you actually going into the asylum with them?"

"Nah," Olivia started. "We're just giving them a lift then heading back."

Vistaer nodded, straightened himself and hollered. "MIKE!"

The young man was at our table in seconds, "What's up?" He looked at me. "Who slapped you?"

"Olivia and Sean are dropping these three off near Morbal's," Michael started.

"WHAT?" Mike exclaimed, turning from Michael to look at me. "Again? You're going there again? You're nuts!"

Michael snorted. "Pay attention! I want you to be ready to port them back here." He looked at Fier, Lilly and me. "Make sure you have phones and Mike's number. Call him as soon as you're ready to get back here, ok?"

I narrowed my eyes, still thinking about Vistaer's sudden change in outlook. "This time, if I run into Morbal, if he's there, I'm killing him."

"Do what you have to do." Michael said. "I won't stop you this time. The bastard deserves to die and he's of no more use to us. Tehlasrin is already tearing itself apart." He looked at Fier, Lilly and then me. "Go with God."

I let out a light, almost sarcastic chuckle then glanced over the group, nodding my head. "Let's get ready."

Chapter 14

"We need to stay together, the three of us." Lilly said in her soft dreamy voice. "If we stick close, within arms reach, I'll be able to extend Richard's enchant."

"Enchant?" Fier spat, skeptically. "What the hell are you talking about?"

It was beyond obvious, Fier didn't care for Lilly. The woman's tone was a dead giveaway but not nearly as telling as her body language. Arms crossed, jaw set, eyes rolling every time Lilly spoke. Yep, all signs pointed to a grown woman who didn't like someone and wasn't afraid to show it. I looked at the two, searching for any clues into their thoughts. Lilly seemed relaxed, calm and her face showed a slight smile; looking quite at peace. Fier, on the other hand, was now giving the other woman an intense, untrusting, angry stare. Great.

Lilly opened her mouth to answer but I beat her to it, hoping to draw Fier's gaze. "Richard put some kind of illusion bubble around me before the last time I went to Morbal's. The spell keeps others from really noticing me." I shook my head. "Beats me how it works, but it does."

The five of us were traveling in Sean Lee's van, headed down a street that lead to Morbal's asylum. He sat in the front and Olivia was behind the wheel. The rest of us were in the back checking our weapons and the Kevlar vests we each wore under our respective outer garments. Fier pulled a somewhat baggy, white sweater over hers that she'd borrowed from Marie. Lilly had a flimsy, blue vinyl jacket over her vest and I wore a black suede coat that Chris leant me. Michael insisted we wear the things. I wasn't sure why but I was glad to see some of his old cautious self show up again.

All set and ready to head back into Morbal's, I blocked out the awkwardness of sharing the ride with Fier and Lilly as best I could and glanced out the nearest window.

Traffic was extremely light but there were people out and about everywhere. It was just shy of two o'clock, the Sun was blazing down on the city and people were congregating in groups on streets and sidewalks. It was a far cry from the usual buttoned up, no talking, keep moving martial law rule of the Union.

Several surveillance cameras were toppled over and in some cases I even saw uniformed Tehlasrin troops intermingling with the citizens, engaged in what seemed to be friendly banter. I could hardly believe it, it looked like the strict rules of the world's overlords were falling away. Olivia couldn't keep from commenting the whole time. She loved telling everyone what she knew. According to her, nearly all of Morbal's troops had moved out to engage Ark's army. She also shared that Michael had called in several freedom groups from the surrounding areas to help secure the area.

That's not to say everything was completely happy go lucky. Gunfire rattled off in the distance and every now and then I saw men and woman running through the streets and gutters, screaming and either chasing others or being chased themselves. There were also car fires and brawls scattered about.

Whatever, given all that, it was encouraging to see the GU's noose loosen. I swallowed, hoping the luck would hold and I'd find David safe and sound.

Fier's left eye twitched. "Ok. So it still works? This enchant?"

I nodded at Lilly and pulled myself back to the present. "Yea, I think so."

"So let's stay close." Lilly repeated. "Jason, give me your…" She trailed off while studying my face. "Come here." I didn't move but instead made a confused and untrusting face. Lilly laughed and moved closer to me. "Hold still." She spoke in a whisper.

Her right hand came up to my face and I instinctively jerked back. Fier growled. "What are you doing?"

Lilly smiled. "Stop moving."

I reluctantly obeyed and let the young woman plant her soft hand, gently on my cheek, the same cheek Fier had slapped. There was a hint of warmth that didn't come naturally from Lilly's touch and after a few seconds she pulled back, nodded and spoke with satisfaction "There. All gone. That hand print just looked ridiculous."

"I didn't know you were a healer too." Fier said, folding her arms again. "You get that from your *mother*?"

Lilly looked at her and blinked.

Fier turned to me. "You know, right? I found out a little bit ago that she's Samantha Forrest's daughter."

"Yea, I know." I said, quietly.

"Who?" Sean asked, reminding me he was still in the van.

Fier raised an eyebrow. "And you know about hailiorea bonding?"

Olivia laughed. "Hey, don't sweat it. Lilly's mom went nuts but one of my ancestors was an osilea. It's all good. We're our own people, we're NOT our parents."

"I told Jason all about that." Lilly said, calmly. "Give me your hands. Both of you."

"No thanks." Fier blurted.

Lilly just looked at Fier, gazing at her like she was looking into the other woman's brain. Hell, I bet she was. She sighed and spoke ever so softly. "I want to help. Fier. You don't need to be jealous." She looked at me then back at the other woman. "Jason and I are friends. It's obvious he cares about you. He felt sick about leaving without saying goodbye, mentioned it a bunch."

Fier looked at me and I blushed. "It's true. But now's not the time for all that. We're almost at the asylum."

"And any fool could tell," Lilly continued, "that he has feelings for you." She laughed. "I don't think Jason Sworn would allow just any woman to slap him in the face without some sort of come back."

"Whatever!" Fier nearly yelled. "You want my hand? Fine, here."

She put her right hand out, palm up and I did the same. Lilly took our hands in hers while closing her eyes. Her lips mouthed words I couldn't hear. After a short time, my previously nervous and pounding heart slowed to a relaxing, comfortable pace. I breathed deep, in and out, over and over.

God damn. Here, in the middle of a rebellion, hunting for my lost, captured and possibly hurt friend, now, more than ever I felt a deep caring for Fier Wren. My eyes locked onto hers and for the briefest of seconds it felt like we were truly together, at peace, far away from any conflict, danger or pain. I felt silly. It was hard to grasp how dumb and blind I'd been for not seeing this before. Now, I was afraid it was too late. I sighed. What the eff...

Fier held her stare on me and her face softened. "It'll be ok, Jason."

I smiled, realizing she wasn't dwelling on her own thoughts and feelings but had instead been concerned about mine. Shoot, it'd be nice to end the race and the fight right here so we could run off and live happily ever after. I'd felt that way about Lilly but this was much deeper. With Lilly, the feelings were mostly from lust and my desire to protect the once seemingly innocent and defenseless woman. With Fier? Christ, I didn't know how to explain it. Even if I did know, even if I could understand my own feelings, I wouldn't know how to put them into words. I wasn't that bright.

"Hey." Fier smirked. "It'll be ok. Alright?"

I drew in one last deep breath and nodded, bringing myself back to the present again. "Right." David needed our help… our help? I looked deep into Fier's big, hazel eyes again, suddenly feeling like I wasn't in this alone. Whether I liked it or not, I was changing. The whole damn world was changing.

"Ok!" Lilly said while releasing our hands. "We should be cloaked a bit for now as long as we stay close. Jason is the beacon." She sat down and tucked the etherpistol I'd given her into her pocket. There was a smile on her face. "It's a hard world. I really hope you two can make it together."

I blushed again, blinking away from both women's eyes. I considered coming clean. Telling Fier that Lilly and I had sex but now wasn't really the time. I wasn't looking forward to telling her but I hoped the chance came soon, feeling guilty about the whole thing was getting old. I let out a labored sigh that drew Fier's attention. I shook my head. "Nothing."

"Hey!" Olivia interjected. "Love finds a way, right, sweetie?"

I saw Sean nod his head.

"Enough of all this." Fier said. She finally laughed and when I looked at her she was smiling too. "We're headed into a serious mess here so let's focus."

On cue, Olivia pulled the van over to the side of the street and looked back at us. "Ladies and gentleman, here's your stop." She gave an especially toothy grin. "Good luck. You all better get your asses back safe or I'll be angry."

-

It was like we'd entered another dimension. Morbal's asylum was wide open and filled with men and women, soldiers, keepers, inmates and others standing and sitting around together in groups. They talked, ate and drank. Some were even sleeping. People ran up and down the white corridors shouting, smiling and laughing. One of them wasn't wearing a stitch of clothing. The place was littered with trash and no one seemed to care in the slightest.

Lilly, Fier and I moved through the groups, too amazed and confused to talk. All I could do was wonder what the eff was going on.

Lilly broke the silence with a soft whisper only she could manage, sending her words out like a gentle wind. "They're lost in their own heads." She glanced at several people we passed. "Like they're stuck in a maze of bliss and confusion, all their cares have been ripped out of them." I saw her shake her head and she let out a little sigh. "This way."

"What?" Fier asked, sounding abrasive in contrast to Lilly's voice. "Where?"

"Morbal's office." The younger woman answered.

I cut my eyes around to meet Fier's. She swallowed then glanced down at a group of keepers, four young men sitting in a circle playing a game of cards. "Look." She whispered.

After a quick scan I recognized a plastic sandwich bag filled with small, white, rice sized tablets. Clear. So, that explained some of it. They were all high as kites off the stuff. Now the question was how they'd gotten it and why they were allowed to shun their duties along with any sense of order. I nodded at Fier and we moved on before I spoke. "Why the office?"

"That's were David is." Lilly hummed, eyes fixed straight ahead.

Fier grunted. "How do you know?"

"We're almost there." Lilly didn't answer the question.

A disheveled woman in nothing but a cheaply made, dirty nightgown and beat up slippers shuffled up to us. She smiled with half closed eyes. "Hey, want some? It's all free now." She held a shaky fist out as several pellets of clear dropped through her fingers.

I brought my mouth close to Lilly's ear. "How can she see us?"

"It must be the drug." She said, studying the half asleep looking woman. "It opens them up a bit but they're so stoned I don't think they really know what's going on."

"Want some?" The woman asked again.

"No." Fier snapped.

The three of us moved on, following Lilly's lead until I saw, of all people, old man Tom half laying on the ground with his shoulders and head propped against a wall. His normally white hair was black and grey, covered in dirt and his clothes were filthy. He smiled, staring off into empty space. That was, at least until I came around. He looked at me and perked his head up. "Jason. You're back again? Come, have some." He waved his own stash of clear pellets in the air.

I slowed and Fier grabbed my hand. "Come on." She said. "Let's keep moving."

I didn't listen and pulled my hand free, blindly walking over to Tom and kneeling beside him. "God damn, Tom. You too?" I shook my head, pointing at the bag, grimacing and swore under my breath. "You know how this stuff is made, right?"

He giggled. "Yep. I didn't want any at first but they made me. Boy, am I glad they did." He moaned, closed his eyes and stretched his neck, turning his head from side to side. "It's so wonderful."

"Jason!" Fier said in an urgent yet quiet voice. "Let's go!"

"He moved too far out of the circle." Lilly said, calmly.

I looked at her and saw she was focused on a pair of men who'd taken notice of us. They were keepers who weren't smiling like the others. It was only a matter of seconds before they were headed toward us, arming their shock gloves.

"You three!" One of them yelled. "Don't move."

I looked at the two women. "Fier, on my lead. Strong stun."

"If you going to be here you need your medicine. Doctor's orders." The other guard said. "On your knees, mouths open!"

The pair moved a few steps closer then I pulled out my pistol, aiming it at one of the men, Fier was aiming hers at the other. The two stopped in their tracks. "Oh eff! They're armed!" They turned to run but didn't make it far. Two shots, one from me and one from Fier quickly shut them up.

I tucked my gun away as Tom spoke. "Why? You should've taken it. Here, have some of mine. Join us."

My eyes locked with the old man's. His stare was once so bright and powerful, lively despite his age and years of torture, but now it was cloudy, weak and dull. I slumped my shoulders, frowning. "I'm sorry."

"Christ, will you stop?" Fier asked while pulling on my arm. "There might be more of them."

I gave Tom one last, sympathetic look before moving on with the women, finally making it to Maledro's office a couple minutes later. Uneasiness, both excited and nervous, clenched my stomach. I pulled out my pistol and spoke as I positioned myself between the door and Fier, Lilly was in the back. "I'll go through first. Be careful."

I placed my sweaty left hand on the doorknob and gave it a twist, expecting it to be locked. It wasn't. The door swung open with a slight nudge and I bolted through followed quickly by Fier and Lilly. My eyes darted around like a spooked cat in the night, scanning the office. It was mostly dark so it didn't take long to zero in on the lone source of light, a lamp resting on what looked like a large desk. The light gave off a weak, soft, gold light that bounced off many surfaces. One of those surfaces was Maledro Morbal, seated behind the desk. I couldn't see the details of his face but I knew his silhouette all too well. His dark, beady eyes reflected the light like a rat in the dark.

I was just barely aware that Fier had closed the door behind us. My attention was on Morbal and my weapon was aimed, point blank at his head. "I'm back, you son of a bitch. Don't you dare effing move."

He didn't budge but I thought I heard a faint snicker. Fier had her weapon aimed at the controller too. I saw Lilly out of the corner of my eye, staring, intently studying the man.

"Where's David?" I sneered between clenched teeth. I wanted to fire, Christ, I wanted to shoot so badly.

Again, Morbal stayed quiet. Fier had enough. "ANSWER HIM!"

A laugh came from behind Morbal then something lobbed itself over the controller's head, landing with a splat at our feet. I didn't take my eyes off the doctor. "Lilly, what is it?"

The woman gasped, finally drawing my gaze. Glancing down I saw a bloody, beat up piece of flesh which I soon recognized as a human heart. The blood drained from my face and my own heart pounded against my recently healed ribs.

"WHAT THE EFF!?" Fier yelled, repositioning her weapon. "That's it!"

I knew she was about to fire but before she could, Morbal leaned to his left, fell out of his chair and crashed to the floor with a thud. The lights in the room suddenly blared awake, burning my eyes and a figure stood up from behind the doctor's chair. After adjusting to the light, I stared in disbelief, my mouth dropped open and the weight from my etherpistol pulled my arm down. David was there, smiling at me.

"Hi Jason!" He said, happily. "Good to see you." His eyes danced over the two women. "And you two. Fier? How nice."

"David?" Fier asked.

I wasn't able to speak. It was David but he looked different. He looked old. He looked horrible. His face was lined with scars that appeared to have healed much longer ago than they possibly could have. His eyes had dark rings around them and his hair, which was scraggly and impossibly long given the short time since I'd seen him last, was gray. It sat on his head like a dirty mop, long enough to cover his ears.

"No, *Captain*," he giggled, a gesture in itself that looked alien and twisted, "David went away a long time ago. My name is Divad."

I made an attempt to speak but only managed a guttural sound as air passed through my vocal chords and lips. I shook my head.

"What's wrong?" David raised his eyebrows and put his arms out wide as he rounded the desk, drawing a few steps closer to us. "Surprise! Hey! You made it! You're here! About god damned time. The wait was driving me crazy."

"DON'T MOVE!" Fier barked.

I turned to her, surprised all over again. She aimed her weapon right at my friend. The muscles in my face strained and pulled it into an odd expression. "Fier. It's David. Put the gun down."

Neither her hand nor her weapon budged. She only shook her head. "No, that's not David."

"What?" I asked, furrowing my brow at the woman. I turned back to my friend.

"Aww," David started with a phony sad, hurt face. "What? No hug and kiss? It's been a while." Then he started giggling and smiling.

Hmm, maybe I could understand where Fier was coming from. Something was seriously wrong here. I let out a deep breath. "What happened to you?"

He laughed, long and loud. "Oh man. What *hasn't* happened? So much it's hard to even know where to start." He stepped closer.

"I mean it!" Fier said. "One more step…"

"This is my place now, Fier. You're right though. I'm not David. I'm Divad." He nodded and smirked. "And I'm getting sick of reminding everyone."

I tore my gaze away from David and looked at the two women. Fier was ready to blast David down right then and there. Lilly on the other hand, looked like a statue, staring, unblinkingly at my friend.

"And who," David started, pulling my gaze back to him, "are you?" He pointed at Lilly then smiled at me. "Oh. You brought some candy for the party?"

"What?" I asked again, sharper this time.

David gestured Lilly. "What a delicious little beauty. I was out of the game for a long time but I'm all better now. We can rip into that one all night long. Sorry, Fier, you're a bit outdated now." More laughter. "This one's much fresher."

That did it. David's tone along with the not so subtle context of his words set me off. I tucked my weapon in my pocket and moved up to David, puffing my chest out, taking up as much space as I could. "What do you mean? Don't be an asshole. That's Lilly, she's my friend. She's Cross's friend and part of the resistance."

Now that we were close enough, David reached out and pulled me in for a large, powerful hug. He laughed again. "Oh, it's good to see you."

I felt awkward but hugged him back. When we released, David smiled. Now that I was so close, I took a better look at the deep scars that covered his face. I asked again, "What happened to your face?"

"But come on…" He chuckled, ignoring my question. "The resistance? What are you resisting? The Union? It's all but dead." He raised his eyebrows. "It's time for something new and we're going to bring it to life, Jason. You and me."

My eyes narrowed while my brain fought to make sense of everything. He glanced at the two women. "You two can stick around if you want. There aren't any rules here."

I grabbed his shoulders and shook him, drawing his gaze. "What are you talking about?"

"We're going to change things, for the better. The world is ours, buddy." He pulled away from my grip, smiled wide and nodded his head. "This place, the asylum is just the beginning. It's a starting point. We'll show them how to live, how things should really be."

"What did you do here?" Fier hissed in a tone that was filled with venom and accusation. Her eyebrows were pulled down so low, seeing it made my face hurt. "WHAT did you do to those people?"

Before he could answer, I grabbed David's left shoulder with my right hand. My thoughts raced, cluttered with all the warnings I'd heard telling me David was shattered, that there was no way back. I didn't want to believe them and fought the haunting words out of my head. "What the eff are you talking about? We need to get out of here. You need help."

"Jason!" Fier said, loudly. "Move out of the way."

I turned to the woman, her weapon was aimed at David and her finger was already squeezing the trigger. "Hold it." I looked back at David. "Let's get you back to Aswain. Maybe Cross can help. We can work through this."

"I see." David sighed. "I didn't kill that rat bastard over there," he pointed at Morbal's bloody corpse, "and take over his operations just to run off to Cross's magic island. No," he gritted his teeth, "we're going to ravage the Union and everyone else who thinks they're going to control us. We're going to take what we want and burn the rest. And when we're done, people will finally be free. No laws, no sick, suppressive order, no society. Mankind will be wild. Like it should be." He nodded and sucked in a lungful of air through clenched teeth. "It'll be beautiful."

"Jesus Christ." I shook my head as frustration and anger started to boil under my skin. "That's insane. You can't mean it. Come on, it's me." I shook him. "Let's go. You told me yourself that Aswain was special. You love it there. People can actually *live*."

David chuckled. "Go? Why would I want to go anywhere? The world is a violent hurricane and we're in the eye. Don't be afraid, amigo. They can't hurt me. They can't hurt us when we're together. The Union," he spat on the ground, "the rebellion, the hailiorea, the osilea, none of them. You're safe as long as you're with me. All of you." He nodded, glanced over the three of us then winked at me. "We're brothers. Trust me."

"JASON," Fier started, "NOW! I mean it!"

I turned again toward the woman. "Put the gun d -"

The next thing I knew, in a move that took incredible strength and speed, David tossed me aside and I crashed hard against the nearest wall. My shoulder stung after it plowed into and knocked down one of Morbal's shelves, adorned with certificates and licenses. By the time I was able to scramble to my feet, Fier had shot off an ether blast that missed her target. David was on her and knocked the weapon out of her hand, punched her in the gut, picked her up and tossed her with ease through the air. She landed hard behind Morbal's desk.

"HEY!" I yelled, nearly livid beyond control. This wasn't how things were supposed to be. David was confused and wounded, acting like a wild animal. I pulled my weapon out and had a hard time aiming it at my best friend, the man who'd saved my life time and time again. But he had to be stopped. A strong stun setting should be good enough…

Amazingly, David was back in front of me, almost teleporting through the air. He knocked the pistol out of my hand and pushed me back against the wall. "See? No, Jason. You don't get it. You never see the world around you. I'll show you. By god, you're going to learn!" Another laugh.

Now I was angry, thinking they'd all been right about David. He was broken. He was dangerous. I roared and charged my best friend, wrapped my arms around him, jumped and slammed him to the ground, positioning myself on top of him. "Shut up! You don't know what you're saying!" I growled, punching him square in his jaw. Anger, fear and sadness powered my blows. I was desperate and tried to beat the failure of the situation out of my friend. "Just stop! I came here to save you!"

I reached back and swung again. This time David caught my fist in his hand and twisted my wrist. He stood up with ease and spun me around before planting his own right fist flush against my cheek. I'd been punched a lot but never that hard. I heard a crack and thought for an instant that my head had snapped clean off my neck. My vision blurred, I stumbled backward and then fell to the floor, landing flat on my ass. The whole world rocked and I nearly passed out, maybe I did for a few seconds, it was hard to tell.

By the time I could see clearly again, David was standing over me. He had all three etherpistols in his hands. My eyes darted over to Lilly who was now on the ground. He must have knocked her down and taken her weapon while I was dazed. I saw Fier was back on her feet behind David. She was panting, holding her head with one hand and leaning on the desk with the other.

Rage burned deep within my gut. Even though I couldn't forget who David was, even though I cared for him and risked everything for him, I fought to block out my feelings. He was a threat to our lives. With surprising speed, I bellowed and sprung to my feet. My right fist connected flush against David's chin with as much force as I could muster. Any other man would've fallen to the ground but not him.

Instead, David repositioned himself and quickly rammed his forehead smack against my nose. I saw my own blood splatter on David's face. He smiled, licking his lips. "This is fun."

My eyes were blurred with tears and blood but I pressed another attack, slamming my left fist into David's gut then planting my right against his face. All my efforts had such little effect I almost couldn't believe it. I felt like I was stuck in a nightmare where nothing worked, where my gun jammed at exactly the wrong moment, or my legs turned to jelly as I tried to run from some ravenous beast. I felt completely powerless.

With an oddly out of place sigh, one people make when they're bored or fed up, David dropped the three weapons at our feet, grabbed my shoulders, spun me around then held me in a tight headlock. He turned me so I faced the two women.

"Listen, Jason." David spoke right into my ear. "I see how it is. I know what you feel for them and for others. The world is trying to separate us but you're my brother. We're not going to let them stop us."

I grunted and struggled to free myself. Again, useless. My struggles only further tired me out. The headlock was cutting off the blood to my brain and the more I fought the closer I grew to passing out.

"Let him go, or I swear I'll kill you!" Fier yelled. Now she was standing on her own holding the lamp that was on the desk. She looked ready to charge and take a swing at David.

"Shut up, dummy." David hissed in a wicked yet almost happy tone. "You're such a stupid bitch, I swear."

I struggled again, against my better judgment but I couldn't stand the man calling Fier names. He held tight and continued, "You're the worst of them all. Taking us to that little island, filling our heads with your delusions. You'll never learn and I've had much better than you." I heard him laugh and guessed from Fier's glance that David gestured Lilly. "So can Jason. Hell, he already has."

"Let them go." I fought to say. "Don't hurt them, dickhead."

David eased his grip a little. "Why? I do what I want."

"Divad." Lilly said, calmly. She was standing now, staring at the man. "Let him go, right now."

Suddenly David started to quiver and he loosened his grip a little more.

Lilly stepped closer, speaking coldly and powerfully. "You're mine. You know it. I broke you on Aswain. You pledged yourself to me. I am your Mistress."

David hummed. "Ah." And threw me to the ground. "So little Miss Samantha Forrest has come back to make me her pet, huh? Sorry, babe. That spell's broken."

I looked up at my friend and rubbed my sore neck as blood continued to trickle down my face. I tried to whip up some sort of plan. It quickly became clear I was only fooling myself. I didn't know what to do. What could I do? Fight him? Kill him? He was my best friend and from our brief skirmish, it was obvious he was a lot stronger than me and borderline insane. Suddenly Kara, the shattered agent on Aswain popped into my head and then so did the naked, wildly crazy Erica. David wasn't like them. He couldn't be.

"I am your Mistress!" Lilly said in a royal, demanding tone. "You will obey!"

David reached down and picked up one of the etherpistols. "Is that so?" He aimed the weapon and stepped on the other two which were just an arm span away from me. Despite his bold tone, I could see his hand, the one holding the weapon start to shake.

I looked at Lilly, put my arm out in a 'get back' gesture and spoke in a defeated tone. "Don't. He'll hurt you."

She stopped moving closer but otherwise didn't flinch. "You can't kill me. You can't hurt me. You're mine. Not the osilea's, not Morbal's. Mine."

David drew in a deep, loud breath through his nose. He looked like he was struggling with himself.

"You can't shoot me." Lilly let out a small chuckle. "I own you. Your madness will end here and now. Your pain will empty." I saw Fier start to make her move but Lilly stopped her. "No. Stay back."

David realigned his weapon so it was pointed at Fier. "Maybe I can't kill you, Forrest, but I can kill her."

"No!" I shouted. A surge of adrenaline ripped through my veins, shooting me to my feet. I planted myself between the barrel and Fier.

Fier hissed. "Get down, Jason."

"Eff that." I said. My eyes locked on David who, to everyone's surprise, suddenly laughed.

"Oh this is just amazing." He looked at the three of us in turn. "Quite a standoff."

"Lower your weapon and give it to me." Lilly said in her cool, dreamy voice.

David's eyes were back on her and his expression went from amused to a mix of uncertainty and anger. "No. You don't rule me. No one does. I'm done being led around like a pathetic little dog. I call the shots now. I have the will."

My brain raced to put things together. Lilly was bonded with Forrest and therefore had some strange sway over David. I wasn't sure what her aims were but right now it seemed she only wanted to keep him from hurting anyone. David was shattered, yes, I had to admit it, and seemed to want me to stay with him for some insane reason. Fier wanted to kill David, seeing him as a threat.

And me… what did I want? Eff. I wanted to get Lilly to safety, help David get better and share my remaining time with Fier the way normal couples did, or at least the way couples did before the world went to hell. David was right though. This was a standoff. "What do *you* want?" I asked finally, breaking the brief silence in the room.

"I want you to stay with me." He smiled and his eyes beamed. "I'd like to kill her but I can't seem to do it." He pointed a lazy finger at Lilly then shrugged. "Would you do it for me? After all the times I saved your life? You owe me."

I balled my hands into fists and gritted my teeth. "I'm not going to hurt her. I'm not going to hurt her or Fier. So eff that."

"Thanks." David rolled his eyes then set his stare back on Lilly. "Be careful, little girl, I'm getting better and stronger all the time. I'm nearly over your mom's little spell. You stick around me and you'll get hurt. You eff with me and you'll feel pain you never dreamed, not even in your worst nightmares. I've been through it. I know what real *pain* is." He shrugged. "But I'm not going to give some sad story. That which didn't kill me only made me stronger," he tapped his left index finger on the side of his head, "and smarter."

Lilly stepped closer. "Fine. Do it, Divad. Kill me or drop to your knees like you know you want to. You willingly gave yourself to me. I know you remember. You remember how *good* it feels."

David spat. "You're not Forrest. You're just a shadow of her. You're just a spoiled little girl who thinks she can play in the big leagues. Eff you!"

My breathing hastened. Lilly was in over her head. I saw David's finger start to squeeze the trigger and panicked. "Ok, ok!" I yelled suddenly, raising my arms in the air. "Let them go and I'll stay."

The man looked at me and scoffed. "They won't leave. What are you playing at, Jason? Always trying to protect others. Always stupidly wishing for a happy, fairy tale ending? Don't be an idiot. The world doesn't work that way."

"You sound like I used to. I was so pessimistic." I started, speaking slowly. "But you taught me to have hope. You taught me to open my eyes so I could see things beyond my bad attitude." I turned to the two women. "Fier, Lilly, go. It's the only way to avoid anyone getting hurt."

Both women protested but Fier spoke first. "I'm not leaving you with this madman."

"Divad's a danger to the world." Lilly said. "He's growing more dangerous every day. He's a weapon for the coming darkness. Can't you see it? Everything he touches burns and dies. Only I can control him. I can't leave."

"Oh lord." David said. "No one and nothing controls me, you clueless twit."

"You're going to die if you stay here. Don't be stupid. Leave!" I said, growing even more frustrated.

Fier looked into my eyes as tears welled up in hers. She shook her head and hissed, speaking through her teeth. "He'll hurt you, change you. I can't take it. I won't!" The last bit was a growl.

I swallowed. "Fier, please." I gave her the best smile I could manage and failed miserably. "This is how it has to be. For now. Take Lilly out of here."

"Jason, I'm not leaving." Lilly said. "This is my purpose. Everything has a reason. My mother bonded with me for this."

David burst into laughter again. "Everything has a reason? God, women are so dumb. There's no *reason* behind anything. And you know what? I'm feeling a lot better already." He'd been progressively slouching more and more as time passed. Now he bolted straight aiming his weapon at Lilly's forehead with renewed vigor.

I quickly put myself right in front of David, pressing my chest against the barrel of his weapon. "You're NOT going to kill them!"

"Interesting." David looked into my eyes. "If this is how it's got to be, then fine. Little Forrest wants to rule me. Fier thinks she can kill me and you want to save me." He laughed. "Give a guy a chance. I'll change all your minds."

"You crazy son of a bitch." Fier slurred, kicking Morbal's dead body. "I cared for you once. But you're just as effed up as this dead controller."

"But first," David started, ignoring Fier, "we need to move somewhere a little more private." He raised his eyebrows. "We wouldn't want big bad Michael Vistaer and his little minions crashing the party."

My eyes narrowed. "What are you talking about?"

"Don't worry about it." He said, winking again. "We're going to have some fun."

I saw him quickly thumb down the power level on the etherpistol in his hand then he fired, hitting me square in my chest. I felt a jolt then everything went black.

Chapter 15

A thick, dark, smoky fog surrounded me. It was impossible to be sure but it felt like I was in a large, empty space. I wanted to cough the smoke out of my lungs even though it didn't actually bother me. I figured it was all mental.

Light came from directly ahead where David sat, quietly smiling at me. I couldn't tell if the light came from behind him, above him or what. Nothing made sense. Eventually, it dawned on me I was dreaming again.

He looked like he was waiting for me to say something but I didn't know what to say. I wasn't even sure I could speak any words at all. I felt so confused and lost, curious what my friend was doing. His hand gently patted a box that sat on the ground in front of him, resting between his legs. It looked to be made out of some sort of smooth black glass. I played with obsidian once when I was a kid, cut the hell out my hand. The box was as shiny and mysterious as the rock only it gave off a hauntingly mesmerizing glow.

My eyes moved from the box to David's face. He just stared back and looked old, beat up and tired but somehow, happy. He slowly pressed the palm of his right hand down on the top of the box and whispered one word which slowly echoed through the empty, foggy room, "Secrets."

I looked at the box and thought I heard a voice coming from it. It was difficult to make out any words at first but as time went on the voice grew to an audible whisper. It repeated itself, saying the same thing over and over. "Let me out. Let me in." All the while, two red dots appeared that eventually morphed into eyes made of flame.

My body tensed with a cold, fearful uncertainty which took a fierce grip of my heart and squeezed. Drops of cold sweat beaded up on my forehead while others ran down my spine. The box hissed, a bit louder than before. "Let me out. Let me in."

A strange sensation began tickling the back of my head. It felt like a tiny, freezing, sharp icicle was digging through my skull, slowly driving itself into my brain. The feeling sent odd, sickening, tickling ripples through my body. I shivered but kept my gaze fixed on the box.

"Let me out. Let me in!" The voice grew bold and powerful while the red eyes blazed even brighter than Olivia's when she was excited. I couldn't tell if the thing was sinister or not and could only stare, curiously into the wavy red flames, tucked deep within the dark glass.

It spoke again, loud enough to hurt my ears. "LET ME OUT! LET ME IN!"

The sound jarred me from my nearly hypnotized state. I blinked and pulled back, collecting myself before finally speaking in as brave a tone as I could manage, "Why? What do you want?"

The eyes vanished and then I woke up.

"Ah, there we go!" David said in as merry a voice as I'd ever heard him use.

I fought to get my bearings and had to look up to meet his eyes. He was standing over me, smiling and breathing heavily. I swallowed and looked down, realizing I was sitting in a chair at what looked like a very elaborate dining room table. The thing was rectangular, long, and black. I wasn't sure what it was made out of but it looked heavy and expensive. It dawned on me the table appeared to be made of the same material as the box from my dream. "What? Where are we?"

David patted me on my back. "Safe."

"This is one of Morbal's houses." Lilly's voice called out, demanding my attention. She seemed as cool and calm as ever, seated at the table to my left. I did notice, though, that her usually bright blue eyes looked oddly dull, tired and heavy. I turned my still groggy head and saw Fier sitting to my right, across from Lilly. I was at the head of the table with an empty chair at the opposite end. No doubt that was David's chair. "Most don't know about this one. It's like a secret hideaway." Lilly went on.

"That's right." David said approvingly. "Nice, private and sort of cozy."

My eyes quickly glanced over the area, taking everything in. All the walls were painted red, decorated with more of Morbal's demented artwork made of skulls, death and decay. There were also sculptures placed here and there on marble pillars. The images were of nightmarish, twisted humans and creatures showing tortured expressions. I couldn't believe it when I saw a pair of shrunken heads each atop their own thin platforms in the corner of the creepy room. I knew better than to doubt their authenticity. Cozy? Good god.

At that point, as I tried to rub my throbbing head, I realized I was loosely bound to my chair. My legs were tied and so was my left wrist. I could lift my right hand just far enough to place it on the table. A slew of unfavorable memories threatened to flood my brain. The set up was oddly familiar to the way I was tied up during my daily therapy sessions at the asylum. I looked at David. "Really? You're keeping us bound? What the hell?"

"I'll let you loose after you calm down and relax." He said with a nod. He shrugged. "Sorry for stunning you but it was the easiest way to get you here. You might've come on your own but I didn't feel like taking the chance." He turned to Fier and chuckled. "I'm not at all sorry for knocking you out.

You definitely would've been trouble. Carrying you both was a chore but I managed." He turned to Lilly. "Thank you, little mistress for being so cooperative to come on your own." David laughed.

He continued. "I took your weapons and phones for safe keeping. We wouldn't want you inviting any unwelcome guests. This party is by reservation only." He smiled at us, turning lastly to Fier.

I looked at her and saw the cold stare she aimed directly at David's face. It didn't take a genius to see the woman was wholeheartedly pissed. She was stuck in the same contraption I was in, tied to her chair with her right hand a bit more free. "Eff you." She spat.

It also dawned on me that the bullet proof vests the three of us had been wearing were all removed. I sat at the table in my jeans, sneakers and a simple white undershirt. Fier wore a somewhat skimpy red tank top that showed off her attractive skin and lengthy, toned arms. Lilly wore a long sleeve, robin's egg blue, cotton shirt on that she'd been wearing under her vest.

"Sure." David nodded. "If you want too. I'm easy." He looked at me and moved his gray eyebrows up and down then focused back on the Captain before I could respond. He knew full well I wasn't happy with his innuendo. "Seriously though, I probably made a mistake bringing you here. You're too uptight. Ah well, it doesn't really matter and could prove entertaining." David rested a hand on Fier's shoulder.

"Get your hand off her." I rumbled. My patience was at its end. Although I loved David like a brother, right now I didn't trust him. "Let her go; her and Lilly."

He took his hand off Fier's shoulder and rolled his eyes. "And also," he continued, all but ignoring me, "Jason likes having you around. When he's happy, I'm happy." David gestured Lilly, lazily waving a hand at her. "She seems pleased to be here. She doesn't even need any restraints. Right?"

I turned and noticed the young woman wasn't bound like Fier and me. The realization grew more disturbing the deeper I thought about it. I was partly envious of her freedom and another part suspected her again of betraying me. Was she with David all along? Was this some sort of plan?

I flexed my muscles and gritted my teeth, trying to tug my way to freedom. "Ok, god damn it, let us loose!" I pulled and struggled against the tough plastic ropes that were wrapped around my wrists and ankles. The damn bindings hardly budged. I let out a defeated breath and looked at David again.

He shook his head. "You finished? I told you I'd let you loose after you calmed down." He cursed under his breath. "Aren't you ever be happy? You found me. Isn't that what you wanted?"

"I want to help you." My eyes narrowed. "David. You're seriously effed up. What the hell are you doing here?"

"Good. You want to help. That's great. I want to help you too. We're unstoppable together, Jason. Remember the break out? When we killed Forate? The attack on Krane and the assault on Aswain's power plant? We were perfect together!" His impossibly large smile slowly faded. "Oh and one more time. Please. Call me Divad. David is gone."

"What does that even mean?" I snarled and fought against my restraints all over again. "Can you even hear yourself? You're losing your mind, just like Kara."

"I'm not restrained because I wouldn't allow it." Lilly said in a neutral tone, bringing my thoughts back. It took an effort to realize she was just now responding to David's comments from before.

I looked at her. "What? Wouldn't allow it? But you let us get tied up?" I gestured Fier and myself.

Lilly looked into my eyes for a half second before her gaze shifted back to David. "Why don't you tell Jason about how you were just inside his head before he woke up? How you were trying to plant ideas and how you were picking through his memories? What're you afraid of? Why don't you tell us about what you've done to all those people back at the asylum? What about Everiel?"

"Inside my head?" I asked, suddenly feeling betrayed and embarrassed.

"What did you do to the others?" Fier asked. "The People at Morbal's?"

Divad ignored my hard stare and my questions. Instead he looked down on Fier. "I'm sure it'll be hard for a dimwitted, riled up, little female like you to understand. But I helped them. I freed them."

I growled, angry with being ignored and even more pissed at the insults he hurled at Fier. She seemed to move past it and asked, "How? How'd you free them?" Her eyes darted back and forth between Lilly and David.

"In Doctor Morbal's absence, I've taken over the clear trade." He raised his eyebrows and smiled, biting his bottom lip, looking as proud and happy as could be. "I made a few improvements to the stuff so now," he laughed, seemingly beyond thrilled with his work, "it doesn't just make you feel great, it changes you're whole outlook on life. There's a little piece of me in all those people now and they're free from all their old concerns and fears. They see beyond the lies of a controlled civilization." He chuckled. "Ha! *Civilization*. What a joke."

I swallowed, too confused now to be angry. "But you hate clear. You know how it's made. That's what set you off back on Aswain. They torture hailiorea to make the stuff!"

"Hey, I stopped the torturing." David finally looked at me. "Doesn't that count for anything? Morbal had more than enough supplies backed up to keep the factory running a long time." He smiled, wickedly and rocked on the balls of his feet. "It's all free now, so everyone, rich and poor, young and old, sexy and ugly can get their fair share. No rules, no class system, all fair."

"You're poisoning the world with your own tainted blood," Lilly accused in a matter of fact tone that carried a hint of sadness.

"The world was already poisoned." David stated. "I'm making it better."

"You've contaminated it and now you're sending it around the world." She went on before pausing to shake her head, giving me a moment to absorb everything. "You really think you're doing this for yourself, for the greater good?" She grinned, ironically. "You're so wrong."

David laughed with a manic sparkle in his eye. The man's demeanor completely shifted in the span of a couple seconds. "Lilly, Claire, Samantha… whatever you want to be called. You really think you're something special don't you?" He glided around the table, moved next to the young woman then dropped down to one knee so they were at eye level. "You had me once. Then you died. You failed. Now," he cupped her head in his hands and I saw fear, real fear in Lilly's eyes for the first time.

"David!" I called. "Don't."

"If I wanted to, I could squeeze all the yummy, juicy life from your little body." He spoke with clenched teeth, visually seething with anger and hatred. "You have no power over me. Now you're mine." The last word was a low, rumbling growl.

"Enough! David, stop!" I shouted.

He turned around and abruptly slapped my head. The hit was hard enough to nearly knock me and the chair over. "My name is Divad."

I realigned myself and cut my eyes around to look at Fier. Her chest was heaving up and down, her jaw was set and her eyes bounced back and forth between David and me. I looked my friend in his eyes then spoke in a cool, threatening tone. "If I'm loose the next time you hit me, mothereffer, you better kill me."

He laughed heartily and placed his hands on his stomach. "Oh, I love you, Jason." He wiped tears of laughter from his eyes. "I love you so much! It's true. I'd be much better off if I didn't but I can't lie to myself." He squeezed my shoulder and gave me a little shake then headed off toward what looked like the kitchen. "Just remember. DIVAD!" He yelled, raising a pointed index finger into the air.

Holy Christ. How could I be so angry and distrustful of David while at the same time be so relieved and happy to see him. I felt trapped on a bumpy rollercoaster, like the old, broken down deathtraps my brother, Mark, used to sneak me onto at fairs when we were kids. The ups and downs hit me when I least expected them leaving me confused, thrilled and sick to my stomach.

There were so many questions I had to ask I didn't even know where to start. It was hard trying to manage just one clear thought. The air was thick and heavy, pressing down on me the same way it did at David's mother's house. Only here it was worse. "Ok fine." I said finally. "Divad. What the eff is going on? What're you trying to do?"

"Revolution is going on, buddy." He spoke as he waltzed into the kitchen with a very noticeable spring in his step.

I locked eyes with Fier and she shook her head, whispering, "We have to get out of here."

David, no Divad called from the other room. "Or didn't you notice?" A laugh. "The world is ripe for the taking. Thanks in part to the weak, cowardly controllers, that pussy August Cross, the so called resistance and that moron rebel, Vistaer."

He came back into the room carrying a large bowl of something steamy that smelled like cheese. As Divad walked past the three of us, he filled our bowls with generous portions of macaroni and cheese, yes, I couldn't believe it… macaroni and cheese. To top things off, we were each given bottles of beer.

Nothing, absolutely nothing made sense. It was just like the dream, hell all the dreams I'd been having lately. Things were becoming more insane every day. Damn, the world made more sense during my time in Morbal's asylum. At least there the bastards had a purpose. Here, everything seemed pointless. As infuriating and frustrating as it all was though, at the same time I was relieved to have finally found my friend, even in his condition. Yep, damn roller coaster ride.

Divad finished filling his own bowl then sat down and started downing scoops of the macaroni into his mouth. He looked around and raised an eyebrow. "Eat up. Don't worry, this stuff is clean. None of that contaminated garbage Tehlasrin feeds the masses." He talked while he chewed. "Can you believe all that crap? The poison they put in our food, water and the air? God, they're so desperate to control us. Makes me sick."

The last thing I felt like doing was eating. My stomach was twisted in knots. I sighed, now knowing why my right hand had a little more freedom. My crazy ass friend wanted to feed us. "What happened on that island" I asked, quickly, before the thought vanished from my spinning head.

"Everiel?" He asked, looking around at the three of us.

I nodded and gave a 'no duh' look. "Yea, Everiel."

Divad smacked his lips, "It blew up."

"You did that." Lilly said in a soft voice.

He glared at her. "Oh? Did I?" Then he smiled. "You don't know anything."

"Were you there when it blew?" I asked, grabbing my beer without thinking and taking a drink. It was hard to do so with such limited mobility but I managed.

Divad looked pleased I'd taken a drink. I glanced at Fier who looked quite the opposite. Her icy stare was aimed at me, eyes like daggers. He shrugged. "That's all in the past."

"From there you went and met Erica Wood." I pressed.

The man across from me set his fork down, slumped his shoulders and sighed. "Yes, then I visited my mother and sisters. Happy? Or do you want a nicely packaged chronology of my entire life?"

"Actually, that would be great." I said with attitude. "Nothing makes sense. I met your mother. Lilly and I were there. She's crazy, tried to kill us."

Divad laughed, nearly choking on his food. "She's always been high spirited." He picked up his bottle and gave me a light salute before downing a gulp. "Damn, that's good beer."

"You did that to your mother. You drove her insane." Lilly accused. "And before that, you hurt Erica."

"You know, you're really boring me, girl." Divad said, setting his drink down. He looked around at us again. "Will you all EFFING EAT? I don't cook often so take what you can get."

I don't know why but I took in a few scoops of the food. It tasted ok but the flavor of the food was the least of my concerns. Lilly and Fier did likewise.

"I had to see my mother, Jason." Divad spoke with a full mouth. The sort of thing usually annoyed the hell out of me but right now I was so far over the edge I hardly even noticed.

"Why?" I asked.

The man considered me for a moment. "Hailiorea are strange. I learned we can unlock some of our strength by, um," he gave a strange smile, like a kid who'd found a hidden stash of chocolate, "connecting with our parents."

"How'd you learn about that?" I asked. Divad shrugged. I looked at Fier who stared at her food, shaking her head. Her jaw was clenched so tight I was afraid she might shatter her own teeth.

When I turned to Lilly I saw her grimace. "You were after a boon."

I furrowed my brow. "A what?"

"Boon." Divad said, merrily. "We can pull some unlocked energy to the surface especially from blood relatives who've been unaware of their own traits. It's like they've been sitting on a gold mine all their lives and had no idea. I needed to do it. I thought it would help." He pointed his fork at me before I could ask what he meant by 'help.' "We should find your parents. I did some research. They're still alive in the old Detroit area."

"Why?" I asked again. "So I can turn them into dangerous lunatics like your mom?"

"Don't be a dick." Divad said the words in a way that sucked the air from my lungs. The tone and the way he said it reminded me of the man I knew, the one I wanted to save. I studied how he was now; dangerous, impulsive, disturbed, erratic, seemingly insane, secretive, mysterious, forceful and oddly aged. This was what I came back for. Eff...

"I didn't *turn* my mother into anything." He went on. "I helped her grow and she couldn't handle it. It's her fault, not mine. She was weak. And you know what? Even if it was my fault, I don't effing care. I'm free now." He nodded then scooped another forkful of food while studying his plate. "And you will be too. Soon."

"Why do you look so old?" I threw the blunt question out there, again while it was fresh in my head. I think everyone was more than done hearing about his screwed up mother or any more BS about me being 'free.'

Divad raised his eyebrows like the question caught him off guard. "There's no simple way to answer that so I'll just tell you. You won't believe me though."

"Tell him." Lilly said while she dug the prongs of her fork through some macaroni.

He looked at her and made an annoyed face. "Will you shut your god damned yap?" He turned to me. "How can you stand this bitch? Jesus, both of them." Divad waved his fork between Lilly and Fier. "Rude and ruder."

I only squinted, not pleased with the continued insults. In fact, my brain imagined taking that fork Divad was waving around and sticking it through his cheek.

He huffed. "Fine. To answer your question, I've grown up. I've seen lots of things, learned the way the world works and became stronger."

Fier sighed and tossed her fork into her bowl making a series of clanging sounds. "This is ridiculous. What do you want with us? Just get it over with."

"Hush." Divad said, raising his index finger. "Put simply. I've been to hell and back. I don't know. It seems little miss know-it-all here has the answers." He nodded toward Lilly. "The travel was outside time so to speak. It felt like a couple months but was really a couple decades but here... only a couple minutes." He grabbed his beer again and shook his head before drinking. "Messed up stuff."

I listened, trying to decide if he was being honest or had completely lost his mind. He did age, a lot, so there was evidence something bizarre happened. "So you're telling me, you're telling us you actually went to Hell?"

"It wasn't Hell as we define it." Lilly commented. "He was pulled into the osilea's dimension."

Fier growled. "This is useless. It's all bull. I can't take anymore." She looked at me. "He obviously aged from some sort of chemical reaction. Either he did it to himself or that crazy son of a bitch Morbal did it to him. Hell. Give me a break."

"My body aged and the place took its toll." David spoke in a labored tone before turning to Fier. "What's your effing problem? You can't handle learning about anything outside the pitiful little box you call reality? You afraid? So desperate to get back to Aswain and play the almighty Captain? Cross's little slut?" He raised his eyebrows, pausing a second. "Just relax and shut your mouth or I'll stun you again. Got it?"

"No." I said, uncontrollably, feeling my blood pressure rise.

Divad smiled. "Listen. Things are going to change. I'm offering you all a chance to make it in the world that's coming. If you want to survive you better wise up and listen to me."

"Why?" I asked. "Why do you even care about us?"

He belched then took another drink. "I told you. I've got a soft spot, a weakness and, SUPRISE, you're it." Divad pointed a sturdy finger at me and narrowed his eyes. Then he smiled. "We're friends, nothing will change that."

"Ok, so what about Fier and Lilly?" I pressed.

Divad looked at the women and made a dismissive 'pft' sound with his lips. "Well I could say I care because they're both so devilishly sexy. Really, god damn. So hot, strong and good looking. Those bodies…" He licked his lips then snapped out of the brief lust filled thoughts. "But no. They're here, unharmed because you wish it that way. Everything I've done has been for you and me."

"I'm here because I choose to be." Lilly said. "Prove me wrong. Hurt me."

He pointed his fork at her and spoke in a foreboding tone. "Don't tempt me."

"And I'm here because don't want to lose another friend." Fier said.

"That sounds about right." Divad said. "Though I thought we were friends too, Fier." He laughed. "No? Fine then, whatever."

"Yes," Fier said, "we were friends but you let yourself get effed over."

Divad sighed, mostly ignoring her. "In the new world there won't be any order or rules. There won't be any laws or control freaks who knock others down so they can prop themselves up."

"So you're still fighting the GU?" I asked, desperate to reach some sort of common ground.

"Of course!" Divad smirked. "I'm fighting everything. It's all got to go. It's all got to burn. The only answer is pure anarchy. No rules, expectations or predictions. Blatant, blissful chaos. True freedom. Some people won't be able to handle it. They'll either need to take my clear, wise up or simply go away." He sighed in a dreamy way. "Just think of it. Real freedom. By whatever gods there may be, it'll be beautiful."

Fier scoffed, resting her head as best she could in her right hand.

The man scowled. "You don't understand. You still believe in society." Divad made quote marks with his fingers when he said the last word. "You put your trust in governments. What a child, Wren. Grow up. You think things can go back to the way they were? Well then you're a fool, too." He sat up straight, beaming. "Even during the *good* times the world was a breeding ground for corruption and greed. No. What I'm after, what the world is going to be, is fair. Fair and free. You'll see… or you'll die." He focused back on his food and shrugged his shoulders. "Either way it's going to be one hell of a ride."

I thought about what he said then skipped ahead. "So, what? We all live like wild animals? No economy, no order? People will starve. It'll be a whole different kind of hell." I shook my head, glancing at Fier and Lilly for support. "Besides, humans, as messed up as we can be, aren't built that way. We're not made to live alone. We form families, packs, groups, nations."

"Well," Divad chuckled, "then they'll be destroyed too. You're logic makes sense, though." He giggled. "You're smarter than I remember. You see anarchy eventually giving way to the strong bullying and ruling the weak. That sounds right, in an outdated way." His eyes locked onto mine. "But you don't have all the information. You don't know."

It was madness, all of it. "You're just…"

"Insane." Fier finished. She turned to me. "I told you. Didn't you even hear him talking about how he's drugged everyone with some new super crazy kind of clear? He's effing nuts." She shook her head and looked back at Divad. "So this is what you've become? This is your *grand* revelation? Anarchy? You're type has been around forever. You're nothing special. You haven't gained any profound wisdom. You're just a delusional man who's going to die extremely disappointed."

Lilly drew in a deep breath. "He's not an anarchist. He's a shattered servant of the osilea." She looked at Divad and shook her head. "He just doesn't know it yet."

"Oh, I don't think my type has been around before, Wren. But I'm glad you joined the conversation." Divad smiled and then glared at Lilly. It looked like he was about to continue when a doorbell sounded. He raised his voice and turned to face a doorway that led out of the dinning room. "Insect! Check the door."

I made a confused face. "Insect?"

Divad rolled his eyes. "You'll see."

A moment later a uniformed Tehlasrin officer entered the room, setting off all sorts of alarms in my head. My eyes, which I presumed were wide as saucers, beamed back and forth between the soldier and Divad. My disturbed friend only smiled.

The officer looked to be in his late forties with thinning hair, pointed sideburns and a thick moustache. Another man, in dirty, civilian clothes, stood behind the soldier. He looked to be about my age, a couple inches shorter than David with a thin but muscular build. He had buzzed short blond hair, dark eyes and a beat up, black and blue face. He seemed like a normal guy except for the black eyes and bruised jaw. He glanced at the three of us in turn. When he looked at Lilly, the woman gasped. "My name's Isaac. Not Insect."

"Hello, Major." Divad said. "You have something for the Doctor?"

The officer nodded. "Yes sir." He eyed Lilly, Fier and me. "Is it safe to speak?"

"Speak." Divad ordered. "These are my guests and friends of Dr. Morbal."

"Very good." The Major said, though still with a suspicious look. No wonder, seeing as Fier and I were bound to our chairs. "We have reports that an expeditionary force of Ark's has moved into the area. We believe a strike on the city is imminent."

I turned to Divad who raised an eyebrow. He was suddenly all business, looking cool and calculating. "We'll see about that." He cocked his head to the side. "Where are our forces?"

"Stationed a click away, Sir. Major Yee reports she has our squad ready to move in." The man stood straight as an arrow. "Shall we engage?"

Divad looked at me and winked. I didn't know how to take the gesture. "No. Tell her to hold tight for now. Understood?"

"Understood, Sir."

"Do you have an intel file for the Doctor?" Divad asked.

The man nodded and quickly presented a small information disk. "Yes, Sir." The disk was quickly snatched by the young man standing near the officer. He smiled and waved it in the air.

"Thank you, Major." Divad said in a slightly labored tone. "Are all operations at the rehabilitation center still running smoothly?"

"Yes, sir." The officer confirmed. "The Doctor's next shipment will be ready for delivery soon. Our teams are overseeing everything."

"Good. You may leave." Divad gave a half assed salute.

Fier turned to the soldier. "Morbal's dead, you know." She gestured Divad. "He killed him."

I whipped my head around to look at the officer. His face went ghost white. "What?" He looked at Divad, his hand reaching for the pistol on his hip. "You said he's resting and handed operation command over to you. I should've known."

If I'd tried, I couldn't have said 'one Mississippi' before Divad launched from his seat, flew across the room produced a knife from his pocket and drove it into the Major's throat. The guy died gurgling and choking on his own blood as he slid down to the ground, bleeding out a puddle on the floor.

Lilly gasped and I grimaced, turning to look at Fier. She closed her eyes and shook her head.

"Good one, Wren." Divad said, throwing the knife and sticking its blade into the wall behind the chair he'd been seated at. "The man was a useful tool and followed orders well. Insect, clean up the mess." He snatched the info disk out of the other's hand.

The man started scooping up the dead body. He looked at Fier, Lilly and me. "Isaac. My name's Isaac."

Divad abruptly hauled off and punched Isaac in his face. "Shut up!" From there he went back to his seat, sat down and continued eating. The rest of us remained silent for a piece of time while Isaac worked.

"What's the matter?" Divad asked finally. "What? Curious about Insect?"

Fier swallowed and spoke with as much attitude as she could. "What is he, your slave? I thought you said people would be free."

I followed her lead, trying to ignore the murder we just witnessed. "Yea. And what are you doing? Leading Morbal's forces? You just said you were against any 'leaders' or control."

Divad groaned. "Means to an end. No, he's not my slave. He's more like my baggage. I hate the bastard but he's here."

"You can't kill him can you?" Lilly asked. "Just like you can't kill me."

He rubbed his head. "I'm getting real sick of all your questions. It doesn't matter where I've been or what I've been through. I'm here now." He slapped his chest with both hands. "This is who I am."

"Then who is he?" I asked, gesturing Isaac. I hoped Divad wasn't shattering people himself. I couldn't take it if he'd become like Forrest or Morbal.

Divad looked at me and I could tell he was getting annoyed. "He used to work for Ark but now he works with me."

"Steven Ark, the controller?"

He sighed again. "Yes."

"He's connected to the osilea like you." Lilly said in a startled tone as if she were reading a book and had just come across a shocking realization. "Xolzv." Her eyes grew wide as she looked at Fier and me.

"What?" Fier asked, confused as hell.

"I'm not connected to anything." Divad growled.

Isaac came back to the room with a mop and bucket then started cleaning up the blood. I watched Lilly study him.

Desperate for more information, I spoke. "I've heard that name before. Xolzv. Erica mentioned it before she died."

Isaac laughed and I looked at him. He was staring back at Lilly, smiling. The look was especially twisted.

Divad growled and was on Isaac again, pounding the smaller man to the floor, beating him into submission. The sounds and sights were barbaric and painfully disturbing. "I didn't say you could laugh or even look at my guests! You piece of…" Isaac curled up into a fetal position and took several kicks to his back.

"STOP!" I yelled, unable to bear seeing a defenseless man being beaten.

Divad turned to me and the wicked look on his face subsided. "Don't fee sorry for Insect. The prick is a talented healer. He fixed up your broken nose while you were out and cleaned the blood off." He looked back at Isaac and spit on him. "His healing stings like a bitch though, not like those fancy little hailiorea doctors on Aswain."

To my surprise, Isaac uncurled himself and smiled. He stood up with a labored grunt, nodding at me. "I do what I can."

"You're just as cruel as the rest of them." Fier said to Divad.

He looked at her. "You don't know anything." He'd said that before. "None of you. You'll see though."

"Right." I said bluntly, sick to death of being in the dark. My head had a moment of clarity so I quickly spat out what I could. "Then tell us. What happened to your mom? What did you do to Erica? Who's Xolzv? Why are you torturing Isaac? What does that new clear really do to people? What's your plan?"

Divad just looked at me with an unreadable face. It was easier for him to hide his thoughts behind the scars and long, dirty, messy hair. I was good at reading his expressions before but now he looked and acted so different I didn't know what the hell he was thinking. His eyes narrowed.

"Damn it, answer me!" I fought my restraints again.

"I'm done answering questions." Divad said in an oddly calm tone. "What about you? Why don't you tell some of your secrets?"

I furrowed my brow. "What? What secrets?"

"Why don't you tell Fier about how you and Lilly had sex not once but twice on your little trip? Huh?" Divad smiled after seeing the horrified look on my face.

A wave of heat ran through my body and even though I didn't want to look at her, my eyes were drawn to Fier's face. The woman stared with her mouth open, looking at me like I'd just sprouted horns and a tail.

"See." Divad said, followed by a laugh. "It's not fun having others pry into your personal life, is it?"

"How do you know about that?" I asked.

Lilly sighed. "He was in your head and read your thoughts."

"Shut up." Fier hissed. "Just shut your mouth."

"You're not the only one playing mind games, little mistress." Divad said. He looked over the three of us. "I'm leaving you to Insect. Don't try anything or he'll stun you. He's a masochistic push over but does enjoy dishing out pain here and there."

The other man smiled and showed off one of our etherpistols.

"And he doesn't sleep." Divad went on.

"Where are you going?" I asked, surprised I even had the strength to speak. Fier was still looking at me, now with tears in her eyes. The weight from her stare made it hard to breathe. I felt like a piece of trash at the bottom of a super city dump.

Divad looked at me and smiled. "Don't worry." He shook his head in an expression of disbelief. "Damn it's good to see you."

-

Isaac eventually moved the three of us into the sickly decorated house's living room where we were sat down on one of Morbal's grossly expensive, plush suede couches. Fier and I still had our hands bound and Lilly remained free. The young woman showed no signs of wanting to fight or escape.

The room was big with lots of open space even though it was well furnished and decorated in a sadistic, horrific way. A large fireplace took up most of one wall and several windows showed the Sun was beginning to set. I hadn't realized so much time had passed.

We sat in silence for a while with Isaac keeping a lazy watch. I pressed Lilly. Not only to gain whatever information she had but also to keep from thinking about how betrayed Fier felt and how angry she was with me. "Alright." I started, staring into her blue eyes. "What do you know about Divad?"

Lilly cut her eyes around to look at Isaac.

"Forget him!" I said, raising my voice. "Tell me."

"Yes." Isaac called from the doorway that led back into the kitchen. "Tell him."

She turned, looking back and forth between Fier and me. "I had to be here, close to him so I could pick up on his thoughts and aims."

"You're little go at controlling him totally sucked." Fier spat.

Lilly shook her head. "Not really."

I saw Fier shake her head and squint her eyes at the other woman. "You're an effing idiot. Just like your mother."

"Fier." I said in as soft a tone as I could muster.

"Don't." She started, looking at me and snorting. "I'm not in the mood to hear you take sides with *her*."

My guilt started to give way to anger. "Well too bad. I'm not going to roll over and play dead. Not now, not ever." She gritted her teeth and sighed, turning away from me. "So what? Lilly and were together. It's done. That was before I knew she was Forrest's daughter and before I knew you had feelings for me."

"You're an idiot too." Fier said with a slight quiver in her voice.

I could feel my temperature rise. "God damn it, this isn't the time. Stop acting like a baby. We had sex."

She shook her head, violently, trying to shake the words out of her brain.

"Yea, we did but we're past that." I worked to calm myself down. "What claim or right do you have anyways? We weren't together. If you had such strong feelings for me, you should've told me when you had the chance." I'll be damned, the same could've been said about me but I tried not to think about it.

Fier turned toward me, locking her eyes onto mine. "You're an asshole, Jason."

"Oh yea?" I snapped back. "Well congratulations on finally figuring that out. I never hid who I was. If you're going to pout about it then go ahead but remember where we are and try to be of some god damn use to us."

"I know where I am!" Fier was almost yelling now. "I'm here because of you. I'm here because I fell for you back on Aswain, because I couldn't stand the thought of you wasting your life on such a stupid thing as helping someone who can't be helped. I should've told you? If you weren't such a blind, self centered prick you would've seen it."

"STOP IT!" Lilly yelled and both Fier and I were startled by how powerful her voice became. "This is what he wants. This is *It* wants, what the darkness wants, what the osilea wants, what Xolzv wants! Can't you see that?"

"David was right." Fier started. "You don't know anything. Maybe you're crazier than all the rest of them."

Lilly collected herself. "I'm not crazy. I'm a hailiorea. Do you even know why we exist?" Neither of us answered. "We exist to fight the darkness. To serve life. To serve the only thing that goes on immortally. Love."

I breathed deeply, not believing or agreeing with Lilly but unable to debate her.

"The only way to remove the darkness is with light." Lilly said before giving up and leaning back into her seat. "Any fool knows that, only you've both forgotten."

Fier looked like she was about to speak but stopped herself. Instead she looked at me. Her face was an awful blend of pain and sadness.

I felt sick to my stomach. I wanted to cave, to tell her how much I cared for her. Eff it, I wanted to tell her I loved her but I just wasn't strong enough. I was a coward.

"You two need to get over this." Lilly started again. "Everything Divad does, every move he makes has a purpose. We're all here for a reason. He acts like he behaves on a whim or that nothing matters to him but it's a lie. A lie he's trying to convince himself of. But deep down, he knows the truth."

"What truth?" I asked, finding my tongue.

Lilly looked at me. "That he's broken. He's shattered. No hailiorea has ever come back after they've been shattered. But deep down, he's raging against it. Deep down, he's desperate for his own freedom. His own salvation."

"You knew all this all along?" Fier asked with attitude.

The younger woman shook her head. "No. I'm learning. That's why I'm here. I'm here to stop him. Divad plans to do unspeakable things. He's inadvertently serving the dark, he may even be its embodiment but he's deliberately ignorant to it." She paused and then spoke quietly. "Like I said, that's why I had sex with you. You and David, or Divad rather are connected. I spent that time with you to better understand and read him. I'm sorry." She looked at Fier. "Jason's feelings for me are nothing like the feelings he has for you. You know that."

My thoughts were split between Fier and David, Divad. I didn't know which one to devote my energy to. The man who I'd returned to save may very well be gone for good but Fier was here and the same as she's always been.

I looked at her not at all sure what to say. "Fier. I -"

"Ok." Isaac called from the other side of the room. His voice made me jump. "You all seem so interested in Divad I know you'll love to watch this."

I looked at him not at all liking the arrogant, wicked tone of his voice. "What?"

The man headed over to a large telescreen and inserted a disk into the media player. "This. Divad's therapy sessions. They're so wonderful."

I shook my head. "No. No, you can't make us watch. Don't turn that crap on."

"Oh," Isaac nodded his head, "I will make you. Divad tolerates you but that doesn't mean I have to. You will watch."

I turned to Lilly then locked my eyes on Fier. She looked horrified, confused, sad, hurt and almost, on some strange level, at peace. That was until Isaac started talking. Lilly stared at the man with a curious expression.

"I won't watch it." Fier said. "Who wants to watch someone being tortured?"

Isaac punched a couple buttons then turned around, aiming his stolen etherpistol at us. "If you don't watch, I'll torture one of the others, the one each of you cares for most." He tucked the gun away and pulled out an especially lethal looking blade. "I'll cut you and cut you again, then heal you and cut you some more. It's wonderful being able to heal others, isn't it?"

I drew in a deep breath wondering if I could take Isaac out even though I was bound. Divad seemed to believe the man would be able to keep us in check so I guessed I didn't have much of a chance. Still anything sounded better than sitting here for the guy's amusement.

"I see the wheels spinning, Sworn." Isaac said with a laugh. "Any of you try anything and the stuff you see in this video will be like a fun filled amusement park compared to what I'll do to you."

"Why the eff do you even help *him*?" Fier asked with a raised tone. "He beats you, hurts you and abuses you."

Isaac smiled. "Divad isn't abusing me. He's raging against his own slavery. He's such a fool." The man let out a sick, joyous laugh followed by a moan mixed with a sigh. "He's growing into his intended role. He's a bigger slave than all the rest of you. He's a slave to his own delusions, a slave to Lilly and a slave to Xolzv. I'm here to make sure he stays that way."

I looked at Fier and she looked back at me. "I'm sorry." The words seeped out from my lips.

"Shush! No talking!" Isaac said, gleefully. "Anyone talks and I'll gag you. The movie's starting."

I braced myself as the video played. Watching David's torment was just like the sessions Morbal and Forate used to put me though only this was much worse. Not only was a good man who'd done nothing wrong being tortured and tormented but that man happened to be the one I loved like a brother.

The atrocities Morbal put him through were god awful and I only wished the rat faced bastard was alive again so I could kill him myself. In the video, which seemed to never end, David wailed in agony, cutting himself, scratching himself, beating his own body, especially his genitals. The doctor had picked up where Forrest left off and took devilish delight in his subject's pain.

On Morbal's command, David was forced to cut and mutilate others, mostly women. He cried in horror the whole time, begging for his own death. I realized then that this was the same thing Morbal had done to Forate, turning the large, beast of a man into his sadistic, ruthless, uncaring plaything.

Fier quivered in disgust as we watched the video. Lilly remained motionless like nothing surprised her. I nearly vomited, especially when Fier lost what little of the macaroni and cheese she'd eaten. By the time the video was over all I wanted to do was kill Isaac but I was too deflated and powerless to even move.

In the end, I searched desperately for something… I turned to Fier as a sole spark of light glittered in my brain. "David won in the end." I spoke, barely above a whisper. "He beat Morbal, killed him. He wasn't taken like Forate."

She looked at me and smiled even though her face was grim and sapped of color. I reached out with my bound hands and found Fier's. Our fingers interlocked with each others and for the briefest of moments the crazy world around me felt tolerable. That was, at least, until Isaac spoke.

"Hey!" he said, not at all happy with even the slightest positive spin anyone could put on the video. "Everything Divad has done is according to Xolzv's plan. You remember that." He nodded and smirked. "Time for you three to sleep."

I looked at the man, as full of rage as my body could manage. "I hate you."

"Good." Isaac smiled and aimed the etherpistol at me then fired. The pain knocked me into unconsciousness.

Chapter 16

"Drink this." Divad shoved a hot cup of what smelled like coffee into my numb, sleepy hands. Some of the liquid spilled over the rim and burned my fingers, waking them up. The sting brought to my attention that my hands weren't bound anymore. My eyes drifted up to meet his stare. He nodded, expectantly. "Hurry."

I took a drink and fought to gather my wits, willing away the cobwebs that cluttered my brain. I'd been dreaming again before Divad jolted me awake with a hard shove to my head and water sprayed on my face. Normally I would've been furious but right now, it didn't matter.

The dream was as strange as the rest, I remembered. This time I was in my parents' old house, the one they had when I was a kid. Only I was an adult and I was alone. That was until a group of faceless men broke in and somehow planted strange black seeds beneath the house's floorboards. The seeds sprouted twisted black vines that reached the ceiling… It was odd but whatever, it wasn't important.

I drank more of the bland coffee and looked around Morbal's living room. Lilly and Fier were both asleep, each on their own couch. Fier's face showed an especially painful expression and I could see her eyes moving beneath her lids. She was dreaming too, and not happily it seemed. Lilly was silent and still, laying in a mummy's pose. Arms crossed over her chest, face calm and expressionless. She almost looked dead. I panicked for the briefest of moments until I finally saw the young woman's chest move. She was breathing, she was alive. But… for how long? I looked at my unbound wrists again and weighed my options.

David stepped up to me, smiling. I glanced at him and then looked around the room again. Windows showed it was dark outside. "What time is it?"

"Two a.m." Divad said, joyfully. Then he tossed a helmet and what looked like a gas mask at me. "Get dressed. Full assault gear. It's time to rock and roll."

I swallowed. "Two? I've been asleep that long?"

"Insect drugged you, all three of you." Divad spit and looked off in the distance. I bet the other man was standing there but I didn't feel like checking. The last thing I wanted to see was that bastard's face. "I guess the no good, son of a bitch got tired of watching you."

"Work smarter, not harder." I heard Isaac say from another room.

Divad snarled before turning to me, suddenly looking very annoyed. He shoved his hand against my head. "Get dressed! Gear up!"

"Why?" I asked. "Slow the eff down. What's going on?"

My friend sighed. "Ark is about to burn Denver. He's going to wipe it clean then declare himself Lord of North America and end the infighting."

"WHAT?" Now I was really starting to wake up.

"This little war has been good for us all." Divad said. "Even your idiot buddy, the mighty Michael Vistaer," he said the name with ridiculously, mocking emphasis, "knows that. The more they all weaken each other, the better. Damn, I should've killed Ark too." He looked at the floor, considering, as if killing another controller had been an afterthought. His eyes were back on me and he smiled. "Oh well! What's done is done. What isn't, will be."

I stood up and looked at the assortment of gear David, er Divad had laid out; combat boots, armored pads, bulletproof armor… My eyes studied the stuff while I inadvertently began taking off my clothes. "Why don't you just send in those troops that Major you killed was talking about?"

"Because I don't trust them and they'd fail, giving Ark his final green light to waste the city." Divad worked on his own gear as he spoke.

I blinked. "Green light?"

"Oh Christ!" Divad yelled. "Ark has been petitioning for permission from Union command in Europe to take out Morbal's home base. Until now they've been hesitant but since they haven't heard from the Doctor in days," he smiled then giggled a little, "they're finally siding with Ark."

Now I could feel the urgency of the situation burning in my gut. Strangely, I seemed to plug into Divad's anxiety and desires. I worked quicker to get suited up. "How? How is he going to destroy the city?"

"Ark can't use ranged missiles, that shield thing of Cross's would stop him. So, he's going to use a newly designed little 'mini-nuke' his team of scientists created. They're going to sneak it in, set it up and then fire it off. The puke doesn't think anyone knows about his plan." A laugh. "He's wrong."

"Jesus." I said with a sigh. "He'll kill millions."

Divad stopped to think for a moment. "Yes. Balls of steel on that one; Ark."

My brain raced and I had to slow things down. Everything Divad did had a reason behind it, Lilly said. From the way he'd been acting, I couldn't understand why he was so desperate to save lives. Perhaps this was proof Divad wasn't insane, he wasn't shattered or evil. Images from his torture sessions played through my head.

"Wake up!" He shouted. "We don't have much time."

I looked at him. "Why do you care?"

"Jason, I'm not a monster." Divad said in a mildly hurt tone. "And I can't allow that prick to refortify the GU. Not here. Not now. We need to stop him. You and me."

"Why us?" I asked. "I mean, why us... alone?"

Divad's eyes boggled. "What? You need a reason? Why not us?" He paused, hands held out in front of him, palms up, like he wanted it all to dawn on me. Then he gave up, shrugged and winked. "Besides. It'll be fun. They can't stop us. You and me, man. You and me."

You and me. The words rang through my head and vibrated through my blood. There was so much meaning and power I had trouble comprehending it all. Divad and I were more than friends, we were more than brothers. I didn't know how it happened or why but it finally dawned on me that the two of us had really created a bond others couldn't understand. It was almost like we were the same person...

"Oh my god, man." Divad said, snapping me from my daze. "If you're going to keep spacing out, you might as well just consider everyone back in the city dead already and declare the esteemed Steven Ark your lord and master."

Isaac chimed in. "Not a bad thing if you ask me. That part about everyone in the city being dead. They're useless feeders. Let 'em die."

"EFF YOU, INSECT!" Divad roared, sending a hot mist of venomous spit from his mouth. He snorted and turned away from the other man, then checked over a lethally impressive set of weapons which included a wicked looking knife, a pair of etherpistols and a military grade automatic carbine.

"Sorry." I said, focusing back on my gear. "Won't this spark a greater resistance? I mean if Ark levels a city, won't more people go against him?" I shook my head. "It's just so insane, I don't see what Ark hopes to get out of this."

"Power and control." Divad said. "The same thing every tyrant drools over and lusts for. The same thing the effing osilea dream of." He picked up one of Morbal's glass ornaments off a nearby table and threw it at Isaac's head.

Unfortunately, the bastard ducked just in time. "And the so called rebel leaders, and August Cross. It's all about domination. You think the resistance would grow stronger? Hell, Tehlasrin plans on blaming the whole thing on Vistaer. They'll spin their little media fear machine and get all the drugged down, brain dead masses to fall in line." He let out a sarcastic chuckle. "Come on, you know better. Don't be a moron."

It was a lot to absorb especially after everything I'd been through. "How do *you* know all this? How do you know what Ark is going to do?"

Divad groaned. "That's one of the advantages of keeping Insect around. He still has ties to Ark's intelligence line. The data the Major brought confirmed the move. The controller has been seriously begging to strike the city for two days now. While most of his forces are at war with the resistance and Morbal's men, he plans to hit here."

"Ok, fine." I said, giving in. "So, the two of us are taking them down? All of them?" Now I laughed. "You are nuts."

I had all my gear on and assembled then Divad handed me a set of weapons that matched his own. He shot a menacing glance at Fier. "She may be right, I may be psychotic but I think I'm the sanest asshole in the world. And now it's time to have some fun. It's time for you to step up. It's time for you to accept that you're changing and growing with me. It's time we worked together to make a real difference. This isn't a dream, this isn't a fantasy. This is real! We're better than the rest and I'm going to prove it to you. That's why Morbal wanted us, why Forrest wanted us, why Cross wanted us, why Vistaer wants you and why Blondie over there," he gestured Lilly, "wants me. *You and me*."

A series of thoughts whizzed through my head the moment I was armed. I considered what Divad said while looking at Fier and Lilly, drugged and still sleeping. I could take Divad and Isaac out now. I could get the two women and make a run for it. But… What would've been the point of everything? After everything I'd been through, I'd hurt or kill my friend, abandon him and run back to Aswain? The thought sounded especially stupid, backward and wasteful. Besides, I couldn't let that son of a bitch Ark slaughter millions. Distant memories of August Cross telling me I was a hailiorum warrior, a guardian, a protector, played through my thoughts. I couldn't puss out and turn aside.

At that moment, the reality of the situation hit me like a sack of bricks. War. My adrenaline shot into overdrive again and I wondered how much of this my body, my heart could take. The odds sounded impossible, like a hopeless suicide mission. Could I really trust him? I remembered how strange David, no Divad had become. I remembered how manic he looked after he tossed Morbal's dead body aside. I remembered how quickly and coldly he murdered that Tehlasrin officer. My brain replayed everything he'd said, all the talk about burning away any semblance of order. Then there was his bizarre account of how he'd aged. I thought of how he'd kept Fier and me bound and how strange things had become back at the asylum.

At that moment, as my doubts mounted to a near tipping point, a strange newfound strength surged through my veins. It may have just been my imagination but I felt more powerful and pumped up than I could remember. I seemed to believe, no, I knew that I was more focused and attuned with my own abilities than I'd ever been before. *His consciousness is growing.* A voice, Richard's voice, spoke in my head.

It never stopped, everything playing at once. Eff it. There was a job to do and Divad and I were going to do it. I nodded and gained control of my breathing. "Alright. But don't think this is fun. Do you have a plan? Any strategy?"

"Ark is like a tiger." Divad said, catching me off guard. "He likes to kill quickly and cleanly. Big explosions are his ways." He pointed at the helmet and mask resting on the couch. "Put them on and be sure to set up the mic and earphone correctly."

I blew out a deep breath and reached for the mask.

"Morbal…" Divad said, "was like a demented hellhound. He liked to torture people, prolong their pain. He liked making them suffer."

I shook my head, clueless where he was going with all this. "Ok."

"Ark has his toys, like his new little bomb." Divad spat. "Morbal had his own nasty goodies and we're going to use them. What was the good Doctor's is now ours. Don't forget the earplug in your other ear."

"Maybe we should bring Fier." I said, meekly. "She's a soldier. She could help."

To that, Divad laughed, loud and jovial. "She'd put a bullet in the back of my head the second she had the chance."

He was right and the realization left a terribly cold sting in my chest. Maybe she'd be right to do so. No. No, that can't be true. Also, on second thought, I wouldn't want to subject her to our mad mission. My rational brain didn't expect to survive the night and I didn't want to put her in the same danger.

We both had our headgear on and when I looked at Divad, he reminded me of a masked villain from the movies. Face covered, wearing all black, armed to the teeth. Eff, I knew I looked just the same.

"Test, test." Divad's voice said in my ear.

I nodded my covered head. "Good. Can you hear me?"

"Yea." My friend said and with that we were suddenly partners again, soldiers off to fight another battle. The situation reminded me of our defense of Eaglebase back on Aswain. Only this time we were going it alone. I cursed under my breath.

Isaac spoke and had to raise his voice for us to hear. "You shouldn't do this. Let Ark bring the city down. Xolzv wills it."

The hair on the back of my neck stood up at the mention of the demonic name and now that I was armed and loaded, I was about to kill the sick man. Before I could aim my weapon though, Divad was on him, beating him to the floor. He punched the other's face, kicked him several times then started punching him again. All the while I could hear my friend's voice in my right ear, his slurs, his grunts, cursing the other man over and over. Finally, he looked at me.

"Let's go. I have a van waiting." Divad kicked Isaac one more time then scooped up what looked like a grenade launcher. "Insect, watch the women."

-

Divad crept our armored van to a rolling stop. The lights had been killed minutes ago and the vehicle stalked through the night air like a prowling cat. He pointed outward, through the windshield, at something beyond. "They're there, in that security station."

I looked down the road about a half mile away. The building looked poorly lit and unoccupied. "Are you sure?" I asked. "Wouldn't they have spotted us?"

"I'm sure. Trust me. They're laying low." I saw Divad nod his head while his electronic voice spoke through the microphone in my ear. "They don't want to risk drawing any unnecessary attention to themselves. Even whatever moron commander they have there is smart enough to know to not blow cover over one approaching vehicle."

I exhaled sharply and clenched my gloved hands into tight fists. The thirty minute drive over was a quiet one and that suited me fine, even though I still had a million questions for Divad. No, instead of speaking, I left myself to the whim of my thoughts. I fought to calm my nerves, prepared myself for battle and readied myself for death. There wasn't any turning back now. The part of me that was driven to protect others had taken over. My hailiorum blood ran fast and hot.

"Still, we move any closer and they won't be able to ignore us." Divad went on. "We'll strike soon."

I let out a deep breath that quivered through my lips. "What's the plan?"

"I told you Morbal had some wicked toys." Divad's voice was especially cold and menacing but I could tell he was smiling as he spoke. That was one of the advantages of knowing someone as well as Divad and I knew each other. I knew his face as well as my own and knew exactly how he looked based on the tone of his voice, even after it had aged so bizarrely. "First, we're going to blow their eardrums out. This baby," he patted the van's dashboard, "has a fully powered ear killer equipped on it."

I swallowed.

"Once they get a taste of that we move in." Divad went on. "Then they'll get round two of Morbal's welcome."

"What's that?" I had to ask but didn't really want to know.

"That launcher is loaded with a lethal, poisonous gas." Divad turned to me and now I wished I could see his face. When you're best friend is happily talking about the brutal murder of dozens of people, you want to see their eyes, to see just how insane they'd become or if there was even the slightest touch of sadness, of regret... of humanity. No such luck. "It was Ark's stuff some of Morbal's, now my men, nabbed after a battle. Time for the bastard's servants to get a taste of their own medicine."

"This is too much." I shook my head.

"Shush!" Divad cut me off. "We'll gas them, move in and clean out what's left. Then take out the nuke."

It felt wrong, it felt evil but I couldn't turn back. The best I could manage was, "How will this stop Ark? We take out this team, who's to say he won't just try again somewhere else?"

"One step at a time, brother. One step at a time." Divad whispered. "Ark's an ego maniac, a raving control freak. I imagine the humiliation alone will cause him to look to other methods of attack."

I sighed as my head started to pound, violently.

"I don't plan on letting the effer live long enough to try." His gloved hand suddenly pushed against my helmet. "Hey! Sharpen up." Divad turned to look forward again. "No hesitation. It's us or them. They win and millions die."

I watched Divad pull out what looked like a cell phone and saw him punch in several numbers. Curious, I turned and scanned as much of the world outside the van as I could, eyes wide as dinner plates. Something moved off to my right. Not something, someone. A closer look showed several figures scurrying through the dark, ducking for cover. "There're people out there."

"Stay focused." Divad droned. "We're moving in 60 seconds."

I looked harder, unable to ignore a strange buzz in the back of my head. A faint spec of light bounced off something metal and shiny that sat on one of the blurry figures' backs. Vistaer. It was Michael Vistaer. He was here! Without thinking, I opened the door and ran from the van, toward the shadowy figures, ripping my helmet, earplugs and mask off in the process. Divad's voice screamed in my ear but I ignored it.

I ran further, knowing full well the others had their weapons aimed at me. Unsure what else to do, I called out, too desperate to care if Ark's troops could hear me. "Michael! It's me, Jason!"

"Shut up and stay low." I recognized Chin's voice coming from directly behind me.

Without turning or acknowledging the amazingly stealthy man, we moved toward the small group and when I reached them Michael's eyes nearly bulged out of their sockets. "What on God's Earth? Where're Fier and Lilly?"

I waved my hands in the air. "There's no time. Get your people out of here, now!"

"What?" The big man looked at me like I was a raving lunatic, not far from the truth at this point. "That group up there has something especially dangerous. I'm not sure what but an informant inside Ark's team -"

"Shut up!" I snapped. "I know about that. You need to go, right now! Don't talk, don't think. Just effing go!"

I could tell Vistaer was well beyond annoyed or curious; he looked pissed. "I don't know what you're up to, but we're stopping them."

"GOD DAMN IT!" I gritted my teeth, pulled my fist back then punched Vistaer square in his jaw. The others, Chin, Chris, Drew and Olivia all had the barrels of the guns pointed at me. "Get out! You're going to die!"

Vistaer, who faltered back a bit after my blow, realigned himself and spat what I knew was spit mixed with blood. "You've gotten stronger." He moved his massive frame an inch from me as his nostrils flared. I could feel the hot air from his lungs blast my face. I thought he was going to hit me back but instead... instead he hugged me.

"I'll trust you, little brother." He said in my ear. "We'll pull back. But why?"

I shook my head and pulled away from the big man's hold. "There's no time. Just go." I gulped, realizing how foolish my next words sounded. "I'll explain some other time. Go now."

"You heard him, team. Let's move." The group started away before Michael turned to me. "Fier, Lilly. Are they alive? Where are they?"

I nodded. "Yes, they're alive." Before he could ask more questions I turned and started back for the van.

"Jason!" Michael called in an elevated whisper and I turned back toward him. "Go with God. Don't lose yourself."

I grimaced and hurried back, plugging my ears again before tugging my mask and helmet on as quickly and efficiently as I could.

Divad spoke as I grew close. "Touching." He sounded disappointed.

"Shut up." I lashed back.

"You need to wise up." Divad said in a low tone. "Now we're behind schedule. Look."

I saw a group of soldiers moving in on the station. They were attacking. "Who?"

"Morbal's team." Divad said. "Game time."

"You said -"

Divad hauled off with his left fist and slammed it into my chest. The hit managed to knock the air out of my lungs even through the protection I wore. "No more of that. Clear your head."

He shifted the van into drive and floored the gas. We blazed toward the station where gunfire started to erupt. A second later, Divad flipped a switch on the van's dash and I could hear a deviously penetrating sound come from the vehicle, even through my state of the art earplugs.

The men and woman we drew closer to suddenly fell to the ground, clasping their hands over their ears. Soldiers on both sides surrendered to the screeching sound waves that hammered them. I couldn't hear their screams and thanked whatever fictitious deity people prayed to. I didn't want to hear their agony, seeing it was bad enough.

Divad slammed the van to a jarring stop, kicked his door open and leapt out into the fray. "Move!" His voice boomed in my ear. "Knock them out, all of them. They can still kill us."

I exited the van and looked around at the helpless people, seeing the tortured, painful expressions on their faces. Then I saw flashes of deep blue that came from Divad's etherpistols. He was coldly plunking the downed men and women square in their heads as he passed by.

My heart sunk and my muscles locked. Executing these people like this didn't sit well in my gut at all. They may have been soldiers, warriors, even domineering, sadistic, villains that served the Union but the repeated sound waves turned them into defenseless victims, terrified and writhing in pain. Divad didn't care in the slightest. I watched him bring the poison gas filled grenade launcher to bear and knew he was about to fire. "DIVAD! DON'T!"

He didn't listen. Instead, a series of small explosions went off around and within the station. Divad had launched several grenades and some of them blasted through the station's windows, clearing out whatever poor creatures were inside.

Now, I had to watch in horror as the men and women around me forgot the misery in their ears and began choking on the foggy air around them. I didn't know what exactly the fumes were made of but it was obviously a wicked concoction. The poor bastards who breathed in the gas writhed in spasms on the ground. I nearly threw up.

Then a bullet whirled past my ear. It was followed by another, then a third. I turned to see several figures that somehow managed to get to their feet and were now zeroing in on me with their weapons. My brain blanked and my body froze. Divad's etherpistol lit the night and burned away the last pieces of life in a couple soldiers. "FOR CHRIST'S SAKE!" He yelled in my ear. "DO SOMETHING!"

Next, bullets started flying toward Divad and that, seeing him in danger, finally broke me from my trance. I was NOT going to let these pathetic losers kill my friend. As usual, as he'd done a dozen times or more, either through words or by his actions, Divad managed to tug me back to the present and probably saved my life.

"NO!" I roared, gritting my teeth and growling like an animal. I lifted both of my etherpistols and fired them at anything that moved. My body went into autopilot, full attack mode, barely leaving room to think. I was a machine now, blasting away at our enemies, one after another. It was hard to know how many I killed and I didn't care to keep count. They were nothing but an obstacle now and we were going to overcome it.

Divad laughed in my ear. The sound was full of thrilled exhilaration. "Way to go! That's it! Fry those effers! Woohoo!"

I glided across the ground, ducking, weaving and dodging incoming shots all without missing any of my own targets.

Divad and I, seemingly unstoppable, moved through the dangerously open space and cleared the area out, all without a scratch on either of us.

He moved up along side me while I surveyed the collection of corpses, lying in the smoky fog surrounded by the continued buzz from the van. "Let's head in." Divad's voice tickled my ear. "Watch it. Some of them had masks on." He kicked something and I looked down at his booted foot. Sure enough, there was a man, a dead man wearing a gas mask.

I nodded and followed Divad's lead. We both un-slung our carbines then headed into the station building. The place was well lit but pockets of poisonous fog still lingered in the air. Sweat dripped over my eyebrows and into my eyes. Some of the drops splashed onto the goggles of my mask which created obscured pockets of vision.

A man moved and Divad opened up on him before I could act, no doubt pumping a dozen rounds into his body. A few steps later and a screaming, now raving lunatic lunged at me. He wrapped his arms around my body and pulled me to the ground. I dropped my carbine and struggled with the man. At the same time, bullets came at us, drawing Divad's attention. He was too busy with the others to help me.

Rather than going for my carbine or one of the two etherpistols, each resting in their own holsters on their respective hips, I reached for the knife tucked away in its own holster, dangling from my belt. The man, who was bleeding from his eyes and ears, fought to get his sweaty, bloody fingers around my throat. Normally I'd easily be able to knock a guy of his size off me but this one was fueled by his desperate madness and I was already weighed down by the gear I wore. It was hard to catch my breath due to all the crap I had on my head and face. I drove my left fist smack into his face while my right hand worked for the knife. My punch had little effect and the man's hands were now around my throat, starting to squeeze.

Finally, I freed the knife; pulled my right hand back a few inches then stuck the blade as deep as it could go into the man's gut. His grip loosened immediately and I was able to toss his body off me. Now back on my feet, I quickly kicked the guard in his face and seemed to knock him out. Between the gas and the gaping wound, I guessed the man would be gone very shortly.

Divad had stopped shooting and handed me my dropped weapon. "You showed him." He laughed and pointed at the demolished wreckage ahead of us. I saw a few dead bodies sprawled on the ground. "Sorry I couldn't help but I was a little busy."

I rubbed my neck, unsure what to think so I didn't. I shut everything off. "Let's keep moving."

"Damn I missed you."

We moved on and soon crept down a long, narrow hallway with a door at the end. I had just enough time to consider the danger of our situation, stuck in a narrow passage without cover, before the door opened up and death itself rained down on us. Bullets smacked hard against my armored chest, sending me back and knocking me to the ground.

Divad dropped back and fell down too. He quickly unloaded his weapon at our foes. I did the same, ignoring the deafening sounds of rapid and repeated gunfire going off in such an enclosed space. Even with the earplugs, it was loud.

Our enemies backed off and my clip emptied quickly. Luckily, Divad had replaced his before mine was dry. So I slapped in a new clip into my weapon while my friend continued blasting away. We progressed that way, covering each other, keeping our adversaries ducked down. All the while, we inched closer and closer to the door.

I ignored everything but my weapon and the bodies of our targets. I knew my brain was racing, faster than ever, I knew my heart was ready to explode, I knew that on so many levels I was the aggressor, the bad guy, ruthlessly plowing through men and women who were trapped, following orders or facing death. I ignored it all. Hell, everyone had a choice, always. These people didn't have to serve the controllers. They could've surrendered or helped the resistance but no, they decided to play it safe, to serve their manipulative, evil masters. Eff them...

Those were the thoughts that played through my head as we, Divad and I, miraculously made it to and through the doorway. The brain works quickly when death is only a breath away and mine instantly counted five others in the room with us. We took care of four of them impossibly fast before the pathetic pricks even knew what hit them. The last one tried to run away, out the door we came in through. I ran my shoulder into his, checking him hard like a pissed off hockey player. The hit knocked the man off his feet and he crashed to the ground.

I aimed my carbine at his head and squeezed the trigger. Nothing happened, the gun was out of bullets. It was then that the machine that had taken over my body and thoughts finally turned off. I looked into the frightened soldier's eyes and felt his terror. Holy... I was about to bury a bullet in his face. It felt like someone dropped buckets of ice chips over every inch of my body. What the eff had I done?

Divad was there in a flash. He aimed an etherpistol at the man's face, having shucked his own carbine, and fired. The killing shot made me jump. I'd been through several battles and had seen lots of death but this one was especially difficult to deal with.

And then, everything was quiet. Everything except a menacing ringing in my head, the sound of my own, heavy breathing and the drum of my heart thumping against my ribs.

"Looks clear." Divad's voice said as he slapped his hand against my shoulder. "Great work!" Again, he sounded giddy and again I knew he was smiling. "I knew we could do it. Now let's get the goods and get the hell out before more of these bastards show up."

I turned to look at my friend's back. He wasn't fazed at all by what we'd done. It wasn't a guess, I absolutely knew it. He was happy, proud. The whole thing was fun for him. He reveled in our victory, the conquest, the final judgment we'd brought down on the men and women, both serving Ark and Morbal. Eff, he *loved* it. I knew that if Vistaer and his team were here, Divad would've of killed them just as quickly without a second thought.

He walked over and opened a case that rested in the corner of the room, studying what was inside. "Here it is." His voice had a dreamy hum to it. "Help me carry this."

"You said you were going to destroy it." I spoke without moving an inch.

He turned to me. "I can't do anything here."

"You're going to keep it, aren't you?" My right hand reflexively slid toward the etherpistol resting in its holster on my right hip. I wasn't sure what I was going to do, what I was willing to do, but alarms sounded through my head and I started to seriously freak out. Love or not, Divad was psychotic. The fact was painfully obvious. The thought of him with a weapon that could wipe out a city nearly drove *me* insane.

Divad spoke, a lot it seemed, no doubt defending himself or telling me I was wrong. I wasn't listening. Instead I was imagining him on Everiel, helping with the destruction of the island and everyone on it. My brain fought with itself, denying that my friend could ever do such a thing. But... denial could only go so far after what I'd seen and done. The dead bodies around me demanded the truth be known.

There wasn't any time for debating. He had to be stopped, taken away from the explosives, and taken somewhere safe where he could get some help. I pulled the pistol out, thumbed the power level down to a low stun and fired, hitting Divad square in his chest. He only stepped back but stayed on his feet. My mouth dropped open. "Jason..." He said in a warning voice.

I sneered and upped the power level to a high stun then fired again. He had to go down, I had to stop him, for everyone's sake. After the second shot, Divad only grunted into his microphone and put his arms in front of his body in an X shape. The blast pegged him but again he didn't fall. It was strange, like his body absorbed the shot. The blast stopped in front of him, formed a ball of light then, I could only watch as the energy, the light slowly soaked into his crossed arms. What the eff?

"Stop it, Jason." Divad spoke in a calm but slightly labored voice. "That stings. You can't stun me. I don't sleep, like Insect. I'm only either alive or dead. If you want to stop me, you'll have to do better."

Now I growled and finally switched the weapon to full kill mode, aiming it at Divad. "You lit up Everiel, didn't you? You killed all of them, just like you killed everyone here."

To my surprise, he removed his helmet, mask and earplugs. "The air's clear now."

"Answer me!" I took my own head gear off and gripped my weapon tighter. The ear shattering buzz from the van was gone and the back of my mind guessed the thing was on a timer.

Divad raised an eyebrow and to my utter shock, smiled then laughed. "You killed everyone here too. They were our enemies. Would you rather have died?"

"ADMIT IT!" I screamed.

My friend's lip curled and for the first time he looked angry. "No! You... either shoot me or drop the weapon. NOW!"

His shout made me jump again, my muscles shook and my right hand, the one holding the gun quivered. I brought my left hand up to help, now holding the gun with both.

"We're past the pathetic, sick, safe middle ground. It's time to decide." Divad went on. "No more *half way* crap. Decide now. Either you're in or out."

"Lilly was right about you." I said between rapid breaths.

He scoffed. "You're seriously effed in the head if you believe that spaced out bimbo. Look at what we just did. We won! Again! God damn it, don't you see?" He gritted his teeth, gestured himself and me as he moved a step closer. "We're better than them; better than the osilea and hailiorea. We don't play by their rules."

"I'm effed in the head?" I asked in a mocking tone, feeling my eyebrows rise to the top of my head. "You're the one who nearly tore your own face off while Morbal ripped your brain to shreds. Insect showed us the videos."

Divad's eyes narrowed. "Yea, and you opened your own throat up. Or have you forgotten? We're the same. Accept it."

I swallowed, remembering how utterly destroyed I was that day during my last 'therapy' session at the asylum.

"Jason," he started, speaking calmly again, "you've let people like Cross and Vistaer twist your mind. You've never found your real purpose, your true potential. I've been to Hell and back. I know now. You're just finally beginning to grow."

I shook my head and snorted. "You're insane. You're sick. That's all I know."

"Believe what you want. But we need each other." He took another step.

I gritted my teeth and moved a step closer to him myself, reaffirming my aim right at his forehead. "Take another step and I'll kill you."

He smiled, an especially vile and twisted look given the situation. "Then do it. One or the other. Shoot, or lower your gun. Time to choose, amigo."

A million thoughts circled through my head until I had to finally decide. For the sake of my own sanity I knew I couldn't go through with it. My shoulders slumped and I dropped the pistol on the ground. I couldn't kill him. It was too much.

Divad walked up to me, picking up the downed weapon on the way, and rested a hand on my shoulder while pulling the other pistol from the holster on my left hip. "Now let's get the bomb and go. I'm proud of you." He shook me. "Hey. This is a happy time. A time of change. Cheer up!"

My eyes met his. The man I'd come back to save was gone and I was too weak to do anything about it. I cursed myself. *Coward. Weak. Loser.*

"Great things are coming," he said, happily. "But I never said it'd be easy."

Chapter 17

We loaded the case with the mini nuke into the back of our van and fled the carnage we helped create. Divad drove while happily prattled on and on about 'true liberty,' talking about how governments were unnatural and how societies were guises for the few to control the many. I blocked it out. My thoughts were stuck on the war we'd just been though. It went quick but the memories would linger. I'd remember how ruthlessly cold and efficient I was, tearing through the Union troops. I remembered their faces, imagining their screams. All of it. Most of all, I couldn't get the haunting image of that last guard Divad killed out of my mind.

The poor guy... I turned to look out the window, away from Divad, threatened by the possibility that a string of tears would roll down my face. A blur of images and lights danced by as I eventually realized, undoubtedly, that I wasn't going to cry. The sadness was there but so was an odd sense of victory and uncaring.

No, he wasn't a poor guy. He was a Tehlasrin soldier who was helping an evil, murderous controller try to level a city full of people. He deserved to die. Maybe Divad let him off too easily. Maybe he should've suffered more, felt the pain he deserved for his crimes. Hell, maybe we were too nice.

No. Damn it, that wasn't right either. It seemed impossible to know what to feel. My natural instincts were twisted up, nearly lost amidst uncertainty. I wondered what Vistaer would say. He was a hailiorum warrior like me. We weren't killers. I remembered the way he ended that controller, Brenner; clean, quick and painless. He'd said torturing others was evil and I agreed. There was a difference between justice and cruelty; a difference between a soldier and a murderer.

Well then why did it feel right to have that last bastard die in such horrible anguish? I saw his eyes, blood crusted and terrified. They showed how much he suffered.

Around and around my thoughts whirled. Eff, put simply, I was confused. Not confused with the strange intricacies of the hailiorea or the osilea nor with the GU or the resistance. No, now I was confused with myself. I didn't know who or what I was anymore. I'd been changing ever since I got off that boat, ever since old man Richard played with my head. Now, I was lost.

I didn't know how much time had passed but I finally pulled myself to the present when Divad brought the van down a long, unkempt, rocky driveway. The stretch was overgrown with long grass and weeds. He pulled up to a metal gate and pressed several buttons on a control panel planted into the vehicle's dashboard. The gate opened and we drove through it. A modest little house sat about fifty meters down a bumpy, dirt trail. The structure looked dark, dank and unoccupied.

"Where are we?" I asked in a measly voice.

Divad looked at me, shook his head and sighed. "Oh my god, will you snap out of it? Lord!"

"This isn't the house from before." I stated, feeling urgency stir in my gut. "What about Fier and Lilly?"

"You could use some time away from those two." He spoke in a cheerful voice. "You need to unwind. It's hard to relax with two women bickering and pestering you every second."

I didn't feel like 'unwinding' with Divad. "No. No, screw this. Take me back to them now!"

"Shut up." Divad said with attitude. "They're fine. Insect is watching them."

That didn't help at all. My heart raced again and my hands clenched into fists. "This is bull, all of it! I'm done with you. I'm leaving."

"You don't mean that." He parked the vehicle and looked at me. "Come inside and have a beer or two. Let's visit, just the two of us, no distractions."

I roared with frustration feeling like I was losing my mind. I couldn't argue and didn't really want to. I wished I could say I truly wanted to see Fier and Lilly but in reality they were the last people I wanted to see. I didn't know how I'd be able to face Fier after the rampage I'd just went through. I felt, I don't know, less than the man I wanted to be, less than the man I should be. Enduring Fier's judgment would be too painful. In the end I surrendered, to baffled, confused and bewildered to fight anymore.

We carried the case with the bomb into the house which, once lit, was especially bare. Nothing was inside the small building except a couch, a couple chairs, a telescreen and a small kitchen with the usual appliances. Divad worked a security panel inside the house that was pressed against the wall near the door.

"That gate may look flimsy," he started, "but it packs quite a punch for anyone dumb enough to try to get through. Have a seat."

I collapsed on the firm, uncomfortable couch and worked to get my battle gear off. I noticed several bullets were still lodged in my vest before tossing it aside. Divad walked into the kitchen and pulled two beers out of the refrigerator. He opened them, handed me one then sat down in a chair.

"What's this place?" I asked, not really caring.

He took a drink. "Another one of Morbal's places. My place now. He had it tucked away as a hideout."

I took a drink and sighed, feeling the weight of the world press down on my shoulders. It was a battle just keeping my eyes open.

"It'll get easier." Divad started. "We still have a long way to go but trust me, we're making the world a better place."

"A better place, huh? I don't know what happened to you but you're a completely sick son of a bitch, you know that?" I glared at him.

He laughed, nearly spitting a mouthful of beer. Then he nodded. "You're right. You're totally right. But that's the price I have to pay to be willing and able to do what's necessary. The world's a sick place, diseased with delusions and fear."

"Don't spin that crap with me." I said. "We just…" I swallowed and fought for breath. "We just slaughtered a bunch of people who did nothing to us."

Divad's brow furrowed. "Jesus. You act like you've never killed anyone before. Grow up! Did you feel this way after we took care of Forate?"

"That was different."

"It was?" He shook his head. "Those *people* we killed were about to wipe out every man, woman and child in Denver. They were going to make Ark even more powerful and influential, practically giving him the entire continent."

My gaze dropped down to the ground. He had a point but why did I feel so awful about it all? Why, why, why? I looked up at Divad as a possible answer formed in my head. "But why did you seem to enjoy it so much? We're warriors, not killers. There's a difference."

"Oh, I see." Divad leaned back in his chair and looked up at the ceiling. "It makes sense now. That's August Cross talk. Or you've been listening to Mr. High and Mighty, Vistaer too much. Now you're plagued by that pesky conscience of yours. Sorry, buddy, but mine went bye-bye a long time ago. I have no issues doing what needs to be done."

I wasn't sure what to say. Maybe Divad was right. It was just so hard to connect with him no matter how badly I wanted to. I wished I had his free spirit and carefree attitude so I could just rip through the world like he did, like an indiscriminate tornado plowing through homes. But I couldn't. I looked at him. "We're not the same."

"Give it time." He smiled and raised his eyebrows. "You'll come around."

"What if I can't?" I asked, hearing the sadness in my own voice.

Divad waved a hand in the air, dismissively. "Bah. You worry too much."

I numbly drank my beer.

"You did great tonight." He nodded. "I could feel our bond grow a lot stronger while we were going through those guys. It was awesome and gave me hope." His voice trailed off at the end. "Jason."

I blinked, curious and caught off guard by the change in his tone.

"I need your help." He started. We need each other. Don't you see that? There's a seriously messed up wave headed our way and you're the only one who can help me. You're the only one who I connect with. I thought I could find support from my mother and sisters but I effed that up. They can't help me. Only you can."

I looked Divad in his eyes. "What are you talking about? What wave? I helped you tonight by wasting all those people?"

He let out a nervous laugh. "That girl, Lilly, is an annoying little bitch but she's right. The osilea are going to make their move. Soon. That thing you killed on Ravenfall, and I'm sorry, I should've been there with you, was nothing compared to what's coming."

Sirens went off in my head. This was a trick, a way for Divad to get me to lower my guard. I didn't say anything.

He made an expectant face. "Nothing? You don't have any questions?"

I only stared, blankly, trying to find some way to ground myself. It felt like sanity, clarity and salvation was just around the corner but I couldn't reach it. The world was a mess and everyone, Cross, Divad, Vistaer, Morbal, the osilea, each had their own ideas on how to fix it. What did I think? How could I cope with the events I'd been through?

Divad seemed uncomfortable with my silence. "Ok. You take your time." He smiled. "But damn we dominated tonight. You and I are going to keep knocking down anything that tries to impose its will on the world. I wish you could feel proud of what we did tonight."

"I do too." I said finally. "But I can't. It feels wrong."

"It didn't seem wrong when you were in your zone. Man, we were incredible." Divad said that with a big smile. The look, in the dimly lit house, almost resembled the young looking David I knew so well.

He went on. "Listen, things will get better. Right now, crate after crate of free clear is traveling across the war torn continent. People need it, more than ever. It'll help ease their pain and losses. The more people that take it, the more will be like us. Free. No more fear. They'll wake up and snap out of the spell the controllers weaved over them for centuries."

"You know damn well there're lots of people that won't use that junk." I said. "What are you planning on doing with them?"

Divad raised an eyebrow. "We'll see when the time comes."

"You'll kill them too?"

To that he laughed hysterically. "Yep! And what's wrong with that? Oh I know, you're morality will say, 'Divad, we can't just kill all of them,' but yes we can and yes we'll have to. How else will things ever get better if we're not willing to make sacrifices? I'm beyond compromise. I'm sick of it. It doesn't work. It's an old joke that's not funny anymore. I'm done laughing." Then he stood up. "Need another one?"

I looked at my bottle with an especially ugly expression on my face. I was surprised to see it was empty. "Sure."

A few moments later he handed me a new, full, cold bottle. "You're so hung up on the killing thing. I only kill what needs to be killed, like a lion killing for food in order to survive. I'm no different and neither are you. You just don't want to accept it." He shrugged. "That's ok. It took a while for me to grasp it too but I eventually came around."

"When? While you were in Hell?" I asked, half mockingly.

He smiled. "Bingo. I told you, I was there a long time. It prepared me for this, showed me what our would-be controllers, those on all sides, Jason, will lead us too. I'm not going to let that happen."

"What the hell are you doing to me?" I asked, suddenly becoming aware that my nerves were calming. I *wanted* to agree with Divad and believe in him so bad… I knew something was wrong. Somehow I knew I was being played, manipulated.

Divad scratched his head and made a goofy face. "What do you mean? I'm not doing anything to you. There's a lot of magic in the world and some of that shows itself when we're together. I told you, we need each other."

"Must've been some sort of bond we created in the asylum," I mumbled under my breath, imagining old man Richard was here saying it.

My friend took a drink. "Mmmhmm." He nodded. "That's where it started. That's why you're here and not back, sitting on your ass on that island, being Cross's little lap dog." He let out a satisfactory sigh. "Hell of a thing being a hailiorum."

"Alright." I said, staring blankly at Divad's face. Whether it was intentional or not, I let my guard down. Even though he'd acted insane, psychotic, cruel even, he did seem to have things figured out. My brain started to grow especially foggy and it was hard to think. That was ok, though, I didn't really want to think. All I knew was Divad had the answers and he was able to cope with things. I envied that. He could help me deal with everything. We didn't need anyone else.

And then, there she was again… Fier. She popped into my head, blowing the fog away like a crisp, clean, breeze. I furrowed my brow. "We have to let Fier go. And Lilly." The younger woman was an afterthought.

Divad smirked and shook his head the way people do when the person across from them 'just doesn't get it.' "You really do love her don't you?"

"I don't know." I swallowed.

He took a drink. "Yes, you do. You think you love her at least." He rolled his eyes. "Nothing but pain there, buddy. Suit yourself."

"We have to let her go." I repeated.

"Sure thing." He said. "In the morning though. For now, I just want to get drunk. I would say get drunk and pass out but I don't sleep anymore. I sort of miss it…"

The last bit didn't sit well. He didn't sleep. What the hell was with that? How could he not need to sleep? The concept was so inhuman, so alien it was hard to feel comfortable the rest of the night. Divad eventually flipped on the telescreen and we learned that riots and revolts were springing up in nearly every super city. The media wasn't holding back and it was obvious things had gotten too out of hand for the GU to keep their shroud of lies and propaganda over everything.

I made it through several more beers before everything shut down and I fell asleep.

-

When I woke up the first thing I noticed was how weak the light was that seeped through the windows. The second was that Divad still sat in his chair, having shucked his armor, he was barefoot wearing a pair of jeans and a thin, light blue tee-shirt. He turned away from the still running telescreen and looked at me. The third thing I noticed was how absolutely awake and alert I felt, like I hadn't been sleeping at all but I wasn't the least bit tired or sleepy. My brain didn't hurt and my body felt good. I sat up.

"Rise and shine." Divad said, happily. "Feel good?"

I looked at him and thought for a second before answering. "Yea, I feel ok but I don't think 'good' would describe it."

"Why not? Better than good? Head clear? Well rested? Ready to take on the world?" Divad nodded then laughed.

I'll be damned, that was exactly how I felt but I didn't want to confess it. "How long was I out for?"

"Oh, about four hours."

I sprung off the couch and looked down on my friend. "What? After not hardly sleeping for days, being drugged, spending everything I had in that battle, pounding down seven or eight beers, not eating... I feel like this after four hours of sleep?"

"Do you think a butterfly asks itself how it can fly after hatching from its cocoon?" Divad chuckled. "Don't over think it. You're changing. Simple as that."

I considered his words before considering myself. I remembered, or rather acknowledged, for the first time how powerful, precise and deadly I was during the attack on the station. The whole thing played over in my head. My movements, reactions, speed... it wasn't normal. Damn myself, I smiled.

"Feels good, doesn't it?" Divad asked, standing up.

I scratched my chin, absentmindedly thinking I needed to shave. "I guess so." I stared the man in his eye. "No more BS, tell me how. How is this happening?"

He sighed. "I'm no professor but there's something to be said about the mind-body connection. Combine that with being a powerful hailiorum with your potential and there you are. I bet just being around me has upped your H level. You're feeling the effects and don't need as much rest time anymore."

A week ago I wouldn't have believed it, three weeks ago and I would have thought the man was out of his mind crazy but now, I believed him, instantly. "Why us? Why the two of us? And how do you know this stuff?"

"The hailiorea were meant to fight together, in teams. That's where we shine. The early ones found their battle partners, teamed up and kicked ass. That's why those junk sucking controllers are so desperate to break other hailiorea. They can't find their own partner so they try to twist and corrupt others into a surrogate of sorts." Divad snorted and gritted his teeth. "Effers." He looked at me. "I learned all this while I was with the osilea. They weren't teaching me, more like pulling information out of me. Information that we instinctively know but either keep tucked away or choose to forget."

I squinted, trying to follow along. He sounded weird talking this way, almost metaphysical and suddenly very serious. It felt out of character and reminded me that Divad's brain was fragile, his thoughts and actions were erratic and unpredictable. Dangerous...

"Eff, I don't know." Divad laughed, no doubt sensing my concerns. "It's like we all have a safe filled with information, locked deep in our heads. Once we become aware of it, we unlock it and the knowledge moves front and center."

"So we're partners." I gestured Divad and myself.

He nodded. "Damn straight."

I liked my lips. "And we can help each other. Grow stronger..." I raised an eyebrow. "And saner?"

"Oh man!" Divad roared with laughter. "I'm not insane! Stop worrying."

I was about to comment when the other man's expression changed again, only much more abruptly. He appeared keenly alert and stood up straighter than normal, turning to look out through the nearby windows. The house security siren went off a split second later. It let out a light buzzing sound that wasn't terribly abrasive. I was instantly on edge and on my feet.

"Follow behind me." Divad said, now extremely serious, pulling an etherpistol from his pocket.

I realized I was unarmed. "Hey! Where's my gun?"

"Not now -" Divad began before a light flashed outside followed by a powerfully loud sound that was a mix of a buzz and a crack. "The fence!"

He quickly punched a code into the security panel, opened the door and flew outside, barefoot and all. I followed right on his tail, running in my socks. I barely noticed it was raining outside, focused instead on the potential danger.

Thinking back, I thought Divad would've wanted to be a bit more careful, moving under cover, but no. He bolted headlong in the wide open, right for the fence. I followed, being the fool I was. He even roared then shouted. "Show yourself, mothereffers!"

We were answered with silence and sprinted up to the gate, now powered down and especially flimsy looking. I stepped through it after Divad. My eyes quickly locked onto a man lying in a dirty pool. His stomach was tore wide open and a small stream of blood ran from his gut, mixing in with the rain and the mud. It only took a second to recognize him. Chin. I raced over to his side and dropped to my knees.

"Jesus!" I panted, unsure what to do, all I could think of was to put my hand on the man's dirty, wet forehead. I looked down at the gross, gaping hole in his belly. Shredded flesh and gore mixed with the man's sweater and undershirt. "What happened? What are you doing here?"

Chin couldn't speak. He only looked at me, tears running from his eyes, his face contorted to show the excruciating pain he was in.

"Chin!" I shouted in the rain as a rumble of thunder rolled through the clouds. I turned to Divad. "Can you heal him?"

My friend didn't move. He was knelt down on one knee, studying what looked like a small pile of grey dirt, or maybe ash, near the gate. He scooped up a handful, brought it to his nose, sniffed it, and then let the chunky, muddy clumps slip through his fingers. It was hard to see clearly, but it looked like he held on to something small that he'd sifted out of the mud. Something small and shiny. "This one hit the fence, got fried."

"DIVAD!" I roared. "He needs help!"

"He's dead, Jason." Divad's voice was a flat blend of defeat and cold, quiet anger. He stood and studied the ground then looked off down the dirt driveway that led to the road. His stare was intense and his nostrils flared like a hound dog that had caught a scent. "Dead. All dead."

I looked back down on Chin to see his eyes had rolled back into his head. "Eff that! Come on! Do something. Let's get him to a healer."

Divad drew closer, I could see him out of the corner of my eye. He swore, loudly and violently as he walked up behind me. I turned just in time to see the barrel of his etherpistol aimed at Chin's face. He fired before I could flinch. The man, Chin, my team mate, according to Michael Vistaer, was gone.

I bolted to my feet, gritted my teeth, felt my disgust filled anger surge then pushed Divad as hard as I could, driving the palms of both my hands flush against his chest. He stumbled back, slipped in the mud then fell on his ass. Without a word or the slightest protest, he stood back up.

"You killed him!" I shouted.

Divad finally looked at me. He looked confused. "Was he your friend?"

I felt like he'd slapped me across my face. "No, but –"

"Did you love him?"

"God damn it, no." I snarled. "But that doesn't mean you should've -" I stopped, getting a good look at the small object in Divad's hand. A gold ring? A wedding ring maybe? I pointed at it. "What the eff is that?"

"Ok then." He interrupted. "Let's go back in, get our shoes and keys and head back to the other house."

He turned around and started quickly back up the dirt road. I ran after him and shouted, "Hey! I'm not done here!"

Divad stopped and turned to me. "WHAT?" He yelled as drops of rain bounced off his odd, aged face. His look was intense, wild and angry. "What do you want from me? He was done, dying, finished. You should thank me for putting him out of his misery. I did that for you. Grow the eff up!"

He was headed off for the house again before I could respond. I was so angry I roared with rage. Most annoying of all, I realized I was pissed because I knew Divad was right.

-

My friend drove like a madman, speeding down streets, nearly plowing into other vehicles or running over pedestrians. Luckily, the roads were mostly empty, giving us a somewhat clear path. The number of people seemed odd but I didn't really care to think about it. Divad muttered curses under his breath, staring intently ahead, angry and obsessed.

"What the hell?" I started again. He'd been ignoring me the whole time since leaving the hideaway house. "What happened to Chin? What did that to him?"

"Shut up!" He snapped. "I'm thinking."

Now I was swearing under my breath, agitated and tired of the nonstop runaround. Soon Divad pulled the van up another driveway, through another security gate and up to Morbal's house where Fier and Lilly were trapped.

Divad got out of the van and marched through the house door without a word. The whole thing reminded me of his angry dash back on Aswain, back to intelligence headquarters after he learned clear was made from the tissue of tortured hailiorea. Christ, that felt like a lifetime ago. I followed, demanding, almost pleading he stop and explain things. No such luck.

After I was in the house, Divad boomed. "INSECT!"

Isaac rounded a corner and looked at us, he was smiling. "How nice. I missed you. Have fun last night?"

Divad shoved past the man and barged into the house's family room. I looked around noticing several pieces of furniture were overturned.

"Oh, sorry about the redecorating." Isaac started. "But our guest was misbehaving. Don't worry, I calmed her down."

My eyes darted around the room, searching... There, I found Lilly hunched over Fier who was lying on the floor. I rushed over to her, shoving aside an overturned chair that was in my way. Fier's nose was bleeding and her left eye had a dark, swollen ring around it.

I crouched down next to her, gently rubbing my fingers across her swollen eye and cheek. The woman's wrists were still bound and now, so were her ankles. It was a battle to maintain any semblance of control but my voice remained calm. "Are you ok?"

Fier gave me a sassy look. Somehow, given everything going on, the expression was still sexy. "I've been better."

"She tried to escape, to go after you. To save you." Lilly purred. "Isaac did this. I've been trying to heal her."

My heart seemed to stop and turned to a cold piece of stone. Rage surged through me like it did the day I learned my brother was murdered. I stood and turned to Isaac, staring at him with absolute hate. I was going to kill him.

Divad was standing within an inch of smaller man, shoving his nose in his face. "So," he started in a calm tone, "you have something to tell me?"

"Like what?" Isaac smiled, making my skin crawl.

Divad growled and punched the other square in his face with enough force to send him reeling backward, crashing into a wall several feet behind him. My friend was on him, punching and kicking. "YOU TAINTED THE CLEAR! DIDN'T YOU?" He screamed and attacked harder and faster.

Isaac swore in pain and protested, finally speaking when Divad let up on his blows. "You couldn't do it so I did."

"YOU EFFING… You ruined EVERYTHING!" Divad tugged the etherpistol out of his pocket and pressed the barrel against Isaac's head.

I nodded, filled with such bloodlust and savage hatred for the man I couldn't wait for Divad to pull the trigger. "DO IT!" I roared.

Isaac's voice was a cold, mocking hiss. "I didn't ruin anything. I did what *our master* commanded." He looked at the gun. "Come on, do it. Pull the trigger."

"How?" Divad growled. "How'd they change so fast? Two effing days?"

My lip curled when I saw Isaac's smug expression. "I'm just that potent. Yes, two days was all it took. They set out last night, here and all over the continent. They're still changing, you know… They're not done *cooking* yet."

I had no idea what the prick was talking about but I didn't care. "Shoot him!"

Isaac went on, now taunting Divad. "You're so dense, so preoccupied with your own stupidity; your own little agenda. How'd you finally figure it out?"

"There was one of them outside my house this morning. It killed one of Vistaer's guys." Divad said.

"What?" Lilly called, turning to me. "Who died? Jason?"

I hardly acknowledged her but she picked my brain anyways. "Chin's dead?" She looked at Divad, reading his thoughts next. "Your clear was corrupted, turning the people into something… inhuman."

My friend looked at her and barked "Shut up!"

Isaac only glared at Divad. "They'll serve the master. You did your part well. Now, squeeze that trigger and take the next step."

"KILL HIM!" I bellowed, squeezing my hands into tight fists and almost jumping up and down, hell maybe I did jump, I couldn't tell.

Divad gritted his teeth. He pushed the gun harder against Isaac's head until his hand started shaking so violently it looked like it was going snap clean off his wrist. With a frustrated bellow, he tossed the gun away, stood up and started destroying everything in the house.

My friend ripped the demonic artwork off the walls, tearing through it and tossing it around the room. Next he kicked over pillars and demolished the sick, perverted sculptures that had been sitting there. Everything in his path, the shrunken heads, tables, chairs, dishes, everything, destroyed and wrecked. He punched holes clean through the wall, screaming and ranting.

As impressive as the display was, my brain was coldly focused on the tossed aside etherpistol. I walked over, quietly, to the gun and picked it up, feeling the power of the weapon flow through my body.

"Throw your little tantrum, *Divad.*" Isaac said, laughing again. "But you know you can't hurt me. How's it feel to be so helpless? So weak?"

I walked up to Isaac and aimed the pistol at his head. "Maybe he can't kill you. But I can."

From somewhere in the back of my head, I heard Lilly scream at me, begging me not to do it. It might've been real, it might not have. I didn't care. Isaac looked at me, nodded and then winked, the son of a bitch actually winked.

I fired and burned a hole right through his head. Lilly screamed and this time I heard her for sure, "NO!"

It may have been my imagination, but a strange, murky, blurry shadow rippled out from the now dead, Isaac's head. The distortion thrummed through me and through the house. I threw up, all over the man's lifeless body. The reaction didn't deter me at all. I spat the last bit of bile out of my mouth, onto Isaac.

Divad was on me in a second. "YOU DID IT!" He hugged me and, unbelievable as it may seem, started dancing around in circles, like a kid who got his favorite present for Christmas. I only let out a deep breath. There was no remorse, no guilt in what I'd done. No, I felt... nothing.

"I knew you could!" Divad went on. "Oh thank you, Jason, thank you!" He hugged me again, tighter this time.

I pulled back. "Ok, ok."

Divad let go and I rushed back over to Fier. She looked at me with an expression I wasn't skilled enough to read. It looked both impressed and terrified. "Jason." She whispered.

"Don't." I said. "He was evil. He showed us those videos. He hurt you. Eff him."

"Oh." Divad started, only partially grabbing my attention. I didn't turn away from Fier. "By the way, about those videos. Morbal only broke me because I was so messed up and weak from Forrest and her death."

I finally looked at him, not at all caring. "What?"

Divad put his hands up palms out. "Just saying."

He was actually embarrassed, defending himself. "Who cares?"

"Right." He said. "Isaac put a serious kink in my plans, though. Get ready, we need to get back to the asylum."

"Why?" I asked.

"I need to fix this as best I can." With that, Divad was off toward one of the house's other rooms.

I looked back at Fier. "Are you ok?" I asked again.

"What happened to you?" She asked, raising an eyebrow. I could tell she was both surprised and concerned. "You've changed."

"Nothing happened."

"No." Lilly said. I'd nearly forgotten she was even there. "You have changed. You *are* changing. Divad is shattering you. Can't you see that? Can't you can feel it?"

I scowled at the woman who suddenly didn't look as beautiful as I remembered. "What? No he's not. You don't know anything about it." I hissed. "I've almost been broken before. I know what it's like. Divad and I are brothers, we're together."

"Jason." Lilly said in as calm and sickeningly sweet a voice she could muster. "You *are* being shattered. Of course you can't see it, that's why I know it's true. You have to find your way back. You have to find yourself."

Don't lose yourself. I remembered Michael say back at the station. My heart pounded against my chest.

I fought the thoughts away and looked back at Fier. "We're going to get you out of here and free."

Fier let out a labored sigh and blinked, slowly. "Jason. Listen to me. I can't lose you. It'd kill me. Please." She shook her head, now looking more disappointed than anything. "Effing snap out of it!"

"Hey," I said while untying the bonds around her ankles. "I'm ok. Trust me."

"You've been his plan all along." Lilly said, like a voice in the far distance. "He's using you, for himself. Divad believes that only you can save him from Xolzv. I know that now, when you killed Isaac, I felt it."

I didn't even look at her and remained focused on Fier. "Anything broken? Are you in pain?"

"I'm fine." Fier snapped. "Will you effing listen to Lilly?"

That got me. I knew Fier didn't care for the other woman or put much stock in her words. The fact that she wanted me to pay heed to Lilly sank in. I turned to the younger woman, looking at her tired, blue eyes. "What do you mean? Why?"

She smiled and her face showed a look of relief. "Isaac and Divad have been feeding the darkness. They're the placenta the unborn osilea have been feeding off of. That's why the two have been here; causing pain and havoc everywhere they go, hurting and deforming people. That's why they were spared on Everiel." She paused, letting the information sink in. "Divad used you to kill Isaac. He couldn't do it himself, his hailiorum blood wouldn't allow it because he knew… he knew killing Isaac would release Xolzv. The two of them were keeping the osilea sealed away, even while feeding the things at the same time. Now, the darkness is loose, you set it free. He used you." She blinked and took a breath. "Divad opened up and accidently let down his guard when he was thrashing around. I know now. Part of him, the outside part hates the osilea but the other part, deep down serves evil. Killing Isaac satisfied both sides of Divad. He's trapped in denial, thinking he can free himself with your help. He needs your love."

I swallowed, oddly uncomfortable with the conversation and the word 'love.' I shielded myself, refusing to buy or accept any responsibility regarding whatever this Xolzv thing was. "Ok, fine. Then I'll help him. That's what I'm here for, to help David."

"Jason." Fier said with a downbeat. "Don't be an idiot. Please? Let's just go."

I looked at her and then turned to Lilly. "I can't go. Neither of you understand. I have to try."

Lilly shook her head. "At what cost? You'll lose yourself. You can't help him." I was about to respond and Lilly shook her head. "No. Shut up and think. What have you done and how have you felt since you've been around him? You're a good, strong man, don't lie to yourself. Divad is a psychotic, dangerous, murdering, manipulative lunatic who can't even see his own actions are working to bring Hell on Earth." Her eyes narrowed. "I'm sorry but it's painfully clear. Ask yourself why you can't see it."

"No!" I said, feeling my blood pressure rise again. "You're wrong. You were wrong about thinking you could control David and you're wrong about this. I'm so sick -" I was about to go on when Divad entered the room.

"Let's get moving." He said. "All of us, together."

I looked at him and saw he was armed with another etherpistol. Seeing him cleared my brain. Lilly was wrong. Divad was my friend, we were growing together. I was going to help him. Isaac was just the beginning.

"Mind giving me that gun back, buddy?" He asked.

I smiled and shook my head. "Eff that. I'm tired of being paraded around. I'm helping you because I want to, not because you're making me."

"Thank god!" Divad said, letting out a fulfilled sigh. "It's about damn time." He looked at Fier. "Better help her up and keep the rope around her wrists." He raised his eyebrows and smiled. "Sorry, dear. But you're a wildcat and we can't quite trust you yet." He turned to me. "That ok, Jason?"

I turned from Divad to Fier. He was right. "I'm sorry. But it's for the best."

The woman squinted her beautiful, hazel eyes at me. "You're throwing it all away, aren't you?" She shook her head. "Everything. For what?"

I fought the sudden lump in my throat and gently helped Fier get to her feet. Lilly was right beside her. After turning back to Divad, I nodded. "Let's go."

Chapter 18

The four of us loaded into Divad's van and headed off down a string of roads. The rain had picked up and flashes of lightning flickered through heavy, grey clouds. I sat in the front passenger seat while Lilly and Fier silently occupied the back. I'm not sure why I even cared but I guessed it was around 11am. There were fewer numbers of people out and about than before, most likely sheltered away from the storm. Those I did see wandering about were armed and none of them wore Tehlasrin uniforms. It seemed the union didn't have any presence in the city at all. If I had the strength or slightest drive to care, I'd be both happy and amazed.

I turned to Divad. "You gonna to tell me what's going on or what?"

He spared a brief glance my way. "Don't worry about it. Minor set back." He shook his head and muttered under his breath. "Didn't need them anyways. Eff it."

"Didn't need who?" I asked.

Lilly spoke. "His disciples."

I saw Divad tighten his grip on the steering wheel. "The people I was trying to wake up with my clear. Insect messed them all up." He snorted. "Whatever, it's done."

"That's who attacked Chin? One of the people who took your clear?" My brain fought to put everything together. Damn it was hard to think.

Divad surprised me with a laugh. "Doesn't matter. They'll still help cause a ruckus. We'll just let them stir the pot a bit more. It'll be ok."

"God damn it!" My temper flared. "What is it? What happened?"

"I told you." Lilly said, calmly. "Isaac did something to the clear and it's caused horrible changes in the poor people who ate it."

My friend snarled. "Shut your mouth! I swear, you keep talking and I'll ask Jason to kill you."

The statement sucked the air from my lungs and I physically pulled back, glancing between Lilly, Fier and Divad. I wanted to say I'd never do such a thing, I'd never kill a defenseless woman but couldn't get the words out.

He brought the van to a sudden, screeching stop outside the asylum. It was a good thing everyone had on their seatbelts. Flying through the windshield wouldn't help anything. "Out." Divad barked. "Follow me."

I helped Fier out of the back of the van then the four of us headed through the institution's front gate. The thing was completely demolished, decorated with bullet holes. The adjacent walls and security booths were also destroyed; burned and shot up, splashed here and there with blood stains. The sight was unsettling but it was nothing compared to what we saw inside the asylum. It was quiet as a tomb only messier and filled with more corpses. Junk, bottles, blood and gore covered the floor.

"What the eff…" Fier murmured.

I tried to ignore the sights but couldn't help focus on one dead man's face. "Stop." I ordered, moving over the body. The skin… it looked burnt or scaled or something. Its eyes were open, staring a lifeless gaze into space. He looked alien. The white part of his eyes had turned red and black. I swallowed, studying the body, seeing several gunshot wounds in its chest and gut. The man's hands and feet were black and charred like his face only they had thick, long nails that resembled, dirty, grotesque claws.

"What the hell did you do?" I asked, fighting to catch my breath.

Divad stepped up behind me. "It was Isaac. He did this. Not me."

I looked at him, considering his lack of concern. His blaming of Isaac, his lack of any accountability sickened me. "Divad…"

"Come on!" He roared, his voice echoing down the empty halls. "There's no time. You wanna stop this? This way."

We pressed on, down a few more hallways until Divad punched in a security code on a panel outside two large doors. After a beep he opened it up and led us into a large conference room. "Stay here." He said. "Watch them and I'll be back."

I shook my head, unsure I wanted to trust Divad anymore.

He put a steady hand on my shoulder. "Jason. It's fine. Get a hold of yourself. I'll be right back. If anyone or anything else comes in here, kill it."

"I can't." I shook my head. "This is effed up."

"Yes you can!" He shook me. "It'll be ok. Remember our bond, think about it. This'll be over soon."

I let out a deep breath and nodded. "Ok." My strength trickled back. "Go."

Divad darted out through the large double doors and shut them behind him. Now that I felt a bit more collected, I noticed the huge table that took up the middle of the room. About fifty chairs were placed around it. Beyond that were large oval shaped windows that showed the wet, grey outside beyond.

Fier sat down and huffed. "Still going along with this?"

Hearing her voice, her disapproval nearly set me off all over again. God, she could be so effing annoying! Anyone else and I wouldn't have cared. With Fier… I did care because I loved her. Yes, it was true and I knew it. I locked onto her face and caved, slumping my shoulders. "I don't know. I guess so. Do I really have a choice?"

I fell into one of the chairs and felt the weight of the world pressing down on me. "Nothing makes sense, nothing feels right. He's my friend! Don't you understand? MY FRIEND!" I slammed my fist hard on the table and felt the whole thing vibrate. Tears threatened to well up in my eyes but I was too angry to let them. "This place…" I was back on my feet. "I HATE IT!"

I had my gun out now and didn't even remember pulling it from its holster. "This place nearly destroyed my life."

"And now Divad is destroying it." I would've thought that was something Lilly would say but no, it was Fier. "Yes, he was your friend but not anymore."

My heart raced, feeling like it was about to explode and the pressure on my brain was awful. I panicked for a couple seconds, thinking my skull was about to crack. I brought my hands up and squeezed my palms hard against my temples, roaring in pain.

"Jason, stop!" Fier yelled, standing back up. "It's not that hard, damn it. LISTEN TO ME!"

I turned to her, breathing heavily through my nose.

"Yes, it's your choice." She spoke, calmly. How could anyone be calm? "He was serious when he said he'd have you kill Lilly. He'll have you kill me too. I know it. I've seen men and women shatter, so have you, Jason. It's how they work. They're crazy." She blinked and graced me with a smile. "It's your life, your choice."

I held quiet for a chunk of time before dropping my hands to my sides. They were shaking, violently, involuntarily curling themselves into fists. "I'm not going to kill either of you! I can't believe you'd even say that?"

She looked at Lilly. The young woman nodded then Fier turned back to me. "I know. *Jason* wouldn't hurt us. But you're turning into someone who isn't Jason."

Eff, she was probably right but I still fought to deny it. "No. You're wrong. You don't know me." Fier was about to speak again and I stopped her. "Shush! LET ME EFFING THINK!"

Stupid. Thinking was the last thing I wanted do. Thinking only brought more pain. It was better not to think, not to think ever again.

While the whirl of conflicting thoughts spiraled through my head, a sudden explosion erupted outside the double doors. The damn things fell clean off their hinges. When the smoke and debris cleared, Michael Vistaer's massive frame took up the space. The handles of the blades pressed against his back shot up over his shoulders.

I drew in a deep breath and instantly raised my gun, aiming it right at the big man's chest. His gold eyes glanced quickly at the three of us then settled on my face, seemingly ignoring the weapon. His brow furrowed. "Oh God almighty. Jason?" He spoke uncannily soft.

"Don't move." I said in a shaky but lethal voice. Seeing him embarrassed me. The man was going to judge me, demean me, and tell me I was weak. I couldn't handle it and I thought of killing him quickly before he could bully me. "He told me to kill anyone who came around."

Vistaer frowned. "He? David? I don't doubt it. I'm sure he's told you lots of things and you believe him because you love him. Your love has been his main weapon against you. I bet he's turning you against yourself."

"I've heard enough of that crap from these two." I made the slightest gesture at the women. "I'm not going to take it from you."

"I've loved lots of people." He said. "Trust me, it's a good thing. I'm glad you love your friend. It shows you have a strong heart. Just don't lose yourself to it."

I squinted before another explosion went off from somewhere else, far off in the building.

"Don't you love Fier too? And Lilly? What about me?" Michael said. "Aren't we friends? Partners? Brothers?"

I shook my head. "Not like David." It dawned me that I didn't say Divad but I couldn't dwell on it. Vistaer was trying to weaken me. I gripped the etherpistol's handle tighter.

"Right." He put his hand out, palms up. "I haven't had the chance to thank you for saving my life last night. He would've killed us all too."

"Divad didn't know you were going to be there." I spat.

Vistaer grimaced. "No, he did. He was the one who tipped us off. I learned that this morning."

"Bull!" I growled.

"Jason, I'm not afraid to die. I'm not going to lie to you in order to protect myself. I'm going to tell you exactly the way things are. You deserve that much. We all do." The man straightened himself, suddenly looking even bigger and more powerful than normal. "David planned the whole thing. He gave Ark the *safe* and available location, he brought in Morbal's troops and also tried to lure us in."

"Why?" I asked, skeptically.

Lilly spoke in a voice louder than normal. "He did it too shatter you. It's all about destroying the good man in you so he can pull you down to his level, to his way of thinking, to his consciousness."

It didn't make sense and I wasn't buying it. "No, it's too far fetched."

"Believe what you will, little brother." Michael said, softly. "I just want to know what you want to do now."

I thought for what felt an eternity. After, I lowered my weapon without saying a word. Michael smiled and started toward me when a blur of movement behind him caught my eye. The big man saw my expression and dove for cover a micro second before a dark blue beam of energy soared through the air he'd been occupying.

From the ground, Michael yelled, "DOWN!"

Lilly and Fier dropped low as a barrage of shots filled the air. They were aimed at Michael but would easily hurt or kill anyone else in their path. Divad deliberately and boldly strode into the room, firing his weapon nonstop. Vistaer rolled, jumped and sprinted out of the way of each shot.

I shouted. "DIVAD STOP!"

He spared a glance at me and in that split second, Vistaer was on him, knocking the pistol away then landing a hard punch to Divad's jaw. The blow knocked the man off his feet. Now I was yelling at Michael, unsure who to help.

Divad sprung up and barreled into Vistaer, manhandling the bigger man to the ground. The two traded blows, bloodying each other's faces until I'd finally had enough.

With a surge of rage and frustration, I charged, hooked my arms around Divad's waste and tossed him off Vistaer, slamming his body, sideways into the nearest wall. Michael stood up and I punched him square in his nose. The big man stumbled back but didn't fall.

Divad was back up again, charging Michael who pulled out one of his blades. Seeing the weapon, I kicked with as much force as I could, landing my foot right against Vistaer's wrist, knocking the deadly weapon out of his hand.

I saw Divad lunge for it and scoop it up, pointing it at Michael. He would've drove the blade straight through the bigger man's heart had I not, with speed I couldn't believe I had, sidestepped, grabbed Divad's arm, pulled and spun him away, topping it off with a good punch to his jaw.

He growled then ran his fist hard into my gut. I fought for my breath as my friend slammed his right fist flush against the side of my head. I dropped to my knees.

Now, Vistaer was back on the attack, armed with his other sword. He drove it down fast but Divad moved just in the nick of time, only suffering a nasty looking gash to his left side, just above his waist. Michael continued his assault and was about to make a killing blow until I grabbed his thick wrist, pulled the blade backward and then yanked it from his hands before dropping it to the floor.

Vistaer snarled at me, pissed as all hell, then drove his forehead into my face. "STAY THE EFF DOWN!" He roared.

I spat and shook my head. "Stop fighting!" Free of any care or respect for my own fatigue and injuries, I, quite amazingly, grabbed Michael by his shirt and belt, hoisted his massive body over my head and threw him clear across the room. He crashed through several chairs before smacking against the wall. "It's done!"

Divad laughed. "Nice toss."

"You stay the eff back!" I warned my friend.

He squinted. "No." Divad nodded at Michael. "He dies."

I yelled something incoherent then charged my friend, ramming my shoulder into his side, driving him to the floor. We both got to our feet, struggling until Divad brought his knee up and drove it into my stomach, knocking the wind out of me again.

My friend looked at me with blazing eyes. I didn't even notice him pull the pistol from my holster, I wasn't sure how it got back in there. Quickly, he thumbed the power down and shot me in my stomach. I gasped and fell to the ground, remaining conscious but in pain and unable to use my muscles.

Fier screamed and charged Divad, bound hands and all. The man zeroed the weapon on her and fired again, knocking her to the ground. Thank whatever god may exist, he forgot to up the power setting.

Divad swore, realizing his error then worked to adjust the gun's setting.

Vistaer's form flew through the space between him and Divad, again, knocking the gun away. He picked up the sword I'd ripped from his hands and then stared at Divad who stood two meters away. My friend picked up Michael's other sword and they fought.

There they were, two men, two of my friends, two dangerous, wounded, passionate, bloody and powerful hailiorea, each armed with a sword, locked onto each other. And all I could do was watch.

Michael snarled. "You killed Chin. You twisted and ripped out the souls of thousands of people. You murder, rape and destroy everyone you touch. In God's name I'm going to kill you."

Divad panted out a laugh. "You stupid, old eff. I haven't been through all this to be stopped by a warped clown like you. You can't kill me. You don't have what it takes. Get ready, Jason. You'll want to see this."

He swung his sword, fast and hard, aimed at Michael's throat. The big man parried the swing then made a killing blow of his own that only hit air. Divad ducked and made another strike, jutting the point of his blade at Vistaer's heart. That was blocked too.

The men danced around the room, swinging, jumping, dodging, blocking and ducking. Neither was a master at swordplay but their hailiorea blood moved them in inhuman ways. My eyes strained to keep up. Mostly though, I was concentrating on my own body, willing my muscles to come back to me.

Now that I was able to, I scooted over to an etherpistol resting on the floor near Fier's feet. It took every ounce of willpower and energy I had. My body protested every move, only wanting to lay still and rest. I grunted and pressed on across the ground.

Fier's eyes were on me. She groaned and managed enough motion to kick the gun, sliding it perfectly into my outstretched hand. I gripped the weapon, thumbed the energy to full and with newfound resilience, somehow managed to pull myself to my feet. It wouldn't take much, a strong breeze even, to knock me back to the floor. I hoped nothing or no one came my way.

I aimed the weapon in the direction of the two whirling bodies, catching glimpses of blood flying through the air from where blades tore into flesh. The two managed to cut each other's shoulders and arms. They also each ran the tips of their swords across each other's chests.

"ENOUGH!" I roared. Both men stopped and looked at me as they gasped for air. The two spread out to a vaguely safe distance from each other. "Stop, or so help me I'll kill both of you! I'M SICK OF THIS! I'm sick of being on the outside. I'm sick of watching. I'm sick of letting others make all the choices!" My eyes danced between the two. I shook my head and gritted my teeth. "No more. It's my way now."

Divad and Michael exchanged glances then turned back to me. My friend smiled. "Good." He laughed. "Do what's right. Kill him. Do him like you killed Isaac. Do it for us. Right in his head. Blamo."

I didn't budge until my eyes cut over to Vistaer. He blinked, nostrils flaring like a ravenous dragon. "I tried to help. But like I told you, I'm done telling others how to live or what to do. You have to do what's right."

"Maybe I won't kill either of you." I sneered. "Maybe that's my choice."

"Jason, Jason, Jason." Divad smirked. "Don't be a fool. You can only stop me by killing me, remember? We went over this last night." He smiled, wide and toothy. "You don't want that. You don't want to kill me." His eyes fell on Michael. "And if you don't kill the old man now, I will. He's weak, spent, ready to go down. I can feel it."

Michael spat a mouthful of blood. "He may be right. I can't tell you what to do but let me tell you what's in store for you with *him*." His eyes blazed with a mix of power and sympathy. "A life of pain and murder. A life of tortured servitude. You're a free man, Jason. Freedom is what matters. Freedom and love." He paused. "Don't lose yourself."

"Oh Christ." Divad mocked. "Fine, stand there and let me end this sack of crap."

"NO!" I hollered when I saw Divad take a step toward Michael.

He sighed. "This is boring. Look at me! You know me. I'm your best friend, your brother! You can't turn on me." He liked his lips and gave me a serious look, shaking his head. "It's me! David!"

Things were so tense I didn't even notice Lilly had stepped up along side me until it was too late. The young woman yelled at the top of her lungs. "JASON! SEE!"

She planted both hands on my head. I felt a sudden jolt; a flash of lightning that ricocheted around in my brain. The blast was like a cool splash of water, washing away the confusion, the indecision, the blurry webs that clogged my thoughts. She fell to the ground, seemingly knocked out.

It's difficult to describe what I can only call 'the speed of thought' but in the course of a second I saw everything David had done. I knew the truth and realized I'd known it all along. Now I was finally able to convince myself to believe it.

My friend's torture and torment at the hands of Morbal and Forrest played over in the back of my mind. From there I saw how he killed all the people on Everiel, he was the one who set off the explosion. I saw the pact he made with the darkness.

I saw how he molested Erica Wood. He ravaged her body before injecting her with a maddening, corrupt blend of his own twisted blood and clear. He was instructed to take her down since the osilea knew she had a real chance at bringing liberty and life back to North America. She was freedom's best shot and Divad destroyed her.

Then I saw Divad psychically rip his own mother's brain to shreds, casting her off into insanity. I learned about his plans to lure the groups of men and women we annihilated together at the station. I felt his delight that came from drugging the world with his clear. I felt the pleasure he gained from tearing Morbal's perverted heart from his lungs.

I knew his goals. He planned to murder millions more, killing anyone who might block his dreams of what he considered true freedom. He'd gladly cast the globe into a state of panic, pain, fear and chaos. He'd do all this and he wanted me to do it with him.

Even then, knowing all that, I couldn't choose. I couldn't bring myself to kill him. Then, finally, I saw his plans for Fier. He wanted her dead and he wanted me to kill her, for what he truly believed was my own good.

I looked between the two men, sparing a glance at Fier who was now regaining her own mobility. I was aware of Lilly's defenseless body on the ground near my feet. Fier and Michael were right. It was my choice.

I'm not proud of my own selfishness, but the only real choice that mattered to me was between Fier and the man David had become. The rest of it, Michael, Lilly, the world, didn't measure up.

I looked into David's strangely deformed and aged eyes. "You're right." I swallowed. "I can't kill David. But you said it yourself. David is gone."

I aimed my weapon and fired, burning a hole in Divad's chest. He flew backward and plowed into the windowed wall behind him, cracking the glass before crumpling to the floor.

Time held still for a series of heartbeats. I stood there, panting as sweat dribbled down the sides of my face. It was hard, so damn hard to grasp what I'd done.

Michael let out a sigh before speaking. "Thank you. But we need to hit his head, it's usually the only sure way to kill powerful hailiorea." He gave me a slight bow. "I'll finish him."

A horrible rumble came from Divad's direction and before I could even think, the man was on his feet, bellowing with animal rage. He darted away from Michael, hunched over and favoring the smoking, smoldering burn on his chest. He gave me a single look that I struggled to understand. The expression, his eyes showed betrayal, anger, humor and a hint of pride. I didn't know what to think.

Then with unbelievable strength, fueled by some unearthly rage, Divad ripped the massive table top off its frame and swung it. I had just enough sense and speed to lunge at Fier, pulling her to the floor, out of the slab's path.

I barely saw Vistaer duck just in time before Divad plowed the giant table top clean through the wall separating the room from the rainy outside. The sound was horribly loud but I thought I actually still heard Divad holler, "WHAT AN EFFING JOKE!" After that, I believe he laughed, rather hysterically, leapt through the hole and then he was gone.

A second or two later, after the debris settled, Michael and I stood up. He forced his way through the mess and, with his sword in hand, cut the restraints around Fier's wrists.

I swayed on my feet, quite ready to collapse. Fier was there. She wrapped her arms around me and squeezed, becoming an anchor of sorts. I wanted to cry like a damn baby but the tears weren't there. I was too blocked up, my brain was such a mess I could only stand there, numb.

After scooping up Lilly with a grunt, Michael hobbled over to me and gestured the young woman. "She's fine, just passed out. She sent quite a blast through you."

I squinted and turned to stare out through the massive hole in the wall.

"Let's go." Vistaer whispered. "Jason. Next time, strike the head."

I glared at him.

He grimaced. "Sorry."

-

My bed in the old toy factory was small, but there was enough room for Fier and me to manage to lie down together, holding each other for what seemed a couple hours. She wore a comfortable pair of shorts and a light tank top, I was in nothing but a pair of underwear and jeans.

We embraced and kissed, enjoying the rare moments of peace and quiet. I particularly enjoyed watching Fier breath and feeling her body work as it was pressed against mine. The time was exactly what the doctor ordered and helped quiet my brain.

She whispered in my ear. "You did the right thing."

It took a moment to pull my head out of the clouds. She meant Divad. I nodded. "Yea, I know. Still, I should've gotten you away sooner." My eyes locked onto hers. "I'm sorry."

"Shut up." Fier smiled. "I'm a big girl, remember?"

I thought about her charging Divad with her hands bound, brave and unconcerned with her own safety. A quick laugh slipped out. Yea, she was a fighter for sure. That was part of what I loved about her. I felt guilty for going along with keeping her captive. It wasn't my plan or intent but I didn't fight it. Hell, had Michael not found us, I don't know how things would've turned out. Vistaer had Olivia staked out at the asylum. The part osilea woman called him the second she saw us arrive at the hospital.

The five of us, Fier, Olivia, Lilly, Michael and me, made it back to the makeshift base shortly after leaving the asylum. The streets were mostly empty, still peppered with scattered violent outbreaks. It seemed some of Morbal's forces had returned with pockets of Ark's troops on their heels. Resistance teams worked to fight them both off in three way skirmishes.

I knew Michael wanted to get directly involved but he was just as beaten and bruised as the rest of us. He wasn't in any condition for more fighting. He and Divad, and me for that matter, did quite a number on each other.

Once we got back, Fier and I took turns receiving a quick healing from Marie and then getting cleaned up as best as we could. It had been a couple days since I'd shaved and between the dull razor and my shaky nerves, I made a mess of my face and neck, nicking it with stinging, bloody cuts here and there. After that we ate a very nutritious and tasteless, vitamin filled meal. The rest of the group was happy to see Lilly back but sad about the loss of Chin. As with Sally, the group each mourned in their own way.

I threw the bloody, sweat stained clothes I'd been wearing the last day and a half in the trash. The things were filthy and tossing them out helped remove some of the pain and confusion I'd been through in a cathartic way. Granted, not all the experiences were horrible… having sex with Lilly, as hallow as it turned out to be, was nice but it didn't feel right thinking about it, especially right now with Fier in my arms.

Chickadis was on me the second I stepped back into the base. I couldn't understand why the dog was so attached to me but she yowled and frantically wagged her tail upon seeing me, licking my hands every chance she had. She pretty much ignored everyone else, including Michael. The animal even scratched and pawed at the bathroom door while I was getting cleaned up and then sat next to me as I ate. Now she was in the room with Fier and me, lying on the floor.

I kissed Fier's forehead. "Yea, I remember."

"So what are you going to do now?" She raised her eyebrows. "Come back to Aswain with me. You still have a home and a job there."

"With you as my commanding officer?" I laughed, gently running my nails up and down Fier's soft, smooth shoulder and arm. "I'm crazy but I'm not *that* crazy."

She huffed. "Ass."

I thought about going back but I wasn't sure it was the right move. I'd defied Cross, left after he told me not too. I felt like I betrayed him and wondered if I really deserved to go back. That and there was still a war going on here. Damn it all to hell, I realized now I truly believed in the revolution. Part of me wanted to help Michael.

But then again, Fier was going back and she'd told me Cross didn't hold any grudges. What good would I be to Michael and the others anyways? The reason I came here at all, David, didn't turn out how I'd planned.

I tried as best I could to not think about the man my friend had become. If I dwelled on it too long, the thoughts would rip me to pieces. I worked to convince myself that his fate was out of my hands. What happened to him wasn't my fault. I tried to help, I tried my best and it wasn't enough.

The war wasn't going to be contained to North America. It was everywhere. Maybe Aswain needed me since it would likely soon be a target. Deep down, I'd figured that would happen for a long time.

"Well?" Fier asked, seemingly tired of waiting.

I didn't normally follow my heart, I was more whimsical, erratic and stubborn. However, given the situation and the look in the woman's eyes, the feel of her touch and my own tired, worn out brain, I nodded. "Ok. Ok, I'll go back. Just keep Chief off my case, alright?"

There was a tap on the room's door that snapped my attention away from Fier. I grimaced. "Yea?"

The door slowly creaked open and old man Richard popped his head into the room. "Jason? May I come in?"

"Sure." I said, drawing in a deep breath.

He entered and sat himself in the chair next to the bed Michael had used a couple nights before. "Sorry to interrupt but I wanted to talk with you. I wanted to tell you I was wrong."

I furrowed my brow. "Wrong? About what?"

"Back in the van, the day we picked you up from the docks, when I read you." He swallowed then gave a little smile. "I said you weren't ready. I thought you weren't strong enough to have yourself opened up. I was wrong."

I studied the man's face, trying to make sense of what he was saying. "Ok. No big deal, though I still don't know what that all really means."

"Yes you do, Mr. Sworn." Richard nodded. "You're much more intelligent than you give yourself credit."

Fier pinched my bare chest and I flinched, giving her an awkward look. "I don't know about that." She laughed.

"I went over, well everything with Lilly." Richard went on, calling back my gaze. "She's right. David and Isaac were empowering the osilea but their very being, their deep rooted hailiorea blood kept the darkness locked in its shadowy realm."

I snorted, not really in the mood for riddles, myths or theories. Fier beat me to the punch. She said, "What does that mean? How is that all possible?"

"Morbal sent Divad to Everiel and Ark sent Isaac." Richard sat up straighter than normal, seemingly enjoying the lesson. I bet he'd be right at home working as a college professor. That is, if most people were allowed or could even afford college. "The island had been a shrine for the osilea, a sort of energy collector for the dark. They both, Morbal and Ark, knew it was nearly time for the osilea to materialize so they sent their pets there to gain favor over the other, to help each of them gain an advantage."

"What about the thing that was on Aswain?" I asked.

Richard put a hand up in the air. "Please, let me finish. One thing at a time." He smiled. "Divad and Isaac made contact and in their shattered, twisted and overwhelmed states, they joined with the osilea, the thing some call Xolzv." He paused. "But, both of them were still powerful hailiorea so the pact had some, hmm, stipulations, shall we say. The better part of the two men, the good part, the human, hailiorea part was able to contain the evil even though they were still doing its bidding."

I shook my head. "It just doesn't make any sense."

"Maybe." Richard shrugged. "Or maybe it makes perfect sense. I suppose it all depends on what one believes. Lilly felt the barrier break when Isaac died."

I appreciated him leaving the part out where I was the one who killed Isaac.

"David or Divad can't keep the gate closed on his own. The seal was a partnership." Richard's eyes narrowed. "Now the thing is loose, somewhere, perhaps already with a physical form." His eyes bounced back and forth between Fier and me. "We'll know soon enough."

I let out a deep breath and turned to Fier. "Great."

"As for the demon you helped kill on Ravenfall." Richard went on. "Well, that one was summoned by Morbal and Lilly's mother. I'm not sure on the specifics but they gave the thing a jump on the rest, swearing allegiance to it." He sighed. "I do know that the creature was merely a servant of the greater darkness, charged with destroying Aswain before it could further strengthen us, the hailiorea."

"Jesus." I said, staring off into empty space, remembering how hard the thing was to kill and how it ripped Forrest up.

Fier called my attention back. "And what about the people who took that drug, the contaminated clear?"

"Their bodies, minds and spirits have been poisoned." Richard said, grimly. "They're becoming raving, murdering monsters." He shook his head and curled his lip. "It sickens me. Such an abomination, a twisted, perversion of nature."

I wasn't sure what to say. Now, on top of everything else, evil itself was coming to town and groups of creatures were running around.

"Anyways, Jason," Richard began, giving me a light slap on my leg before standing up, "I just wanted to say I'm proud of you and I was wrong. You were ready, you're as strong as I hoped." He looked down on Fier and me, smiling. "Also, you may not want to believe it but you were shattered. Divad had you and you broke free. To my knowledge, that makes you the only hailiorea to ever come back."

I blinked, trying to understand the significance of everything. All I got out was, "Thanks."

"I'll leave you be." Richard cocked his head to the side. "I knew when Chin died. I could feel it and told the others immediately. Unfortunately, I couldn't figure out where exactly he went. He followed you and David after the battle. He went out on his own to find and save Lilly. He loved her." The old man huffed then smiled. "Anyways that's beside the point. The point is I knew. Just like I know and can feel two souls headed this way, coming to see you." With that, he gave a little bow and left.

"That guy is something else." Fier said, laying the full weight of her head on my chest while dancing her fingers over my belly, sending delightful tickling waves through my skin.

I returned the favor and snuck my fingers under Fier's tank top, lightly running my fingernails over her side just above her waist. She giggled. "I don't really feel like I should believe him, but I do."

Sure enough, not five minutes later, there was another knock on the door.

Fier and I looked at each other and both smiled. "Come in." She said.

It was Lilly and Lilly alone. "Hey, sorry." Her eyes danced over the two us, tangled together in minimal clothing. She beamed. "How... awesome."

"Anyone else with you?" I asked.

Lilly gave me a confused look. "No, just me."

Fier cleared her throat. "What's up?"

"Oh yea!" Lilly said again, with more enthusiasm. "Michael needs to see you guys, when you're ready." She turned to leave then looked back at us. "Actually, if you could hurry it up a bit, that would be best."

Lilly left and I gave Fier one more squeeze. "I knew this couldn't last forever."

"Let's go see what the guy wants." Fier said with a laugh.

Chapter 19

I knocked on Michael's office door and opened it after hearing the man's deep voice bellow, "Come in."

Fier and I entered both having dressed ourselves more appropriately. We were each wearing pants, t-shirts and shoes.

I shut the door behind me and Chickadis complained about being left outside the office. Michael sat in his chair behind his desk, tugging on his bottom lip with his left hand. Chris stood behind him, arms folded. Both had serious expressions on their faces. The four of us weren't alone, the Hispanic man I'd met in Seattle was there, seated across from Vistaer.

The guy spoke. "Brass won't like this one bit."

"Well I can't get a hold of him and I'm not waiting." Michael's eyes beamed with intensity, he turned to me. "Jason, you've met Martin." He gestured the man and then looked at Fier. "This is Martin Gomez. He's been leading the resistance throughout Mexico and the southern parts of the US."

Gomez turned and looked back at us, forcing a smile. "Good evening." He turned back to Michael. "The former US you mean."

The big man instinctively reached for his small, well read and battered copy of the United States Constitution, gently stroking it. "Not for long, my friend."

"Hello." Fier said in what was almost a question, her voice sounding just as curious as I felt.

"Hannah and Aiden Kasire are on the phone." Michael said. "Jason, I wanted to ask you about that explosive device," he paused before saying the name, "David took. It's still operational? He didn't destroy it, did he?"

I shook my head and swallowed, feeling ashamed and embarrassed. I helped him carry the damn thing back to his van. "No. It still works as far as I know."

Michael snorted and locked eyes with Gomez. "See? You hear that?"

Both Hannah and the other man, Kasire, whose face I couldn't remember, each replied with their own "Yes" over the speakerphone.

"So we have a serious problem. I've put the word out to our people to keep an eye out for Mr. Holt though I'm not sure what good that'll do." Michael raised an eyebrow. "That and I have no doubt Ark will try again." His eyes narrowed. "It's not safe here. It's not safe in any city. They're each potential mass death traps. They have to be cleared out."

I stirred, thinking of Divad… David. Now he was on the run from the Union and the resistance. Good lord.

"I agree, but Michael, please." Gomez said in a polite tone. "You really should contact the other leaders, especially Brass."

"I've tried! That's what we're here for." Michael groaned, visibly working to calm himself. "I give the man credit, Rigel that is. He's actually leading his forces, fighting against the Union. Not sitting back barking orders into a radio. But, he should be accessible."

"We're also busy working on securing and stabilizing the continent's power grids and communication lines." Kasire's voice said. "The bastards might try to shut them down. We can't afford to go dark."

The prospect hadn't dawned on me. I imagined how horrible it'd be if there suddenly wasn't any electricity anywhere. Damn. I turned to Fier and we gave each other concerned glances.

"Right." Vistaer said in his deep, bold tone. "That's my point. Rigel is busy. He doesn't have all the information." He curled his lip. "We have to act. Now."

"I agree." Hannah said through the phone. "I've already worked on my areas, calling in on all the help and favors I can get. People will need safe shelter in the areas surrounding Seattle, and all the other cities."

Gomez sighed. "Oh man." He ran a shaky hand through his dark, wavy hair. "I'm with you, amigo, but it's not going to be pretty."

"We don't have a choice." Michael looked around at everyone for confirmation. "We can't allow Ark or anyone else the opportunity to instigate any further catastrophes. Everyone needs to be warned."

"Ok." Gomez said, nodding. "My teams are spread out. What do you need?"

"We need your help. Protect as many people and as large an area as you can." Michael nodded his head as he spoke. "We need to help as much as possible. Chris." He turned to look at the man. "How's our guest?"

"She's… contained." The other said with his southern accent. The words came out heavy.

I chewed on my lip a second before asking, "Guest?"

"Jason," Michael looked at me, "I know you're worn out like the rest of us and I know you plan on heading back to Aswain with Fier." A hint of disappointment dressed his tone. "But I was wondering if you two would come with me tonight."

I looked at Fier then turned back to Michael. "Come where?"

"All the arrangements are made." He said. "I'm going to make another broadcast. We're sending the message out over radios and telescreens throughout the continent."

"You're going to the media central building?" Fier asked, surprised.

Michael smirked. "Well, I hope you are too." His eyes flashed between the two of us. "Jason? Are you in? I could use your help, both of you."

I let out a deep breath through my nose. The whole thing sounded insane and extremely risky but Michael was right, people had to be warned and his plan seemed to be the best way. Plus, he'd helped me, several times. I owed him. "Yea, I'm in."

Fier let out a small growl. "Fine."

"Don't worry." Michael said, sounding especially dumb. Don't worry? "The area is mostly free of Tehlasrin control. With a little luck, we won't run into any complications."

"Unlike last time." Chris said, shaking his head and looking down at his feet.

Michael laughed. "Come on. What's life without risk?" Quiet hung in the air a few moments. "We'll be fine."

"But," Gomez said, "I'm telling you, Brass and the others... they'll be pissed."

"Bah, so what else is new?" Michael said, rolling his gold eyes. "Aiden, send the word along to your people and let me know if you pick up any rumblings afterward."

"Will do." The man's voice said. "Good luck." I heard him sign off.

"Martin." Michael said with a light chuckle. "Relax. You just focus on yourself and your people."

"Ok."

Hannah's voice came through loud and clear. "We're all in this together, each doing our parts. Rigel has the numbers, the support and the money but he's not our lord and savior. Michael, Hun. We're behind you all the way."

The big man smiled. "Thanks, Dear. Kiss our girls for me. Love you."

"Love you too." With that she was off.

Michael pressed the 'end call' button on his phone then stood up. Gomez followed then nodded at Chris and Vistaer before turning to Fier and me. "Nice seeing you again, Jason. Fier." He brushed past us, opened the door and headed off.

Chickadis promptly moved into the office and licked my hand. I smiled and scratched behind her soft ears.

"Traitor." Michael said to the dog, playfully furrowing his brow. He shifted his gaze up to Fier and me. "Jason, I wanted to thank you."

I made an odd face. "Thank me? For what?"

"Oh, maybe for not killing me back at Morbal's. But more so, for showing me that people can come back from dark places. For showing that no matter how horrible and painful things may be, or how deep a hole someone's in, they can still make the right choices." Michael smiled and looked down at the desktop, suddenly seeming bashful. "You helped restore my faith and resolve." His eyes were back on me, then Fier, then me again. He grinned. "The old Michael Vistaer is back and you can only blame yourself."

I wasn't sure what to say and didn't feel like mentioning the main reason I didn't side with Divad was Fier. In the end though, I don't think that really mattered to Michael. I think he just appreciated my standing up to the mad man my friend had become. "Ok then. You're welcome."

Vistaer nodded and puffed his chest out. "Good. Enough of that. Time to kick ass and I've got a newscast to prepare. Show time is 10pm; three hours from now. We'll head out in two. Chris."

"Sir?"

Michael planted his right palm on the man's shoulder. "I want everything ready on your end. Take Drew with you."

Chris nodded. "Got it."

-

"You're on in three, two…" The man standing behind the large camera gave a 'one' gesture with his finger before quickly pointing it at Vistaer. Michael sat up straight behind an immaculate, glossy, royal blue desk. His face was rigid and his eyes burned brighter than Olivia's. He wore a tight, red shirt and had his hands clasped in front of him, resting on the table. The handles of two blades peered over his shoulders, giving him an even more intense look. There were several discolored, swollen patches on his face from his fight with Divad even though Marie did her best to heal him up. The bruises only added to his serious, tough as nails look.

"Hello. Most of you know who I am by now." He smirked. "For those who don't, my name is Michael Vistaer and I'm here to tell you we've been given a second chance. I'm no different, better or worse than any of you. I'm just a man with a purpose I've sworn my life to. I'm driven to resist and fight against the tyranny that's darkened our world for nearly a decade. Our differences, those between you and me, might be seen in my willingness to take action. There are many who've fought and continue to fight for that which make's life worth living: Freedom. Some of you haven't found the will or courage to take the necessary steps. Others have been resisting the controlling, domineering monsters that have killed, demeaned and weakened us for years even before the birth of the Global Union. To those brave souls, I say thank you from the bottom of my heart. For the others… I'm here tonight to tell you that now, this very day, this very instant; it's time to join the fight."

I shifted my weight from one foot to the other, dividing my attention between Michael and the dozen or so others, most of them strangers, that shared the large news room. Getting into the building was easier than I ever dared dream. Resistance soldiers, men and women, had the place well secured and the people who worked here seemed more than willing to accept us. The air still set me on edge though. I worried that at any moment, a squad of Tehlasrin soldiers would come barging into the room, opening fire on everyone in attendance.

Fier stood by my side. She sensed my agitation and quickly clasped her right hand with my left, making me aware of how much my palms were sweating. I looked at her, unblinking, and swallowed. She smiled before turning back to Vistaer.

Olivia, who'd driven us over to the building in Sean's van, was standing to my right. As usual, the woman was beyond excited with the whole situation. Of the whole group, I decided she was the craziest.

"We need to stop being afraid of the Union. All their cunning, murdering controllers, save one, are gone." Michael nodded and paused a second, smiling. "Some of their underlings are fighting, futilely, for the power of their removed masters but they can't possibly succeed. The poor, misguided fools don't stand a chance against the light and spirit of liberty that has finally risen."

His eyes dropped from the camera for a moment, showing the wheels in his brain were spinning, thinking as he went along. He continued when his stare met with the lenses again. "To those who still fight for the corrupt, greedy government body that seeks to rob us of our rights, to take our children away and turn them against us, to poison us and sicken us, I say this. The choice is yours. It always was and always will be. The lives we live are our own and it's never, NEVER too late to do the right thing. I don't want to fight you. But if you continue to throw your honor and dignity away, striving to harm and rule others, then we're enemies. I'm sorry."

Damn it all to hell, I thought of David. Now, after everything we'd been through together, it felt like he and I were enemies. I did what I had to do but doubted he'd ever trust me again even though his own madness forced my hand. I sighed, again telling myself I'd made the right choice and squeezed Fier's hand.

"To those of you watching me on telescreens or listening to my ramblings over radio waves across the continent, I ask you this question: What do you want from life?" Michael's eye's narrowed. "What are you afraid of? Death? Some throughout time have said that humanity's knowledge of our own mortality has been a nightmare that's plagued us from our start. No. I say it's the most liberating gift we could ever have. We know, each and every one of us, that'll we'll die. It's inevitable. So, these dilutions of security and the sacrificial slaughter of our freedoms to protect us from unseen dangers is a shameful waste. In the end, the life you know of will end no matter what you do or who you are. Instead of cowering in fear and surrendering to the torment of tyrannical men and women, why not devote our time on this planet and our energy to making life as prosperous and free we possibly can? Therein and therein alone is the key to happiness."

He gave the camera a deep, meaningful look. "Or maybe you fear imprisonment or torture. Is that how you want to live? In constant fear? Damn it, if we can work together to restore liberty the dangers and pains of such cruelty will vanish in the face of true justice. The Union and the powers that serve it can't do anything unless we, the people allow it. Can't you see? We're the ones giving life to the bastards. Their entire twisted government is a house of cards we hold together. We gave it life. We created our own cage. Our parents, children, loved ones, friends, enemies all together gave the GU strength. By God, now it's time we take it back! Without us, they're nothing. Absolutely nothing!"

Michael drew in a deep breath and blew it out, forcefully. "I'm no fool. I understand fear and I understand pain. I've lost friends and loved ones. I'm a father and the thought of harm coming to my children is nearly unbearable. But even more unbearable, is the prospect of my children rolling over and living in a world of misery, fear and slavery. I can not and will not accept that, ever!"

He was gritting his teeth now as blood rushed to his head, turning his ears red. It took Michael a couple seconds to calm himself. He went on. "So I've decided, like others, to dedicate my life and everything I have to freedom. I can't do anything on my own. The group I fight with can't do anything on their own. The only way for freedom to blossom and for any shot at happiness is through all of us working together. Each and every one of you, together with your fellows can truly make a difference in the world. Failing to believe that is equal to surrendering to the lies the monsters have spat at us. I'm merely a beacon to remind you all of what, deep down, you already know."

I watched Michael lick his lips as he glanced around at the faces staring back at him. When he looked back at the camera, he raised an eyebrow. "Thanks to those who've fought against the beast that Tehlasrin truly is, the risk now is minimal. We've won. Their control net is smashed. You've seen it. You've noticed it in the streets first hand. There's no denying that most of the continent is free from GU control." He nodded. "But here is our greatest challenge. What are we going to do now? Allow other tyrants to replace the ones we've removed? Give Tehlasrin a foothold to sweep back in and regain control?"

Vistaer drew in a quick, deep breath. "I'm a warrior, not an esteemed intellectual of any merit. I don't know all the correct steps that we need to take. But I do know where to begin. First we need to accept the truth that for nearly the entire continent, *OUR* continent, the Union has no sway. From there we need to bond together, held true by our universal desires for what much wiser men than me labeled, life, liberty and the pursuit of happiness. We need to search deep down for the love, respect and compassion we inheritably feel for our fellows, for our families, for our kids. We need to be strong and brave. We need to be willing to stand up for our own dignity. We need to be prepared to fight. We need to accept the fact that evil can not win."

I felt the weight of Michael Vistaer's words fill the room, this room and millions of rooms throughout North America. As he went on, I found myself nodding in agreement. It was like he put into words the jumbled up thoughts I'd had scrambled in my brain for years.

"From there, we need to unite and help each other." Michael nodded and his eyes showed a type of sympathy, a pleading look I hadn't seen from the large, strong man before. "Maybe that, along with this little document," he held up his familiar copy of the Constitution, "as a guide can lead us to something we've forgotten, to something we've lost, to something special."

He smiled and shook his head, turning to look at the small book. "People have said this document is old, irrelevant, outdated." He turned back to the camera. "What's their alternative? These words," he shook the book, "are the newest, freshest and most liberating ideas humanity has come up with. It's not perfect. Hell, we're human, nothing we do is perfect. But what's the alternative? Fascism, Communism, Feudalism, Dictatorship?" He closed his eyes for a brief moment and smiled. "All those lead to the exact same state of affairs we've been trapped under. Tyranny. Again, I'm not a scholar or a bright political mind but I know my history and I've seen where their *alternatives* lead. They lead to pain, fear and slavery for nearly every man, woman and child."

Michael was quiet for more than a few seconds and I thought he was done. I let out a breath I hadn't realized I'd been holding and relaxed my shoulders, turning to look at Fier.

Her eyes were wide and there was a little smile on her face. She was impressed and so was I.

"I mentioned all the controllers except one have been removed from power." Michael started again and I quickly turned to look at him, remembering the deaths of Morbal, Erica and that controller, Vistaer himself ended with a bullet to the head. "Steven Ark still holds sway over the northeastern coast. The man, an especially cold and evil ruler, is a serious danger to all of us. Just last night, he planned to completely destroy the city of Denver. I have no reason to lie to any of you and my intention isn't to scare anyone. Eff." He swore then looked mildly embarrassed having done so. "Fear is one of our major obstacles we need to overcome and one of the things I fight hardest against. No, scare tactics aren't my aim. My aim is prosperity. Having a raving, homicidal, psychopath still on the loose is something I need to warn everyone about."

God damn it! I thought of David again.

"I don't know what else he's capable of but until he and his forces are overtaken, I advise everyone living in these giant cities across North America to vacate and spread out." Michael blinked, giving himself a moment to think. "Don't make yourselves easy targets. Move out into the vast open expanses surrounding the cities and build better lives for yourselves. Those of us with the resistance will do everything we can to help but again, whether we succeed in creating a better world isn't up to me or the resistance. It's up to you."

He nodded. "We're good people. I truly believe that and I believe we can overcome any challenge together. All we need is a little trust and a little companionship along with respect for each other's rights as human beings. My colleagues have been working to make sure there's enough food and living space for us all. It'll be hard but things will get better so long as we keep our aims true. Still, we have to fan out. The Union is capable of any number of horrific acts."

I imagined what was going on throughout the continent. Were people panicking? Were they dismissing Michael? Or were they preparing to file out of cities across the continent? Hmm, probably all three.

"Chris, Drew." Michael waved to the two men who'd been standing off in an especially dark corner of the large newsroom. I didn't even know they were there until now. Vistaer continued. "There's one other thing I need to tell you about while I have your attention. Whether you believe it or not, there are evil, truly evil forces working against us."

The two men stopped just outside the camera's eye. They had a third person with them. I couldn't see anything of the other since he or she was covered in a large brown coat with a masked face and a hat on his or her head. My brow furrowed, curiously.

"I know some of you have already had the unfortunate experience to see this." Michael grimaced. "To those who've lost friends and family, I'm truly sorry. To those who don't know let me give a most urgent and sincere warning. Do not, ever take the drug clear. The latest shipment sent out through the world is contaminated. It's been," he swallowed, "turning its users into something no longer human."

He turned to Chris and nodded. The other man, along with Drew, brought the cloaked figure over to Michael, now visible on screen. Vistaer stood and turned to the camera. "Forgive me but you all need to see this. For those listening over the radio, I implore you, do not ever use the drug."

"Now." Michael said, queuing Chris to remove the hat, mask and coat from what looked like a woman, judging by what appeared to be breasts and long hair. Her skin was completely dried up, brown and wrinkled. The face was horrific, her lips were, well gone, showing black, rotting and inhumanely sharp teeth. Her hands were tipped with long, lethally looking sharp claws and her eyes, most noticeable of all, looked to be nothing but sunken in, small balls of gel sitting far back in otherwise empty sockets.

My mouth dropped open while Fier's grip on my hand became almost painfully strong. There was a collective gasp from the others in the room. The thing reminded me of the creature that died on Ravenfall.

I could only watch as the woman the thing used to be, struggled against Chris's and Drew's grip. It looked into the camera and let out a series of sounds that ranged from a growl to a hiss to a shriek. It was a monster and I felt an utter hatred coming from it. The thing wanted to kill.

"This is what happens. This is a product of the aims from the forces behind those who run Tehlasrin." Michael said, speaking over the thing without taking his eyes off it. "As God is my witness, I wish she could be helped, saved. I want to feel pity for her but it's too late. The drug has changed her into a deranged creature. Her humanity, probably even her soul is gone."

I managed to tear my eyes off the writhing, squirming, shrieking thing to see Michael shake his head. His face frowned and I thought for a moment he was going to burst into tears. He turned to the camera.

"It's too late for her. This one was captured hunched over corpses of several people it killed." Michael snorted. "Don't underestimate them. They're intelligent, calculating and dangerous despite their frail look."

Chris grunted, visibly straining to contain the creature. It fought for freedom. I pulled my etherpistol out of its holster on my right hip, ready for the thing to break loose.

Michael followed suit and tugged one of his blades free from its home across his back. "I promise you, these things are no longer human and beyond redemption. A human, or most animals couldn't survive this."

With that, Vistaer quickly and cleanly severed the thing's head from its neck. People in attendance gasped and grunted in disgust. All the slice managed to do to the thing was end its shrieks, growls, grumbles and hisses. The body continued to fight for freedom while its head, which landed on the news desk, still bit at the air.

I only barely believed what I was seeing. It was headless but still alive. Anger and revulsion surged through my body. "KILL IT!" I roared.

"For whatever reason, somehow," Michael said, now speaking again in his calm voice, "removing its head doesn't end it. No, it doesn't die until it's either burned or it's sufficiently shot or stabbed through the gut, between the stomach and waste."

From there, the big man drove his sword into the creature's stomach, turned and twisted the blade then pulled it out. The thing's now lifeless form crumpled to the floor. Its head stopped still with an especially grotesque expression and Chris and Drew gasped for breath.

Michael turned back to the camera. "I don't know how many of these are out there but I beg you to not contribute to their numbers. They seem terrifying but don't let them diminish your reemerging spirit. That's what they want to do. Don't let them win."

He drew in a deep breath, sheathed his weapon and stood up straighter than normal. "Regardless of whatever challenges we face, and I know in my heart there will be many, we need to keep true to our purpose. We need to help each other. If we can do that, there's nothing that can destroy our inherent right to freedom and liberty. Only we can do that to ourselves. It's our choice: Freedom and the potential for happiness or slavery under tyranny."

Michael sat back down. "Deep down, I trust all of you to make the right decision. Overcome your fears, help others and together we can resurrect a new union under the principles of justice, equality and freedom. I believe in you all and I salute your willingness to fight for the good in all of us. It's time we stand up and fight for each other. Together we can save ourselves. Thank you for your time." He smiled. "God Bless. For a better tomorrow."

Chapter 20

"That was a great speech," Olivia said in her usual peppy, upbeat tone, exhaling a plum of smoke from the latest hit of her cigarette, "but you probably should've started with the bad stuff." She was driving the van back to the toy store with Michael sitting in the front passenger seat. Chris, Drew, Fier and I were in the back.

It was nearly 11pm and the streets were mostly quiet. The rain from earlier had ended and I gazed out the window, wondering where David was in all this. The thought sent an odd warning through my brain.

Fier put her hand on top of mine and I turned to her. She smiled.

"Hmm," Chris started, "I thought it was fine. If you'd started with that creature I doubt anyone would've paid any attention to rest of what you had to say."

I saw Michael nod his head. "That's what I thought too. I just hope I made sense."

"You did good." I said finally, before swearing under my breath. "You moved me, that's for sure."

The big man laughed. "I can live with that. Thanks."

A phone rang and Drew quickly answered it. "Drew." He held quiet for a moment and I could hear the faint voice on the other end. It was a man's voice and it sounded alarmed.

"WHAT?" Drew bellowed. "IS EVERYONE ALRIGHT? WHAT DID YOU -"

"Give me the phone, NOW!" Michael interrupted as he outstretched an open hand. Drew obediently handed it over, cursing up a storm and suddenly checking over his weapons.

"What the hell's going on?" I asked.

Fier gave me an alarmed look and shook her head. "What now?"

"Mike, MIKE!" Vistaer said. "Calm down! Is everyone ok? Anyone hurt?"

Michael was quiet for a few moments, nodding his head and shifting in his seat. "Ok," he said finally, "we'll be right there." He ended the call and threw the phone back to Drew.

"What is it?" Chris asked, sounding concerned but calm at the same time.

Michael turned to Olivia. His voice was deep and cold. "Go. Step on it."

-

Olivia parked the van in a lot a half a block from the store and the six of us rushed in, quickly covering the distance. Drew and Michael said next to nothing the rest of the drive but it was obvious, as soon as we moved through the back room that the team's base had been attacked. Fresh bullet holes dotted the walls and I saw a trail of blood leading out of through the warehouse.

Chickadis jumped up on me and I pushed her down. "No! Not now!" I felt something wet on my hands and looked at them, noticing fresh blood. I turned to the dog, her scruffy beard was covered red. "What the eff?"

Mike and Andres came around a corner, meeting us in the large open room I'd teleported into a couple times. The young man was cradling his right arm and his brown eyes were enormous behind his thick glasses. "He took it! He took the teleporter!"

"WHO?!?" I roared.

Andres put his hands out. "Please, calm down! We're ok."

"Richard, Lilly!" Michael hollered. "Marie, get out here!"

The three rushed into the room, moving beside Mike. Vistaer bolted over to them, studying inquisitively. A second later, he blew out a sigh of relief, finally convinced his team hadn't suffered any more losses. He turned to Richard last. "Where is he?"

"He ran off." The old man said, still gasping for air. "Lilly tried to subdue him. She failed at first but I channeled my energy through her. We scattered his mind a bit and he fled." He swallowed. "He would've killed us all."

"Who?" Both Fier and Chris asked at the same time.

Michael, Lilly and Richard all looked at me. Vistaer spoke. "Divad."

My mouth dropped open and I shook my head. "No." I couldn't believe it. "He was here? He attacked you? How? How did he know where to find you?"

"He knew how to find us from you." Lilly purred. "He pulled the knowledge from your mind."

"I knew it!" Drew roared. "You led him here, you son of a bitch!" The man sped over to me and landed a punch square against my jaw. I reeled back, fighting off the blow and working to gather my wits.

Michael roared, "DREW!"

Chickadis let out a series of barks and growls.

Fier snarled and started for Drew, pissed as hell.

I regained my composure just quick enough to dodge another strike. Fier was close and I didn't want her to get involved. With speed and strength I was amazed I had, I grabbed Drew by his shoulders and tossed him through the air behind me, away from Fier.

He was back on his feet quickly, charging me. I stood my ground and puffed out my chest. When he was close enough I made a quick, little sidestep and then returned the punch he'd given me, right to his chin. I thought I heard something crack. The man groaned and fell to a knee. I punched him again, as hard as I could and he fell flat on the floor.

Chickadis was on Drew, snarling and barking, looking for an opening to sink her teeth into the man's skin.

"STOP!" Michael hollered from directly behind me. The man hooked his arms around my wrist before I could punch Drew again and then he and Chris were on me, holding me back ordering me to control myself.

Lilly wrapped her arms around Chickadis, working to calm the dog down.

Fier stood behind them. "Get off him!"

Andres, Olivia and Marie were by Drew, checking to make sure he was ok and making sure he wasn't going to do anything stupid like attacking me again.

"I'm alright!" I yelled through clenched teeth. "Let me go!"

Michael nodded at Chris and the two released their grips. I turned to Drew. "Don't EVER cheap shot me like that again, you effing hear me?"

The man was sitting on the floor, glancing up at me with a scowl on his face. "Eff you."

Olivia slapped Drew on the top of his head. "Mind your manners!"

"It's ok, girl." Lilly cooed in Chickadis's ear. I looked at her and the woman smiled. "She bit Divad, helped drive him off."

Olivia laughed. "Awesome. Even the dog is a hero!"

I turned to Richard. "He was really here?"

"Yes." He let out a groan before finding a seat to plop himself into. "Lilly got into his head just in the nick of time. I used the roadway to help disorient him. That's when Chickadis attacked."

Mike cleared his throat. "But that was after… after he grabbed the teleporter."

The full weight of everything hit me all at once. The teleporter... Now David could be anywhere at anytime. I couldn't think of all the havoc the man could create across the globe.

"I tried to hit him." Andres said, showing off his pistol. "But he was too god damned fast."

At that instant a sound came from the computer terminal station that was parked next to a couple clothes lines holding a few articles of dry laundry. The sound was a mix of beeps and rings which startled all of us. The sounds went through three series then the answering device picked up, booming the call over speaker throughout the toy store's backroom.

"MICHAEL! GOD DAMN IT!" The voice roared. It took a couple seconds for me to recognize the speaker as Rigel Brass. "Michael, pick up the phone! I don't know what the hell you were thinking but you've just seriously sent the world into a tailspin." I could hear the man gritting his teeth on the other end. "The others are furious! You really forced my hand this time." Another growl. "Don't leave your base, don't go anywhere. I'm coming your way." Judging by the loud bang that echoed through the room, Rigel must have slammed the phone down on his end as hard as he could.

Michael scratched his chin. "We've got a whole new series of problems to deal with." He shook his head. "Good God."

"We found him in your room." Marie said, focusing on me, seeming oblivious to the phone call. "Divad. He'd already snuck around, somehow getting through our security systems, and found the teleporter. Mike saw him first. That's when Divad broke his arm."

I winced. "My room?"

Fier grabbed my hand. "Come on."

We rushed to my small room. When we got there I immediately noticed writing on the wall over the head of my bed. The words were written in black marker and said, "You didn't give up on me and I'm not giving up on you." It was signed, "Your friend, Divad."

Icy needles ran up the back of my neck and goosebumps popped up on my arms. I wasn't sure what to feel. Amazed? Angry? Frightened? Threatened? Relieved in some odd way? As hard as it was to think clearly, it was impossible to speak.

Fier was there and she spoke for me in a low, soft, slow tone. "Holy eff…"

About the Author

This is Adam's third completed novel and the second in the *Hailiorea* series. He is currently working on the next segment, *Hailiorea Clearing* before moving on to an unrelated project titled *Trial of Ascension*. Adam lives outside Phoenix, Arizona and works in advertising sales. Aside from writing, Adam's interests are music, nature, history and fiction, both stories and games. Above it all, he enjoys spending time with friends and family and helping his daughter continue to grow.